# Mysterious
# Aisles

The narrative pinballs non-stop through a large cast of unique personalities—clock in with your attention at the ready. Plenty of scope for future adventures in South Hertling, as the action dashes to a close.

For lovers of the witty and absurd, this novel is a jubilant escapade into delirious weirdness.

**- Clare Rhoden, Aurealis Magazine**

**** This is one quirky book… the jokes were as frequent as they were funny.

**- Jess, Goodreads**

**** But plot is not what we come for in these books. We come for the funny and the weird. That's what this book delivers. Boy, does it deliver.

**- Julie Porter, Goodreads**

**** Ya, it's a lot, but also a lot of fun! I genuinely enjoyed most of the silliness but loved and appreciated the undertones of inclusivity & LGBTQ+ representation in the characters.

**- Dain, Goodreads**

# Mysterious Aisles

## The South Hertling Chronicles Book 1

### BG Hilton

BGHilton.com

# Dedication

To my sister, Catherine.

# Also by BG Hilton

*Champagne Charlie and the Amazing Gladys*

*The Terror of London, or, Spring-Heeled Jack*

ISBN (print) – 978-0-6454919-0-6
ISBN (ebook) - 978-0-6454919-1-3

Cover illustrations by Joel Tarling - www.joeltarling.com

Editing by Pamela Willson at the Picky Bookworm - thepickybookworm.com

NATIONAL
LIBRARY
OF AUSTRALIA

A catalogue record for this book is available from the National Library of Australia

# Contents

# Cast of Characters

**Adam** — Handy Pavilion staffer. Works in Outdoor Furnishings.

**Ali** — Handy Pavilion department manager, in charge of Power Tools. Bald, divorced.

**Angela McGregor** — a sinister employee of the Handy Pavilion. Manager of the Blinds and Shutters section. Twin sister to Sadie Mcgregor.

**Axel Platzoff** — Aka 'Professor Devistato.' A former supervillain. An employee of the Handy Pavilion.

**Belinda** — An extremely annoying member of the Handy Pavilion staff.

**Bruce** — Former concreter, now a ghost. Bruce haunts the Handy Pavilion.

**Buck Dusty** — cowboy and Handy Pavilion employee. Works in Power Tools.

**Captain Stellar** — aka Vincent Pizano. Superhero, long-time enemy of Axel. Initially in relationship with Cycloman, and a member of the Vigilancers

**Carlos** — Pavilion employee, works in Key Cutting. Friend of Laura.

**Carol** — Hipster and barista. Runs a café in the Super Centre.

Fond of Zorbar.

**Cycloman** — aka 'Len.' Captain Stellar's partner; later his ex.

**Donna Saheco** — Works in the Handy Pavilion lighting section. Disciple of Sadie.

**Fanaka** — Brilliant engineer from an alternate Afrofuturist/Steampunk timeline.

**Fiona** — A rather timid employee of the Handy Pavilion. Works in plumbing. Has water powers. Reason for this: unclear.

**Gwen Harper** — Employee of Handy Pavilion with a magical connection to wood.

**Jasu Shan** — see Ms Shan.

**Jane Nguyen** — Works in Equipment Hire. Seems basically normal, but is actually a werewolf. Honestly, this doesn't come up very much, so forget I mentioned it.

**Karl Wintergreen** — Owner of the Super Centre stationery shop. Karl run's the Centre's newsletter and is an inveterate conspiracy theorist.

**Laura Cho** — a young employee of the Handy Pavilion. Later becomes the superheroine, Voyager.

**Maria and Luigina** — Dimension-hopping plumber heroes.

**Mrs Liselle** — Claudia Liselle. Manager of the Super Centre and ally of the Pavilion. In love with Ms Shan.

**Lumpy-looking Customer, the** — A customer of the Handy Pavilion who is a bit lumpy looking and who needs a pulley.

**Marlon Dillinger** — Duty manager at Handy Pavilion. A basically normal person.

**Mr Smith**—Senior Manager at the DIY Barn. A bad person.

**Nalda Teheintausand**—A killer cyborg from the future. Works in the Arts and Crafts section.

**Norman Leamington**—A young man who works in the Pavilion. Seems basically normal, but probably isn't.

**Ma Dusty**—Buck Dusty's mother. A cowgirl and member of a sinister conspiracy.

**Ms Shan, Jasu**—manager of the Handy Pavilion. A corporate type who finds herself increasingly plagued with 'empathy' and 'loyalty'. In love with Mrs Liselle.

**Phantasm, The**—A mysterious black-cloaked devoted to sabotaging the Handy Pavilion. Real identity unknown (though really not that hard to figure out).

**Professor Devistato**—see *Axel Platzoff*

**Richard Pennington**—An alchemist. Not directly involved in the Pavilion/Barn struggle.

**Sadie McGregor**—An extremely moral member of the Handy Pavilion staff. Manager of the Lighting section. Twin sister to Angela McGregor.

**Seamus O'Consolodatedshanghaipotteryworks**—A garden gnome and outdated ethnic stereotype. Comes to life under the full moon.

**Vincent Pizano**—see Captain Stellar.

**Voyager**—see Laura Cho.

**Stavros Theopolos**—Owner of a kebab shop in the Super Centre.

**Wellsey**—Department manager in Handy Pavilion Plumbing section. Real surname: Popplewell, real first name:

unclear.

**Zeus** — Greek deity. King of Olympus. Horndog.

**Zorbar Ofthechimps** — A former Handy Pavilion staff member, notable in that he was raised by chimpanzees. In love with Carol.

# 1 The Reunion

It was a Saturday morning, and the merciless Australian sun beat down on the broad roof of the Handy Pavilion. Inside, enormous ceiling fans struggled to put up a fight against the rising heat, but it was still anyone's battle.

The Handy Pavilion was the sort of building could have been an aircraft hangar — enormous and lightly built. Unlike a hangar, however, little of the internal space was empty. Huge shelving units — spaced about two metres apart, packed with paint and chainsaws, pliers and charcoal bricks — towered up towards the vast skylights and fluorescents. Enormous trolleys traversed these aisles, moving these wares to the neat row of registers out the front.

At the end of Aisle 12, Axel Platzoff was restocking a shelf of caulking guns, when out of the corner of his eye he spotted a familiar face. It was a handsome face, screwed up in an expression of concentration. It belonged to a big man, who was examining the label on a can of exterior varnish with the intensity of a bomb-disposal expert, wondering which wire to snip.

There was something about the man... Something familiar... Oh, dear Lord! It was Captain Stellar. Not in his uniform—just a t-shirt, shorts, and sandshoes—but Captain Stellar nonetheless.

*Please,* Axel thought. *Please don't let him recognise me.*

Before he could get away, Stellar was approaching: "Excuse me, is this okay to use this on spruce... Oh, my God! Professor Devistato! Haha! How are you?"

"Hello, Captain," Axel mumbled.

The Captain stared at him for a moment before grinning. "Professor? Oh, small world! Of course, not as small as it would be if I hadn't destroyed your shrink ray! Been up to your old tricks?"

"No," Axel sighed. "I've been legit since escaping the Barrier Dimension."

Stellar grimaced. "Yeah. Look, I'm sorry I had to imprison you there, but if that gluon bomb had..."

His apology was cut short by a teenager asking Axel for directions to the spray paint.

"So, anyway," Stellar said when the pimply youth had gone, "I guess you landed on your feet? Working at Handy Pavilion? Must be a blast for someone who's as into DIY as you are."

There was a long pause, underscored by the distant whine of a bandsaw demonstration.

"There's an assistant shift supervisor position coming up," Axel said. "I was thinking of applying."

"That's great. I might be moving into management myself. The chairmanship of the Vigilancers will be opening up, once Aquaticwoman returns to Lost Lemuria."

There was another pause, more awkward than the first. It was broken by the sudden arrival of a man carrying a huge terracotta planter like it was made of paper-mâché.

"Vincent, did you get the varnish?" he called. "How long..."

"Len! look who I ran into?" Stellar replied. "Professor Devistato!"

"Pleased to meet you, Professor," the newcomer said. "I'm Cycloman, the Human Cyclone. Vincent told me all about you. You must have nearly conquered the world, what, six times?"

"Seven," Axel sighed. "Nice to meet you, Cycloman."

Yet another pause. The expectant silence gnawed at Axel's brain. *Must... make... small-talk...*

"So are you two... you know... uh..."

"That's right," Stellar said. "Five years, come August."

"Hm. It's just that I always assumed that... uh... you and Galactic Lad..."

Cycloman stifled a laugh. Captain Stellar reddened. "I really don't know how these things start," Stellar said. "He's a minor, he's my nephew, and he's straight. You do the maths."

"I think Rory... I mean Galactic Lad is dating Swamp Girl from the Teen Brigade," Cycloman added.

"No, they broke up. He's been seeing Atomicina, lately."

"Good. She's more his type."

"You think? I always thought he and Senorita Ocelota..."

Axel sighed a sigh of the damned. Stellar didn't seem to

notice, but Cycloman diplomatically drew the encounter to a close. "Sorry, Professor," he said. "Listen to us gossiping! You have work to do, and we have to get going if we're going to make it to lunch at the Astoundings'. See you!"

Axel forced a smile, and the pair left. The instant they were gone, he quick-marched to the break room. Locking himself in the staff toilet, he propped himself against the sink, hyperventilating.

For the hundredth time that day, an unbidden thought rose from the depths of his mind: an image of himself, seated on a throne of skulls that rose from a sea of blood on a burning Earth. For the hundredth time that day, he pushed the image down, down, down.

He wanted a cigarette. He wanted a vodka. Most of all, he wanted to lock Captain Stellar in a sealed room, and laugh and laugh as the room slowly filled with water. He shook his head hard to clear it, took a deep breath, and splashed some water on his face.

Back in the break room, he ran into Marlon, the floor manager. Marlon was a big man with a face like a mugshot. He sat smoking at the Formica table, occasionally flicking his ashes into an ashtray that he'd made from the room's 'no smoking' sign.

"Slow day, huh?" he asked. Axel nodded automatically.

"It's that new DIY Barn that opened down the road," Marlon said. "They're cutting into our business badly. Between you and me, I might have to let some of the newer people go."

Axel breathed in sharply. His eyes closed. When they

opened again, they were full of icy fire.

He reached out and took a cigarette from Marlon's pack. His hands no longer shook. Ignoring his supervisor's disapproving glare, he lit up and breathed in the blue smoke. Cheap supermarket cigarettes. Good enough for now.

"The DIY Barn comes for what is ours," he said. "Let them come. They will be... dealt with."

"Dealt with?" Marlon laughed.

"Oh, yes," Axel said. "Most severely."

Marlon cast an appraising eye over Axel, and what he saw made him frown. "Axel," he said. He spoke evenly, carefully. He may have looked like an extra from a gangster picture, but Axel knew Marlon was a diplomat at heart.

"Axel, you know what your probation officer told you. You know what she told *me*, for God's sake. Maybe turn it down a notch, yeah? You're beginning to scare me."

His words withered under Axel's glare.

"Of course," Axel said, half a smile on his lips. "No need to make a big deal of things."

Marlon nodded uncertainly. For a moment, it looked as if he might say something else — but only for a moment.

## 2 A Wooden Chorus

The wood sang its sweet song to Gwendolyn Harper, but for once she could not listen.

Most days, she could hear little else. Her ears filled with a thousand tunes, and she was happy. Now there was no room in her broken heart for the timber's joy.

It was Sunday morning, and the crowds were yet to arrive. Gwen worked in the timber section of Handy Pavilion, amongst the vast shelves of potential. Rough long baulks of framing pine, neat thin strips of hardwood decking, huge pallets overloaded with sheets of plywood and MDF. This was her kingdom, and these were her people—and yet she would give it all away for one sweet kiss from the man she loved from afar.

Norman, his name was. Norman. Nor-man. He was fairly new at the Pavilion. Worked in Power Tools. He was a young man of perhaps twenty, perhaps less. He had a tufty little beard that didn't suit him, yet could not obscure his beauty. There were tattoos up and down his arms. She wondered how far they extended beneath his shirt, under his apron.

Gwen had goggle eyes and was shaped like a barrel. She

knew people thought her about fifty years old, and half-Maori. That probably made her half white, but people didn't bother saying that part. It didn't matter. She was not fifty, nor Maori, nor white, nor, for that matter, human.

A burst of singing startled her from her thoughts. A middle-aged white man in a polo shirt was looking with a critical eye at a pallet of 3mm plywood. He picked up a piece and inspected it. Not a professional, but not a complete amateur either. Gwen had not seen him before but imagined him as a maker of bird feeders or dollhouses. The plywood sheets seemed to like him. They sang sweetly, their voices strong even in the vast echoing cavern of the Handy Pavilion. Too bad the man could not hear them.

Sighing, she looked back to Norman, who was in deep conversation with Axel Platzoff. Axel had been acting weirdly lately, but Gwen didn't give that much thought. She only had eyes for Norman. Norman with his stringy hair and his tight, tight jeans.

Gwen's parents had never cared for her to become involved in the selling of timber. They were old school. They loved the *trees*. And why should they not? Trees are wonderful, important things. But they are not the *only* things. There are houses and bookshelves and coffee tables. There are birdhouses and clocks and chairs and garden furniture. A tree is a tree. Timber is *potential*. Timber is a tree nearly grown up and wondering what to do with its life.

The man in the polo shirt picked a sheet of plywood that seemed to meet his requirements, then noticed something and

21

approached Gwen. Was he going to ask for a discount over some flaw? No. The label had worn away, and the barcode was unreadable. It was an easy fix, but it made people uncertain.

"No worries," she said. "We can fix that at the counter."

"Thank you so much," the man said. From his voice and manner, he was extremely middle-class and exceptionally polite. Probably one of those lefty types, happy to have a black woman to be polite to because it proved something. "He's a nice lad," the man added.

"Who?" Gwen asked. She knew who he meant. Her question was an implication that it was none of his business, rather than a request for information.

"Well, it's none of my business," he said.

There was a 'but' coming.

"*But* I see you looking at the lad," he added. "Shave him and wash him, and he'd be a handsome kid."

"He's not a lad and not a kid," Gwen said. "He's a grown man."

The man laughed. "Of course. No offence meant. He's a smart fellow, too. Bought one of the new Dremels from his department the other day, and he really knew his stuff. Don't know if he's single. But let's be honest, do you think you'd be his first choice?"

Gwen flinched as if he'd thrown a punch at her. She recovered, humiliated by his words, humiliated by her reaction.

"Okay, take your plywood and get the fuck out," she said. She was breaching half a dozen company regulations, talking to him like this, but she didn't care.

The man smiled and nodded apologetically. "I've spoken out of turn," he said. "I'm sorry I did that. Here, take my card. I owe you a favour. Feel free to call anytime and I'll do what I can. No charge."

He passed her the card. Blinking back stinging tears, she took it, fearful of breaking further regulations. When the man was out of sight, tried to tear the card into confetti. It resisted her attempt, remaining stubbornly whole. She grabbed it tighter and tore harder. Not only did it not rip, it left a shallow cut in the tips of her left fingers as the edge passed through them.

Only then did she look at the card. It read 'Richard Pennington'. Beneath the man's name, she expected to see that he was a solicitor or maybe a dentist. Perhaps she thought it might say 'The Devil' — but then she'd be the first to admit she was rather prone to cliché.

Instead, the little piece of white card read 'Richard Pennington, M.Phil, Master Alchemist'.

The Pavilion was beginning to fill with the Sunday crowd. Every week they seemed to arrive earlier, all trying to beat the crowd. Humans. Pack behaviour defined them. Gwen looked down at the card in her hand and looked up at Norman. To his obvious relief, a customer had given him the chance to get away from Axel. Now he was showing a cordless drill to a baffled looking young man.

Gwendolyn Harper listened to the song of the timber, audible even as the Pavilion filled with noise. Once again, she found that she could appreciate its beauty.

# 3 A Mystic Spring

The sink was overflowing.

Overflowing sinks were not supposed to be Wellsey's problem. The Handy Pavilion was like any other shop, in that if there was a problem with a sink or toilet, then a plumber should be called. But Marlon—cheap bastard that he was— would generally call on Wellsey to fix leaks in the grimy Pavilion bathroom. Wellsey could, and did, argue that this was not his duty. He was the senior staff member in the Plumbing section, sure, but that didn't make him a licensed plumber—or even, you know, a competent plumber.

So Wellsey would object, and Marlon would usually respond by glancing around and saying, "Well, it's not like you're busy."

It was often. A lot of customers didn't enjoy talking to Wellsey. Not so much the tradies; they didn't mind him. But the middle-class mums and dads who came into his section always gave him funny looks. Fair enough, he looked like he was bad news. He was a big man, and even though he was pushing fifty, he looked like he could dish out some damage if he wanted to. A shaven head, a facial scar, a missing front tooth, and an armful of tattoos all seemed to confirm the inevitable first impression that Wellsey was a dangerous customer.

In fact, Wellsey was mostly harmless. He had been wild enough in his youth, but age had tamed him. His scars and missing tooth all came from the same teenage motorcycle crash, while the tattoos had come during a stay in prison in his twenties for growing marijuana. The skin-head look was just his reaction to male pattern baldness. He was not a fighting man, not anymore.

Looking the way he did, he didn't have to be.

Marlon saw through Wellsey's tough exterior to the gentle soul beneath and pushed Wellsey around mercilessly.

But this time it wasn't Marlon who propelled Wellsey towards some spilled water. It was Fiona, the most junior of Wellsey's staff.

She had come rushing over while Wellsey was in the middle of a three-way conversation with Axel Platzoff and a customer. The customer was a pleasant-looking middle-aged woman hunting for some shower curtains. Inevitably, she looked past Wellsey and asked Axel. It amused Wellsey that the woman saw *him* as a threat, but implicitly trusted the quiet little fellow who had once tried to blow up the Hoover Dam.

"Next aisle, left-hand side, about halfway down," Axel said.

The pleasant-looking woman thanked him, smiled, and left, before remembering to be polite to Wellsey too. She turned, forced a smile, and carried on her way. As she went, Wellsey saw Fiona standing back, clearly excited by something, and yet too deferential to break into the conversation between her senior co-workers.

Wellsey ignored her and concentrated on Axel. Was there something about him lately, since he'd taken up smoking again? Something different? Something strange and nasty? Wellsey shook his head. No. No, that was just the drugs talking. He had been clean for over twenty years, and he was mostly over the side effects—but every now and then the paranoia would return. He just had to ride it out when it did. Axel was okay. Probably.

"So, I've been thinking about this 2IC position, and I'd like..." Axel began, but he was cut off by Fiona, whose excitement had reached a bursting point.

Axel sighed. Wellsey sighed.

Fiona... Fiona meant well. Handy Pavilion was her first job after dropping out of high school. She'd had a raft of references and letters of commendation, and it wasn't hard to understand how she'd gotten them. She was friendly and good-natured, and she tried so hard at everything she did. It seemed unfair that she was so bloody useless.

"Mr Popplewell," she said. She shifted from one foot to another.

"Wellsey, Fiona. I'm not your teacher. Everyone calls me Wellsey."

Fiona paused a second, perhaps wondering whether to address him as Mr Wellsey. In the end, she simply said: "There's a problem with the sink. There's water going everywhere."

Axel swore and pointed at the floor. Looking down, Wellsey saw a pool of water seeping under the heavy shelving unit, soaking into the cardboard of some boxes of toilet seats that lay on the floor.

Fiona blushed brightly. "It's going everywhere, sir."

How long had it been overflowing? There was only one toilet for staff and customers, halfway across the cavernous Pavilion. How had the water spread so far before anyone noticed it?

Fiona grabbed Wellsey by the sleeve and with surprising strength dragged him into the next aisle, to a neat display of half a dozen gleaming new bathroom sinks. They stood lined neatly in an alcove in one of the massive shelves which cut up the space in the store. Sure enough, an embarrassed-looking woman was trying to turn off the tap on a midrange Swedish unit, while water spilled out over her open-toed shoes.

"How?" Wellsey said.

"I don't..." the woman said, completely flustered. "That young woman... I said I didn't need her to show me..." she added accusingly.

Fiona blushed an even deeper shade of red, from her mousy hair to her gold-rimmed glasses to the green collar of her shirt.

"How did you do that?' Wellsey asked her. "Those sinks aren't plumbed in."

"Oh. Is that why it's overflowing?"

"Is that? No! That's the opposite of why, Fiona."

Grabbing the tap in his calloused hands, Wellsey wrenched it into the off position. Still, the water came. He looked at his coworkers for assistance. Fiona merely goggled at the tap and hopped from one foot to another. Axel stared at the flowing water, nothing on his face but confusion. If a genius like Axel couldn't figure it out, that didn't leave Wellsey with much confidence he could manage.

Wellsey tried again. He slowly turned the tap on, then manfully wrenched it closed. The flow of the water did not alter. The customer was still there, so Wellsey bit down on a mouthful of curses before they left his lips. He tried again. Nothing.

"I tried that," the customer said. God save us from helpful customers!

"So *you* turned it on, Fiona?" Axel said.

"Yes."

"Have you tried to turn it off?"

This seemed to Wellsey a silly question to ask, but then there was nothing sensible about the situation. "Give it a go, Fiona," he shrugged.

Fiona looked up as if seeking inspiration in the vast ceiling fans. Stepping forward, she grasped the tap and turned. The flow of water ceased immediately.

"Interesting," Axel said.

"Holy living crap," Wellsey said.

"That's what I said," Axel said. "Try turning it on, Fiona."

Blushing like a stop-light, Fiona opened the tap a half-turn, and a little stream trickled from the minimalist Scandinavian device. She quickly turned it off.

"Huh," Axel said. He reached out and turned the tap, but nothing came out. He tried the sink next to it, a (frankly overpriced) Japanese unit. Nothing happened. "Fiona?" Fiona also turned the tap, but nothing happened.

"How about the hot tap on the original unit?" asked the customer, who seemed to have gotten over her initial embarrassment and was becoming curious.

"I don't know..." Wellsey said, but he must not have said it loud enough because Fiona opened said tap, and more water poured out.

Axel put his hand in the stream. "Not hot," he said. A moment later he said, "Ouch!" and pulled his fingers away. "Just needed a moment to run hot, I guess."

Wellsey rubbed his beard. "All right. All right."

All eyes were on him now. He hadn't pulled himself up from the gutter for this, but fate had given this to him to deal with, anyway. It was going to take all of his management skills, all his leadership, to deal with this.

"Fiona, mop up," he said. "Never touch this unit again. Understand? This did not happen. This absolutely did not happen. I'm not a tough bloke to work for; I reckon I can say that. But I'm not letting *any* laws of science get broken in my section. Sorry, Missus, about the problem. If you need compensation for your shoes, I'll make it happen even if I have to pay out of my own pocket. But this did not happen, all right?"

Fiona nodded with enthusiasm. The customer looked doubtful, but also seemed keener to get new shoes than to investigate an unnatural phenomenon. And Axel... Axel just looked thoughtful.

# 4 Coffee Break

Gwen sipped her coffee in the break room that smelled of smoke, but she didn't light up herself. She did smoke, but she did not care for tobacco. For all his laxness on OHS, Marlon did not like people smoking illicit substances on his watch.

The room itself was like most break rooms. A cheap table. Some indifferently washed coffee mugs. A zip boiler with a little rim of scale around the spout. A corkboard covered with papers—urgent policy updates side by side with party invitations from three years before and a faded group photo of people in Pavilion uniforms, most of whom had left long ago. A bicycle was perpetually parked in a free corner. No one knew if it was left there every day by the same early riser, or if it was long abandoned.

Gwen drummed her fingers on the plastic of the table. There was much on her mind. She lived a simple life and seldom found herself with great moral choices to make. What Pennington offered… It can't have been right to do as he suggested. And yet, how could she say no? Legally, Pennington's plan was probably okay. No law against it—or if there was, it was part of some old law against witchcraft, something that remained on the books even though no one had cared since the dark ages. No, there was no law against it exactly, but there were similar things — modern things — that were pretty damn illegal.

She needed to distract herself. Someone had left a *Woman's Day* on the table, but the crossword had been finished. The only other thing to read was the South Hertling Super Centre newsletter, which was usually pretty dull. There was no one to chat with, so she picked it up.

"New Carpet Shop Opening!" read the headline. After that was a brief paragraph explaining how Majestic Carpets would be opening in the shop next to the Place O' Pets.

What had that shop been that used to be there? Oh, that's right, it had been Royal Carpets. Gwen sighed. A story about a new carpet shop opening on the site of a former carpet shop might just be the dullest thing she had ever read. Besides, after the first paragraph, it just trailed off into ramblings about the Illuminati and alien conspiracies — as bloody usual. For the hundredth time, she wondered who wrote the newsletter and for the hundredth time, she decided she'd rather not know.

"Poor tree," she whispered to the page. "You could have been anything, and they made you into this."

Fiona, the new girl, walked in and nodded an awkward greeting. She took her coffee cup with its picture of some boy band and put a tea bag in it. She hesitated before flipping the tap of the hot water boiler. That was a new one, Gwen thought. Another awkward mannerism to add to a long list.

"How you settling in?" Gwen said.

Fiona looked at her, startled, as if she'd only just noticed

Gwen. "I'm okay," she said. But she said it in a defensive way, as if she'd just been unjustly accused of not being okay.

Gwen considered pressing the conversation, but instead, she took mercy and let Fiona be. The girl picked up the newsletter and read, ostentatiously focusing all of her attention on it. Gwen considered playing a game on her phone, but the battery was low. She sighed and sipped her coffee. The hot water contained the echo of the beans, long dead and yet alive, their spirits trapped in freeze-dried granules. Gwen coaxed them into a final song before they went to their reward.

When she looked up, she saw Fiona staring at the newsletter in bewilderment, shaking her head. The one good thing about the ridiculous paper was watching new staff puzzling over it. Fiona was literally scratching her head. Soon she laid the letter down on the table, gently, as if it might go off.

"Who writes that stuff?" she wondered.

"No idea."

"How long have you worked here?"

"Too long."

"Have you worked in other places?"

Gwen paused a moment before answering. "Yes," she said. Technically, that was true.

"Is this a good place to work?"

"You tell me."

"I mean, compared to other places?"

"Better than some," Gwen said. "Worse than others."

"It's just... I don't know if I like it here."

"This your first job, love?"

"Yes," Fiona said. "My parents wanted me to stay in school, but my teacher talked them out of it. They tried to get me an apprenticeship, but."

"But?"

"But it didn't work out."

Gwen tried to imagine Fiona wiring a house or using a circular saw, or even a kitchen knife. Each image she brought to mind made her wince. Fiona — and those around her — were probably safest when she was stocking shelves. It was a sad destiny in life, but there are worse ones.

"Well, you're young," Gwen said. "This might not be a job for life, but you shouldn't give up just yet. Stick around a bit. You'll know better after a month."

"That's what my parents said," Fiona moaned.

"Yeah, parents," Gwen said. "They want what's best for you, and that's the problem. Means their advice is no good. You can just think, 'what's the best for me'? and get the same answer. Might as well not bother talking to them."

Fiona's eyebrows huddled together like possums on seeking warmth on a winter night. "Yes, I see what you mean."

"Who you should ask is your grandmother," Gwen said. "Or your granddad. They'll do what grandparents always do — what they wanted to do for their kids, but couldn't 'cause... Well, 'cause they're their kids. Grandparents don't always give the best advice, but you can always get *different* advice."

Gwen hoped she was making sense. She wasn't sure

that she was until Fiona nodded slowly.

"That's a good idea, Rachel," Fiona said. The girl never got anyone's name right, even though they were all wearing nametags. "I'll ask Nan. See what she says." Fiona sipped her tea, deep in thought.

Gwen sighed and swirled her coffee around her chipped enamel mug. The air in the room felt muggy and stale. It always had been muggy and stale, she thought, but now she *felt* it. She took a sip, and examined the design on her cup: Geeveston, Tasmania, it read, over a picture of a tree.

Sometimes in life, you know what it is that you ought to do, but you don't know until you say it out loud. Grandmother. There was nothing for it but to ask grandmother.

Reaching into her pocket, Gwen withdrew a crumpled paper bag containing a small bottle. A handwritten label read, 'Love Potion.'

Grandmother. Definitely.

# 5 The Shirts

Axel sat in the loading dock. It was nearly midday, and it was as hot as an oven. A little drop of sweat made its way down his face to the point of his chin. It hung there for a moment, then dropped down to the green collar of his Handy Pavilion shirt, where it soaked into the fabric. Axel ignored it. His eyes were focused on a spot between the Place O' Pets' building and a parked truck. He could only see a little sliver through this gap—a busy roadway, and beyond that a small section of concrete wall painted an unpleasant yellow.

The DIY Barn.

The enemy.

"Hot out, eh?"

Axel was aware of the voice in the same way he was aware of the drops of sweat down his face—present, but distant from his thoughts. He heard his own voice reply: "Going to get hotter, they say."

"Sounds about bloody right."

Axel did not look around. The other voice belonged to Norman, an affable idiot who worked in Power Tools. From what Axel could gather, Norman had wanted to work in hardware ever since he had been a small child. Is a man who has achieved his life's ambition at the age of twenty a man to be envied or pitied? Axel didn't know, and he didn't care to think about it.

Norman continued to make polite conversation, and Axel devoted as little brainpower as possible to replying. Fortunately, the boy was only talking about tennis. Axel had long since developed a simple algorithm for holding his own in tennis conversations. Lucky the lad wasn't keen on cricket. Even with all his genius, Axel found cricket simply baffling.

Axel's mouth was saying something about clay courts when he saw it—the armoured van. He checked his watch. 11.43. The van was not quite regular, varying its arrival time by as much as twenty minutes. That would have to be accounted for in the plan.

Not that the plan was well formed at this point. It couldn't be close to any of his previous schemes or he'd be the prime suspect. Something low-key then. Sleeping gas? No, security guards tended to carry re-breathers these days... what then?

"Freeze rays?" Norman said.

Axel reddened, realising he'd been muttering out loud.

"It's nothing," Axel said.

"Don't worry, mate. You should hear some of the shit that goes on in my head when I have a brain fart, hey?"

Charming. Still, the lad didn't seem concerned or curious, and that was what mattered.

The van left. It had been there for five minutes fewer than usual. Axel shook his head. This was why, back in his supervillain days, he'd stuck to world domination. Conquest took big, grandiose schemes, not the sort of Swiss-watch timing you need for a heist.

Axel took a cigarette and offered another to Norman, who declined.

"Oh," Norman said. "That big guy was asking after you."

Axel's spine went cold. "Which big guy?"

"Don't know his name. He's in here pretty often. He keeps breaking shit and claiming it was like that when he bought it. You know, you were talking to him last week. He looks a bit like Captain Stellar — if Stellar wore glasses, but."

"What did you tell him?"

"He asked about your promotion. I said that you pretty much had it, since Gino quit when they cut his hours, and Mags went over to the DIY Barn. He seemed pretty stoked for you."

Axel relaxed.

The door opened, and Marlon stuck his head out. "Norman? A word."

The lad popped back inside. To his surprise, Axel felt sorry to see him go. There was something about the *shirts* that Handy Pavilion made its employees wear. In some troublesome way, it made the wearers more... solid? That wasn't quite the right word, but it would do. People wearing them held Axel's attention in a way that most people did not.

Axel sucked angrily on his cigarette. It was confusing.

Axel finished his smoke and stubbed it out with the toe of his work boot. As he did, the cracked red fire door opened again, and Norman slumped out. Something was wrong. To his surprise, Axel found himself asking what the problem was even before working out how to use Norman's state to his advantage.

"They're going to fire me," Norman said. He was clearly holding back tears. Axel wasn't quite sure how to react.

"Aren't they happy with the job you're doing?"

"It's not that. It's DIY Barn." He seemed to have more to say, but clamped his mouth shut. Axel knew what he meant. Layoffs. Last on, first off. That put two heads right on the chopping block—Norman's and Fiona's.

That gave Axel two immediate allies. Norman would be of moderate value, but Fiona could be a real help to his plan. He smiled. His desire to help the wearers of the shirts seemed to be coming back into line with his more natural desires. He wiped the sweat off his brow with the back of his hand. Yes, Norman and Fiona could be easily persuaded.

Depending on how many people Marlon would be firing at once, Donna in Lighting would be next in line. But recruiting her would mean crossing Sadie, the formidable Lighting team leader, and Axel wasn't ready for that. Not yet. Belinda? The checkout operator with the terrible jokes? Marlon would be happy to let go of her, but she had seniority over a number of the people in Gardening...

"So, you planning on robbing the DIY Barn?"

It wasn't just the words that made Axel flinch; it was Norman's tone. It was conversational—as if he were asking what Axel was doing on the weekend, or whether he could lend him twenty until payday.

"What?"

"Mate, I might not be the sharpest tool in the shed," Norman said, "But you see a supervillain eyeing armoured cars and talking about freeze rays; you don't need a calculator to do the maths on that one. If you're going for it, I'm in. Don't worry, I don't want the money. You got to launder it and shit, like on *Breaking Bad*. Looks complicated. No, I just want to take those smug bastards down a peg."

Behind Axel's sternum, and above his solar plexus, he felt an unfamiliar warm feeling. It felt odd, wrong, out of place, and yet it was strangely pleasant. Against his will, he felt his face crinkle into a smile.

What was it about those shirts?

# 6 Luminiferous

"Will this take an LED bulb?"

Sadie McGregor looked up from the manifest she had been checking, to see a huge fat man. At first, she took him for a glutton, but a closer look told her he was not. Perhaps he had a glandular condition? It didn't matter. What mattered was that he was thrusting a standard lamp at her.

"It will take any bulb with a standard Edison screw," she said.

"You sure? I don't want to have to bring it back."

Sadie looked up from her manifest and gave the man her full attention. His eyes widened, and he swallowed hard. This often happened to people on the receiving end of Sadie's full attention. She gazed deeper into his eyes. His soul was in relatively good shape, other than some mild office pilfering and... ah. A short, doomed affair that he'd never told his wife about. He really *should* tell her.

"Here,' she said. "I will show you."

"Uh, if you say it will work, I'm sure you know..."

"I will *show* you. Behold!"

She pointed at a line of shelves, packed high with all shapes and sizes of bulbs. She took an LED bulb from its box and screwed it into the lamp. Then, she unplugged an ugly plastic reading lamp in the display area, plugged the big man's standard lamp into the empty socket, and switched it on. A warm feeling rose inside her as the LEDs flared into life, and the lamp gave off a pleasant glow. She smiled at the big man, who seemed to relax.

"Do you see?" Sadie demanded. "Do you see the *light*?"

The man gave a nervous laugh. "Yes, thank you. I'll take it. And the bulb. They cost almost as much as the lamps, these days. More, sometimes."

"LED lamps give off more light than the old bulbs," Sadie said. "So much more. And they last longer. Use less electricity."

"So I guess you make your money back in the end?"

Sadie could see the big man's fear. Not immediate fear, like the pedestrian who sees a truck coming, or the swimmer who realises—a moment too late—that the dorsal fin he has been watching does not belong to a dolphin. No, it was just the day-to-day uneasiness of a man who does not know what to make of something.

"It is not about money," she said. "It is about light. That is what matters. Can I help you with anything else?"

"I'm good," he said, quickly. "Thanks a heap!"

He scurried off towards the cashiers, casting worried glances backwards.

Sadie went back to checking her manifest against the shelves of bulbs. Everything was correct, but it was her duty to check, so she checked. All the bulbs and globes, all the tubes and downlights, all the halogens and LEDs, and all those cool-looking but dim Edison bulbs that all the hipsters seemed to love. It was a huge range, spreading over two lanes of tall shelving. She had seen strong men brought to helpless confusion by the bewildering array, unable to find which of the hundreds of products could replace the missing bulb in a ten-year-old fridge.

But Sadie was always there to help them. Help them find the light.

Sadie's junior, Donna, scuttled over. She always seemed to move that way, in a sort of half-sideways walk, like a crab that refuses to commit. The girl was an inveterate liar. She occasionally drove drunk and was addicted to a particularly revolting form of Japanese pornography. Still, she had not been under Sadie's tutelage for long. She would learn.

"Hey, boss lady," she said. "You hear the goss? Central office wanted to lay off a bunch of us, but Marlon managed to get them to change their minds. They are cutting our hours instead — a lot of hours."

Donna did not seem overly concerned about this change. She was a student and her parents were quite wealthy. She only worked at the Pavilion in order to earn enough money to make purchases that did not show up on her parents' credit card bill. To the other youngsters, this blow would cut deep.

"How many hours?"

"I'm basically down to Saturdays and Thursday nights. It sucks."

"Language," Sadie said. "Well, I suppose I can do

without you Sundays."

Sadie could have done without her at all. She could have run the whole department herself, from 7 am open to 7 pm close. Her team existed purely because Head Office believed them necessary.

"Well, at least it means I can stay up later Saturday night if I don't have to be in early Sunday," Donna said.

"You mean you won't get in trouble for turning up late and hungover anymore," Sadie said.

Donna laughed. She seemed to find all of her moral failings amusing. It did not matter. She was young. She would *learn*.

As if determined to prove Sadie right, Donna shook her head in that awkward way she did when she wanted to do something right. "You, uh, you were going to explain about the floodlights to me?"

Sadie did not smile, yet she was pleased. They always came around in the end. No matter how hard they worked to deny it, the human soul is drawn to light like a moth to the flame.

She looked down the aisle that ran across the back of the Pavilion. Down several aisles, past hand tools, past mailboxes, past doors, door numbers, and doormats stood her twin sister: Angela, team leader in charge of Curtains, Blinds, and Shutters. Sadie bristled as she saw that Angela was demonstrating shut-out blinds to the big man with the standard lamp.

Angela realised that she was being watched. She looked up and for a moment, her eye met Sadie's. With a gesture of her head, she directed Sadie's gaze further down the corridor, where Axel Platzoff was shaking the hand of Marlon Dillinger, Acting Manager.

Now? So soon? Her shock must have shown, because Angela smirked at her, before returning to her hideous business.

# 7 Diversion

"Ow!"

Captain Stellar had a couple of lengths of two-by-four in his trolley. When he reached the cashier, he realised he'd put them in the wrong way around, and the woman at the checkout couldn't get at the barcodes. It was a stupid mistake. Cycloman always did that, and Stellar would always correct him. Now, here was Stellar doing it himself.

Annoyed, he'd flipped the two-bees end-over-end. He must have whacked the poor cashier while he was doing it. Her eyes were shut tight in pain and she clutched her temple.

"Oh! I'm so sorry!" Stellar said. "How careless! Here, let me..."

Let me what? Apply a tourniquet? Kiss it better? What could he do? What could he do?

The cashier let go of her forehead and grinned. There was no bruise, no cut. "Nah, I'm fine," she said. "You're the third person I got with that one."

Someone in the queue behind Stellar gave a short, mirthless laugh. A joke. A cruel, unnecessary joke. Stellar forced a smile. Jokes are the unkindest form of cruelty. You have to pretend to be a good sport about them.

The woman rang up his two-bees, his Ant-Rid, and his ferns. Cycloman had always hated ferns. Guess that didn't matter anymore.

Cycloman...

He pushed his trolley out towards the car park. He'd been so out of it that morning that he'd nearly driven the Stellar Wagon into the Handy Pavilion. The day before, he'd almost gone to his day job in his mask. Concentrate! Needed to concentrate. Hold it together. He was better off without that rat bastard anyway...

He checked his phone. No messages in the three minutes since he checked it last. Good. If Cycloman called, he'd get a piece of Stellar's mind. Coward probably knew that, and that was why he wasn't calling, and... Oh. Terrific. There, by the entrance, checking people's purchases, was Professor bloody Devistato.

"Captain," the Professor smiled.

"Professor," the Captain sighed, showing his receipt.

"Oh, don't worry about that," the Professor said, waving the paper away. "If I can't trust *you* not to steal, who *can* I trust? And please, call me Axel."

The little man turned away to check the receipt of a teenaged boy carrying a box of spray paints. Stellar glowered at the kid. Graffiti was usually beneath his notice, but right then, he would have accepted even the most trivial call to justice.

Axel laughed. The sound surprised Stellar. He'd heard Axel's evil supervillain laugh often enough, but this was the first time he'd heard the man laugh in genuine amusement.

"Don't worry about the lad, Captain. He's with the drama club at the local high school. Uses those spray paints to make scenery and backdrops. Quite a promising artist, I'm told."

Why is it that the people who you least want to talk to are always the keenest to chat? Why can't they see that they're being nuisances?

"I wish you wouldn't call me Captain," Stellar said.

"I don't know your name."

"It's Vincent."

"Is Vince okay?"

"No."

"Vincent it is. I got my promotion, by the way."

"So, why are you watching the door?"

"The guy rostered on for today called in sick and, well, rank has its duties as well as its privileges. How's Cycloman?"

"How the Hell should I know?"

Axel had been smiling. Not a genuinely happy smile, Stellar thought, but that dutiful customer service smile. The smile faded, to be replaced by a look of concern. "Yeah," he said. "I feel the same way about Empress Zagona of Ceres. She... it's... look, I know that you and I have had our differences, but if you need to..."

"No! I don't 'need to!'" Stellar snapped. "I don't need to 'talk', I don't need to 'take some time', I don't need 'some space' or 'some help' or any bloody thing. *I help people.* That's the way help works. *You* don't help *me*, understand? You, *especially,* of *all people,* do not help me!"

Axel backed away a step, his expression carefully neutral. "Of course. It was wrong of me to presume. Forgive me."

"If you want to help, tell that damn cashier over there not to make jokes at customers' expense," Stellar said, relenting slightly. "She made me think I accidentally hit her! That's not funny, playing with people's empathy like that. It's just mean."

"Would you like it to be a formal warning or informal?"

"What's the difference?"

"Three formal warnings and she's fired. She's already on two."

Stellar sighed. Sometimes a good person was the worst thing to be. "No," he said. "Just tell her to pull her head in."

Axel nodded. "I will. She knows she's on thin ice."

"Thanks." A million thoughts crowded Stellar's mind. He was sorry he snapped at Axel. It was wrong to take out his frustrations on others. He wanted to apologise, but couldn't force the words out of his mouth.

"I got to go," he said.

"Watch out for the Wellington Rd exit," Axel said. "It's usually the quickest way back onto the Hurley Rd, but the lunch rush is starting now, so it's easier if you go by Kurrawong."

"Thanks."

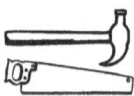

Axel watched Stellar push his trolley away. It was

loaded with heavy items, and Stellar ought to push it slowly to emphasise the fact that he was an ordinary man. Instead, he just barrelled along as if the cart was empty. How was it that no one ever put two and two together and figured out his secret identity?

Perhaps no one cared. Maybe that was it. Maybe superheroes put all that effort into protecting their secrets, and everyone else just went about their lives as if it didn't matter.

Stellar's presence had been an unexpected complication, but Axel was good at thinking on his feet. He checked his watch. If Stellar took the Kurrawong Ln exit, he'd miss the armoured car heist by minutes. Still, he did feel bad for the big galoot, nasty breakup, and everything. Perhaps Empress Zagona would know how to help. If he called…

Axel gave a rueful smile. The heart and its tricks! Just when you think you know them all, it tries to pull another one. He looked over to the checkout and gave Belinda, the girl with the bad jokes, a thumbs up. She gave a thumbs-up back to him, and they both went about their business.

# 8 The Newsletter

From the South Hertling Super Centre Newsletter February 29th, 2016:

## Robbery Nearly Strikes Super Centre

By Karl Wintergreen

Last week, an armoured car was robbed on Wellington Rd, mere moments away from the South Hertling Supercentre. Had it been a mere fifty metres south, the car would have been within the precincts of our beloved Supercentre. This, apparently, would have justified the expense of an additional issue of this newsletter, to write about the exciting crime. But, since it took place a *whole* fifty metres away, I was unable to write about it until now. Also, I am not allowed to devote the entire issue to the crime, since I still have to make space for that piece about how Place 'O Pets teamed up with the local high school to raise money for Guide Dogs.

Some of you are probably interested in that crap. Sheeple.

Last week on the day in question, an armoured car servicing the DIY Barn across the street at South Bannerman

Mega Centre was robbed in broad daylight. Around ten:17 o'clock in the morning of that day, a water pipe burst, spilling water onto Wellington Road. I was there later to take photos and interview the guy from the water department, who was unable to explicitly prove that the Trilateral Commission was uninvolved saying, quote, "don't know what you mean, bro,' end quote new paragraph.

At about a few hours later, the armoured car was barrelling along, unaware of the fate that was in store for it. I didn't know either, being as I was in the can when the first exciting thing ever happened near here happened. According to NSW Police, the water on the Wellinfton road froze, sending the armoured car into a spin, and blocking traffic on Wellington. Then, two person or people unknown rushed the van, blew the door off with an incendiary device and knocked the already disorientatedted guards out with tasers. They took bags containing approx. 1 (one) (I) metric buttload of cash into a car and accelerated away on the traffic-free Wellington Rd.

As I said, I didn't see this. A police spokesman said this to a bunch of simpering toadies from the "so-called" lamestream media, and I wasn't even aloud to ask my question, viz, is it true that the NSW Police Force's has been infiltrated by the MK ULTRA/Illuminati conspiracy and is the commissioner really a reptilian shapeshifter? But that jerk from Channel Seven got to ask his stupid, insipid question about what the getaway car looked like. Pathetic.

At this point I returned to the can (the effect of CIA microwave satellites, or else last night's curry repeating on me?).

Later I asked DIY Barn Operations Manager John Smith about the robbery. He was very nice, and he offered me a cup of instant coffee and a biscuit. I turned down the coffee, because the freeze-drying process which is supposed to keep the coffee fresh actually releases psychotropic mind control drugs. Mr Smith said ok, then how about the biscuit? I said that was probably ok.

Mr Smith said that the robbery was the work of criminals who should be brought to justice, which is a good point. He also said that the robbery would not impact on DIY Barn operations. The DIY Barn was too strong to be affected by such nonsense and the DIY Barn would prevail. When they came to write the history of the DIY Barn, they would write of glory, of strength, of victory after victory, and not, NOT this little setback, this pointless little act of simpering cowards and perverts. What was a few dollars to the DIY Barn? What? Did the savages; the filthy, crawling scum behind this dastardly but pointless act think they were even in a position hurt the DIY Barn? If they thought so, they were wrong, sorely wrong. For the DIY Barn would triumph for a thousand years! All the petty thieves in the world should attack it, and they would be crushed, crushed beneath the Barn, as beneath the wheels of mighty Juggernaut!

I said thank you for the biscuits. They were gingernuts.

About two days or so later, give or take, the alleged car used by the robbers allegedly was found by police abandoned in a local creek, possibly Sloane creek. The spokespolice was still refusing to take my calls, but told my friend Rita that enquiries were proceeding and that an announcement would be made soon. He or she did not answer my question about Roswell, because Rita refused to ask it.

**Weather to-day:** Cloudy.

**Charity for Guide Dogs Not Just Random Luck!**

Students from Local High School teamed up with the Place O' Pets in order to raise money for the Guide Dog Association. The school kids organised a sponsored pet-wash at their school, in which people brought in their pets and the kids washed them for money. This amount of money was matched by the Place O' Pets. Asked why they'd chosen to support the Guide Dog Association rather than UFO Abductees for 9/11 Truth, the Place O' Petts CEO was cagey and evasive, in a manner typically associated with the higher degrees of Masonry.

I would of taken a photo of the kids giving a check to the Guide Dog people, but it was just a regular cheque not one of those cool giant checcques, so screw 'em.

Local High School is named after Sir Robert Local, inventor of the self-adhesive envelope. It is also a high school local to this area, a fact that causes more bemusement than confusion.

# 9 The Phial

A man was looking at melamine boards. He checked their lengths for defects, then raised them to eye height and held them straight ahead to see if they were straight. He was doing a terrible job of it, taking far too long and picking a bunch of boards that Gwen could see, even from five metres away, were sub-par.

The customer had probably never had to check boards before. He'd probably learned the technique out of a book or a YouTube video. Men who were just starting in on woodwork tended to be like that. There seemed to be a weird belief amongst men that woodworking is in the blood, and so asking for help was admitting that something was wrong with them.

They seemed perfectly okay with asking about paint, though. Colours. Women's stuff. A bloke could be forgiven for not knowing.

The man took his substandard timber and walked away with an artificial, knowing look. Gwen sighed. It's easy to be contemptuous about people who pretend to know what they're doing—but that's all of us, sooner or later. At least the timber was happy; its song grew brighter as he left.

Visiting home had been a disappointment. Gwen's

parents had been hostile, as they had been ever since she'd left. Nanna though... she was always sympathetic to Gwen, but when Gwen had sat down and explained her plan, Nanna had told her in no uncertain terms that it was wrong.

"A love potion is a thing of evil," Nanna had said over tea and scones. "Love doesn't come out of a bottle. Something that looks like love might, but the real thing never does. It's a cruel thing to keep someone in a state like that, of making them have fake love so you can have the real thing. You tell this Pennington to go stuff himself."

She was right, of course, but it hadn't been what Gwen had wanted to hear. She had told herself that what she wanted from Nanna was advice. In truth, what she wanted was *permission*. She'd have to give the potion back to Pennington when...

As if answering a silent call, Pennington crossed into the timber section, his trolley loaded with cleaning chemicals and plastic tubes. He looked up at Gwen as if surprised to see her and gave a friendly wave.

"Hello, Gwen," he said. "I've missed you around here the last few days. Been away?"

Gwen reached into her jeans pocket and extracted a small glass phial. "Here. I've changed my mind."

"Keep it," Pennington shrugged. "You might change your mind again."

"I won't," Gwen said. "I don't need it. I'm going to march up to Norman and ask him out, and if he says no, I'm just going to bloody cop it."

Pennington's smile faded. "I have to admit, Gwendolyn, I'm feeling a little insulted. I give you a very valuable product, completely free of charge, and you throw it in my face. Do you know what I usually charge for something like that? More than you paid for your car, probably. I'm not a generous man by nature, and I think it's wrong to throw such generosity aside, lightly."

Gwen snarled at him. She guessed that if she pressed the phial on him, he'd refuse it, so she stepped forward and slipped it into the pocket of his grey business shirt.

"I. Don't. Want. It."

Pennington turned his head from side to side, taking Gwen in from all angles. The song of the timber became low and ominous as the boards and beams became caught up in the suspense.

The alchemist shrugged theatrically. "Very well," he said. "If you change your mind, be aware that the next one will not be free. Good morning."

The song of the wood took on a relieved tone, and Pennington pushed his trolley towards the checkout. Gwen stood back, her arms folded. A teenaged girl approached Gwen with a sheet of 3mm MDF, but caught the look on her face and backed away.

Gwen breathed out slowly. She'd done the right thing. She knew it, because it felt as disheartening and disappointing as doing the right thing so often does. What now? What now? How she felt about Norman hadn't changed. She'd arrived this morning, and he'd given her a big smile and she'd almost fainted. She knew the smile was not for her; it was just that he was in a good mood, but even so…

Had she meant what she said to Pennington? Had she meant it about marching up to Norman and asking him out? She should. She should, damn it. He would say no. Almost certainly, he would. But then she could move on, get past him. Fuck it, why not? In saying 'no' to Pennington, she'd just given up her last chance of being with Norman. Why not make it official?

She strode out of Timber and into Power Tools. Anticlimax. Norman wasn't there. Gwen almost slunk away, but gritted her teeth and asked Norman's supervisor, Ali, where he was.

"I think I saw him out in Seasonal with Axel," Ali said. "You see him, tell him to get his arse back here; he's not on a break."

Gwen marched off to Seasonal, which was in the process of clearing out the air conditioners to replace them with heaters. There, between a pile of Dyson fans and a drift of Easter merchandise, was Norman, talking to Axel and Fiona from Plumbing. Axel said something Gwen couldn't hear, but it made the kids jump with glee when they heard it. Axel pressed his finger to his lips and swaggered off. Norman put his arms around Fiona. She hugged him back, then the two released one another and strolled off to their respective departments.

The DIY Barn was a big building. Now it seemed bigger. The walls seemed further away, the tin roof seemed miles overhead. The shoppers seemed like a sea, a river in which little gnome-like staff members bobbed and floated.

It only lasted a moment, before Gwen shook her head clear.

"Righty-o," she said, before rushing for the exit. If she hurried, she might catch Pennington in the car park.

# 10 A Dilemma for Wellsey

Wellsey watched Fiona with horrified interest. Here was a woman who, not that long ago, could barely tell one end of a plunger from another. Hell, a fortnight ago he'd seen her reduced to mumbling incoherence by a simple question about bath plugs. Now she was selling like Arthur Daley on steroids.

"Sure, this one's top of the line," she said. "But you've got to ask yourself, 'do I need top of the line', yeah? You're doing one of those dream-home sort of projects, you've got money to burn, then yeah, get this one. But for a place the size you're talking about, I'd suggest the one over here. Looks good, solidly built, nine-year guarantee, and half the price of the one you were looking at."

"Yeah, but you know, it's top of the line," the customer said. He was a nervous-looking man with a ginger moustache, who wouldn't stop scratching at an earlobe.

"Sometimes top quality is worth it," Fiona nodded. "But bottom line, any sink will get your hands clean."

"So, what's wrong with that cheap one?"

"That? Nothing. My dad has one of those. Keeps it in the garage for cleaning himself up after working on a car. But the one in his bathroom, the one that visitors see? He likes something better, yeah?"

The back and forth went on for another two minutes, before the man with the ginger moustache gave up and took the sink unit that Fiona recommended.

Wellsey hadn't thought that Fiona had seen him, but she didn't seem surprised when he stepped forward. "If he bought the one he wanted, he'd have been back in a week to exchange it," she said. "Saves us on admin work."

She was probably right, but that was the problem. Fiona was a well-intentioned incompetent. How had that changed, and why was it so disturbing that she had?

"That's good work, Fiona," Wellsey said. "You've been improving a lot lately, and I appreciate it."

Had she changed her hair? As a married man, Wellsey had painstakingly trained himself to notice when his *wife* had her hair done, but still found it difficult to tell when other women had. Fiona had done something with her appearance, anyway. The girl was still somewhere in that vast grey area between 'attractive' and 'unattractive', but she seemed more... professional, somehow?

Maybe it *was* her hair.

Wellsey gritted his teeth. Her hair wasn't the issue. He was only focusing on it as a way to avoid thinking about what he wanted to ask.

"I... I notice you're hanging around with Norman a lot," he said.

"Yeah," Fiona said. "He's a good guy. We've got to be good friends over the last couple of weeks. He's like a brother to me."

"And both of you are hanging around with Axel."

Fiona looked a little more guarded at that. "Yeah," she said. "He's been… giving me help with my work."

"What, like sales tips?"

"No, no," Fiona said quickly. "That's your job. Axel respects that. He's been helping me with my confidence, my self-esteem."

Was that good or bad? That was the trouble. It could easily be either. "What I mean is…" Wellsey began, "look, Axel and I have something in common, in that we both got in trouble with the law. A lot. And now we're both out of trouble and moving on with our lives, right? But… but it doesn't always work like that. Sometimes people get in trouble and they never get out. They end up in jail forever, or dead, or worse."

Fiona said nothing. She regarded him, as if trying to make sense of what he was saying. What had he been expecting? A guilty look? A poker face? Either of those things would have said something.

He continued: "What I mean is… what I mean is, don't make the mistakes we made, I guess. You know what I mean? You're getting advice from two former criminals. I just hope we're only giving you good advice."

"I see what you mean," Fiona said.

"Do you?" Wellsey said, not certain what he meant himself. "Do you?"

"Yes," Fiona said. "It's okay. I'll keep out of trouble."

He wanted to say more, but a customer was calling. He

waved Fiona on her way and stood, deep in thought.

"It's the water, the water on the road," came a voice from behind him. "That's the little detail that's bothering you."

Turning, Wellsey saw Sadie McGregor. He didn't much like Sadie. There was something about her eyes, something judgy that Wellsey didn't care for. On the other hand, she *was* right. That *was* what had been bothering him, way in the back of his brain.

The armoured car robbery. The water on the road. Fiona hadn't demonstrated her strange ability with water since the incident with the sink. But Wellsey hadn't forgotten.

"Shit," he said. "Do you think Fiona was involved?"

"Do *you*?"

"I… I don't know," Wellsey said. He'd tried to forget all about the stupid incident with the sink … Tried to reject the obvious conclusion that there was something weird about Fiona. But then, random water from nowhere… But it didn't mean anything. Sometimes there was water on the road. So what? It didn't implicate a strange young woman in an armed robbery.

Did it?

"Wait a second," Wellsey said. "What's it got to do with you?"

"Nothing," Sadie said. "What's it got to do with you?"

"Not a thing," Wellsey said. "I'm her supervisor. Not her Dad, not her teacher, not her parole officer, not her priest. If she's misbehaving off the clock, why is it any business of mine?"

"If you believe that," Sadie said. "If, in your heart of hearts, you *truly* believe that, then carry on as you were. Stand back and let her do as she will."

Wellsey slumped and ran his hand over his bald head. There had been a time in his life when he'd been convinced that he would die young. It was sort of a relief, the thought that he might be gone before he ever had to worry about the long-term consequences of actions. Stubbornly, though, he'd survived, and now he had a responsibility to Fiona. Not a contractual or a legal responsibility. It was the other sort of responsibility, the sort that no one enforces – and that is the worst sort of all.

He looked up to talk to Sadie, but she was walking away. She had a stiff walk, like a wind-up toy. Perhaps there was something wrong with her knees.

## 11 Silver Men in Moonlight

The full moon shone down on the Handy Pavilion's Garden Centre as Seamus awoke. He yawned and stretched, though even at full extension his arms didn't go very far. He smacked his lips and put his pipe in between his teeth, though he could not light it.

Standing, he began his inspection. All the neat rows of plants, all the trees and seedlings, all the ferns and that little corner full of bonsais. Walking slowly on his little legs, he began his methodical rounds, examining the leaves, testing the dampness of the soil, squinting in the moonlight for any sign of aphids or thrips.

He had one night to do his job. He had to make it count.

There was a sound, a tiny sound at the very edge of Seamus' hearing. Either a cat or... no. There, crouched on top of the wall between the Garden section and the carpark. It was Zorbar. The big man moved cautiously, glancing around for any sign of danger. Lithe as a panther, he slipped to the ground. Even in the night and the distance, Seamus could see that Zorbar wore nothing but a pair of shorts. He shuddered. Perhaps Seamus was old-fashioned, but was it too much to ask a man to wear a tunic? And a pair of long pants and some buckled shoes? And a hat? Was that too much?

"Seamus," Zorbar called. "You awake?"

"Sure and so I am," Seamus said. "And what is that to ye?"

"Zorbar see if you still here. Make sure you all right."

The great soft bastard! Zorbar may have been made of solid muscle over a skeleton of even more muscle but he had a heart of... well, a heart of muscle, Seamus guessed. But that meant a strong heart, didn't it, and that was basically what Seamus was getting at.

Seamus wasn't good at metaphors. That was why he kept most of them to himself.

"Faith, but you're fooling no one here, Zorbar. You're doing what I am. You're checking on the bloody plants."

Zorbar looked down on Seamus. In the moonlight, Seamus could make out the big man's handsome features under his long, greasy brown hair. A sheepish smile spread across Zorbar's face. "It true. Handy Pavilion fire Zorbar. Say no money for Zorbar! Zorbar not care. Zorbar promise take care plant. Zorbar take care plant."

"Sure and you've also been living in that display treehouse over there," Seamus said. "Don't deny it, now. I've been asleep for a month now, but I passed by a minute ago. The smell is unmistakable."

Zorbar cast his eyes towards the ground to avoid eye contact. Since Seamus was only six inches tall, the manoeuvre failed.

"How do you even fit in that thing? Blessed Saints, it's a

kids' tree-house, you blatherskite."

"I curl up. Zorbar not care for comfort!"

Seamus threw up his little hands. Sometimes he thought he was the only person in the whole Pavilion with a brain in his head — although of course technically his head was hollow.

"Why not move back in with your family? Your real family, I mean. Not them monkeys such as raised you. Aren't your real family rich?"

"They make Zorbar wear collar shirt," Zorbar sulked. "Make Zorbar eat with fork. Won't shut up 'negative gearing.'"

"By all the saints, Zorbar Ofthechimps, sometimes, I wonder what goes on in your head, so and I do."

"Why you use stero-ripe language?" Zorbar said. "It not cool. It pro-mul-gates social ine… inequ… It not cool."

Seamus rolled his eyes, making a noise like terracotta tiles rubbing together. "You been talking with that girl from the coffee shop again? Faith, and it don't matter how PC you try to be, she'd still not going to let you… What's that?"

"Zorbar think Seamus being unfair Carol… What that?"

"That's what I said, ye feckin' eejit. Shush!"

Seamus strained his ceramic ears. A motor? Sometimes kids drove into the Centre carpark after hours to do doughnuts and burnouts and stupid stuff like that. This motor sound was too quiet. Seamus looked up at Zorbar, who reached down and picked him up. With catlike stealth, he crept them both towards the door to the carpark before setting him back down.

Peeking out under the iron door, Seamus saw a small van, gleaming black under the moon and parking lot lights. Its rear door hung open and a long hose pipe protruded from the interior. It coiled across the ground, extending to a hatch in the ground.

"It water pipe workers," Zorbar said, looking out through the cutaway door handle. "Probably just fix pipes. Work after time of sun. Less traffic. Overtime rates."

A man came around from the back of the van and tapped on the driver's side door. The door opened to reveal another figure seated behind the wheel. Both men were dressed in silver one-piece uniforms with black belts across their torsos. Both wore heavy plastic helmets with shaded masks and respirators that completely hid their faces.

"Those don't look like the water supply people to me," Seamus said.

"Then who they? *Eugh!*"

Seamus smelled it a moment after Zorbar. Shit. That was the word for it. The smell of human waste was welling up from the nearest drain in the garden centre's concrete floor.

"I see what they're doing!" Seamus said. "Those feckin' bastards are trying to back the sewage up through our drains!"

"Why?"

"Who gives a shite why? I don't care who these people are, or what they're about. Nobody messes with me plants! We've got to get those buggers!"

If he'd taken a moment longer to think, Seamus might have given a more precise order. Before he could reconsider it, Zorbar had grabbed him in a huge hand. In a second they were both on top of the wall, Seamus' curses drowned into inaudibility by the Zorbar's bloodcurdling scream. The next he knew he was in freefall.

Had he been dropped? No, he was still in Zorbar's hand, swinging back and forth like an enraged pendulum as Zorbar charged the silver men.

"Please, let me go before you punch someone," Seamus whimpered.

Zorbar went one better than that. Seamus flew through the air as Zorbar hurled him at the driver of the van. The driver's helmet visor shattered, pierced by Seamus' pointy hat. The man cried out in pain as Seamus slipped, dazed, to the seat. Outside, he could hear sounds of shrieking and screaming — terrible, wet blows of fist on flesh — the occasional crack of bone.

The driver was fumbling with the handbrake. In a moment he'd try to close the door, Seamus realised. Quick as he could, he lowered himself to the floor, then dropped down to the tarmac, chipping his hat in the process. Behind him was a squeal of tires. He turned, and before his painted eyes, he saw smoke rising from behind the rear wheels as the panicked driver accelerated too quickly and in the wrong gear.

Seamus rolled out of the way, fearful of being crushed once the drive wheels gained some traction. His motion came to a stop against something fleshy. Above him, he heard a yelp, and then something heavy was pinning him to the ground.

Seamus pulled himself out and dusted himself off. The van was squealing away in the distance, its rear doors flapping open and the second silver man holding with one arm to the pumping equipment inside. The pipes had fallen right out of the pump and lay on the ground, oozing noxious sludge. Seamus heard a groan, and realised what had happened. Zorbar had tripped over him, and the big man lay moaning on the tarmac.

"Zorbar think he bite tongue. Ouch."

"Oh, be quiet ye big baby," Seamus said. He scratched the glaze of his beard. What had just happened? Well, he'd just saved his beloved plants, sure as eggs. On the other hand, who had those people been, and why were they threatening the Pavilion?

"Faith, and sure you did a number on that one you was fighting. Poor bugger didn't stand a chance."

"Zorbar learn fight from apes—not Marquis bloody Queensbury."

Seamus smiled. In spite of himself, he liked the big galoot. "Well, I'm lucky I'm still in one piece, and all, after the way you threw me."

"Seamus have luck of Irish."

The little gnome laughed a big belly laugh. He sat on the ground and extended a leg to show Zorbar the bottom of his left shoe.

"M... mad-e..." Zorbar read. "*Made*. Made in kuh-huh... Chuh... China. Made in China."

"Faith and begorrah, sure and I don't have the luck of the Irish," Seamus said. "I'm a feckin' Chinaman."

Zorbar gasped. "That not acceptable ethnic..."

"Just get me back home, lad. And keep an eye out for

them gobshites in future. Unless they come back on the full moon, I won't be able to help you."

Zorbar jumped them back over the fence. Back home. Seamus didn't like being away, though technically the carpark was part of the Pavilion.

The smell was already clearing and the plants were safe, undefiled by sewage, for now. Again, Seamus wondered what this was all about, who the silver men were, and why they had tried what they had tried. Again, he had no answer.

Yodelling a yawn, Zorbar returned to his treehouse to sleep. Seamus bid him good night and went back to his rounds, checking his plants. Only they weren't his plants, were they? Over the course of a month, there must have been a huge turnover, especially of the seedlings. How often did he see the same plant twice?

Seamus pushed the thought from his mind. They were still his plants. This was his garden, and looking after the plants was what his kind did. The full moon was on the horizon, and it would set soon. Seamus returned to his spot under a sign reading 'Not for sale.' He adjusted his pipe in his hand, assumed his pose, and slipped silently back into sleep.

# 12 Tea and Scandal

Marlon had never liked Ms Jasu Shan. She never remembered anyone's name; she was abrasive, and she talked over him, often changing the topic of conversation right in the middle of one of his sentences. Unfortunately, there wasn't a damned thing he could do about it; she was the General Manager and he was just the Duty Manager.

When Ms Shan had taken ill, Marlon had been quietly pleased. He'd expected corporate to put someone else in charge for a while, preferably some quiet little pen-pusher who would take care of the big picture stuff and leave Marlon to the rest. In fact, head office had made Marlon acting manager. He'd been doing double duty as General Manager and Duty Manager in exchange for a nominal — and temporary — raise in salary.

Even that he might have coped with, had sales not started tanking when the DIY Barn opened. That had put him in the awkward position of being both the good-guy boss he liked to believe himself to be — champion of his staff against the penny-pinchers at head office — while simultaneously acting as a penny-pincher from head office. It was vexing.

Now Ms Shan was back. Supposedly, she'd made a

complete recovery, but Marlon doubted it. She seemed slower and weaker than she had been when she'd left. There had been a time when Marlon would have welcomed this change, but weakness is never welcome in the person you hope will shoulder your burdens.

"So you cut hours, rather than lay off staff?" Ms Shan said. She was from Mumbai, originally, but had come to Australia by way of Canada and the US, and had the strangest accent Marlon had ever heard.

"Mostly. I had to let Zorbar go."

"Zorbar? Malay guy? Outdoor furnishings?"

"Ape-man. Garden Centre."

"Oh, him," Ms Shan said with a shrug. "Well, I have to hand it to you: if there are any layoffs, they will blame me, not you."

Marlon considered defending himself from the implication, before deciding that it was pretty fair. "Does that bother you?"

Ms Shan shrugged. "More than you'd think."

A pang of guilt struck Marlon. He'd always thought of Ms Shan as a pure corporate robot with a spreadsheet for a heart. Perhaps her brush with mortality had changed her. Then again, perhaps he had misunderstood her from the start.

They passed through Paints, with its tiers of colourful metal tubs towering up towards the roof. As if in proof of her humanity, Ms Shan smiled at Nalda Teheintausand, who worked in that section, and ran the Kids Kraft Korner on Saturdays. "Good morning, Nalda."

"Greeting acknowledged," Nalda replied.

"How's the Kraft Korner going?"

"Der number off human children in attendance has been decreasing," Nalda said. "Suggestion: rename der Kraft Korner with der correct English spelling. Increased linguistic precision may result in increased human children activities. End suggestion."

Ms Shan blinked confusedly. Marlon wondered if she'd ever had such a long conversation with Nalda before. "How are those new paper-mâché products moving, Nalda?" he said.

"Sales levels adequate. Request additional hearts on sticks. They are romantic and in much demand for pair-bonding ceremonies."

"You mean weddings, Nalda?"

"Vedd-inks, ja. Correction acknowledged."

Marlon smiled and moved on. "Where's she from?" Ms Shan said.

"It's not a 'where'," Marlon said. "More of a 'when.'"

Ms Shan kicked a stray bag of steel wool that lay on the floor. Definitely changed by her ordeal, Marlon thought. Before, she would never have let that much emotion through the corporate mask.

"Tell me, Marlon," she said. "Besides you and me, is anyone here a normal person?"

"Adam's pretty down-to-earth."

"Adam?"

"Malay guy. Works in Outdoor Furnishings."

They walked into the break room, causing an outbreak

of guilty looks. There's nothing like managers walking into the break room to make completely blameless employees wonder if they're doing something wrong.

"As you were," Marlon said.

"Everything okay?" Ms Shan said. The response was nothing but a round of vague grunts, but that seemed to be what she expected, so she just moved on towards the hot water boiler. She sniffed the air, which reeked of air freshener. When word arrived that she had recovered, Marlon had been forced to reinstate the 'no-smoking' policy, and spared no expense in concealing the evidence of past indiscretions.

Gwen, who seemed guiltier than most, was handing out coffees. "Belinda," she said. "One sugar, right? Adam, that's yours."

As Marlon watched, Gwen paused and swallowed before handing a steaming mug to Norman. Marlon sighed. He'd always known that she was a little sweet on the boy, but she seemed to have gotten worse.

"Oh, cheers, Gwen," he said. Gwen looked at Norman expectantly, but the lad just blew on the surface of his tea and kept reading the centre newsletter.

"What's an MK-Ultra?" he asked. "Like a type of gun or something?" There was a round of shrugs, and Norman returned to his reading.

Ms Shan sat at the table; everyone drew back as she did so. "So you're feeling better then?" Adam asked.

"Oh, much," Ms Shan said. "By the way, thanks everyone for that get well soon card."

Marlon observed another round of guilty looks as the team members struggled to remember if they'd signed. Smiling, Marlon helped himself to a coffee and sat in a plastic chair at the table as the break-room chatter resumed its usual pattern of everyone talking over everyone else.

"How's your tea, Norman?"

"Still a little hot, thanks, Gwen."

"It was pretty bad for a while, but they say I've made a complete recovery."

"Oi, Marlon, is there any chance of getting next Tuesday off?"

"Anyone know where some place called Roswell is?"

"They had to make an incision here, and siphon out about a litre of…"

"Go on, it'll get cold."

"Tuesday? What for?"

"And who's Adam Weisshaupt?"

"Yes?"

"No, Adam *Weisshaupt*."

"Oh."

"Dental appointment."

"Oh, shit, is that the time? I'd better drink up."

Norman stood up quickly, slurping down his tea as he did so. Gwen grinned expectantly. Ms Shan was holding both of her arms out sideways, like an exaggerating fisherman, to demonstrate the size of whatever it was that had been removed from her abdomen. Her arm struck Norman as he rose, catching him off guard and making him lose his balance. His feet slipped under the table, his chair tumbled over and he fell into a seated position on the fetid break-room floor.

Ms Shan reached down to help the stricken lad. "Are you alright?" she asked, with what seemed to Marlon like genuine concern.

Norman looked up, annoyed. His face went slack. A big silly grin spread across his olive features.

"Yes," he said. "Yes, I'm fine, Ms Shan. I've never been better."

Marlon hadn't quite puzzled out the meaning of this before Gwen rose and ran, sobbing, from the room.

# 13 Axel's Day

"Have you noticed Ms Shan's hair?"

Axel looked up from the cans of grout he was stacking. It was Norman who had spoken. He leant against the mighty shelves a wistful smile on his gormless face.

"I have not noticed Ms Shan's hair, particularly," Axel said. "What is it about her hair that I ought to have noticed?"

"It's very black," Norman said.

"Well, she is of Indian descent," Axel said. "Black hair rather comes with the territory."

"*So* black," Norman sighed. "Like a really black car. But not one of those matte black ones, though. Her hair is shiny."

"I quite like those matte black cars," Axel said. "I'm thinking of buying one, as soon as the International Court of Justice at The Hague finally reinstates my driver's license."

"Why did...?"

"Don't ask."

"It's not that sort of black anyway," Norman said, tetchily. "It's shiny black. Like... like a really black stereo."

Axel dusted his hands and stood. "Norman, I may not be the *smartest* man in the world. That honour belongs to Brainekles. In fact, on the World Intelligence Rankings, I come in at a distant fourth—tied with Dr Escapement, the Man with the Clockwork Mind. Given my limited cognitive resources, it might be better if you just explained yourself directly, rather than leaving me to guess."

"Yeah, I get it," Norman said. "You aren't interested in her hair. But have you noticed her eyes?"

Axel stopped dead where he stood. "Norman, are you in love?"

"No!" Norman said. "Yes. Well, maybe. No. A bit."

"The reason I ask, is that you've known Ms Shan for over a year now, and this is the first time I've ever heard you say anything positive about her," Axel said. "The last time you mentioned her at all, she'd just turned down your request for leave and you said some unkind things about her. Very unkind. And frankly, a little racist."

Norman reddened in anger. "Well, I didn't know her then!"

"You plan on working today, Norm?" Norman's supervisor Ali called from the end of the aisle. "That something you think you might want to do?"

"Yeah, keep your hair on," Norman said, hiking up his pants and strolling off.

Axel shook his head. The stupid boy was growing on him—but this was foolish even by his standards. Ms Shan was twice his age and out of his league in every way—smarter, richer, more professional. Then there was the religious issue. Ms Shan was a non-practising Hindu, whereas Norman came from a very different background indeed.

Putting the issue aside as a young man's folly, Axel went back to his work. It was a middling busy day, and there was a lot to do. He buried himself in the mundane detail of his menial work, and for a while he was happy. Then he met the man in the white suit.

He'd seen the fellow around the centre, and thought little of him except that he disliked the man's taste in clothes. Now the man walked right up to him and tipped his ridiculous little straw hat.

"Excuse me, are you Axel Platzoff?"

"That's right," Axel said.

"I'm Karl Wintergreen. I write the centre newsletter."

Axel had never cared for journalists. When there was some matter he wished to put before the public, he had always preferred to simply take over all the television broadcasts and deliver his ultimatum that way.

"Oh, you're the guy," Axel said.

"Yes. Mostly, I'm owner/manager of the Stationary Station, over by the kebab shop, but I'm also on the Centre management committee, and of course, I put out the newsletter."

"Stationary...?" Axel mused. "Oh, yes, the stuff we used before we had devices. How's that going? Shift a lot of... It's so hard to remember... Shift a lot of parchment? Typewriter ribbon? Sealing wax?"

"Your hostility is unnecessary."

"But fun."

"I wanted to ask you about the heist the other week."

Axel's poker face became so hard it could have stopped bullets. Seriously? The police, the real media, Captain Stellar, all of them had overlooked Axel as a suspect. And this idiot figures it out?

"I assume you are referring to my past," he said. "I am a law-abiding citizen, and in addition, I can account for my whereabouts…"

"No, no, no, you have me all wrong," Karl said. "No, I just wanted your insight on the crime. As an expert witness as it were. I didn't think you *did* it, Mr Platzoff. You? The man who tried to crash the International Space Station into the Beijing Olympics? The man who forced President Obama to fight President Dracula from Monster Earth? No, surely no such villain of your standing would commit such a petty and mundane crime."

It took all of Axel's self-control to keep himself from laughing. The old ego-trap? Badmouth the crime, until the villain begins to stand up for it? That trick was old when Dick Tracy was in short pants. One smart guess, that was all Wintergreen had. He didn't have the investigative chops to back it up.

"Ah, I see what you mean," Axel said. "Well, I'd like to help, but I am trying to put all that sort of stuff in the past. Perhaps if you put me down as an unnamed source?"

"That does somewhat detract from the 'straight from the horse's mouth' aspect I was going for," Karl said.

"I see. Well, I'm sorry to disappoint you."

Axel watched Karl turn and walk away. So that was the

standard of arch-nemesis you got when you were committing crimes of this low level. What was worse, he had found he had to clench his teeth to avoid boasting about his dastardly crime.

Because that was the thing about the ego-trap. It *worked*.

The rest of the day was busy, so busy that Axel barely had another thought for either Norman or Karl again. A customer dropped and broke a fertilizer bag, and Axel had to organise a group to clean up the mess before it stank up the place. What was worse was that one of the big ceiling fans faltered and died and the rising heat met the rising stink, which made nobody happy.

At last, weary, exhausted, Axel managed to find some time to sneak out the back amongst the splintery piles of palates for a well-deserved smoke. He had the place to himself, and he looked through the gaps in the buildings towards the DIY Barn, but he was too exhausted to consider the next stage in his campaign. Sighing, he drew a cigarette from his pocket. No sooner had he wrapped his lips about the paper tube than he fell to the ground, stars before his eyes.

He struggled back to his knees, before being dragged upright. Out of the corner of his eye, he saw a flash of silver, like a fire blanket or something. In front of him, though, was a short bald man in a white shirt and grey pants.

"Ah, Mr Platzoff, we meet at last," the man said.

Seriously? If Axel could have laughed, he would have. You do *not* pull the old "we meet at last" dressed in business casual.

Still, play along for now. "I believe you have the

advantage, Mr…"

"Smith," the man said. "I am Senior Manager at the DIY Barn."

"Nice to see you, Smith," Axel said. "Now I won't have to walk to the Barn to complain about the faulty Dremel you sold me."

Smith nodded to the man in the corner of Axel's vision, in the silver uniform, who swung around and punched Axel in the gut.

"You wouldn't happen to know anything about an armoured car heist would you, Mr Platzoff?" Smith said. His voice was high and nasal. Without his goon—who knew how to throw a punch, all right—Smith would seem no more threatening than a sponge.

"Only what I read in the newsletter," Axel said. Damn! The newsletter. If Wintergreen was investigating, he might have told his suspicions to Smith. Still, the man had nothing to go on but a hunch, which meant Smith had nothing to go on except hearsay of a hunch, and that had to be even less…

The rear door of the DIY Pavilion opened and Nalda from Paints came out, clutching something that looked like a steel cigarette with an antenna sticking out of it.

"Vat is going on?" she said.

Smith glared at the silver-clad man. "I thought I told you to secure the door?"

"Oh," the silver man said, muffled by his helmet. "*Sercure that* door."

"It's okay, Nalda," Axel said. "Just an amateurish

shakedown."

"Which door did you think I meant?"

"I thought you were saying that my fly was open. 'Secure the door', yeah?"

"Oh for…" Smith ran a hand over his bald head. "Okay, Platzoff. Consider this a warning. We're not Captain Stellar, okay? Cross us, and you'll get worse than a little punch on the jaw and a short prison stay, savvy?"

"Yeah," the silver man said. "We'll mess you up— dreadfully!"

"Dreadfully," Smith sighed. "Come on!"

Smith and his goon made their exit towards the Place O' Pets carpark.

Nalda seemed to be over her initial shock, and was down the stairs to Axel in a moment. "Are you all right?"

"Fine, thanks, Nalda," he said. "Just a small problem, easily fixed. Thanks for showing up when you did."

"If there is a problem, I could travel backwards in time and kill…"

"Thank you, Nalda, I don't think that'll be necessary," Axel said. He watched Smith and his goon vanish and shook his head.

"They didn't know anything," he said out loud. "Not really. This was just a fishing expedition. But they'll keep looking, and if they find proof…"

Nalda's donned a pair of dark glasses. "Dey'll be back."

"Yes, Nalda," Axel said. "Yes, I daresay they will."

# 14 Zorbar and the Ute

"Zorbar?"

In a second, Zorbar Ofthechimps was wide awake, his knife pressed against the flesh of the intruder's throat … Oh, wait, it was only Norman. Zorbar sheathed his blade.

"Holy shit, Zorbar," Norman said, rubbing his neck.

"Zorbar sorry, Norman."

"You nearly cut me head off, Zorb. I don't think 'sorry' covers it."

"Please not call Zorbar 'Zorb.'"

"I mean, I was just doing you a favour, waking you up before Adam gets in. You know how pissed off he was last time he caught you sleeping in the treehouse."

"Adam jerk," Zorbar said, pulling on a pair of pants in the tiny space.

"Well to be fair, you did nearly slit *his* throat when he woke you."

Zorbar stretched and yodelled quietly. "How things inside?"

Norman shook his head. "Going downhill fast," he said. "We're not losing so much business to the DIY Barn, but still enough to hurt. Ms Shan's back."

"Ms Shan less soft-hearted than Marlon," Zorbar said. "Maybe more layoffs."

"She's not as bad as people think," Norman snapped. "I don't know why everyone's always down on her. I reckon it's racism."

"Didn't Norman call Ms Shan a bloody curry—"

Norman straightened, banging his head on the low pine rafters of the treehouse ceiling. "That was before I got to know her," he said, rubbing his crown with the hand that wasn't rubbing his neck.

"Still racism. It not cool thing. It perpetuate social…"

"Spare me, mate. This isn't bloody Twitter. I get enough of that stuff online."

Zorbar put his pants on, to Norman's obvious relief. People who were raised by humans worried too much about trousers.

"You know, I hear there's a job going at the liquor place," Norman said

"Which? Emile's Fine Vintage Cellar?" Zorbar said. "Or Harry's House of Ethanol Based 'Beverages'?"

"Harry's."

"Ugh," Zorbar said. "Not it matter. Zorbar not have RSA."

"Maybe Carol could get you something at the coffee shop."

Zorbar felt himself blush beneath his tan. Not long ago, Norman had rolled his eyes whenever Zorbar mentioned Carol or even reacted to the mention of her. Now Normy just nodded sympathetically at Zorbar's discomfort.

"Come on, mate let's go," Norman said. For a moment, he looked guilty, like a small child considering an assault on a lolly jar. "Slide?" he said.

"Slide," Zorbar said.

They both came down via the little slide that led from the treehouse to the concrete floor of the Garden Centre. It trembled under their weight, but held.

"How is Mrs Leamington?"

"Mum's doing well," Norman said. "Had the flu, but now she's over it. She said you could sleep on the spare bed for a while, if you want to."

"That nice of her."

"She thinks the world of you, Zorbar. We all do. You need to just move on from this place, you know?"

It was still early, and the Pavilion was in the earliest stages of opening. There was no one else in the Garden Centre, except for Seamus, who was fast asleep. Zorbar picked some leaves off a spinach seedling and ate them.

"It hard find job, when resume say 'raised by chimps' for education," he said.

"Mate, while you were being raised by chimps, I was at an all-boys school," Norman said. "It's not that different."

Norman looked so sincere that Zorbar almost couldn't bear to look at him. "Maybe Zorbar try Place O' Pets. Zorbar good with animals."

"That's the idea!" Norman smiled.

Zorbar ate some silverbeet while he and Norman began

the elaborate process of opening the ancient lock on the Gardening exit.

"Norman," Zorbar asked. "Zorbar never ask: what happen Mr Leamington? He eaten by lions like Zorbar father?"

"Who?" Norman said. "Oh, I get you. There never was a Mr Leamington. Dad's alive, he just didn't stick around after I was born. Never married Mum. I still see him, now and then. Mate, nobody ever looked less like a 'Mr Leamington' than Dad. He's about as Greek as you can get."

"Zorbar sorry bring it up."

"Ah, no worries," Norman shrugged. "Some of us have two parents, some of us have one, some are raised by chimps. It's just life, isn't it, Zorb?"

"Please not call Zorb. In language of chimps, Zorbar mean 'Mighty Warrior, Fleet of Foot.'"

"What does Zorb mean?"

"It mean 'penis of smaller than usual size'," Zorbar said.

"Oh. Okay…"

"Average chimpanzee penis four centimetre long…"

"Okay, okay, you don't have to spell it out." Norman finished with the lock. "There! Got you, you bastard! Well, see you around, Zorbar, mate. If you have to sleep here, try to wake up earlier. And maybe keep the knife out of arm's reach, eh? No leopards around here, mate."

"See Norman later."

Zorbar stood outside the garden fence in the Centre carpark. The morning was overcast, and a cold wind blew across the near-empty tarmac. He'd only ever had one job, watching over the plants and flowers at the Handy Pavilion. It hadn't paid much, but it had allowed him a roof over his head, and had helped him pay his fine that time he'd been caught eating the ducks at the local park. More than that, his friends were there. Seamus, Norman, Donna… even Adam and Belinda. He didn't want to leave.

The wind was cold against the bare skin of his torso. Sighing, he directed his feet towards the Place O' Pets. It might work. He did have a way with animals, and even Marlon had to admit that his customer service skills were surprisingly good. It might not be so bad. With some money, he could move out of the treehouse. Maybe build a treehouse of his own. Maybe even have enough left to ask Carol out. Zorbar took a lungful of cold air, straightened his back, and marched.

He made it almost halfway across the carpark, before he was knocked over by a ute.

# 15 Light and Dark

There were two coffee shops at the South Hertling Super Centre. One of them was quite nice. It was located just in between the Barbecue Imperium and Arthur C. Clock's Timepiece World. The barista there was a slightly annoying, but basically quite nice hipster named Carol, who sold organic coffee and gluten free wraps.

The other was in a dingy little corner of the Handy Pavilion, just by outdoor furniture. It sold second-rate coffee at first-rate coffee prices to those too tired or lazy to walk across the vast car park to Carol's.

Captain Stellar would have liked to go to Carol's, but without his coffee he didn't have the energy.

"Ironic," he said.

"What?" the barista said.

"That I need coffee to get coffee."

"Oh, I thought you were saying that I was ironic," the barista said. "Good thing you weren't, I don't take kindly to insults."

The strangeness of the remark momentarily pulled the Captain out of his funk. "I don't think 'ironic' is an insult."

"Well, you might be okay with being called that sort of

thing," the barista said. "That's your choice. Me, I don't take that sort of crap."

"Didn't you used to work at the checkout counter?" Captain Stellar said.

"That's right," the barista said. "Nearly didn't get this transfer, either. Just one more formal complaint and I'd be stuck on the checkout for another year, at least. Here's your flat white."

"But I ordered a latte... Oh, never mind." The Captain paid the barista and took his coffee. It tasted even worse than he'd expected. Still, it had caffeine, and that gave a little life back to him.

One more formal complaint. Ironic indeed. In his pursuit of justice, Captain Stellar was powered by cosmic rays. In his civilian life, he was powered by the occasional cup of coffee, sleepwalking towards the part of the day when he could finally drift off to sleep in front of a documentary.

Alone.

"May I sit here? There are no more seats."

Stellar could have pointed out the dozens of unused seats in the Outdoor Furniture department just next to the cafe. But he didn't. Instead, he shrugged his massive shoulders. "Feel free," he said, though he hoped she didn't feel any such thing. He didn't feel sociable. He hadn't felt sociable since Cycloman had left.

The woman sitting across from him was red-headed and thirtyish. Was she going to try to make conversation?

"Don't worry," the woman said. "I won't bother you at

all."

Oh, no. She *was* going to try to make conversation.

"I see you around here a lot," she said.

"Do you?" Stellar said. Smartphone! Where was his smartphone? Everyone knew that a man looking at his smartphone is not a man who wants to talk. Right? Crap, did he leave it in the car again? Why don't civilian clothes come with utility belts, damn it!

"Yes. I work here, usually. I'm not wearing the uniform because it's my day off."

"Ah," Stellar sighed, giving in to the inevitable. "Yes, I remember you. You work in lighting, don't you?"

"No, that's my sister," the woman said. "I'm Angela. Work in curtains."

"I see."

"Did anyone ever tell you that you look like Captain Stellar?"

"Ha, yes, I get that all the time," Stellar said. "My name's Vincent. I'm a solicitor. That's stressful enough without fighting the Human Iceberg, ha ha."

Angela sipped at her coffee. "I guess you must work from home. Men who have to go to work usually either shave regularly or grow a beard. Five-day growths are pretty rare, don't you think?"

God damn it. Had he forgotten to shave again? Had he showered at least? Was his shirt fresh, and were his shoes tied? What had he even come to the Handy Pavilion for, anyway? It wasn't like he needed anything in particular. Certainly not bad coffee.

Somewhere inside, rising from the slagheap of his emotions was a chunk of steel. He was better than this. Len... Cycloman had left him. Okay. That was bad, but it happened.

His nostrils flared. Relationships break up every day, all across the world. People, *regular* people, *ordinary* people dealt with it. Here he was, Captain fucking Stellar — the man who'd defeated the Centipede Empire for God's sake — snivelling like a lost puppy. Screw it. Cycloman wanted to move on? His call, his loss. Let him...

"No," Angela said. Stellar had been so lost in his thoughts that he had forgotten her, but now he was staring into her pale blue eyes. Her pupils were tiny. He couldn't pull his eyes away. What was it he saw in there? Something comforting. Something dark.

"I need you to pull yourself together," Angela said. "But not *yet*. Don't let go of your resentment completely. Not now. Can you hold onto it for me?"

It was the single stupidest thing Captain Stellar had ever heard. "Yes," he heard himself say.

Angela smiled, her lips barely less white than her teeth. "There's a lot of light in you, Captain Stellar," she whispered. "A lot of light. But that's where my sister gets it wrong. Sometimes darkness is not about shutting the light out. Sometimes it's about rearranging it. Delaying it. Illumination delayed is illumination denied, you know."

"Yes, yes I see," Stellar said, though he didn't.

"Why do you keep coming back here with nothing to

buy?" Angela said.

"Because I miss Cycloman, and we used to come here together."

"Why, really?"

"Because I am suspicious of Axel Platzoff and I want to keep an eye on him."

"The truth."

"Because I am lonely and I don't like to admit it, so I'm channelling my loneliness into suspicion and resentment."

Why was he saying this? Why was he floating in the pinhole pupils of Angela's eyes, telling her things he could barely admit to himself?

"Now, let's go back to those first two reasons," Angela said. "You have hit the skids because of a disloyal lover and a treacherous foe. You are right to hold onto your anger. Do you understand?"

Stellar's watch started buzzing. All at once, he was out of the eyes and back in his own head, drinking bad coffee. Eyes? What eyes? Why was there a half-empty coffee cup opposite him? Had it been there when he sat down? Didn't they clean the tables in this dump?

But there was no time to worry about that. His Vigilancers signal watch was buzzing, and Captain Stellar was needed in the never-ending fight against evil. Finally! Something to take his mind off of everything. His knuckles itched. He hoped it was Granite Man. Granite Man was invulnerable enough that Stellar could hit him *really hard* without feeling bad about it.

But first, he had to change. Better change in his car, behind its tinted windows. The toilets in the Pavilion were always filthy.

# 16 Management Conference

Jasu Shan closed the door to the office, mixed a cocktail of Paracetamol and Quickeze into her instant coffee, then swilled the whole thing down. Just hold on, Jasu. Darelson promised a position at head office, just as soon as Vickers retired... Old Vickers, who was barely getting by, these days. Just hold on and soon you'll be out of this dump.

Trouble had started almost as soon as she'd arrived that morning. Jane Nguyen from the Equipment Hire counter was one of that section of the staff that Ms Shan thought of as 'the normal people.' She had been showing off her new smartphone, and somehow managed to trigger the self-destruct system on Nalda Teheintausand's internal fission reactor. Axel Platzoff had tried to jerry-rig a carbon-rod dampening system out of charcoal briquettes, but Donna from lighting hacked Nalda's system and initiated shutdown mode before Axel had made much progress.

Near nuclear meltdown in a hardware store, and it was barely half past nine. About the only thing Ms Shan could do was to get Nalda to shut down her WiFi to prevent similar incidents.

She drank down her cocktail. Vickers. So old. So frail.

Couldn't last long. Probably wanted to go play with his grandchildren. She stared at her phone, willing it to ring. Retire! Retire, you senile old bastard!

There was a soft knock on the door, like someone tapping it with a show. Ms Shan looked around her windowless little cubby-hole of an office and sighed. What now? What could it be now?

"Come in," she said, the acid in her stomach rising in anticipation of the latest travesty. But instead of one of her staff members, it was Claudia Liselle, the General Manager of the South Hertling Super Centre, carrying two cups of coffee. Real coffee, not Handy Pavillion coffee.

"Hello Jasu," Mrs Liselle said. "Sorry I haven't come to see you since you've been back."

"Hi, Claudia," Ms Shan said, pointedly not accepting the apology.

"Yeah, it's been a nightmare, lately."

"Has it?"

Mrs Liselle took a seat and handed Ms Shan a coffee cup. Ms Shan stared at the paper cup for a moment, then sighed and took it. The tension in the office faded a little, though not completely.

"Just a heads up," Ms Liselle said. "You know the accident outside, a few days back? Guy hit by a ute?"

"Yeah?"

"He was one of yours," Ms Liselle said, checking her tablet. "A Mr Zorbar… Ofthechimps? Is that right?"

Ms Shan remembered Zorbar. She was fond of feigning

ignorance of her employees' names. Partly this was a deliberate power move and partly just because she enjoyed annoying people but seldom had the opportunity.

"Not one of ours," Ms Shan said. "Used to be, but sacked a few weeks back."

"Well, he was kidnapped."

"What?"

"Some bystanders said the driver of the ute put him in the back, saying that he was taking him to hospital," Ms Liselle said. "But he never arrived. I'm looking into this on a liability level, of course, but if there's a kidnapper about, you should warn your staff. Be careful, park close by, that sort of thing."

Ms Shan glared at Mrs Liselle. "Is that all?"

"No," Mrs Liselle said. "You know Karl Wintergreen?"

"The weird newsletter guy?"

"He wanted to put something in the newsletter suggesting that one of your people was involved in that armoured car heist."

"Who?"

"Uh… Fiona… something."

Ms Shan laughed out loud. Fiona was about as unlikely a robber as could be imagined. She hadn't even talked to Fiona since her return from the hospital, but she remembered the girl — a timid, mousy, semi-competent, who couldn't be trusted for a sandwich run, let alone a payroll heist.

"Yes, well, I told Karl that the centre newsletter shouldn't be used for defamatory purposes," Mrs Liselle said, rolling her eyes. "Then he started claiming local courts only had, uh, maritime authority? Or some nonsense. Anyway, like I said, I just wanted to give you a heads up."

There was another knock on the door. This time it was Norman, who was a nice lad in general but always seemed to be under Ms Shan's feet lately.

"It's Buck Dusty," Norman said.

"Filipino woman?" Ms Shan said. "Works in Cleaning Products?"

"Works in Power Tools," Norman said. "Don't reckon he's Filo. He's some sort of cowboy, I think. Has one of them hats, anyway. He was showing off, twirling a nail gun and…"

"Is he injured?"

"No, just nailed himself to a chainsaw by his sleeve."

"Do we have pliers somewhere?"

Norman looked surprised. "Well, yeah. It's a hardware centre."

"Then bloody use them!" Ms Shan said.

"Yes, Miss," Norman said. He looked downcast, like a kicked dog, but Ms Shan was in no mood to soften the blow.

"And tell him that the cost of the chainsaw is coming out of his pay," she added. Norman's sad backwards glance was almost heartrending.

Ms Shan composed herself and breathed in deeply. She took a long sip of Mrs Liselle's coffee. "Thank you for the heads up. But you could have just emailed me, you know. No need to come in person. You didn't feel the need to come visit me in hospital, after all. But I guess that's different from taking a little stroll across from centre management to talk to me."

Mrs Liselle looked at the ground. "I guess I deserve that. But I have been busy lately. A lot of things going on at work — and at home." She took a deep breath. "And in court. It's finalised, Jasu. My husband… my *ex*-husband… he's stopped making trouble and just signed the paperwork."

"Really?" Ms Shan climbed out of her uncomfortable little office chair. "I… I don't know what to say."

"Then don't say anything."

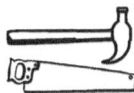

Fiona stood outside the office door, lost in thought. The heist had seemed so… so *fun*. But now dear old Wellsey didn't trust her anymore, and that creep Wintergreen was accusing her of all sorts of things and thugs were assaulting Axel in the carpark… It was too far. It had all gone too far.

She needed to tell someone. Not the police. Not yet, anyway. But someone. Fiona had concluded that the leader of the Handy Pavilion should know what she, Fiona, had wrought. That way Ms Shan could… could…

Fiona didn't know what Ms Shan could do, exactly. She barely knew her at all. She just knew that Ms Shan was in charge and that Norman was always talking about how wise and clever she was. Fiona took a deep breath and opened the door.

Her eyes were drawn downwards, to the desk lamp which lay on the floor, casting its glow across two spilled coffee cups. The ground was strewn with papers and desk ornaments. Fiona brought her eyes up to the level of the desk. Lying on the desktop was Ms Shan, and lying on Ms Shan was...

"Don't you know how to knock?" Ms Shan said.

Fiona closed the door and scurried away.

## 17 A Bad Deal All Round

Gwen watched, her heart squirming in her chest as Norman rushed to pick up a pencil that Ms Shan had dropped. He smiled winningly as he handed it to her. She acknowledged his action with a gesture and moved on, leaving Norman sighing behind her. Gwen bit her hand. What a fool. What a fool she had been! To have given up so much, all for nothing.

All around her were the Handy Pavilion staff, going about their business as if it were just another day. It was a quiet day. Fiona lugged a box of taps. Adam laughed uncomfortably at one of Belinda's jokes. Axel Platzoff, rubbing his eyes, was being lectured by Sadie MacGregor. Marlon and Wellsey were deep in conversation. Customers were few, but present. An elderly man in a tweed jacket staggered under too many cans of paint. A teenaged carpenter's apprentice eyed expensive hammers with a wistful sigh. A short woman and her tall husband pushed a trolley full of plants.

No one looked at Gwen. If the world ends with aliens or fire and brimstone or zombies, then everyone is in on the fight. When the world ends in heartbreak, there you are, alone.

There was only one thing that could have made Gwen's day any worse, so naturally, it happened: Pennington arrived.

Gwen saw him across the counters, in his pressed trousers and polo neck shirt. She lacked the strength to deal with him out the front, so retreated to the safety of the timber section.

Pennington met her minutes later. In his hand was one of those lightweight folding bags. Nothing sinister about bags like that—unless you know what is meant to go in them.

"I can't pay you," Gwen said.

"You can," Pennington said. "You will."

Gwen shook her head. The wood in the timber section sang a brave song to encourage her, but it was not working. Pennington was a soft-looking fellow, but his eyes were like steel.

"But…"

"Gwen, I offered you the love potion for free," he said. "You insulted me by returning it, then you demanded I sell you more. Against my better judgement, I did so. Even now, I would be prepared to accept the return of my product in lieu of payment—but you don't have it anymore. This is unacceptable, and I think you know that."

Gwen looked around. The timber section was an enormous space, but still, it felt like a trap. "It went wrong," she said. "Norman fell in love with someone else."

"Was there a defect in the product?" Pennington said. "I don't think so. It worked exactly as advertised. If you crash your car, the dealership won't return your money. If you burn a chop, you still owe the butcher. If you misuse a potion…"

"But what you're asking…"

"Is the agreed price. Nothing more, nothing less."

Gwen nodded. Deep down, she had known that there would be no way out of this. Really, how could this have gone any other way? She should have listened to her grandmother. She had known…

"Now, if you please," Pennington said, his face like stone.

Gwen looked around to see if anyone was watching, though she was almost past the point at which she cared. She reached up, placing two fingertips within her right earhole. Pushing outward, her ear stretched until there was more room for all her fingers. It burned as she pulled her external ear inside out, revealing her *real* ear, her *true* ear, green and gently glowing beneath the surface. Fighting back tears, she tore the green ear from her head like a mushroom from a tree trunk and handed it to Pennington. The dull brown external ear snapped back into place.

"And the other one," he said. His words were audible on both sides, but the song of the wood could only be heard through her left ear. Gwen almost hesitated, but knew that if she faltered she would not be able to start again. She opened up her left ear and plucked out the green ear within. Instantly the sound of the woodsong died. Deaf. Not human deaf. That would be bad enough. *Dryad* deaf, forever cut off from the songs of tree and wood.

Pennington took a plastic Ziploc from his pocket, and deposited Gwen's ears in it. Sealing it, he slipped it into the lightweight bag. "There you go," he said. "That wasn't so bad, was it?"

"It was worse than you could imagine."

"It may have been bad," Pennington said with a cold smile, "but I'd be willing to bet you any amount that it was *not* worse than *I* could imagine."

A shudder ran up Gwen's back. Creepy bastard was probably right.

"What are you going to do with them?" she asked.

"Wouldn't you be happier not knowing?"

Again, he had a point.

"Well, I can't say it's been a pleasure," Pennington said. "All in all you have been a very ungrateful customer."

"Fuck you."

"See what I mean? But just out of professional interest, who did poor Norman fall for, if not you?"

"You wouldn't know her."

"Probably not," Pennington shrugged. "Goodbye, Gwen."

Gwendolyn Harper stood amidst piles of silent timber. Once again, she thought there was only one way to make her day worse, and once again the universe tested her theory.

"Hey, Gwen," Norman said. "You seen Axel?"

"Axel?" Gwen said. "I'd have thought you'd be looking for Ms Shan."

Norman blushed behind his scraggly beard. "Don't know what you mean," he mumbled.

"Well, you're always fawning over her."

"I'm showing respect to my boss. Maybe if more people did that, this place would work better."

Gwen couldn't stand it any longer. "Norman, you're in love with her."

The lad went fire-engine red, then to Gwen's surprise, burst into laughter. "Yeah, Gwen. I guess maybe I am. Silly, isn't it? She's twice my age, and she's too good for me, and Mum would freak if she saw her. And if what Fiona said is… well, let's just say winning her over would be an uphill run, know what I mean?"

Norman shook his head at his foolishness. "It's a sad thing to be in love and have it going nowhere. But I suppose I'll just have to get over it. What else can you do, hey?"

"You could give her a love potion," Gwen said. "That's how some people would deal with unrequited love."

"Wouldn't that be cool," Norman laughed. "But, seriously, though, you don't want to mess with that shit. My Dad was always pulling that sort of thing, tricking women into liking him. Now there's all these women who he likes, but who hate his guts. How sad is that? And he's all alone, sleeping on his brother's couch… No, love is a pain in the arse, but you've just got to cop what it throws at you."

Involuntarily, Gwen touched her ear.

"What if someone used a love potion on you?" Gwen said.

Norman laughed. "Yeah, nah. Wouldn't work."

"What?"

"Wouldn't work," Norman repeated. "I'm immune to that sort of thing. Dad might be an ass, he gave me some good genes, but. Potions, curses, minor wands. I'm immune. It's all genetic, yeah?"

"Seriously?"

"Yup," Norman said. "In this day and age, I guess you don't have to worry about that shit too much, but I'm lucky not to have to worry at all. Anyway, I need to find Axel. He's been thinking a lot lately… I don't think I should let *him* think too much. See ya!"

And he left, as Gwen stood alone in silent shock.

# 18 From Across the Veil

"Are you sure about this?" Wellsey asked.

"Could you be any more clichéd?" Belinda said. "'Are you sure about this?'" she added in a high-pitched mockery of Wellsey's voice. "Gahd."

The Handy Pavilion was spooky in the dark. No, Wellsey thought, not spooky. Terrifying. The huge shelves towered up into the darkness, dark and ghostly pale in the moonlight that slanted through the skylights. The air hung still and hot, undisturbed by the vast ceiling fans that lay idle beneath the ghostly ceiling. The building seemed at the same time too large and too small, dwarfing Wellsey and yet leaving him all too aware of the many places that some terrible thing might hide. Wellsey stood in the middle of aisle eight, his growing dread focused on the folding table, covered with black candles and surrounded by director chairs.

"Fuck you," he said. "I don't mean, 'are you sure we should be doing this?', I mean, 'are you sure this will work?'"

Belinda laughed. "Of course I'm not. I only done this once. Talked to my Granddad."

"What did he die of?" Fiona said. Her recently improved social skills seemed to be in remission, and Wellsey had no idea if this was a good sign.

"Oh, he's not dead," Belinda said.

"You reached across the veil to contact your *living* Granddad?" Wellsey sighed.

"Hey, he's in a coma," Belinda said. "It was nice to talk to the old guy; don't be a prick about it."

To his surprise, Belinda's admission made Wellsey feel a little better. If Belinda wasn't a real medium, then by implication this wasn't a real séance. Nothing to be scared of then. Just three employees on company property after hours without authorisation. It wasn't even a firing offence, probably.

"Are we going to get started?" Carol said. Okay, bringing an unauthorised non-employee might be more difficult to explain away. Carol was a tall, red-headed woman with crazy hair and serious glasses and a vast excess of beads. There was just enough rebellious youth left deep inside Wellsey for him to admire her style, and yet still he sometimes found himself pursing his lips at her tattoos. Carol ran a little café where she made coffee with Walter White-ian levels of chemical precision. She'd always had a little crush on Zorbar, so when she'd insisted on coming to the séance, Wellsey didn't have the heart to turn her down.

"Let's get started," Wellsey said, though he really wanted to say, "Are you sure about this?" one more time.

They took their seats around the little card table and joined hands. God, holding hands with two younger, female employees. HR had better bloody not find out about this.

"So who are we going to contact?" Fiona asked.

"Bruce," Belinda said.

Wellsey rolled his eyes. Bruce was a myth, a workplace folktale. He was supposedly an electrical contractor who had been involved in building the Handy Pavilion. As the story went, Bruce had an affair with the wife of another contractor, a concreter. The concreter had found out, and now Bruce's body was buried in the foundation of the Pavilion. Bruce's ghost was said to haunt the place, and was blamed every time there was an accident that no one wanted to own up to.

A fake séance for a fake ghost. Wellsey found the corners of his mouth turning up a little. What the hell, it was fun. He closed his eyes.

"Oh, spi-rits! We in-voke and be-seech thy!" Belinda intoned, in a singsong rhythm, partway between a Southern Baptist minister and a Scooby-Doo villain. "We need thee wisdom, here, in the material world."

Wellsey opened his eyes again, to find that Fiona and Carol had opened their eyes too. He glanced back and forth at them, questioningly. Belinda began speaking again and he snapped his eyelids shut, guiltily.

"Bruce, ghost of the Handy Pavilion!" Belinda said. "Show thouself! Reveal thine eternal ectoplasmic... uh... thing!"

"Awright, keep it down," said a strange voice. "I'm dead, not bloody deaf."

At once, Wellsey felt cold, even in the sultry air. His palms began to sweat. Worse, both Belinda and Fiona's palms had started sweating. It was pretty gross.

Summoning all his courage, Wellsey forced a trembling eyelid open. He swore under his breath, opened his eyes and let go of the girls' hands.

"Okay, ha ha big bloody joke," he said. The others all opened their eyes too and saw what Wellsey had—a shortish, plumpish man, hidden under a white sheet, two round holes cut out for eyes.

"Oh, seriously?" Carol said. "I almost shat myself! Who is that under there?"

"Look down, love," came a voice from under the sheet. Carol looked down and gasped. Wellsey couldn't see what she had until he stood. From that angle, he could see that the apparition had no legs.

"What the...?" he began. He searched around for an appropriate swear, but nothing in the whole of his prison-honed vocabulary seemed adequate. "Heck," he finished, unsatisfyingly.

"So what do yez want?" the sheet said. "'Oo dares disturb me eternal slumber, ay?"

"Uh," Belinda said.

"Uh," Wellsey said.

"Buh," Fiona said.

"You, like, see everything that goes on here, right?" Carol said.

"Yeah, nah," the sheet said. "I see a fair bit, but only when I'm watching. Even then, these bloody eyeholes don't give much peripheral, do they, love?"

"So why the sheet?" Wellsey said.

"I'm a bloody ghost," the sheet said. "It's sheets, or dragging chains, and I'm not into that. No judgement, yeah? Just not my thing. And they don't give you a third choice, so... I'm Bruce by the way. And you are... Does your name start with an 'F'? No? Is there anyone here whose name begins with an 'F'?"

"Stop that!" Carol said. "We need to know if you saw what happened to Zorbar."

Bruce raised a shrouded hand to where his mouth would have been, had he had one. "Zorbar... Big guy? Not overly fond of pants? Oh, yeah, I reckon I saw what happened. Hit by a ute, poor bastard."

"We know that!" Fiona said. "Can you tell us anything about the ute? Did you get its license number?"

"You're in luck there," Bruce said. "I happen to be a ute spotter. It's me hobby. Every time I see a ute, I jot down its plate number in me ute spotter's journal."

"Really?"

"Of course not really!"

"Come on Bruce, don't be slack," Wellsey said. "We're worried about our friend, you know? So worried we broke the laws of God and nature to contact you. Be a mate and help us out."

The ghost's shrouded head bent forward. "All right," he said. He waved his right hand, and it began to fill with beams of moonlight, like a carnival worker gathering fairy floss. His fingers moving slowly and with care, the ghost spun the fibres of moonbeam into a small tube—which he tucked between his beshrouded lips.

"Look," Bruce said from the corner of his mouth, "it was a plain-looking ute, and I didn't get the licence plate, but I recognised the driver. He was here last month, dressed in some strange costume. Zorbar was fighting with the driver's mate. Wouldn't have got a look at him, but Seamus broke his helmet. Cool fight, I reckon. Better than watching two mums play tug-of-war with a box of Christmas lights, anyway, and that's usually the level of entertainment I can expect around here. Anyone got a light?"

No one offered the dread apparition a light. It grunted in disgust and pressed a spectral finger to the end of the phantom durry. The end began to burn, creating a cloud of gently glowing smoke, that smelled of not much at all.

Belinda scratched her crazy hair. "So… Who were these people?"

"Never seen 'em before," Bruce said. "You want to know, ask Seamus."

The women all looked at Wellsey, who racked his brains then shrugged. "I don't know a Seamus. There was a Sean, a few years back, worked in cleaning supplies…"

"No, not Sean," Bruce said. "Seamus. He's right there."

Wellsey looked where the ghost pointed. There was nothing there but a box full of assorted garden gnomes. No, there was… something… He couldn't see in the dim light, so he picked up one of the black candles and brought it closer. One of the gnomes wasn't new. It had soil marks, watermarks, some chipping and discolouring. What was it doing amongst the freshly minted lawn ornaments?

A fat drop of black wax fell from the candle and landed on the gnome's nose. Wellsey jumped back as the thing yelped in pain.

"Bloody good one," the gnome said to the ghost, as it wiped the wax away with its coat cuff. "Tell on me, why don't you? Things have come to a fine pass when even the fecking ghosts are informers!"

# 19 Origin Story

It was Laura Cho's first day at the Handy Pavilion, and her trainee badge was pinned to a neatly ironed apron over her polo shirt. Her excitement about starting her new job had been dwindling since Adam had parked her close to the entrance and told her to wait for her supervisor.

That had been half an hour ago. Not only was she bored, but customers also kept coming up to her and asking questions that she couldn't possibly answer, then getting annoyed when she claimed ignorance. She wished she could go hide in the break room, but she didn't even know where that was.

"Excuse me?" came a voice.

"Yeah, no, I'm new here, so…" she turned and nearly jumped to see a little man in a Handy Pavilion uniform. He had slate grey hair, a round pink face, and he stank of tobacco. "Oh, sorry, I thought you were a customer."

"I am your supervisor," he said. He didn't shake her hand, and she realised that he was carrying a metal box, so heavy he needed both hands. "You must be Laura. Bad start, by the way. Never brush off a customer with an inquiry."

Laura blushed. The little man continued: "I'm Axel Platzoff. You're a lucky girl, getting a job here now. They're talking about shedding more positions. The team member you're replacing was working full time, and they've brought you in for ten hours a week, and frankly, you're lucky to get that. Are you going to help me with this box, or what?"

"Woman," Laura said.

Axel scowled. "What?"

"You said I'm a lucky girl," Laura said. "I'm eighteen. Woman, not girl."

To her surprise, the little man nodded solemnly. "Woman, yes," he said. "An error, corrected. I appreciate that. Nonetheless, help me with this damned box."

Laura took one end of the metal box and wondered how he'd been able to carry it on his own.

"So what's your story?" Axel said, as they carried their burden towards the back of the store. "Psychic? Lycanthrope? Revenant?"

Laura laughed nervously. "School leaver?"

"Well, it takes all sorts," Axel grunted. "Tell me a bit about yourself."

"Well, I was born in Taiwan, but grew up here," Laura said. "I want to be a hairdresser, but I need a part-time job while I'm at TAFE; first-year apprenticeships don't..."

"Not that stuff," Axel said. "I mean like what's your favourite movie? Favourite band, TV show, do you have a boyfriend?"

"'*Star Trek: the Motion Picture*', Beyonce, *Nailed It*, and yes, but its early days," she said. "Why...?"

"Because you might be about to die, and I'd like to know

who I'm missing if you do," Axel said. "This way! Wait, *Star Trek*, as in the very first Star Trek movie? Wow, it really does take all sorts."

"What do you mean about...?"

"Never mind, here's Wellsey."

They'd come out the back of the Pavilion to the loading bay, where they met a bald man with tattooed arms. "We're going with this?"

"Yes, of course," Axel said. "We have to, don't we?"

"You'd like to think that, wouldn't you?" the bald man said. "That this is out of your hands. Well, you started this shit with the DIY Barn."

"They started it!" Axel said.

"Should I be writing any of this down?" Laura said.

There was a pallet under a tarpaulin. Axel pulled it off with a flourish, revealing a metal tube on top of a tripod. At one end the tube ended in a metal box, at the other in a brass cone.

"Laura, the isotopes," Axel said.

"WHAT?"

"You came to work at a *very* bad time," Axel said.

"This is the new girl?" Wellsey said. "Seriously?"

"No time to argue," Axel said. He opened the box, which contained a smaller plastic box full of metal pellets. Axel began shovelling them into the box at the end of the tube — which, now that Laura thought of it, looked an awful lot like a death ray.

"Norman's been keeping tabs on Ms Shan," Axel

continued, "and he says she's heading this way. We need for her to have plausible deniability. Besides, Laura here's safer than Carol, and you didn't object to where I stationed *her*."

"I objected for hours! I only said 'yes' to keep you from sending Fiona over!"

All of a sudden, the clouds parted and Laura understood. They were *messing* with her. It was some elaborate version of sending the new trainee for a left-handed screwdriver and a bucket of striped paint. Laura suppressed a smile. What the hell, why not play along? Show the old boys that she had a sense of humour. She dipped her hands into the plastic box and helped Axel scoop the 'isotope' pellets. Wait until she told her parents about this! They'd split their sides laughing. Or, more realistically, they'd glare at her and ask why she didn't go to university. But they *might* laugh.

At the sight of Laura actively helping, Wellsey stopped grousing. "Fine, fine," he muttered. "But are you sure...?"

Axel replied in a silly, high-pitched voice. "'Are you sure?', 'Is it safe?', 'Doesn't this violate the laws of God and nature?'... honestly you sound like a broken record. What you need is a 'can-do' attitude like Laura here."

Laura smiled. What the hell, she was having fun. And the pellets were warm to the touch, which gave the weird situation a surprising touch of authenticity.

"Just to get you up to speed," Axel said, "there was this ape-man who used to work here, but he's been captured. Using information gleaned from a gnome, we've learned that he's been taken by our arch-enemies at the DIY Barn. Carol, who works at the coffee shop across the way (get your coffee there, by the way, not the swill Belinda makes) is over there now. She's figured out where Zorbar is being held, and will be helping us knock the wall off the DIY Barn's secret dungeon. Zorbar can do the rest."

"And Norman?" Laura said, picking a random name to show she was listening.

"Norman is in love with our manager, Ms Shan," Wellsey said. "But he's keeping an eye on her for us even though it breaks his heart to see Ms Shan in the company of the true love of her life. But by doing so, he can help us keep her out of this so that if we're discovered, our actions won't splash back on her, which shows a touching degree of loyalty."

"And the staff lockers?"

"In the staff room, which is at the end of aisle 12," Axel said. "You need to bring your own padlock, or you can just buy a padlock here with your staff discount. Okay, that should be enough."

Axel slammed closed the lid of the box and pressed a sequence of buttons on top. Laura was impressed at the detail they'd put into their death ray. It looked glorious, a crazy art-deco contraption, with real lights — four red lights to be precise. As Laura watched, one blinked off. Oh, like a timer. That was clever. Axel smiled as he checked his phone. "Good old Carol! Range, declination… To think she knew nothing about this a week ago. Never underestimate a hipster's skill when it comes picking up some obscure, practically obsolete skill!"

"Ow fuck!"

120

Laura looked around to see a stout, middle-aged Islander woman rubbing the shin that she'd barked on a small pile of timber. Was she part of the game, or just another employee who'd wandered in?

"Didn't see it?" Laura said, though even as she asked, she knew it wasn't a helpful question.

"Didn't hear it!" the woman snapped.

Definitely part of the act. A second light blinked off.

"What are you wankers up to?" the woman continued, pointing at the death ray.

"Look!" Laura yelled, pointing to a yellow blur in the sky. She thought it was a shooting star, bright enough to be seen in daylight, but it changed direction and in a second resolved itself into the shape of a flying man. With astonishing speed, the shape hit the ground, and... holy crap! Was that Captain Stellar? It was... though it looked like he'd seen better days. He was unshaven, his costume was filthy and he reeked of Scotch. A third light blinked off.

Laura stared open-mouthed as Stellar pointed a gold-clad finger at Axel. "Captain Stellar, we meet again... No, wait, I'm Capt... I mean Profersa Devesto we meet... Ohh, death ray... Sweet..."

"Captain," Axel said; his voice was low, slow and forcedly calm. "Captain Stellar, listen to me very carefully."

Oh, God. Laura's stomach rose to the height of her tonsils. Oh God, it wasn't a joke, was it? What had she walked into?

"Captain, you are standing directly in the path of this

weapon," Axel said, moving towards the controls.

"Touch anything, and I'll *get* you!" Stellar said. "With my powers 'n' abilities. 'N' shit."

Laura began creeping back towards the Pavilion entrance. She'd turned down Kmart for this?

"Stellar, you need to either move out of the way or let me deactivate the weapon."

"Fuck you!" Stellar said. "Always tellin' ever'one what ter do! Well, you know what? You're not so fu…"

Then the last light blinked off and the whole world went bright.

Laura's hearing returned before her eyesight. She heard screaming, running, shouting. Then shapes started resolving themselves. There was the Islander woman—burning, drop stop and roll by a pallet of burning timber. Axel, all sunburned down one side of his face, was pounding on Wellsey's chest, like CPR or something. Miraculously, the tripod stood, but the death ray itself was nowhere to be seen. Stretching away from the tripod were two parallel lines, gouged in the earth, ending in a man-shaped hole in a distant building.

Laura looked down at herself. She was in terrible pain, but she seemed more aware of this on an intellectual level than a visceral one. There were a bunch of holes in her apron, and she was bleeding through all of them. Well, that can't be good. She felt in one of the holes with the tip of a fingernail. Beneath the apron was a flap of skin, and underneath that was a bloody wound with a piece of warm metal at the bottom.

"Well that sucks," she said.

In later years, her gratitude at her own survival was heightened by her happiness that those were not her last words.

## 20 The Return

The Handy Pavilion was packed to the gills with customers. This was often the case on a Saturday — but on this particular Saturday, things were even more hectic thanks to the public appearance of Australia's newest superhero, Voyager — just out the front, downwind of the Rotary Club sausage sizzle.

The scent of sausages and onions made Voyager's mouth water. She couldn't buy a sausage sandwich, though. Her stupid costume didn't have any pockets. Her utility belt was full of crime-fighting gear, but the designer had neglected to include a change pouch. She decided that she should get rid of one of the micro-torches. She could melt steel with her eye beams, what did she need it for anyway?

Voyager took photo after photo with her new fans. "The public loves its newest hero best," Aquaticwoman had told her, with just a touch of bitterness. As her picture was taken by customer after customer, Voyager didn't quite know yet whether she liked the attention.

"Is Captain Stellar coming back?" a teenager in a 'Walking Dead' t-shirt, said.

"Captain Stellar needs some time alone to work some things out," Voyager said, for the hundredth time that day.

"I heard that it was a mind-control ray that made him go crazy," a chubby young woman in flannels said.

Voyager struggled to come up with an answer, but the Vigilancers' publicist stepped in and gave the official story that Stellar's actions were under investigation. Voyager simply nodded. The photo session came to an end, but there was still work to do. Voyager flew up into the sky, turned invisible, then dropped back down to the staff entrance in her work clothes, just plain, everyday Laura Cho.

As she clocked on, she saw Axel Platzoff taking a pack of cigarettes from his locker. She almost choked on her surprise.

"So how come you didn't get fired?" she said.

Axel turned around, to see. "Oh, hello, Laura. I'm a little surprised to see you back here, too. Wellsey told me you dropped in on him in hospital; that was very nice of you, for someone you barely knew."

"I'm still working here because the Vigilancers say I need a day job for my secret identity," Laura said. "But how come you didn't get fired?"

Axel shrugged. "Stellar took all the blame when he sobered up," he said. "He couldn't remember what happened, and like a big hero, he decided it was all his responsibility. You were unconscious, Wellsey was coming around but he didn't dob me in, and Gwen refused to say anything to anyone..."

"So no one knows what you did?"

"No one with the power to fire me," Axel said. "Zorbar got away, for what it's worth. When Stellar went flying, he

125

smashed the room those DIY Barn bastards were holding him in. The Barn hasn't retaliated… yet."

"And what about me?" Laura said.

"You got superpowers from all those isotopes you absorbed," Axel said. "And a nice position on the Vigilancers that came open because Stellar claimed responsibility for the accident. Do you know how seldom positions in the Vigilancers open up? You can dob me in, but that would exonerate Stellar, so…"

Laura felt her teeth hurt, and realised she was grinding them very hard with her superhuman strength. She figured her teeth were pretty invulnerable, but stopped grinding them anyway. "Let's get to work."

They went out onto the floor, and all its horrors. It was worse, far worse than battling subterranean monsters or invasions from space. The people were mostly nice, even if frazzled and impatient. Even though Laura had been studying her product guides diligently, she still didn't know the answers to half the queries put to her. She was supposed to go to Axel when she needed help, yet she felt entirely justified in doing nothing of the sort.

She should tell on him. Seriously. Yeah, she'd lucked out when the ray-gun had exploded but she could just as easily have died. Axel had said as much himself.

"Settling in okay?" Marlon said. Marlon had been there at her interview. She hadn't formed any strong opinions about the man yet, but at least he was a familiar face. Marlon raised a sandwich to his mouth, and Laura drooled at the scent of low-grade sausage mince.

She tried to gather up her nerve to tell on Axel. She should. The only thing stopping her was years of Australian schooling telling her, 'do not dob'.

"I'm doing okay," she said. "But..."

"Glad to hear it," Marlon said, between bites of sandwich. "It's a busy day, chomp, chomp. We're short-staffed, chomp, chomp."

Laura's stomach was kicking her in the hindbrain. Oh God, those onions smelled good! They were overcoming her concentration so badly, and she needed her concentration right then if she was going to...

"Well, don't forget, chomp, you run into any trouble, chomp, talk to me or Axel," Marlon said, before licking the barbeque sauce from his fingers.

A customer came over, a big guy wearing slightly too little in the way of clothing. No, not a customer, Marlon waved to him. Not now! Laura hadn't screwed up the resolve to dob on Axel, yet.

"What's up, Zorbar?" Marlon said to the newcomer.

"Have coffee for Laura," Zorbar said. "From Carol. She say we owe Laura one."

Marlon looked like he was hoping for more information, but Zorbar said nothing. So this was the ape-man she'd unwittingly helped to rescue. She ground her teeth again. Putting a face on Zorbar just made it harder to tell on Axel.

But no. She had to do it. Sure, no one had been hurt, so there was no need to go to the police. But to have to work with a man with so little regard for her safety... it just wasn't right.

"Thanks, Zorbar," she said. "But Marlon, I have something important that I..."

Through the din of the crowd, she heard a creaking noise. Zorbar must have heard it at the same time as she did, because both their heads turned before the others' did. They saw the shelving unit—the huge, heavy shelving unit, that reached three whole metres above the concrete floor of the Pavilion—start to topple and fall.

She shoved Marlon with a fraction of her strength, sending him sprawling into the front aisle. But there were other people threatened by the falling unit, a hipster couple with a trolley full of paint cans... and a small child.

Everything was moving slowly. What would happen when the shelving unit hit the next one? Would the whole Pavilion fall like a row of dominoes? Laura didn't know. But then, Zorbar was moving, bracing the unit, muscles and veins standing out on his arms. He was holding it back, but for how long?

Laura knew she couldn't use her powers where everyone could see... or wasn't supposed to, or something. She needed to think quickly. With a shove from her foot, she sent the hipster family and their trolley reeling backwards. With an invisible eyebeam, she burned through the feet on the shelving unit opposite. It creaked and groaned, and then started toppling the other way.

"Come on!" she grabbed Zorbar's hand and pulled. Freed from his iron grip, it began to fall. The two massive shelves collapsed into one another, then struck in the middle of the aisle, propping each other up.

Laura and Zorbar stood in a space between the leaning shelves that now seemed like the interior of a short, Scandi-designed church. Gingerly, they stepped out from under the huge iron archway.

"What wasn't so bad," Marlon said from the ground. And then all the things started falling off the shelves—tool chests, letterboxes, lawnmowers. In seconds, the place they'd been standing was littered with hazardous debris.

"Marlon," Laura said.

"Yes?" Marlon said, in a 'surprised to be alive' sort of tone.

"Could I take my break now? I really, really, *really* need a sausage sandwich."

# 21 Newsletter Redux

*Here's the draft of my newsletter, Claudia. Once again I must formally protest the fact that this has to be passed by the Commissar for approval before publication –* Karl Wintergreen.

*Objection noted. Here is the amended draft. Change any of my edits I'll shut down your newsletter so fast you won't know what hit you –* Claudia Liselle.

From The South Hertling Super Centre Newsletter, 1 June 2016:

**Mysterious Accidents Plague Handy Pavilion**
by Karl Wintergreen

Mere weeks after the accident out the back of the Handy Pavilion, ~~allegedly~~ caused by the actions of rogue superhero Captain Stellar,~~ but in reality probably caused by a ley-line shift orchestrated by the Trilateral Commission,~~ HP staff and customers have reported a number of serious accidents.

The first such accident involved the collapse of two heavy shelving units, which toppled into each other ~~forming the structure known as a 'shelf pyramid', a little known~~

~~Masonic symbol~~. Though no one was injured, accident investigators ~~were stumped by the inexplicable nature of the event~~ have yet to make a ruling.

A mere day later, Pavillion staffers Buck Dusty and Andrea Teheinthausand were injured when a large industrial ceiling fan fell from the ceiling. Mr Dusty was taken to a hospital, while Ms Teheinthausand was taken to the Jerry's IT Repairs, next to the kebab shop. Since I happened to be nearby purchasing a spanner, I rushed to investigate and found ~~clear~~ possible signs of hacksaw marks on the broken fan. When asked for a statement, Ms Teheinthausand ~~threatened to travel backwards in time and kill me in my crib.~~ declined to comment.

The following day, three HP customers contracted food poisoning, but I think that's more to do with Belinda's coffee than any conspiracy **[I'd like to believe that this is libel, but realistically I don't think there's a jury in the land that would convict you—C]**

In addition to this, an electrical fault developed in the motorised scooter of an elderly customer, causing it to accelerate uncontrollably, dumping its rider into a display children's sandpit that, regrettably, did not contain sufficient sand to soften the impact. The old man claimed to have heard mocking laughter shortly before his accident.

I interviewed Ms Shan, the Manager of the Handy Pavilion, ~~but much of my interview will probably be redacted by Claudia Liselle, who everyone knows is giving it up to Ms Shan.~~ **[How's that for redaction? — C]** Ms Shan claimed that the accidents were a run of bad luck, a statistical blip in what she claims is a very safe shop. I asked about her connection of the Handy Pavilion's CEO to certain esoteric orders, and she said that she didn't know. Maybe she does and maybe she doesn't. Wheels within wheels, man. **[You know what? Fuck it. I'm leaving this in, you idiot. You want to look like a fool, go ahead — C]** Ms Shan then rolled her eyes, and told me that JFK was shot by cricketing great Tiger Pataudi, but that can't be true because JFK was stabbed to death by Jackie, and the man killed in Dallas was a double.

Then I got into an argument with Ms Shan, and forgot to ask the rest of my questions.

I asked Mr Smith of DIY Barn about the accidents. He seemed surprised, but claimed that it was a just punishment by Divine Providence upon the wretched and pitiful Handy Pavilion, which would surely be wiped away by the forces of History. He didn't have any of those biscuits left that I like, though.

~~What we can say about the Pavilion accidents are that they are definitely no accidents. Something mysterious and ghastly is afoot, and I will get to the bottom of it. The explosion allegedly caused by Captain Stellar was just phase one of a Masonic/Illuminati/Royal Surf Life Saving conspiracy to encoil the entire South Hertling Super Centre into its clutches.~~ **[Ok, pulling the plug here. Get a life, Karl! — C]**

Kebab Shop Revamp

**[Ok, I've cut all your crap about One World Governments, and rewritten this completely — C]**

Mr Stavros Theoupolos, owner/manager of the Kebab

Shop has initiated an ambitious revamp.

"Right now, all I have is a drink fridge, beef and chicken doner kebab cookers, and a salad station," he said. "We're closing for a week, and when we reopen there will be new chairs, an additional option of lamb kebab, in addition to the existing options, and a deep fry station for chips."

During the Kebab Shop's hiatus, it is suggested that Super Centre workers who would like to consume kebabs should bring their own from home.

"You can easily make kebabs at home," Mr Theoupolos said. "You just need mincemeat, a skewer and a blowtorch."

The revamped shop will also include an ice-cream freezer and a ten-foot satellite dish on the roof. It will be decorated in a 'stonemason's tools' motif, said Mr Theoupolos, and would host nightly meetings of mysterious robed figures.

**[There, isn't that better? — C]**

## 22 No Way Out

Hot autumn was turning to freezing winter when Wellsey returned to the Pavilion. He stopped just before the automatic doors. He knew exactly where the invisible line was, the one that opened the doors if crossed. He drew a deep breath, held it for the count of ten, let it out slowly, and stepped forward.

Inside, he spotted Axel. He was helping an elderly customer find a cardboard box of an appropriate size for the old girl's gardening supplies. Wellsey felt his eyes narrow.

"Axel," he said, in the most neutral tone he could manage.

"Morning, Wellsey," Axel said.

Wellsey waited for an apology — or at least some sort of acknowledgement that he'd been badly done by. None was forthcoming.

The old girl, clearly nervous about Wellsey, cringed slightly in the direction of Axel. Wellsey scowled and stalked off to the staff room. He was supposed to come in via the rear staff entrance, but as one of the Pavilion's rare full-time permanent employees, he didn't have to clock on, so he came from the front where it was easier to get a parking spot. The flip side of that convenience was that he had to walk through the Pavilion in his work clothes, and he was stopped twice by customers with questions before he even got to the staff room.

Inside, Marlon lounged — or at least lounged as much as is possible on a moulded plastic chair. When Wellsey came in, he sprang to his feet. "How you doing, mate? Good to see you back on your feet."

Wellsey didn't show it, but he was touched. You never really know who your friends are until things go wrong for you. There were people who he'd thought were close to him who never even bothered to visit him in the hospital. Then again, there were people like Marlon. Marlon had always seemed to treat Wellsey like a doormat, but he'd been to visit half a dozen times, once with a huge card signed by everyone, and each time with all the news from the Pavilion.

"Coffee?" Marlon said.

"Got one at Carol's," Wellsey said. Carol had visited him once and promised him free coffee for life for his role in the rescue of Zorbar. Wellsey wasn't entirely comfortable with the gesture, so had left the full price of a flat white in Carol's tip jar. Wellsey sipped at the coffee as he sat and glanced at the supercentre newsletter.

"Don't bother, mate," Marlon said. "It's not funny anymore; not since Ms Shan's special friend started editing it."

"That true then?" Wellsey said. "Ms Shan and Mrs Liselle? Carol said something about that, but you know... People like Carol always think everyone's gay."

"All I know is, Ms Shan was already less of a hard ass

when she got back from the hospital," Marlon shrugged. "Now she's *super* happy all the time. Whatever the reason is for that, it suits me well enough."

"Marlon," Wellsey said. "Thanks."

"For what?"

"For being a friend," Wellsey said. "You were always dumping extra work on me. I didn't think you liked me."

"I respect you and I think you always do a solid job," Marlon said. "That's why when there's something important to do, you usually come to mind."

Wellsey looked at the clock. His shift started in five minutes. Just enough time to finish his coffee.

"Marlon," he said. "You know it didn't go down like they said in the news? Captain Stellar was being an irresponsible ass, like they said, but he didn't cause the problem."

"I know," Marlon said. "I know what Axel has been up to. He's a dangerous man—but he's right about one thing: we need to take the DIY Barn down, and we need to do it before they destroy us."

Wellsey didn't know what to say, so he just nodded and went out onto the floor, straight to Plumbing. Fiona met him there. After her initial shyness and later arrogance, she seemed to have plateaued in the middle. She was stacking toilet seat boxes when she saw him, but she put them down and gave Wellsey a big hug when she saw him.

"I'm so sorry," she said. "I shouldn't have..."

"It wasn't your fault."

"No, but I... there were things I shouldn't have gotten involved in. If I hadn't, maybe it wouldn't have swung out of control so bad."

"I did worse things when I was your age," Wesley said.

"Really?"

"Sure," he lied. "Now come on, those 8703-Bs aren't going to stack themselves."

Wesley smiled at her as she went off about her way, then sighed deeply. He'd tried. While he was recovering, he'd tried to find another job. He'd tried so hard. But he wasn't young, he wasn't educated, and he had big holes in his employment record. Ten years ago—five years, even—he might have been able to retrain, to find something new. He couldn't deal with that now. The idea of going to TAFE, sitting with a bunch of kids half his age who were picking up these new ideas so quickly while he plodded along... No, he couldn't face it. It had to be here. There was nothing else for him. No place else to go.

He caught up on some paperwork. Whoever had been looking after it in his absence had done a real hit-and-miss job. Then he called his shrinking band of team members together to talk about departmental priorities. He talked to customers, he checked the shelves, and he sat behind the special orders desk.

And then he went to talk to Axel.

"So," he said to the little man. "What are your plans for taking those Barn buggers out?"

And Axel smiled.

## 23 The Chase

Nalda scared the crap out of Fiona. Always had. She was tall, way taller and more solid than Fiona. She had this thick European accent, never smiled, and she never looked you quite directly in the eye. And she was strong. Not just 'big person' strong, either. More like 'forklift truck' strong. Nalda wore sunglasses, even at night, and she was forever threatening to travel back in time and kill someone.

On the other hand, she *was* quite good with children.

Belinda—who worked in Paints now—was off sick. Fiona had been temporarily moved from Plumbing to Paints, and every time she went to the spray paint locker, she could see the little open area between the end of aisle fifteen and the rear wall of the Pavilion. There, in a little area behind a short plastic fence, Fiona saw Nalda leading the Saturday morning kids' craft group.

"Ja, you see you are too much glidder using," Nalda said to a girl in a pink fairy princess costume. "Dat is why it is running. Go easy on der glidder, use it to accent, not overpower, der acrylic paints."

"Thanks, Miss Robot!" the child said, hugging Nalda's leg.

"Affection acknowledged," Nalda said. "Now I must deal with dat little dopey boy eating der crayons. As for you: I'll be back."

Fiona smiled. She guessed that deep down in the killer cyborg's cold mechanical heart, Nalda loved her job. Fiona wished she could take such joy from her own work. Maybe she could have, if she hadn't gone along with Axel's plans. Her terrible secret was driving a wedge between her and her coworkers. Norman was the only one she could talk to, and he'd been too cranky to talk much since he'd been transferred to the cafeteria.

"Is that the Kids Kraft Korner?" asked the young mother of an incredibly shy looking four-year-old girl.

"It used to be, until someone figured out the initials meant something unintended and, yeah, we had to change it," Fiona said.

The young woman squinted as she worked this one out.

"Oh, yeah," she said. "I see. What is it now?"

"Nalda there calls it the 'Kinder, Kunst, Kraft.'"

"Uh... Ok. Do you know if there's room for little Bronwyn here?"

"I think so," Fiona said. "Nalda! You have room for one more?"

Nalda walked over. From her immense height, she looked down on little Bronwyn. Fiona thought she saw a red light somewhere behind the lenses of Nalda's sunglasses. The child looked up at the towering apparition before her, seemingly uncertain whether to cry or go straight to soiling herself. Nalda reached down and lifted the tyke by his armpits to her eye level.

"Dis one," she said. "Dis one will be a watercolourist. I am in her eyes seeing it. Dere is *fire*, ja, but also *delicacy*. Ach. Vatercolours. Alles klar?"

With a faint whirr of servos, she took the kid into the little craft area. The child's mother watched, open-mouthed.

"Here are vatercolours. Here ist water. Important to use correct amount of water. Not too much not too little, ja? Now, vat paint you, liebchen?"

"A unicorn?" Bronwyn said, uncertainly.

"Gut. Later ve vill discuss proportion and colour theory. For now, paint!"

The child's mother shot a terrified glance at Fiona. "She's very good, you know," Fiona said. To prove her point, she took from her pocket a key ring, with a pendant in the shape of a perfect Attic vase, black except for the red figure of an Arcadian shepherd playing his pipes. The whole thing was about five centimetres long and made out of polymer clay.

"Did she make that?"

"One of her students did," Fiona said, turning the little vase upside down so the woman could see the base.

"'Timmy, age 5,'" the mother read, relaxing a little. "I hope Bronwyn will be all right," she said. "I've heard bad things about the safety record here. Collapsing shelves and so on."

"We had a run of bad luck," Fiona said. She was parroting the official line, not believing a word she said. "Look, every shop has an accident now and then. Sometimes they just clump together. Like sometimes you can flip a coin ten times and it'll split evenly between heads and tails and sometimes you'll get ten heads or ten tails. Just probability."

"I guess," the mother sighed. "I'd just rather not go back to the DIY Barn again. Their Kids' craft area is creepy." To prove her point, she reached into her handbag, taking out a childish picture of a man's head in profile. The man was jowly and bald, and his face was circled by what looked at first like ivy, but which Fiona quickly realised were wreaths of laurel. Beneath in a scrawled hand was written: "mR SmiTh, ar lEEder."

"Huh," Fiona said.

At this point, Christian ambled past. Fiona didn't care for Christian. He was an extraordinarily pretty young man, who'd started as a cashier not long after the explosion of Axel's deathray. Since then, he'd had a meteoric rise through the ranks. His sales record was second to none, edging Fiona out from her position as the rising young team member — though that was not why she disliked him, she thought.

Christian smiled lazily at her and Fiona forced a smile in return. She was at a loss to understand his success when he always looked half asleep. He didn't stop to talk. Fiona waited until he was out of sight, then sneered at his back.

"That guy's a jerk," she muttered.

She expected Bronwyn's mother to change the subject or walk away. Instead, she smiled and adopted an 'I'm listening' posture.

"He took the job of my friend Norman in Power Tools," Fiona said.

"So Norman was fired?"

"No, that's the thing. They made him manager of the Pavilion Café, which is technically a promotion, but he hates the job. He always wanted to work in the power tool shop, but he's helping to support his mother so he couldn't turn down the extra money."

"That's rough."

"So why are you interested?"

"I haven't worked since Bronwyn was born," the woman said. "I miss office gossip so badly."

That was when the trolley spun out of control.

It was one of the heavier trolleys, loaded up with plants and bags of soil, and being pushed along the rear aisle. The man who'd been pushing it gamely tried to regain control of the handle, but he slipped and fell, leaving the trolley thundering towards the Kid's group. Fiona pushed down every protective urge in her body. Nalda could handle the trolley. She ran the other way. Past the trolley, past the fallen man, and seeking the culprit who had pushed him over.

She'd run through every possibility as to who the mystery saboteur might be; the source of all the accidents. Axel had been a suspect, soon discarded. Whatever else you could say about him, he was fiercely loyal to the Pavilion. Then there had been some staff who'd been fired. One of them might pull a cruel prank, but a weeks-long campaign of terror seemed unlikely. Agents of the DIY Barn? That seemed the most likely contender.

But the time for speculation was over. Now, it was time to find out for real! Fiona skidded on the same slippery patch of floor that had caused the man to lose control of the trolley — a puddle of lubricant. Fiona managed to keep upright, barely, and reflectively reached out with her power. Fortunately, the fluid was water-based. She swept it away with a wave of her hand.

She almost ran past aisle twelve, when a movement caught her eye. A flapping motion, like a flag or... a cloak. A black cloak! A figure in a black cloak and hat was running away, towards the front of the store. The saboteur! It had to be.

"Stop him!" Fiona shouted. "Stop him!"

Adam from Outdoor Furniture made a lunge for the fleeing figure, just by the Enquiries counter. The black-clad form jumped, kicking off the front of the great shelves, passing over Adam's head, and sending the poor guy to the floor. Donna from lighting might have grabbed the fugitive, but she was so shocked by what happened to Adam that her quarry felled her with a quick but effective kick to the shin.

Fiona redoubled her efforts, sprinting as fast as she could, roaring for help at the top of her. She wasn't much of an athlete. Already her lungs felt like twin furnaces and her eyes swam like eggs in curry sauce. Some woman from Indoor Plants whose name Fiona could never remember grabbed the fugitive's left arm, and a burly customer in a Knights jersey grabbed the right. Fiona almost relaxed — until the black-clad villain banged his captors' heads together and ran.

But the incident had slowed him. Fiona was nearly on top of him when she tripped and nearly fell. She looked back to see what she'd tripped on, but saw nothing but Angela McKenzie from Blinds and Curtains.

Fiona thought that the cloaked figure was heading for the Garden Centre to escape. Instead, he veered off and slipped into the toilet. The door was closed with a bang, followed by the sound of the bolt sliding into place. Fiona stood, leaning against the wall, gulping cool air into her burning lungs.

What to do now? She could increase water pressure in the toilet, blow all the gaskets… No, too much. But she was in no state to break down the door with her hands or feet…

"Stand aside, Fiona." It was Nalda, looking just as pissed off as an emotionless cyborg can look.

"Where…" Fiona gasped, "where did you get that leather jacket from?"

"Der Kinder are safe," Nalda said. "Now to get der culprit."

Fiona stood back as Nalda drove her right fist through the door, and unlocked it from the inside. "Come with me — if you want to help me beat der crap out of dis asshole."

Nalda led the way. Through the spots before her eyes, Fiona was dimly aware that there was a large mob of staff and customers behind them. Well, they could just wait their turn. Fiona followed Nalda into the little anteroom between the male and female toilets. An elderly lady emerged from the women's room.

"Have you seen dis man?" Nalda said, holding up a

hastily drawn charcoal sketch of a cloaked figure in a broad-brimmed hat.

"No, love," the old woman said.

"Der men's room. We have him!"

Fiona had been in the men's room before, but only after hours while she and Wellsey had been doing running repairs. She followed Nalda in to find…

Nothing.

The room was empty of people. It contained a grubby urinal and a grubbier sink. The tiny window was closed, and showed no signs of having been opened lately. That left the single, grubby cubicle.

"Wait by the door," Nalda whispered. "He'll try to get past me. If he succeeds, you must stop him."

Fiona took her position. God the room smelt bad. How did men stand it? Nalda crept up to the cubicle door she opened it and called out: "Skynet in Himmel!"

As Fiona watched, Nalda walked into the cubicle. For a second, she held her breath, until the big cyborg woman walked out, holding a black hat with a broad brim. Fiona's heart fell. They'd been close! So close!

"What do you think it means?" she said.

"What it means," Nalda said, "is 'fuck dis noise, I'm not waiting until 11.45. I am taking mein break *now*.'"

"You know what?" Fiona said. "I think it does mean that."

# 24 One Day at a Time

Captain Stellar had been sober for fifty days.

No.

No, not Captain Stellar. Stellar wasn't around anymore. It was *Vincent* who had been sober for fifty days. Only Vincent.

Vincent, off the bottle and here to make amends to the people he'd wronged. He'd written an anonymous cheque for the damage he'd done to the DIY Barn and the Place O'Pets, but that was just impersonal property damage. Now he had to make amends to the real people he'd hurt: Popplewell. Harper. Cho.

Platzoff.

The awful woman who usually made the coffee at the Handy Pavilion was checking purchases at the door. That was something at least. It meant a decent cuppa for once, perhaps? The barista behind the espresso machine was a young man whose scraggly beard was just beginning to fill out. Vincent observed that he was quite a handsome man — or he would be if he didn't have an expression like he was sucking a lemon. His features were even and he was well built. Younger than Vincent, but not *so* much younger; not socially unacceptable younger.

But the observation was purely theoretical. Vincent felt no visceral reaction at the sight of the fellow. No lust, no attraction, no envy even. Just the grey recognition of feelings that weren't there. He ordered his coffee, and watched the young man go through the motions with mechanical precision.

"I'm meant to be working in Power Tools," the young man said. His badge said 'Norman'. Well, at least he wasn't 'Norm.' "This look like power tools?"

"Well technically."

Norman looked at the espresso machine. "Yeah, technically. But not really, you know?"

"Way of the world," Vincent said. "I just lost a job myself. To a younger worker."

Seriously, the Vigilancers had chosen Voyager to replace him? Sure, Vincent felt terrible when he thought of his role in the accident that had granted Voyager her powers. That pang of guilt was balanced by envy at the woman's meteoric rise. But that was sobriety for you—sometimes not enough emotions, sometimes too many.

"Yeah, that's what happened to me," Norman said. "You'd think a man in his twenties wouldn't have to worry about that, you know?"

The little café was empty aside from Vincent and Norman. Vincent considered sitting in the far corner and having his latte and muffin quietly, but suddenly he found the thought of silence terrifying. He took the table closest to the counter, where he could hear Norman muttering as he refilled the cookie jars.

"Hey, do you know Axel Platzoff?" Vincent asked.

"Yeah, he's a friend of yours, right? I've seen you talking to him."

"He's not a friend. More like a former co-worker."

"Don't tell me you were a supervillain too?"

"No, no." Vincent had said too much, damn it. "A different job. A long time ago."

Norman nodded. "Yeah, you don't look the supervillain type. If anything, you look more like Captain Stellar."

"Really?"

"Well except for the glasses. I guess you get that all the time."

"No," Vincent said. "First time."

But it wasn't the first time, was it? Someone had made the observation before… Maybe it had been when he was drunk.

"I liked Captain Stellar," Norman continued. "Seemed like a decent guy, until he flipped out. It's probably nothing, but. It'll turn out to be a mind-control ray that made him do it, or an evil duplicate or something."

Something stirred in Vincent's guts, a desire for… what? Validation? Probably. It was a little pathetic, how badly he needed to hear something nice said about himself. But *damn* did he need it.

"Was he your favourite hero?" Vincent asked.

"No, not *favourite*," Norman said. "I liked Doc Submarine when I was a boy. Still got an autographed photo, somewhere. Might be worth a buck or two on eBay. But

Captain Stellar was pretty cool. My mate Leonard in high school? Stellar was his favourite, but I think that's mostly because Leonard's gay, too. I guess it's good to have role models like that."

Vincent suddenly felt a pang of guilt, along with the depression and regret.

"You okay, mate?" Norman asked.

"I'm fine. I just… I think…"

Norman looked at him in an appraising, thoughtful way. He seemed to be on the verge of saying something, when a red-haired woman walked in. She looked familiar, but Vincent couldn't quite remember where it was that he'd seen her before.

"Hey, Sadie. Soy latte?"

The woman nodded. Norman looked at her for what seemed like a longer time than necessary, before shaking his head to clear it. He breathed deeply twice, seeming to steel his resolve.

"You know, mate," he said to Vincent, "Axel saw what happened with Stellar, out the back of the Pavilion," he said. "If you're interested in… that particular superhero… maybe you should ask Axel about what happened."

"It was in all the papers," Vincent said.

"Not all of it."

Vincent waited for him to say more, but the young man clammed up. What did he mean? What did he mean?

There was only one way to answer that question. Vincent finished his coffee and nodded goodbye to Sadie just in case she was someone he ought to know. Standing, he squared his shoulders and set his jaw, and strode off to confront his archenemy.

# 25 Underground

Christian looked across Outdoor Furniture towards Norman in his little café apron and smirked. So much less manly than his hardware apron! All was proceeding apace. Norman was out and he, *Christian,* was the rising star of the Handy Pavilion!

Just look at Norman there, making coffee for Sadie and that guy with the glasses and big chin! Where would he be in five years' time? Still making coffee! Where would Christian be? 2IC of the Power Tools section! Or even... dare he even dream it? *Manager* of Power Tools!

Of course, his success was not all down to him. He had his mentor to thank...

His shift had ended, so he made his way to the men's toilet and moved the hidden panel in the floor. Beneath was a narrow tunnel, which he descended by means of a ladder of huge cast iron staples. Hanging on one staple was a battered old electric lamp. He turned it on, clipped it to his belt, and continued his descent.

After an eternity of struggling downward, he came to a huge open space, dominated by an underground lake. A gondola was tied to the bottom-most rung of the ladder.

Christian dropped gently into the boat, cast off, and rowed the small vessel across the smooth surface of the water. A thin mist rose from the lake. Other than the faint rhythmic splash of his oars and the occasional drip of water from the ceiling, his journey was silent.

It wasn't long before Christian arrived at a little jetty, poking out of the darkness into the lake. He hitched up the gondola and climbed ashore. Passing down a narrow tunnel, he entered a large underground room. Against one wall was a bookcase, assembled from some antique flat-pack. It was filled from top to bottom in precious tomes— 'Retail for Dummies', 'How to Succeed in Hardware', 'The Customer is Sometimes Right: a New Guide to Selling'. The rest of the room was decked out with slightly wonky lawn furniture and factory second rugs, all arranged in such exquisite taste that it almost made Christian weep. But the *piece de resistance* was the organ, made from an MDF worktable, PVC pipes and an old air compressor.

At the controls to the organ, *she* sat—dressed head to foot in black, and playing the guitar riff from *Slice of Heaven* on keys made from 20x20mm pine.

"How fares the surface world, Christian," she said.

"All goes well, Mistress," Christian said. "Norman has been shamed. Your reign of terror has reduced custom at the Pavilion. The DIY Barn is poised to strike!"

"Excellent," she said.

"Is it not time then, my mistress?" Christian said, eagerly.

"Time?"

"For the next stage of the plan? First, create a crisis, then we step in to fix it. We could be running the place by week's end!"

She turned. Christian looked down, so as not to stare at the bone-white mask of polymer clay that covered over half of her face. "Oh, my pupil. You have learned so much, and yet so little. Yes, the Pavilion will pay dearly for a hand up—but first, it must be *truly* pushed to its knees!"

"But," Christian began. He did not like to argue with the Phantasm. She was so wise, and she had raised him up from nothing to his current status at the Handy Pavilion. And yet… and yet…

"But surely, we must take care not to destroy the Pavilion completely," he said. "What do we gain by taking over, if the Pavilion is past the point of being saved?"

It was always impossible to tell what the Phantasm was thinking. The mask hid her face, and there was never any expression in her eyes. "Of course you are right. The Pavilion wronged me. Because of it, I have lost my false face and my real ears."

Christian shifted uncomfortably. She had said that often, about the ears. He never quite knew what she meant by it, and he was embarrassed to ask.

"But," the Phantasm continued, "you are still correct. We cannot let the Pavilion die. Without it, there is no purgatory for Norman, and no future for you, my protégé. We must bleed the Pavilion *almost* dry. Just not completely."

"So it is time?"

"How little you know."

The Phantasm arose from her seat atop an enormous upturned planter and laid a black-gloved hand on Christian's shoulder. "There will come a time for the next phase. It will come soon. But no, it will not come now."

"Yes, mistress," Christian said. He looked into her eyes, deep in the holes of the mask, brimming with fierce energy. He knew that he could not say no. She was right in this, as she was right in all things.

The Phantasm's eyes flicked sideways, towards the little room that contained her bed — or more accurately, her garden hammock.

"Of course, my mistress," Christian sighed. "But this time... You know, maybe just for a change... could you take the mask off?"

"Hm... Hm... Hmm... Uh... Ahh... Hmmm... No."

"How about the cape?"

"Also no."

"At least take off the gloves?"

"How about one glove?"

"Right hand?"

"Left."

Christian sighed. Well, it was a start.

# 26 The Ghost in the Machine

The trouble with being dead, Bruce thought, was that it was incredibly bloody boring.

Boredom didn't seem to bother the other ghosts. Not that there were many of them around. He was the only one in the Handy Pavilion, and there were just a few others in the Super Centre. Yet these others all seemed to have a *purpose*.

Take young Vinnie. Sixteen-year-old petrol-head. Died after a tire blew out while he was doing burnouts in the carpark late one night, sending his stolen Mazda crashing into an open stormwater drain. His spectral vehicle could still be seen from time to time, doing doughnuts in the moonlight.

Then there was Mr Donovan, the original owner of the carpet shop across the way. He'd had a heart attack part way through his annual stocktake, and now spent every night in a doomed attempt to finish his counting. He was the ghost Bruce saw most, since he sometimes came over to the Pavilion to count their carpets too. He seldom said much, except when he was on his tea break.

Other than that, there was Kylie, who'd OD'd in the toilet beside BBQ Imperium, who spent her time searching for her missing syringe. And then there were some local

Aboriginal people who'd died in a smallpox outbreak just before WWI, and had been buried under what was now Hoonworld Automotive. Bruce found himself too embarrassed to talk to them.

All of those other ghosts *did* things. They recreated the last moments of their life, or searched fruitlessly for lost loves. Even the cloud of dead goldfish that surrounded the Place O'Pets seemed in constant search of fish food.

And Bruce? Bruce just wandered around the Pavilion and smoked imaginary cigarettes. Maybe that was what happened to dead tradies. Always overtime, never payday.

"You must have *some* wisdom from beyond," Carol said.

"Nah," Bruce replied. Ever since Belinda's séance, Carol had come to talk to him pretty regularly. She'd sit on the chained-down pine bench outside the Handy Pavilion's front door, and try to talk about cosmic wisdom. At first, Bruce had been happy for the attention, but he was seriously getting tired of it all.

"Not even a little?" Carol pleaded.

"Eat well," Bruce said. "Be good to your parents. Oh, and don't smoke. Even if it doesn't kill you directly, it'll slow you down and make you easier to murder. Take it from me. Personal experience."

Carol shook her head. "Is that why you're still here, tied to the material world? Because you were murdered?"

"Could be," Bruce said. "I don't know. They don't tell me anything they don't tell you."

"They?" Carol said, sitting up straight. "Who are *they*?"

"Buggered if I know," he said. "They, he, she, it… I don't know. Used to be an Anglican, you know? Got to say, not a very *good* Anglican, but an Anglican. Thought once I'd died I'd get a chat with God, and what have you? 'Hey, Big Fella, thanks for the daffodils *et cetera*, sorry about that whole adultery thing, and thanks for being understanding about it.' That's what I thought. Haven't seen Him yet."

He looked over at Carol. It was a cold night and Carol was dressed head to toe in warm clothes, but through the gap between her Laplander hat and heavy scarf, he could see a look of disapproval.

"I'm sorry," he sighed. "I was an electrician. I liked being an electrician, you know? I liked being an electrician, I liked betting on the greyhounds, I liked a nice cold beer and I liked Mrs Mariana Galukis. I wasn't much interested in the meaning of life, and I'm pretty sure I've missed my chance on figuring out what it was."

Carol shook her head. "I'm sorry," she said. "I just… You're a being of pure spirit. Maybe you have more wisdom than you think?"

"Wouldn't know what to do with wisdom even if I had any."

"You would if you had wisdom."

Beneath his sheet, Bruce frowned. "Yeah, I guess I would, eh?"

Carol sighed and rubbed her eyes. A cool breeze blew under the eaves of the Pavilion, and she pulled her coat tighter about her. Bruce tended to prefer when attractive women wore a lot of clothes. When he'd first discovered that he was a ghost, he'd considered killing the time by ogling women in the toilet. He'd quickly decided that this would be more embarrassing and shameful than erotic, so he'd given up on the idea before carrying it out. These days, he kept well clear of the toilets and—more recently—Ms Shan's office. Honestly, didn't that woman have a bed at home?

"Look, love, I wish I could tell you something," he said. "I wish I could tell you that there's a plan, or that it's all going to be all right or something like that. I do. Bottom line, though, I'm pretty sure I've learned everything I was ever going to learn while I was alive, and it didn't amount to much. I'm just not a curious bloke, you know?"

Carol nodded. Bruce had never liked upsetting people—an attitude that had only been reinforced by the consequences of upsetting *Mr* Galukis. He cast about for something kind to say.

"I reckon it's a good thing. What sort of unfair world would withhold the meaning of life until you don't have a life to even have a meaning?"

Carol sniffed. "You know, that's almost wise?"

"And almost is as close as I'm ever going to get," Bruce said. "How's Zorbar?" he added.

"He's pretty well," Carol said, pointing to the only car in the darkened carpark. "He's recovered from his ordeal at the DIY Barn, or as much as anyone can recover from something like that. He's waiting for me in the car. Says he's scared of ghosts."

To Bruce's surprise, this cheered him a little. A bruiser like Zorbar would never have been scared of the podgy, chain-smoking, middle-aged Bruce when he'd been alive. The thought that he was now the tough guy made him feel magnanimous towards Zorbar, who he'd never much cared for.

"Well, you keep hold of that one," Bruce said. "He's a good man. He's got some issues and all, what with the chimp thing, but."

All at once, Carol was sitting on the ground, the bench bowled over by some terrible shock. Bruce was still in a sitting position, the sudden collapse of the seat meaning little to his spectral body. Standing, he reached down to help Carol to her feet, before remembering that it was a bloody silly thing to do.

He looked up, hoping to see the source of the shock wave. It wasn't hard to spot. Standing in a crater in the carpark was a robot. Not some fancy-looking robot from a modern movie, but a big, clunky thing that looked like it was made out of parts from an FJ Holden. It stood about five meters tall, and it lurched towards the Handy Pavilion on clanging, steel legs.

"Oh, fuck *me*," Bruce said.

Carol lay on the ground. She wasn't dead, or even unconscious, as far as Bruce could tell. A trickle of blood ran from under her Laplander hat, and she was muttering something that Bruce couldn't make out. His ears were ringing from the impact—which didn't make a lot of sense, really, but what can you do?

The robot lurched forward. Bruce could finally hear

what it had to say, and it said: "Crush! Kill! Destroy!"

A streak of tan lightning came hurtling towards the robot. Zorbar! Bruce cursed. Forget the robot, you idiot! Come and help get Carol to safety! Shrieking, Zorbar leapt on the robot's back, clutching on for dear life with one hand, while with the other stabbing at the joint between its head and body with a huge knife.

"No, you bloody idiot!" Bruce said.

Again and again, Zorbar's savage blade struck home. Then it struck home a little too well. The ape-man's long hair stood on end as a shower of sparks cascaded from the robot's neck. Zorbar fell twitching to the ground. Still sparking, the robot marched on.

"Oh, fuck this," Bruce grumbled. Instinct made him want to run away or else rush to help Carol. His immaterial form made the first instinct unnecessary and the second instinct useless. He ran his hand across his shrouded face. "I'm dead, you pricks. Stop fucking with me!"

Other than the shower of sparks, Zorbar's assault didn't seem to have had any effect on the robot. Paralysed with indecision, Bruce watched the sparks fall — and found himself estimating the current and voltage involved. Bits of his mind that he hadn't used since his death clicked into action, calculating amps, watts, hertz, volts, newtons. Unhindered by the meat of his brain, his thoughts raced faster than ever before. By the time the robot reached him, he had a pretty comprehensive model of the thing's wiring.

And then the robot walked into him. And Bruce was

inside the thing's hulking steel frame and he grabbed at the electrons racing through the metal monster as the whole world vanished.

## 27 Terror From Tomorrow!

Fridays were the worst days, Laura decided. No, wait. Saturdays were the worst. Not counting Thursdays. She sighed, and looked at her watch. Only three hours to go. Then she could take off, change into her Voyager costume and go fight some crime.

She grimaced at the thought. She had never really wanted to be a superhero, but the job had grown on her. True, a lot of it was kind of stupid. That whole alien gorilla thing she'd dealt with the previous week... seriously, what had that been about? But sometimes — not always, but sometimes — the people she had to put in prison were very bad indeed. It made the whole thing seem a little less pointless.

"'Scuse me," a customer said. He was a lumpy looking guy in a singlet that left little to the imagination. "Where's pulleys?"

"Two aisles over," Laura said.

"I looked there," the man complained.

"They're right down the end."

"I looked right down the end."

"Right down the *far* end."

The man grunted, narrowed his eyes and lumbered off,

grumbling under his breath. Seriously, what did he think? That she was hiding the pulleys from him? Hoarding them for some reason?

Laura went back to taking recalled air pumps off the shelf. Two hours and fifty-five minutes to the end of her shift. Laura had heard that the Crime Cats were on the loose again. Was it too much to hope that maybe they'd rob a bank or two? They'd been the number one crime gang for years, and now they were laying low. What were they, *pussies*?

Well, of course they were, but…

Laura put her head down and looked busy as Marlon and Ms Shan came walking through. They both looked pretty grim. Laura had heard that the DIY Barn management had been challenging some development plans at the local council. Ostensibly, they were the plans of the Super Centre, but they indirectly affected the Handy Pavilion pretty bad and—oh God, Laura could barely stay awake just thinking about it. She wished she was punching someone. Maybe the Human Sandbag? He was pretty easy on the knuckles.

"I looked," said the lumpy customer.

Laura sighed. "I'll show you…"

"No need, you can just tell me."

"Okay. Two aisles down?"

"Yes."

"That way?"

"Yes."

"Far end?"

"Yes."

"Left hand side, facing the back of the store?"

The lumpy customer seemed to think about this for a moment. "*Left* side. You sure they're there?"

"Positive."

"O-kay," the customer said, those two syllables both dripping distrust. He stumped off again.

She had hardly put her head down, when she heard a noise behind her.

"Look, you go past the collapsible trolleys, and… Oh, my God!" she gasped. Looking up, she did not see the lumpy customer. Instead, she saw a woman who was her exact duplicate — which, quite frankly, was kind of a freakout.

"Evil twin?" Laura said. "Other dimensional duplicate? Me from the future?"

"You from the future," Other Laura said.

"Ah," Laura said. On a closer look, she could see that her other self was beginning to go grey, and had a few extra lines on her face. "You're gonna be annoying and refuse to tell me anything interesting or useful because 'time streams, blah blah blah,' aren't you?"

"Got it in one," Older Laura said.

Laura examined the dress Older Laura was wearing. It was knee length, made of stiff green plastic, and had a high, square collar.

"Is that what we're wearing in twenty years' time?"

"Ten years," Older Laura said, touching her face. "You need to stay out of the sun. And would it hurt you to moisturise?"

"God, you sound like my Mum," Laura said. A moment later, the implications of this hit home. "Awwww!"

"There, there," Older Laura said. "Hey, want to see my Nobel Peace Prize?"

"Hell, yeah!"

"Then work harder on promoting peace," Older Laura laughed. "Hang on, I've got to hide."

To Laura's surprise, her older doppelganger slid sideways between a couple of enormous, wheeled toolboxes, hiding herself in the tiny space between the box and the back of the shelving unit.

"I'm very small, aren't I?" she said. "I knew it, I guess, but it's weird to see it in action."

A second later, she saw who Older Laura was hiding from, as the lumpy customer reappeared. Laura sighed. "Are you sure you don't want me to just lead you..."

"No," the man said. "I'm not stupid. Just tell me."

Laura repeated the instructions, this time adding that the pulleys were on the two middle shelves. Again, the man squinted at her in deep suspicion, and walked off. Older Laura reappeared.

"Please tell me I get a better job," Laura said.

"That's down to you," Older Laura said. "You do the job you have now to the absolute bare minimum that's required. If you think you're going to get a better job that way, go nuts."

"Do you need contacts for that hindsight?" Laura said. "No? It's 20/20, you say? How nice for you. So what did you come backwards in time for, anyway?"

"There's something you do need to know," Older Laura said. "Something important. Something critical. The entire future of the world depends on what happens, right here, right now. I'm breaking a fundamental law of the universe to tell you this, but you *must* know or then entire world may be *doomed*."

Laura's annoyance faded. There was something so earnest about her older self's tone, something so urgent. She scanned Older Laura's face, which she knew almost as well as her own. Yes, she meant it.

"Okay," Laura said. "What do I have to know?"

"Firstly: the DIY Barn," Older Laura said. "You think that it's just a rival hardware store. It's not. It's a force of sheer, unadulterated evil. It must be stopped."

The DIY Barn? Laura knew that Ms Shan and Marlon and that pain-in-the-ass Axel all had bees in their bonnets about the place. The Barnlings had kidnapped Zorbar, after all. But a threat to the entire world? How did that even work?

"What should I do?" Laura said.

"You must thwart the DIY Barn, any chance you get," Older Laura said. Her eyes narrowed. "Any chance, any way, any time."

"And the other thing?" Laura said. "You said 'firstly?'"

"The second thing is, if anything, even more important than the first," Older Laura said. "If you falter in the struggle against the Barn, the world will suffer. If you fail in this second mission, the whole universe will be shaken to its very foundations."

"Yes?" Laura said, helplessly.

Older Laura pointed to the end of the aisle, where the lumpy customer stood, scratching his head.

"You must *never* let that man find the pulleys!"

# 28 Axel's Enemy

Axel looked down at the pile of glass terrarium bottles he'd just unpacked, and realised that he'd put them all on the wrong shelf. In his frustration, he kicked the base of the shelving unit, which hurt his toe far more than it hurt the massive steel strut.

Why? Why didn't Captain Stellar just *fight* him?

That was the thing. A week before, Stellar had confronted Axel about the incident with the death ray. He'd guessed everything. Everything!

Axel ought to have known that Stellar would figure it out eventually, once he'd sobered up and pulled himself together. But he hadn't known; he had been caught flatfooted. Axel mind had raced, searching for some strategy to fight Stellar without causing any damage to the Handy Pavilion. Before he'd even finished ironing out the issues with his third contingency plan, Stellar had given a cold smile, waved goodbye, and walked away.

Ever since that moment, Axel had been off his game.

"Herr Platzoff? Axel?"

Axel shook his head. It sunk into his brain that Nalda was waving a hand in front of his face.

"Sorry. I was miles away."

"Apology accepted," Nalda said. "Metaphor comprehended. Have you been thinking about der issue of der Phantasm?"

The Phantasm! Axel almost smiled. Yes, the Mystery of the Phantasm of the Pavilion. That might serve to distract his mighty brain from Stellar's — what the Hell was Stellar playing at, anyway?

Axel forced himself to concentrate. "Now, you saw this black-clad figure go into the toilets, yes?"

"Ja."

"But didn't come out?"

"Ja."

"And you saw it with your own eyes? This isn't just what Fiona told you?"

Nalda removed her sunglasses. Where her eyes should have been were digital readouts — red, 1980s style digital readouts. "Nein, I see her with my own photoreceptors."

So not a trick of the light, or Fiona's imagination playing on her. "Then the logical solution is that there's a hidden exit from the toilet. And, quite aside from the Phantasm, that's a lawsuit waiting to happen."

"Ja, but dat is der problem. We checked. We tap on ground, tap on wall — nothing. Yesterday, Ms Shan gives permission to remove the tiles, so Adam broke some mit a sledgehammer."

"Adam? Never ceases to amaze me, that guy. What did he find?"

"Nothing. Nothing out of der ordinary at all."

The problem was an intriguing one. Axel was pretty sure that the Phantasm wasn't a real ghost. Bruce would have said something otherwise. Even so, there was clearly something very wrong about Stellar's just walking away like that. That wasn't how this worked. When the hero figures out the villain's plot, there's a fight. Those are just the *rules*.

Axel shook his head again, harder this time. The Phantasm, not Stellar. Focus, Axel. *Focus!*

"Do you think it's *those* folks?" Nalda said. "You know. Der DIY Barn people."

"Not their style," Axel said. "Inasmuch as they have any style at all."

"They make me so angry sometimes, dose Barnlings," Nalda said. "Sometimes, I just want to go backwards in time and kill—"

"This Phantasm," Axel said, as much to focus his mind as to redirect Nalda, "Clearly has some sort of superhuman ability. I suspect that he can't teleport, because then he could have escaped from anywhere, with no need to run into the khazi. Maybe there was some portal in the toilet? Some dimensional gateway? That might explain—"

And then Captain Stellar walked past. Just right past. As he got to the corner of the aisle, he turned a little and nodded in a half-interested way. Every muscle in Axel's body tensed. His stomach churned and his mouth went dry. He ground his teeth so hard they began to squeak. Then Stellar walked on. He turned again and was gone.

Who the hell did Stellar think he was? *Who*? Some nobody, a schnook in glasses who thought he was a big deal because he possessed the Power Cosmogonol? Did he just think he could make his own rules like that? Stellar was a superhero, damn it! His job was to enforce the rules, not *make them up*.

"Are you all right, Axel?"

Nalda looked concerned — though her 'concerned' look was not very different from her 'sad' look, or even her 'angry' look. And honestly all these looks were mere variants on her 'impassive' look.

"Would you like me to…?"

"No, Nalda," Axel snapped. "I would not like you to go backwards in time and kill that man."

"Nein, I mean do you want me to get some bandages for your hand?"

Axel looked down. The glass bottle he'd been holding had broken in two and his hand was bleeding. A moment later, the pain hit his brain and he winced.

"Thank you, Nalda. That would be very kind."

She left him standing there, after assuring him that she'd be back. The riotous whirl of his thoughts prevented his mighty brain from thinking very hard about the question of the Phantasm. His fists clenched and his eyes felt hot.

Kill Stellar? No. Out of the question. There were too many things to do, too many important things. If Stellar attacked, Axel would have to defend himself. But he couldn't voluntarily escalate the conflict with a broken-down retired superhero. And yet, Stellar's presence was making it difficult to do anything. Maybe too difficult.

Calm, Axel thought. That's what I need. I need to calm my thoughts. But how?

Axel looked up at the terrarium bottles and laughed. Of course! It was so simple. The Handy Pavilion itself would be his saviour, just as it had been in the past. Nalda was returning with a sterile dressing, but Axel had already forgotten the gash in his palm. He was looking at the bottles and thinking of the aisles and aisles of wood, paint, glue, and tools.

"I think I need a hobby," he told Nalda.

# 29 Escalation

Ms Shan looked at the letter and found that it had stubbornly refused to change its meaning while she'd been looking away.

"Can we appeal it?" Marlon said

"Yes, easily," Ms Shan said. "I tried to raise the issue with the Minister already, but he didn't seem very willing to chat."

The plan had been simple. The Super Centre had a carpark slightly smaller than that of the neighbouring Mega Centre. This meant that when the Super Centre carpark was full, the Mega Centre got the overflow. By increasing the size of the Super Centre carpark, the situation would be reversed.

The Mega Centre hadn't been happy about this change, but also hadn't felt it necessary to oppose it. Or at least they hadn't *at first*. But then the DIY Barn had campaigned for the Mega Centre management to fight the Super Centre management in council. They had fought, and they'd won in Council. And the now the State Planning Minister had refused to overrule in the Pavilion's favour.

Again, Ms Shan stared at the words on government letterhead paper. Again, they would not change. The increased traffic from the new carpark wasn't projected to increase profits much. 0.25% according to the analysts. But when the bottom line is so damn tight, every 0.25% counts.

"What do we know about them?" Marlon said. "Those DIY Barn people. What do we know? I've looked them up online and all I can find is bland corporate crap. Do you know more about these arseholes? Does head office?"

"Probably not much more than you do," Ms Shan said. "Their parent company was formed in Argentina in 1946. They make jackboots... barbed wire... helmets... that sort of thing. They moved into the hardware business a few years ago and began setting up locally."

"It's pretty bland stuff all around," Marlon said. "Company sees an opportunity and goes for it."

He picked up his teacup off of the desk. Ms Shan noticed his eyes wandering around the cramped little office. They never seemed to settle on the desk. She wondered what, if anything, that meant.

"I'm not the only one doing something about the Barnlings, am I?" Ms Shan asked. Marlon looked almost comically shocked. Ms Shan rolled her eyes. "I'm not stupid, Marlon. I'm a good manager, and like any good manager I know when *not* to see something. But just because I choose not to see something, that doesn't mean I don't know it's there."

Marlon's jaw clenched.

"It's to stop now," Ms Shan said. "Okay? I've learned something from chasing this application through council. And that is, that those DIY Barn bigwigs look like postal workers, dentists or failed artists, but they can be real frigging Nazis."

Marlon said nothing. Ms Shan noted that he had not actually admitted to anything. *Yes! Plausible deniability! Thank you Marlon!*

"I'm responsible for the safety of the people here," Ms Shan continued. "And I don't want anyone else getting hurt. The risks just aren't worth it. Seriously, why die over a low-paying McJob?"

"Do you think that's what this is about?" Marlon snapped. He'd been holding his tongue, Ms Shan realised. Trying not to say what was on his mind. Now, the floodgates were open: "I thought you'd started to understand. I should have known, you corporate types would never would. This isn't about the job. Not the way you see a job anyway—money goes in, labour comes out. No, it's about the smell of fresh cut timber. It's about plants, green and blooming. It's about young couples getting keys cut to their first place together. It's about kids taking home paint-your own models and Venus flytraps. It's about hobbyists taking forever to check wood for defects while the tradies roll their eyes at them. But there's more than that. It's about mates. It's about the people you go to the pub with after work, or just bitch with in the staff room. It's about people, boss. Not economic units, *people*. Some of us are here for the long haul, some just until something better turns up, but it doesn't matter. As long as there's a place here, this is *our* place. And if those fuckers from the DIY Barn want it, then they're going to have to come through us."

Marlon reached down for his tea, carefully not looking

at the desk. Ms Shan stared at him for a while, drumming her fingers on the lid of her laptop.

"You finished?" she said. "Good. Because that was the dumbest thing I ever heard. This place is nothing. Nothing permanent, anyway. It's a temporary feature, a whirlpool between the current of supply and the current of demand. One day it'll be gone with nothing to show for it. Maybe that day will be distant, but probably it will be soon. And nobody will miss it and nobody will care because it was never. Built. To. Last."

Marlon's jaw clenched. "What will you do?"

"Probably go to another Pavilion," Ms Shan said. "Or back to corporate."

"And what about Mrs Liselle?" Marlon said. "You going to miss her?"

Ms Shan felt her face flush. "I'll miss my colleagues here, of course…"

"I know about you and her," Marlon said. "Everybody knows. You try to seem all sooooo professional, but the way you look at each other… Look, I'm not trying to give you grief. What you get up to is your own business. What I mean is, what do you like more about this job? The work or the social connections? The spreadsheets or the fact that you and your girlfriend can just do it in this office?"

*Oh*, Ms Shan thought. *So that's why he can't look at the desk!*

She sighed deeply. "Maybe you do have something," she said. "Maybe. Look, if hypothetically you and some of the others were up to something… well, that would be wrong. Escalation won't help. Okay?"

"People talk big, but nothing will happen," Marlon said, not even bothering to hide the fact that he was lying.

"Good," Ms Shan said. "Oh, by the way, there's a concrete truck in the car park. Been there a few days. Could you move it?"

She went to hand him the keys. For a moment, she imagined herself putting them on the desk in front of Marlon. Was that harassment? Yeah, it probably was. Instead, she tossed them and he caught them.

"Whose truck?" Marlon said. "Park it where?"

"It belongs to Bruce," Ms Shan said. "And just find somewhere for it that isn't here."

"Bruce died years ago," Marlon said. "How did his truck…?"

"Why don't you ask the truck?"

Marlon looked like he was going to say something, but brain went faster than his lips and he kept quiet. "I'll find somewhere," he said.

"Good. And no escalation."

Marlon smiled from ear-to-ear. "That's right, boss. No escalation."

# 30 Showdown at Loading Bay Gulch

Buck Dusty was ringing up a sale in the power tool section when his trigger finger started to itch. He looked up at the time. The hour hand on the clock behind the Key Cutting counter pointed straight up. The minute hand was off by maybe twenty degrees. Three minutes to High Noon. He knew what was coming.

He wanted to hitch up his belt, spit on the floor and mosey out to the stand in front of Mailboxes and Doormats, but the last time he'd done that he'd been given an official warning. Instead, he fought down the squirming in his gut and finished the transaction he was processing.

"Afraid we don't take AmEx, suh," he said to the man in the expensive shirt who was buying an overpriced biscuit joiner.

"No one takes AmEx!" the customer whinged, and produced another credit card.

His duty done, Buck gestured to Christian to take the counter. Then he hitched up his belt, but refrained from spitting at the floor.

Immediately outside of the power tool section, Laura Cho was arguing with a lumpy looking man. "Seriously? You still don't have any pulleys in stock?"

Ordinarily, this conversation would have interested Buck, who'd been wondering himself where the pulleys kept vanishing to. But he didn't have the time now. It was necessary, he thought, for a male person to do that which the world required of them, or else perchance lose some quintessential element of masculinity.

But there had to be a pithier way of saying that.

Just as the hands of the Key Cutters' clock hit twelve, into the store strode a tall woman. She wore a long black coat that reached down past her knees and seemed much too warm for the mild day. On her head was a hat with a broad, flat brim, decorated with a large brown feather in the band. Grey hair fell from the hat in a long plait that reached halfway down her back. Her eyes—barely visible in the shadow of her hat brim—were small and hard, promising swift judgement and little mercy. She stood in the middle of the front aisle by a stack of paint cans, ten yards from Buck, staring intensely.

"Buck," she said.

"Mom," Buck replied.

Tense seconds ticked by before she spoke again.

"Stopped by your place," she said, her voice low and raspy. "Saw that housemate of yours. He said you forgot your lunch. Again."

"Reckon," Buck said.

A hand emerged from underneath her long coat, holding a hessian bag. Buck's eyes flicked to the bag for just a second. He knew that it held a can of pork-and-beans, a fifth of whiskey, a plug of chewing tobacco and a vanilla slice for dessert.

"Got a minute to talk?" Mrs Dusty asked.

Buck turned to Marlon who was hurrying past, shaking his head over some malarkey or other.

"Hey, Marlon," he called. "It ain't busy or nothin'. Can I take my break early?"

"You know the rules. There's to be no..." Marlon glanced up and found himself staring straight into the eyes of Buck's mom. Recoiling a little, he blurted, "Jesus! Go. Just go, go."

Buck and his mother slipped out the back. Fiona and Nalda were working the box crusher, but otherwise the loading dock was empty. Buck opened his beans with his Bowie knife.

"So you ain't wearing that serape I made you," Mrs Dusty said.

"Uniform policy."

"Huh."

Buck ate his beans with a wooden spoon. They were good. Good beans.

"The High Sheriff is a'worried," Mrs Dusty said.

"He oughta be," Buck said. "There are more things goin' on as meets the eye. This here hardware centre ain't just on a mystical nexus, there's extradimensional, trans-temporal, transhuman and spiritual issues all a'swirlin' about this here store, to say nothin' of mundane political/economic..."

"How did I raise you, boy?" Mrs Dusty said. "Tell me more terse, like."

"Uh..." Buck scratched at his moustache as he sought for the words. "Storm's a brewin'?"

Mrs Dusty nodded and cut herself a plug of tobacco. She slipped it into her mouth and began chewing. "Is it time to move yet?"

Buck took a swig of whiskey and shook his head. "Nope. But tell the High Sheriff. When the time comes, I'm gonna need all the help The Grey Barn can spare."

Fiona and Nalda went back inside, nodding as they went. Buck and his mom both touched the brims of their hats in reply.

"So how come they let you wear the hat?" Mrs Dusty said.

Buck shrugged.

A mouse crept out from a pile of broken pallets. With a smooth motion, Mrs Dusty shook a knife from her sleeve and threw it, pinning the helpless rodent against the crumbling pine. She spat on the ground and adjusted her hat.

"Ain't lost your aim none," Buck said.

"They can lay me in the cold, cold ground the day I do," Mrs Dusty said. "'Kay, boy. You keep watch. I'll take your report to the High Sheriff."

"Tell him it ain't urgent yet," Buck said. "But when it is, it's gonna get urgent quick. And then he's gonna have to mobilise the whole Covert Order, Western Battle Operations... Uh... Did he ever figure out how to end that thar acronym?"

"Nope."

"Has to be a 'Y', I figure."

"Reckon."

"How about yokel?"

Mys Dusty frowned beneath her flat-brimmed hat. "You know how I feel 'bout them thar steereo-types." She spat again. "Your paw says 'hey.'"

"Tell him 'hey' back."

With that, Mrs Dusty turned and walked away. It was barely past midday and the sun had only just begun to move to the west—but nonetheless she walked into the sun.

# 31 Crossed Words

Fiona sat in the Handy Pavilion break room, using her powers to make whirlpools in her juice. But whirlpools were easy and she soon tired of them. Water spouts were a little more fun, but only a little. She sighed deeply let the juice fall back into the cup. She concentrated for a minute, and then the tiny figure of a man rose out of the cup, a sculpture in orange.

She concentrated a little longer, and the details of the figure became more focused, more precise. From a rough outline of a human form, it transformed into the figure of a specific man. Wellsey, with his bald head and apron. Fiona made the figure as perfect as she could, willing the molecules of water into polymer chains, willing the chains into solid forms. The shape of Wellsey gave way to a figure of Norman. Then Ms Shan, Norman, Zorbar, Nalda, Donna, dear old Adam, and finally Sadie and Angela.

The last one broke her concentration. She hadn't meant her figure to be either of the MacGregor twins specifically, but somehow she found her little water sculpture breaking into two identical copies. Annoyed, she stopped and let the juice resume to the shape of the cup.

She needed more sleep. That much was certain.

She also needed to decide whether to stay or go. It was a decision she'd been trying to make for months. Chasing the mystery of the Phantasm had kept her too busy to think— which perhaps had been the point of the chase. But lately, the Phantasm seemed to have gone to ground. Everyone seemed to have their own theory on why this was, but all Fiona knew was that the Phantasm's absence left her mind free to consider.

Fiona was a robber. A payroll robber. It had seemed fun, silly, like a big prank. But since then, all the tension between the Handy Pavilion and the DIY Barn had just snowballed...

Sadie McGregor entered the room. Fiona squinted. What was up with the lights? Were they running brighter than usual?

"Fiona," Sadie said.

"Sadie," Fiona said.

Sadie took a seat across the plastic table and opened a copy of *Modern Lighting* magazine. Fiona sighed. She considered moving, but what did it matter? She could be just as lost in thought with Sadie present.

Where was she... Oh, yes. Should she leave? Well, was leaving even really the issue? The issue was surely one of responsibility. She had done wrong. It was only right that her deeds should be exposed. She should do what she wanted to do before and go to the authorities...

The door opened again and in walked Sadie's twin sister, Angela McGregor. Fiona now noticed that the lights had gone back to normal. Sadie shifted a little in her chair as her sister took a seat in a shady corner behind her.

"Angela."

"Fiona."

Angela picked up a copy of the newsletter and munched on an apple. Fiona shut the noise out and returned to her quandary. Of course she couldn't go the authorities. She might deserve punishment for her role in the heist, but what about Norman? The poor guy was just as much under Axel's influence as she'd been. And Axel... in spite of everything, he was on parole. Fiona could claim 'first offense' and maybe she'd be out in a couple of years, but Axel...

Sadie grunted, laid aside her reading and attacked a *Women's' Weekly* crossword with a mechanical pencil. The light flickered. What did it matter if Axel got in trouble? The man had once kidnapped Santa Claus and held him hostage for a fortnight. For most people, an armoured car heist doesn't look good on their resume, for someone with Axel's record, it almost seemed benign.

"'Overreaching,'" Angela called.

"Huh?" Fiona said.

"Twelve letters, fifth is an r," Angela said, pointing to Sadie and her crossword.

Fiona sighed. Ultimately Axel had made his own bed. What he did was between himself and his conscience. And that was the issue, wasn't it? Conscience? After all, Fiona had hurt no one, and the money lost by the Barn had been repaid by their insurers. There were no practical issues that needed addressing. It was all just about Fiona's conscience. Just a token gesture to sooth her feelings, and wasn't that kind of selfish?

"'Sophistry!'" Sadie called. "Ha, that was a tough one!"

Now, as for the Barn/Pavilion conflict... *that was* a practical issue. As long as it was being fought in the dark, the treacherous Barnlings had the advantage. If the heist were to become a police matter and argued in a court of law then who knew what Barnish atrocities might be brought to light?

"'Pathetic,'" Angela said.

Of course that wouldn't happen. If the matter came to court, it would reflect badly on the Pavilion and the Barn would come off Scot free. The armoured car employees were only contractors. There was no reason for Barn personnel to even take the stand. Ah, forget what would happen in court. The question for Fiona was: stay or leave?

"'Cowardish?'" Sadie said. "No, of course not. No such word. It's 'cowardly'."

Maybe it was cowardly. If Fiona wasn't going to the authorities, she owed it to her friends at least to see it through. Even so, she couldn't just keep what she knew to herself. She couldn't talk to Axel, either. Or Norman, or Wellsey; both of them were too pally with Axel. Who did that leave? Nalda? Too scary. Laura? She still wasn't sure about Laura. Ms Shan was too senior. Maybe Carol and Zorbar? They didn't care for the Barn, but Fiona hadn't seen either of them around for a while.

"'Christian,'" Angela said. "'Adherent of major world religion,' starts with C. Christian."

Christian? Maybe... Fiona didn't know him well. He wasn't in Axel's orbit, but he was a bit of a —

"'Sphincter,'" Sadie said. "Tight ring of muscle

186

controlling flow through digestive system."

Yeah, he was one of those things. How about Gwen? No, she had gone and no one seemed to know where.

"Spanish lady, five letters?" Sadie said.

"No not that one, you don't have enough letters," Angela said. "Try 'male deer'. It only needs four letters and you already have a…"

Fiona scraped her chair loudly on the tiles as she stood. "You know, you two aren't the only ones in the break room," she said, tossing back the last slurp of juice. "Did you think other people might like to hear themselves think?"

And even though she had a whole two minutes left on her break, she stomped out of the room and into Plumbing.

## 32 Transformations

It wasn't about the newsletter. Not anymore, not since the enemies of FREE SPEECH had made it clear that nothing important or true could be found there any longer. No, as Karl Wintergreen sat in his old Datsun in the car park seeking the Truth, he knew he'd never be able to tell anyone what he'd learned. Oh, he could put it on the Internet, probably. One more conspiracy theory among thousands; for all the good it would do.

No, Karl Wintergreen was not there to be a reporter. He was there to be a *witness*. He was there because *someone* needed to be there.

The clues had been scattered, but he'd taken them all in. Not long ago, Carol from the coffee shop had arrived at work with a bruise on her face, which she'd attempted, however ineptly, to cover up with makeup. Karl might have suspected her lunkhead boyfriend, Zorbar Ofthechimps, but a) that didn't seem his style and b) Zorbar had turned up for work at the Place O' Pets with his eyebrows singed off, suggesting that something had happened to both of them.

The same day was the first day he saw the concrete truck parked in front of the Handy Pavilion. There was no concreting work going on nearby, but tradies often went to the Pavilion for tools, so there was no reason a concrete truck shouldn't have been there. But it was there the next day and the next day after that—always in a slightly different parking spot, but always a good spot. The spots were too good for the Pavilion management to let some random vehicle park there indefinitely.

So for the last few nights, Karl had watched and waited. He sat in his aging Datsun hatchback with a thermos of herbal coffee and watched the concrete truck.

God, it was boring. But boredom is the basis of truth. That's what all those people who complained about his newsletter failed to understand. That was why it was so easy for *Them* to manipulate everyone — with their *interesting* stories, their *intelligible* news. The real truth was as dull as it was strange.

So Karl watched and waited. Every so often the Super Centre security car drove by, and he ducked down to avoid being seen. More often, a random vehicle came past, taking a shortcut across the Centre carpark to avoid those tricky lights on Dawson St. Karl had timed it once, and found that the shortcut didn't save any time. But people just kept trying. The illusion of control over your own life—a delusion few ever really escape, Karl thought, with a pitying shake of his head.

There was a van in the Pavilion car park. Karl had been so distracted by his thoughts he didn't notice it until the doors opened. As he watched, a half a dozen men got out. They dressed in silver costumes that shimmered in the sodium lights.

It was not what he had been expecting. Nonetheless, Karl took out his camera. An old fashioned one: film, not digital. There would be no hacking his pictures. It was high speed film, so he didn't need to set the shutter too fast, which was good. He caught a couple of nice pictures of the men as they went about their work, removing something from the van. What was it? A Masonic ritual? No, they were setting up some machinery. Something connected to the HAARP array, perhaps, a communications…

No. Simpler than that. It was a mortar. Karl was disappointed for a moment at the mundanity of it. Nothing big, nothing important. Nothing connected to the New World Order, just some goons preparing to blow up a shop. Trivial nonsense.

"Even so," he muttered to himself, "I should probably do something about this."

He didn't carry a mobile, so Google (or as Karl thought of them, **666**-gle) couldn't trace him. He could run to his shop and call the police, but he was pretty sure they were screening calls from his number since a particular incident… Okay, since several incidents.

Could he flag down the security car? No, it had gone by just before the van had turned up. The goons had probably timed that. Nothing for it then, but to keep taking pictures. If he couldn't stop this crime, at least he could record it. Hey, if nothing else, this would give him the newsletter of a lifetime, with enough prestige to win back editorial control from Mrs

Liselle.

Snap! The goons had the base of the mortar set up. Snap! They fitted the barrel. Snap! The concrete truck began to stand up on enormous steel legs.

"Darn!" said Karl, who was so utterly shocked that he had forgotten how to swear properly. "Curses!"

The concrete truck unfolded like a puzzle. Its undercarriage became legs, its sides split into arms. The driver's cabin became its chest and a head popped out of the sunroof, a shining chrome forehead set above scruffy metallic jowls. One mechanical hand reached into its cabin/torso and came back with a huge steel cigarette that it clamped between metallic lips.

Karl snapped away as the silver men desperately altered the angle of the mortar, bringing it low enough to aim at the metal monster. The mortar fired—Karl hoped his camera had caught the flash—and the robot/truck thing grabbed the projectile out of the air. With its other hand, it took the concrete mixing drum from its back and dropped the mortar shell in. It clapped a hand over the end of the drum, and there followed a muffled 'bang'.

"What else ya got?" the robot said.

The silver men were already running back to their van. The robot towards the vehicle, lurching about half a dozen ground-shaking steps before stopping and doubling over in a coughing fit. The van took off in a squeal of tires and a cloud of black smoke.

"You better run!" the robot wheezed. "No, actually,

wait! Hold up..."

Karl wound his film on, but the spool was empty. He had photos of the whole incident. Wasn't that enough? Somewhere deep inside, he knew it wasn't. He turned the key in the ignition and put his car into gear. The van was headed to Wellington Rd, but if Karl went around the Barbecue Imperium, then just maybe he could head them off.

He stomped the accelerator down and geared up, skidding into a handbrake turn in front of the kebab shop. He turned too quickly, almost losing control, but he was just barely able to avoid crashing into Hoonworld Auto. Now that would have been ironic. His wheels found traction, and he sped through the little lane between Carpet Junction and Carpets! Carpets! Carpets! and hit the Super Centre's main throughfare just a moment after the van came speeding past. The van's rear door swung open. Karl's Datsun caught it, sending it spinning into the gutter.

Karl slammed on the brakes. Too late. He mounted the curb, and then the whole world was spinning, round and round, wheels within wheels. He was punched in the face by something white — an airbag, he realised. And then everything went still.

He didn't black out. He was upside down, held in his seat by the belt and the airbag. And then he was moving again. He was turning, rising. Something was lifting his little hatchback, something that was pushing in the metal of the roof and floor…

And then he was right-side up and stationary.

That was probably a good sign, probably. Could go the other way, though...

Gingerly, Karl undid his seatbelt and opened the door. Outside stood the robot.

"I'm Bruce," it said. "Who the fuck are you?"

# 33 Family Business

"Hi, what can I get you?" Norman asked. He was under the counter, taking stock when the customer came in. Why did the Handy Pavilion coffee shop have three times as many small cup lids as it had small cups? It just didn't make any sense.

"Can you do me a Greek coffee?" came a voice.

"Don't have the settup for Turkish coffee."

"I didn't order a Turkish coffee, I said Greek coffee."

"It's all the same sh... Oh, it's you, Dad." Norman rose, dusting his hands with a paper towel. "We're just set up for espresso. I can get you a short black, if you like."

Norman's father was a handsome, broad faced man with thick salt-and-pepper hair and a neatly trimmed grey beard. He was a couple of inches taller than Norman and looked like he worked out. Certainly, the sleeves of his fawn windcheater bulged with muscle.

"Just a cup of tea will be fine," he said, "if I can't get a *proper* coffee."

Norman sighed and poured hot water into a cup and added a teabag. He knew there was no chance his father would pay for his beverage, so this was coming out of his wages. To add insult to injury, this was the point Ms Shan came bustling past. She acknowledged Norman with a curt nod, while Norman tried not to notice the smell of her shampoo. He failed, naturally, and just as naturally his Dad noticed the little wistful look that crossed his face.

"You could do worse, Normie," Dad said.

"Have I ever asked you for relationship advice?" Norman said, a little too sharply. Damn it, he hadn't wanted the old man to know how deeply he felt about Ms Shan. Too late now. "How long since your wife kicked you out? How long have you been sleeping in your brother's spare room?"

The old man shrugged. "A while now. It's not so bad. Just a little damp. You worry too much, Norman. The missus'll take me back, sooner or later."

"She kicked you out for sleeping around," Norman said. "If you stopped sleeping around then maybe—*maybe* she'd take you back. But you won't stop, will you? You're too full of your 'I'm a sexy silver fox' bullshit."

Norman's father waggled a finger at him. "If I didn't sleep around, you wouldn't be here, sonny. But I'm not here to argue, so stop dunking that teabag and take a five-minute break, yeah?"

Every time! Norman always promised he wouldn't let the old letch get to him, but every time he failed. Norman handed him his English Breakfast in a takeaway cup and put up his 'back in 5 min' sign. It was a quiet afternoon, so there was a good chance he'd get away with it.

"What on Earth is this?" Norman's dad said, pointing at the little brass centrepiece on the table.

195

"It's meant to be a steampunk flower-growing machine," Norman said. "My mate Axel makes them. He likes his hobbies when he's stressed out."

Norman's dad looked around the café, which was decorated top to bottom with a Pinterestworth of handicrafts — macrame, polymer clay, crochet, wood-burning pictures and matchstick buildings. "Under a lot of stress, is he?"

"Yeah, a fair bit."

"What he needs is a woman."

"That's your answer to everything, isn't it?" Norman said. "Why deal with life when you could be getting laid?"

"I said I don't want to talk about that. I'm here to talk business. You said you wanted to work here in the power tool department, and I gave my permission."

"What makes you think I need —"

"But now they have you working in the kitchen. Is that any sort of job? Now your cousin —"

"What cousin?"

"You're Greek, boy! You have cousins. Your cousin was going to go kill this five-headed lion, but he threw his back out so I thought you'd…"

Norman raised an eyebrow. "Someone's going to pay me to kill a five-headed lion?"

Norman's dad's lips pursed. "Well, no, not *pay*. But…"

"Of course they aren't. It's 2016. No one pays you to kill lions. You pay other people so they can *get* to kill lions, and then Facebook hates you forever."

"Hey, Norman!" said Fiona, who was walking by

pushing a trolley full of toilet floats. Norman may not have liked the café, but at least it was better than Plumbing.

"Hi, Fiona," Norman said. "Oh, this is my dad — Zeus."

"Hello, Mr Zeus," Fiona said.

"Just Zeus, love, just Zeus," Norman's dad said, cracking a winning smile. Norman kicked him in the shin, but the old man ignored him and turned up the charm another notch.

"Zeus?" Fiona said. "Like the old guy in *Clash of the Titans?*"

The King of Olympus' winning smile faded. "Yeah, like that."

"I liked the metal owl," Fiona said.

"Bubo," Zeus said without much enthusiasm. "Everyone loves Bubo."

As Fiona trotted off, Norman glared at his father. "You can't keep it in your pants? That's your problem. Just don't go cracking onto my friends, alright?"

"Whatever. Where were we?"

"This lion. Is it in driving distance of here?"

Zeus laughed. "No, it's in Central Asia."

"And who's paying for the airfare?"

The old man scratched his silver beard. "You don't have to take a plane. You could get a crew together and a trireme..."

"And *row* there?" Norman said. "No wonder this cousin threw his bloody back out. How do you row from Sydney to Central fucking Asia? And who's paying Mum's rent while I'm away from work? You?"

197

"Okay, you want to shush for a minute and let me get a word in?" Zeus said. "This lion is guarding a treasure, alrighty?"

Norman nodded in a way that he hoped made it clear that he didn't agree. "*Actual* treasure? Like 'I can sell it and make a mint' treasure? Or is it one of those 'symbolic representations of prosperity' deals?"

Zeus' face reddened and the air pressure began dropping rapidly. As an easy-going lad, Norman did not usually like pushing his father so far, but come on! If the old man wanted to help, a couple of sleeves of small coffee cups would be more useful than some dumbass quest.

"Hey, Norman." Now it was Axel's turn to interrupt. Norman's dad glowered silently at the little fellow, who held up a glass globe full of succulents. "You got room for another terrarium?"

Norman blinked hard. This is what he got for being good-natured. Nagged in two directions.

"Not really, mate," he said. He gestured around the café. Surely Axel could see that every possible surface was covered with his handicrafts. There were paper flowers and painted wooden containers and little plaster figures. The quality was highly variable. Axel seemed better at paper crafts than woodwork, and he was better with metals than either. The horribly accurate A3-sized embossed copper portrait of Gary Busey that hung next to the drinks fridge was proof of that.

"Huh," Axel said. "Maybe the key-cutting counter would like it, then."

"Maybe, hey?" Norman said.

Axel scuttled off. His interruption had probably been for the best. It had given Dad time to calm down.

"That was my mate Axel," Norman said. "That was a bit rude of him, talking like you weren't there."

"He's probably an atheist," Zeus shrugged. "They're all like that. Look, I got shit to do. Give me a call when you get bored making coffee, alright?"

Blue electric sparks began crackling across the old man's skin. In an eyeblink his body became a flash of lightning shooting upwards, leaving Norman looking at an empty chair. Other than a small burn-mark in the ceiling, there was no sign that the King of Olympus had ever been there.

"No, you give *me* a call, you old prick," Norman said to the empty chair, "when you can find some way that killing lions will get my rent paid, and not get me sued by the animal rights people!"

But it wasn't a satisfying thing to say. He went back to searching for the coffee cups. Though if he'd just asked Belinda, she could have told him what had happened to them.

# 34 From Bad to Wurst

As with so many Australian big-box hardware stores, the charity sausage sizzle was a weekend tradition at the Pavilion. Service clubs, school groups, social clubs... all of them would take a turn, cooking sausage sandwiches for the Pavilion customers. The organisations would provide the ingredients, their members would provide the volunteer labour and the Pavilion would provide them with a stall and a barbeque, *gratis*.

The Handy Pavilion's weekly sizzle had been going downhill with the Pavilion's customer base. Already the biggest charity groups had decamped to the DIY Barn. The Rotary Club, the Lions Club, Apex, Local High School and the South Hertling Ute Spotters Society... all gone. The last couple of weeks, the sausage sizzle had been run by the Pinecone Awareness League, the Friends of Lithgow, and an obscure church group that alienated its customers by refusing to put two sausages in the same bread.

This week, instead of the usual cheerful, semi-chaotic bustle of volunteers, the little stall was occupied by one person only. It was Nalda Teheinthausand, who was cooking bratwurst with the monstrous efficiency that only comes with being both German *and* a cyborg.

"Kommen sie hier!" she said, waving her tongs at the trickle of early customers. "Ist Oktoberfest, ja?"

Most of the customers skittered by, trying not to look her in the sunglasses. But one short, fiftyish woman came over. She wore jeans and an expensive jacket, from the pocket of which she took a Louis Vuitton wallet.

"Could I have a bacon and egg roll, please?" she said.

"No, it is Oktoberfest," Nalda said. "I am only Oktoberfester food having."

"Isn't Oktoberfest in September?"

"Ja, it is *now*," Nalda said. "Under your primitive flesh-calendar. In der future, we will use a base eight calendar with only one festival, occurring in der eighth month. Hence, Oktoberfest."

The woman gave a baffled smile. "Oh, is this one of those 'fan' things? My daughter used to do something like that. She dressed up as an elf and claimed to come from the Middle Earth. She works in public relations now."

Nalda nodded. "Weight of der world crush her spirit?"

The woman nodded back. "Basically. I think it's better when that happens early, don't you? Saves a lot of time later. But anyway, if you don't have bacon and egg rolls, what do you have?"

"We have selection of sausages," Nalda said. "They lack the imprecision of human-made sausages. Their ingredients are combined to within a tolerance of ±0.34%."

The woman smiled. "My word, those are very precise

manufactured meats. And that sauerkraut! Sliced to perfection! Each strand a little work of engineering."

"I cut der cabbage by hand. Also, I have three types of bread and a selection of mustards. But I can see dat you appreciate high precision food?"

"Oh, yes," the customer said. "I'm chief engineer at a Harrison Food Processing. We're working on increasing precision and control of final product through the creation of a powerful artificial intelligence."

Nalda smirked. "Let me know how dat works out for you. For now, how about a weisswurst on multigrain with Soylent mustard?

"I mean seeded!" she added, hurriedly. "Seeded mustard. Ha ha, mistake acknowledged."

Sausages and money exchanged hands. The seal broken, nervous but hungry customers came and bought food from the terrifying woman in sunglasses, who wore a leather jacket under her apron.

The first workers had arrived at the Pavilion before Nalda had begun cooking, but more filtered past as the morning progressed. They were supposed to enter by the rear staff door, but Ms Shan and Marlon were both off that day, so they came by whichever entrance suited them. Fiona and Donna from lighting came by together and bought a bratwurst roll to share. Thick as thieves lately, those two.

Laura Cho was early for once and bought two bratwurst rolls, tucking into the first while the second was still being assembled. She examined the pile of glossy pamphlets that

Nalda had left next to the serviettes, and which about 95% of the customers had studiously avoided looking at.

"The Malevolent Singularity,'" Laura said, reading out loud from the cover. "'What Does Human Extinction Mean for You?'" She frowned for a moment, shrugged, took her second roll and left just as another customer was strolling up.

He was a tall man with skin of a deep reddish brown. Upon his shaven head sat a circlet of bronze gears. He wore a long, multi-coloured robe and carried in his right hand a mahogany and brass box. He moved the box in an arc in front of him. When it pointed directly at Nalda it began clicking loudly.

Geiger counter? No, Nalda had just upgraded her shielding. A Geiger counter pointed at her wouldn't click *quite* so loudly.

"Ah, hello," the man said. He spoke with an accent Nalda couldn't place. Certainly there was something of Nairobi in it, but also something else. "Are you from the future, if it's not rude to ask?"

"Ja, that is correct," Nalda frowned.

"Good, good! My name is Fanaka. I'm from the past."

"Ja?" Nalda said. It was a good a thing as any to say, she supposed.

"You see, I was a graduate student at the Pan African Institute of Steampunk Technology and Wonderment, about a century and a half ago. In the middle of an experiment into the nature of time, we had a containment breach, and…"

"What? Der never was…"

The man waved her objections away with a gesture. "Yes, yes. The past I'm from doesn't seem to be real any more. I'm trying to track down other time-travellers, to help me find out if this is a parallel-universe-sort-of-a-deal, or more of a mutability-of-the-timelines-thingy."

"Mute... mutable timelines?" Nalda said, her artificial heart falling in her chest. "So if you were from der future, you couldn't just wait for it to come around again?"

"Well, that's one of the things I'm trying to find out," the stranger grinned. "I'm Fanaka, by the way. Or did I say that already? Still not sure what to make of this strange future. So many English speakers! Fortunately, my mother was a Leader in the Mechatank Division. Our family was stationed in England during the last years of the occupation, so..."

Nalda stopped listening, letting Fanaka's words rattle around her mechanical ears, devoid of meaning. He was still prattling when Christian, looking even more hollow-eyed than usual, bought a kransky. Ugh. Kransky. Why did Australians think those horrible things were German? They didn't even sound German.

"...Which would both collapse and — simultaneously — de-collapse the waveform, resulting in a huge surge of anti-time," Fanaka was saying when Nalda finally returned to the here-and-now. "I'd show the maths, but we used a different notation system back at PAISTAW."

"But, bottom line, you don't know if der future is set?"

"Not clear at all," Fanaka said with an airy wave of his hand. "Trying to figure that out. That's what brought me to this place. There are two temporal anomalies here, and both are potential data points."

"Two?" Nalda said.

"That's right," Fanaka said. "One ongoing, one intermittent. I suppose you are the ongoing one?"

Another time traveller. From the future. But from her future or another? Surely Nalda's future, if there was any justice. She liked humans—but, to be fair, they'd *had* their turn. Besides, the survivors would be alright in their reservation matrices. The Age of the Machine was coming. It had to come. That was only right and proper.

But what if it didn't? What if the future never came?

"What if I *won't* be back?" Nalda whispered under her breath.

So who was this other traveller? What did they know? Intermittent? Did that mean that they could... could go back to their future?

"Tell me, Fanaka," she said, "have you somewhere to stay?"

## 35 Toilet Humour

The toilets were out of commission at the Handy Pavilion. That wasn't the terrible thing in Christian's book. There were a couple of porta-loos out the back, so it wasn't like no one could go. It did mean that the customers would be asking questions about the bathrooms all day, in spite of the dozens of big signs explaining the situation. So annoying! But still not the problem.

The problem was that the plumbers would be digging up part of the toilet floor—and in doing so, Christian was certain they'd soon find the passage to the Phantasm's lair. And then what would happen?

Christian stood outside the grotty little toilet anteroom, watching two overall-clad figures sorting out their tools. What to do? He had to protect his mistress and patron, the Phantasm... But on the other hand...

"Christian!" It was his supervisor—Ali, who ran the Power Tools section—glaring at him from near the umbrella stands. "I got an idea, instead of watching plumbers work, why not go back and do your job?"

"Yeah, but..." Christian began. He realised almost immediately that he didn't have a way to end that sentence. Fortunately, Ali jumped in before he had to try.

"Why you want to watch plumbers work, anyway? Never seen a butt-crack before?"

"That's a stereotype!" one of the plumbers said, looking up from her bag of tools.

"Oh," Ali said. "I didn't know you were a woman."

"So it's okay to look at a woman's butt-crack, is it?" the other plumber said. Both Christian and Ali did a double take as they realised that, under a denim boiler suit was another woman.

"No, no, that's wrong too," Ali said, backpedalling with all his might. "I just mean it's not so bad as looking at a bloke's butt-crack."

"So you're a homophobe as well as a sexist?" the first plumber said.

"No, no, what I mean is butt-cracks…"

"Ahem." They all looked around to see Ms Shan glaring at them. "Could you all please stop saying 'butt-crack'? Or at least say it quieter."

Ashen faced, Ali made his retreat back to Power Tools, apparently forgetting about Christian as he went. Finding himself alone with the plumbers, Christian sought for an excuse to stick around and keep an eye on things.

"So what's the problem with the toilet?" he said.

"Big blockage here," the first plumber said. She was a shortish woman, with olive skin and a few tendrils of black hair peeking out from under her cap. "We tried to root it out with a drain-snake but it won't budge, so we're going to have to pull up some floor and replace a bit of pipe."

"Take long?"

"Nah, should be done in under a day, with the two of us," the second plumber said. She looked a lot like the first plumber, but taller and a little thinner.

"You two related?"

"Sisters," the first plumber said. "I'm Maria, this is Luigina."

"Christian."

"Catholic, but we don't get to mass as often as we'd like."

"No, my name is Christian." Damn, but it was one of those days, wasn't it?

He watched as they maneuvered a small jackhammer into place. He should do something! He had to do something. But what? If he spoke up, he'd give himself away. If he didn't they'd cut right down into the Phantasm's lair...

What to do? What to do? Delay? Might work. He knew a lot about Power Tools, maybe he could distract them that way. "That jackhammer a Ryobi, isn't it..." he began, but he was cut off by a terrible racket of hammering and a cloud of choking dust.

Christian closed his eyes, his insides melting from terror. When the horrible din ended, he slowly opened his eyes, fearful of seeing the ladder to the Phantasm's realm, exposed for all the world to see...

Instead, he saw a length of metal pipe at the bottom of a hole in perfectly normal concrete.

"Could you have two things in the same space?" he wondered aloud.

He hadn't been expecting an answer, but Maria said: "Yeah. You could have some sort of spatial warping field.

Christian stared at her. Her dust covered goggles made her look like a big grey beetle.

"Or a hyperspatial pocket," Luigina said, dusting concrete off her clothes.

"You and your hyperspatial pockets!" Maria said. "Hyperspace costs you, sis. You think we're made out of hyperspace?"

"Yeah, nah, hyperspace isn't cheap, but…"

"What the hell are you talking about?" Christian said.

"We're plumbers," Maria said. "We learned all about hyperbolic topology during our apprenticeships."

Christian could literally feel his jaw drop and his eyes bulge, yet there was nothing he could do to stop it.

"I mean, think about it," Maria continued. "You don't want to hit a power cable when you're digging, right? But you also don't want to fall through a dimensional warp into another plane of existence. It's just good OH&S practice, really."

"Still, accidents happen," Luigina said. "Remember that time we fell through the pipes into that fantasy realm?"

"The one with the race cars or the mushrooms?"

"Mushrooms."

"Oh, yeah, and we had to rescue that prince from that tower," Maria said.

"His highness had a tower of his own," Luigina leered.

"You didn't?" Maria laughed. "Dirty cow…"

Christian ignored their blather. His mistress was safe, but what had happened? Was her realm in some other dimension, or a hyperspace pocket or what? Could he get back there? Could she get out? What was causing a spatial anomaly in the goddamn Handy Pavilion?

"Here's your trouble!" Maria said. Her sister held a length of pipe, and she was armpit deep in it, fossicking around. The smell was probably terrible. Christian was glad his nose was too full of dust to tell.

Maria gave a yank and pulled out something big and crusted with filth. "There you go! I tell you, whoever passed that…"

"Alright, shush," Christian said. "I'm getting a bit tired of all this 'Carry on Up the Khazi' stuff, you know? What is it?"

Maria ran the object under a tap. She let up a whistle. "Not every day you see one of these," she said. She turned and held the object in front of her.

The light the object emitted was reflected by the mirror over the sink and nearly-white walls of the little room. The diamond-bright rays seared Christian's retinas. His eyes felt as if they were screaming in their sockets, and even through hastily clamped-down lids he could see the brightness—the terrifying, unearthly brightness, like a thousand suns…

"Hang on, I'll switch it off," Maria said. Instantly, the light went dim. For a while, Christian could see nothing but an afterimage floating before his eyes. An image of a burning skull, faceted like a crystal.

"It's so beautiful," Christian whispered. "Like it was alive, and somehow knows all the secrets of the universe!"

"Nah, that's nothing," Luigina said. "One time we found the Philosopher's Stone in a septic tank."

"Yeah, and don't forget the time we found the Holy Grail. Honestly, the shit people flush isn't just shit..."

"Oh, shut up the pair of you," Christian muttered.

# 36 Where Have all the Pulleys Gone?

In spite of herself, Laura was getting to like Carlos from the key-cutting desk. *Like* like. It was weird. In her other life as the superhero Voyager, Laura spent many of her days hanging around with some of the most desired men on the planet. Tall, handsome, toned... Usually they had cool jobs, like international ace reporter, test pilot or CEO and they somehow managed to keep hold of these positions despite only checking into the office when they felt like it.

And yet Laura found that she had not taken to any of them. Perhaps it was the way they were always gritting their teeth and narrowing their eyes at the slightest provocation. But then again, perhaps it was the way their wives and girlfriends were always being kidnapped. It was kind of a red flag, she thought.

Carlos, though... funny, flabby little Carlos from the key-cutting counter... He would talk non-stop for minutes until the penny dropped that he was being rude, then suddenly blush and fall silent. He always ate the home-cooked Filipino meals his mother made for him, even though she wasn't a good cook. He got this look when he was cutting keys, like he was a scientist watching some brilliant new creature under a microscope, rather than looking at something he'd seen a million times… She really was getting to like him.

The two of them were sitting in the break room, wolfing down lunch. Laura had adjusted her break schedule to synchronise with his without even realising it. God, did she have it that bad already?

Carlos was talking non-stop again, this time about why the second season of *Daredevil* wasn't as good as the first one. Involuntarily, Laura's eyes flicked to the cheap plastic clock above the sink. Carlos reddened and stammered to a halt.

"But what did you think of it?" he said.

"I didn't see it."

"Oh, sorry, I gave so many spoilers!"

"Don't worry. I probably won't see it. I'm not into superhero stuff. Too unrealistic!"

Carlos laughed. "It's supposed to be unrealistic!"

Laura shook her head. The plastic clock said that it was time to go back to work, but she didn't want to go. She didn't think she'd have much choice though, because right then Marlon entered.

"Hey gang," he said. He took a cigarette packet from his jacket, then remembered that Ms Shan had reinstated 'no smoking' in the break room. He sighed like a man whose favourite football team had disowned him. "Oh, Carlos, you remember I was telling you about the missing pulleys?"

Laura froze. Damn it, why hadn't she gone back to work while she'd had the chance? She sat as still as she could and stared at her empty keep-cup, trying not to let her culpability show.

"Yeah, you and everyone else," Carlos said. "Six days a week? All the pulleys you could eat. Then they all just vanish. Poor Mr Williams, he comes in on his only day off looking for them, but they're never there."

"Yeah, well you'll never guess who bought them," Marlon said.

Marlon looked at Carlos expectantly. Carlos responded with a polite smile.

"Well?" Marlon said.

"Well, what?"

"Well guess."

"But you just said I'd never..."

"That's a challenge, not a statement of fact," Marlon grumbled. "The answer is, they're being purchased by Clint Bryan."

Was Laura going red? Oh God, she could feel herself turning red. She willed herself to stay as still as she could. She was sure that both of her co-workers could see guilt written all over her face, yet somehow they didn't say anything. Why? Why were they torturing her like this?

"Clint Bryan?" Carlos said. "The billionaire playboy whose parents were murdered all those years ago? Who lives with his male teenage ward and never marries those society ladies he's always dating and yet — in some indefinable way — is very definitely heterosexual? That Clint Bryan?"

"Not him personally," Marlon said. "Someone using his corporate credit card. Ms Shan finally let me have a look at the credit card records, though I can't tell whether it's Bryan himself or someone with a secondary card for his account. Once a week he comes in and buys every pulley in the place."

Laura ground her teeth with a force that could cleave titanium as Carlos asked the obvious question: "So has one of the checkout operators seen…"

"No," Marlon said. "The transaction always goes through the self-serve checkout. Except one time when Belinda rang it all up. But you know Belinda."

"Yeah, I know Belinda. That's weird. That's all seriously weird," Carlos laughed. "At least someone's buying them, not stealing them. I had my money on it being some new gang initiation. 'Steal all the Handy Pavilion's pulleys and join the Bloody Dagger Gang, or whatever."

Laura stood. She knew how unnaturally she was moving, as she willed every limb to act normally. God, this was so stupid, so embarrassing. But if what her future self had said was true… No, it wasn't worth thinking about.

The boys grunted some goodbyes as she crept out of the break room. Whatever. She didn't have time for manners either. By the entrance to Lawn Care, Axel Platzoff was arguing with a big man in glasses. It wasn't like Axel to get emotional in front of a customer — though the customer didn't seem put out. And yet, when the bespectacled man looked at Laura, he gave *her* a mean look. Laura could hardly bring herself to care.

Keep the pulleys away from the lumpy looking Mr Williams, that's what the Laura from the future had said. It was so much harder than it sounded. She'd tried losing boxes at first, but there was only so long that could go on before anyone noticed. She knew Clint Bryan through her superhero team, The Vigilancers, where he was known as Dr Justice. Laura had mentioned that she needed to buy some pulleys and he'd given her a credit card, without even seeming to think about it. After all, Laura could buy a million pulleys and it would make no more difference to Clint's bottom line than a rounding error.

No, the problem wasn't the money, it was the store. Hardware stores need pulleys. End of story. Sooner or later they'd find a way to keep them on the shelves all week long. And then what would she do?

"Giving up so easily?" Laura turned to find herself face-to-face with Future Laura.

In the distance, a man wearing a circlet of brass gears and a dashiki whirled around to face them, a wooden box in one hand. Laura pointedly refused to notice him.

"I can't," Laura said. "It's impossible."

"Then perhaps you should see what will happen if you give up," Future Laura said.

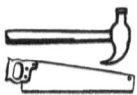

There was no flash of light as the two women vanished. There were no special effects at all. Fanaka stood at the place where he'd seen them last and examined the brass dials on his chrono-detector. He took a pencil from behind his ear, but found that he'd neglected to bring a notepad.

Lacking paper, he did some quick equations in his head, then scribbled his findings on the lid of a carton of whippersnipper cords. He cocked his head from side to side as he double checked his working. When he'd done that, he smiled broadly and wandered off, leaving the next customer to puzzle out the meaning of his sums.

# 37 Intervention

Wellsey had always known about Axel's past. Known about his attempt to rob Fort Knox from orbit. Known about his plan to replace major world leaders with realistic marionettes, to teleport Hobart to the Sahara Desert, to turn the people of Melbourne into walking catfish…

Wellsey knew all that, but still he'd never been afraid of the man. Wellsey was an ex-con. To him, a dangerous man was someone with a shank, a grudge and a guard who owed him a favour. Axel was frightening in a way that Wellsey could barely get his head around.

Now, though… now Wellsey was afraid, but he was afraid *for* his friend, not afraid *of* him.

"Hey, Axel," he said. Axel sat at one end of the break room table, cutting cardboard with a craft knife and a straightedge. He barely looked up to grunt his acknowledgement. At the other end of the Formica table, Adam and Belinda sat, pointedly not looking at the former villain. Wellsey sighed and took a seat next to Axel.

"What are you working on?" he said.

"Wedding decorations."

Wedding… oh, yes. Wellsey had heard that Zorbar and

Carol were finally tying the knot. Zorbar must have finally backed down about making it a traditional chimpanzee ceremony. Last Wellsey had heard, that had been the big sticking point for Carol.

"You've, ah, you've been doing a lot of crafts lately," Wellsey said.

"No, not so much."

Wellsey looked around the formerly austere room. Once, the only feature on the walls had been peeling, off-white paint and the occasional OH&S notice. Now every inch of stained white walls was covered with something. Pastels, oil paints, mosaics, copper engraving, enamelling, polymer clay, macrame. The little food preparation area was almost unusable, groaning under a pile of painted wooden boxes, glass terraria and popsicle-stick houses full of pipe-cleaner people.

"Uh..." Wellsey said.

"Uh..." Axel added.

Wellsey rubbed his eyes and breathed in deeply. He pictured a sunny beach, the way he used to do when he awoke at night in his cell and found the horror of his surroundings too much to bear. It helped for a moment, but when Wellsey opened his eyes, Axel was applying glitter to his cardboard creation.

"Uh," he said.

"I have a hobby," Axel said. "Is it wrong for a man to have a hobby?"

"No, but..."

"Am I violating any staff guidelines?"

"No, but..."

"Am I letting it interfere with my work?"

"Technically no, though it comes pretty..."

"Well, then what's the problem?"

Wellsey felt tired. This place, it was getting to him, wearing him down. Sure, the Phantasm attacks seemed to have stopped suddenly and the DIY Barn had mostly been bleeding the Handy Pavilion through legal means rather than sending their goon squad around — but still, it was hard to be a manager there.

"Axel, I'm not talking to you as a boss. I'm your friend, too. I'm worried about you, mate."

"That's sweet of you," Axel said, not looking up.

"Dammit Axel, what's wrong?" Wellsey snapped.

Axel looked up at Wellsey. Somewhere in the back of his eyes was one of the circles of Hell.

"Wellsey, things are not right," Axel said.

Wellsey nodded and stepped back.

"The world must work a certain way if it is to make sense," Axel said. "It has been said that 'horror is when flowers sing'. Do you see? Something seemingly advantageous can be awful simply by virtue of being... not right."

Adam and Belinda were looking on with horrified curiosity. Wellsey gestured for them to leave. Axel's hands clutched into fists, released, clutched again. His breathing became more strained until he picked up the craft knife and started forming perfect letters from the card, freehand.

"Okay, Axel, spill it," Wellsey said.

"It's Captain Stellar! He knows!"

Wellsey's bald head crinkled. "What, about? Firing that death ray at the DIY Barn? About what happened to Laura?"

"Everything!" Axel said, rifling through a paintbox. "Teal? Maybe teal…"

"Axel!"

"Stellar confronted me. Thought he was going to fight me right there. But he… he just… Wellsey, he walked off."

Wellsey waited for the next part of the story, but Axel fell silent. That was all that had happened. Axel's arch enemy had waked away.

In Wellsey's wilder days, he would have loved to see a cop just ignore his petty crimes and walk away… Or would he? Maybe it would have felt weird. Wrong. Maybe it would have made him paranoid… edgy… wondering when the axe was going to fall?

"I think I see."

"The crafting relaxes me," Axel said.

"Axel," Wellsey said. "Listen. I'm not big on the whole villain/hero thing. Back in the bad old days I was beneath the notice of even the minor supers. But think: when you used to fight Stellar, it was just business. Not personal, yeah? You'd try to… to steal the Eiffel Tower, he'd stop you. Just business — weird, stupid, business."

"Yes?" Axel said.

"This time, Axel, this time it was personal," Wellsey continued. "*You* cost Stellar his career. *You* caused the damage he took the blame for. *You* created the hero that took his place in the Vigilancers. He doesn't just want you back in *prison*. Not this time. He wants to *hurt* you."

Axel rubbed PVC glue off of his fingers. "How?"

"You're supposed to be the genius," Wellsey said. "Can't you see he's already done it?"

Axel's hands shook as he packed his craft supplies away in their carry case. He looked at Wellsey with pleading eyes. For a moment, Wellsey thought his friend might be on the verge of pulling himself together. Then Axel shook his head vigorously and hurried out of the break room.

Sighing, Wellsey sat. His hand brushed the folded cardboard thing that Axel had been making. Wellsey picked it up and opened it. A bunch of brightly coloured letters popped up in 3d.

They read: "HELP ME!"

# 38 Between Two Doors

An important order was late to arrive, so Ms Shan spent her morning in the Trade section, assuring a local builder that his nail plates would be coming soon. When it did turn up, the builder kept complaining about how long he'd been kept waiting, effectively adding another hour to his departure time after the half-hour that the late delivery had cost him.

"It's a bloody outrage! I'm on a deadline, you know," he said at last, grabbing his bored apprentice by the shirtsleeve and pulling him away. "Come on, Gavin, let's get some lunch."

Ms Shan rubbed her weary eyes. At least it was normal. At least an idiot complaining is a normal, mundane thing. Nothing weird, nothing spooky. An everyday jackass was almost a treat.

She turned, and her almost-happiness dissolved. There, lounging awkwardly against a pile of cement sacks was Mr Smith from the DIY Barn.

"Hello, Ms Shan," he said.

"Mr Smith," she said. She thought of asking what she could do for him, before deciding that she didn't have the energy to pretend to care.

"Sorry for dropping in at such a busy time," he said,

looking pointedly around at the tiny number of customers. Ms Shan was not a violent person, but there was something about Smith that made her knuckles itch. She'd heard the term 'punchable face' before, but she'd never understood it until she'd met this man.

She didn't know quite what it was, exactly, that made him so maddening. He was a completely unremarkable-looking fellow. White, slightly red-faced, average height, somewhat overweight, short black hair, noticeably receding. If you asked an unimaginative artist to draw an office manager, Smith was what he'd come up with.

Oh, she knew that her staff suspected Smith and his DIY Barn of all sorts of misdeeds. They accused him of all sorts of crime and mischief. But Ms Shan had never seen a scrap of proof that Smith's bastardry was anything but petty, mundane and perfectly legal.

Ms Shan wondered how hard you had to hit a man to break his nose...

"Don't mention it." She smiled a brittle smile. "What brings you to the Handy Pavilion?" she added, as if she cared.

"Well, it's a funny thing," he said. "There have been some problems at the Barn. Some trouble was caused by water leakage last week, and this week we found that a drain had been blocked with concrete."

Seriously? That was Marlon's idea of escalation? This is what he and his people had been doing at night? Silly pranks like that? Nothing that might *hurt*.

Suddenly very tired, Ms Shan looked at her watch. The

builder had been right about one thing. It *was* lunchtime. She started walking towards the exit, Smith following along.

"We had a run of strange events here, too," she said. "People blamed it on a mysterious 'Phantasm of the Pavilion.'"

There was a crashing noise to her left. She looked left and saw... What was his name? That young guy in Power Tools. He'd dropped that creepy glass skull he used as a paperweight. It hadn't broken, unfortunately.

"But there haven't been any Phantasm sightings lately," she said, glowering at the lad. "Perhaps this Phantasm went over to the DIY Barn?"

Smith smiled a joyless, thin-lipped smile. He was lucky he didn't show any teeth, of Ms Shan probably would have whacked him with a newspaper.

"Perhaps," he said. "But that's not the main reason I'm here. I'm here to talk about the Local High School Fete."

Ms Shan stopped short, just by a cleaning display. She couldn't move forward. Every ounce of self-control was needed to keep herself from picking up a broom handle and beating Smith to within an inch of his life. She knew what he was going to say. She knew it.

"I know that, up until now, the Handy Pavilion has been one of the Fete's major sponsors," he said. "But since things aren't going well for you... It seemed the kindest thing we could do was talk to the school about taking over."

Ms Shan said nothing. She willed her jaw shut so she wouldn't scream. The School Fete... it was surprising how such a small thing hurt so much.

It wasn't so much the Fete itself, which Ms Shan always found rather dull. It was the *standing*. Sponsoring the Fete meant that the Pavilion had standing in the community—that it was as much a part of the neighbourhood as the school. Now... Now the Pavilion was just as she had always known, always said—but never really wanted to accept. The Pavilion was a transient thing. A footnote in a ledger. A column on a database that could be deleted with the press of a key.

"I see," she said. "Well thank you for the thought."

"Not at all," Smith said, smiling his non-smile. "Well, don't let me detain you. I can see that you're busy."

Smith exited through the front of the store. Ms Shan thought of going on her lunch break but decided that she'd lost her appetite. She turned, not quite certain where she was going. The young man in Power Tools was polishing the glass skull. Karl thingamy who ran the Centre newsletter was watching him, thoughtfully. She barely took this in.

She passed by whats-his-name, the cowboy guy, slowly giving directions to an impatient customer. She passed the hipster girl from the coffee shop, who was looking at the DIY decorations and her ape-man boyfriend who was just looking as helpless as an enormous muscle-bound wild-man is capable of looking.

But it wasn't the familiar faces that bothered her. It was the everyday customers. The citizens of the local community, the community she now felt cut off from. It seemed like some sort of wall had sprung up around her, and she wasn't part of anything anymore. Just a corporate asset, ready to be redeployed. Like everyone thought she was. Nothing more.

She didn't cry. That wasn't her sort of thing, but she had to do *something*. She was passing a range of internal doors mounted on hinges for display. She stepped into the display and stood between two solid exterior doors, shutting them on herself, making a little triangular room in which to scream silently and stamp her foot.

It felt good until the door was flung open. Ms Shan stood, mortified, a senior manager caught throwing a tantrum like a toddler. She sought some sort of excuse, but none was forthcoming.

The interloper was Sadie MacGregor from Lighting. Somehow she always remembered *her* name, and never mistook her for her twin sister. Sadie's ginger-lashed eyes were kind but stern.

"Hiding is beneath you," Sadie said.

"I..." Ms Shan began. "I want to hurt them. The Barn. I want to hurt them so badly."

"It may come to that," Sadie said. "But would it not be better to drag them into the light?"

Ms Shan shook her head. "We looked. They're squeaky clean."

"Dig deeper."

"How?"

"Who do you know who has an in with Smith?" Sadie said. "And who is adept at seeing what no one else does?"

"Karl thingummy?" Ms Shan said. "He knows Smith. And yes, he sees what no one else does, but that's just because he's delusional."

"Karl struggles to bring that which is hidden into the light," Sadie said. She grimaced before continuing, "Granted, he's bad at that. Extremely bad. But perhaps if someone put him on the right track?"

Ms Shan shook her head. "But I could just get Marlon to escalate a little more…"

"You can fight them with secrets in the darkness," Sadie said. "But secrets are *their* weapon. Night is *their* battlefield. Think it over."

She walked away, closing the doors as she did. Ms Shan stood between the doors in the display, lost in thought. Yes, it was all very metaphorical wasn't it. Two doors. Two paths. And Sadie had been right, hadn't she? It was better to take the high road. Follow the light…

A door opened—not the one Sadie had opened, the other one.. This time, it was Sadie's sister, Angela.

"Or you could just burn the DIY Barn to the ground," Angela said. "Just sayin'."

# 39 Testing Times

The Handy Pavilion was quiet on a Tuesday morning, allowing Fiona to catch up with some of Wellsey's paperwork. She was increasingly finding herself in de facto charge of the bathroom section since Wellsey was away on errands for Ms Shan so often these days. Fiona covered for him, working out rosters and making orders. The other team members in Plumbing did not dispute this new hierarchy. Most of them spent their quiet moments searching the job websites anyway. No one wanted a promotion—least of all an unofficial promotion that came without a raise.

Fiona muttered under her breath at her nominal boss' childish handwriting, then chuckled at herself. When she'd started working, she'd been considered a hopeless employee, one of the worst the Pavilion had hired. Now here she was criticising the work of her mentor.

It felt good. In a deeply uncomfortable way.

"Hey, Fiona."

It was Donna Saheco. Donna worked in lighting, and in recent weeks had become Fiona's best friend at the Pavilion. She was... she was a good influence on Fiona. It was a weird thing for an adult to think about herself, but there it was. Since she'd assisted in the armoured car heist, Fiona had felt like she had been morally twisting in the wind, floating rudderless on an unpaved road through a whirlpool of increasingly mixed metaphors. Donna's friendship helped to ground her.

"Hey, Donna," Fiona said. "Just be a sec." She stapled a sheath of receipts together with a satisfying clunk. "Break time? Kebab shop?"

"Full moon last night," Donna said. "You know the kebab shop is always closed after a night with a full moon. If you didn't bring a packed lunch, we'll have to go to the café and watch Miss Carob and Captain Monkeyman make sheep eyes at each other while we eat."

"Ugh," Fiona said. Seriously, she was happy for Carol and Zorbar, but even so… "Never mind, Carol makes a pretty decent sandwich. Besides, it doesn't matter. I want to talk about some stuff."

"What's that thing?" Donna said, gesturing to a strange-looking piece of hardware, affixed to the wall above the little desk at the end of Aisle 23 where the Plumbing paperwork was completed. "That electric deally with the green light on top? It goes on whenever I'm talking to you."

"Oh, that's something called a Bechdelmeter," Fiona said. "It's not just you, the light goes on when I'm talking to Belinda or Nalda or Ms Shan. I think it was built by Axel… Oh, the light's gone off."

"Never mind," Donna said. "Let's talk about Axel for a while. He's quite interesting… Huh. Now a red light has come on."

"Weird!" Fiona said. "Anyway, I don't want to talk about Axel. I need to ask you for some advice."

Donna came around behind the orders desk and took a wonky seat with a missing castor. "I'm all ears."

"I... there's something I need to get off my chest," Fiona said. The light on the meter turned pale green.

"It's about a terrible deed I took part in, alongside others," she continued. The light turned yellow. "But mostly it concerns my own role in it and how it affects my personal story." The light began glowing a brightest green.

Frowning, Donna switched the device off. "Sorry, that's distracting. You were saying?"

Fiona took a deep breath and told her friend everything. About her unexpected, unexplained water powers. About her acquiescence to Axel's plan. About pouring water all over the road, ready to be frozen by Norman using Axel's freeze ray.

About a daylight robbery, in short.

Donna whistled. "That's pretty heavy," she said. "I mean, it was only hurting those a-holes at the DIY Barn, but still..."

"What should I do?" Fiona said. "I... I feel so awful about it. But if I confess to the police, won't that just hurt the Pavilion?" She gestured around the near-empty aisles. "Do you think we can take the hit?"

"If you'd asked me a year ago, I'd have said just keep your head down," Donna said. "But since I've been working in lighting, I've been talking to Sadie a lot. You know about morals, ethics, things like that. It's really changed... Hey, I

231

thought I turned that meter thing off. Ugh, the green light is hurting my eyes. Anyway, I think you have only one option open to you. And that is…"

Fiona strained her ears and leaned in close as Donna took a deep breath to speak.

And then they were both on the floor. Fiona's ears rang. Was Donna okay? Was *she* okay? There were papers everywhere… It would take forever to tidy. Gathering all her strength, Fiona pushed herself off the concrete. She seemed to be in one piece. Her nose was bleeding but nothing seemed broken.

The two nearest shelving units had partly collapsed, each one bowed outwards at more or less the same height. Fiona found her eye attracted to the floor between the bends in the shelves. There, cratered in the concrete of the floor, was a glowing red rock.

A meteor? A meteorite? Fiona had used to know the distance. StalagTites came from the Top… No, that is something different…

Donna was standing now. She tapped Fiona's shoulder and said something that couldn't be heard over the ringing. Fiona followed Donna's pointed finger to a hole in the ceiling almost above them. Belatedly, the store sprinklers started. A cloud of white steam flashed into being when the water hit the rock, obscuring Fiona's vision. When it cleared, she saw the monster.

It was a demonic figure, goat-legged and bull-horned. It was human-shaped but bigger than most men. Perhaps even bigger than Dwayne "The Rock" Johnson. And it came out of a rock too. Interesting. Was comparing monsters to actor/wrestlers a sign of concussion? It seemed all too probable that it was.

Donna grabbed Fiona's shoulder and gestured for her to run. That was easier said than done. The splintery ruins of the orders desk blocked easy escape. On unsteady legs, Fiona hobbled away from the glowing red creature as it shambled after them, fury written into every line of its slavering features.

But... was that help ahead? Hurtling through the air towards them and the monster was the sleek figure of the superhero Voyager! Fiona was seeing double. It was as if two Voyagers were zooming towards the creature. There *were* two Voyagers! They hit the thing hard, driving it backwards. Donna cheered and punched her fist in the air. Fiona's hearing came back just in time to hear Donna's 'whoop' of triumph.

The Voyagers fought hard, punch after atomic punch, pushing the Monster back out of the steam, into the clear air of the Seasonal section. All at once, the thing rallied, knocking one Voyager from the air with a fist the size of a lawnmower; grabbing the other by a leg and sending her careening into a pile of Halloween decorations.

"Water!" Donna said. "Don't you see? It's a creature of flame!"

"Well, duh," Fiona said, not happy with being patronised.

She closed her eyes and felt out with her mind. There was water everywhere. She called it to her and settled its agitated molecules. She calmed the waters' fears, and it respected her for that. She opened her eyes.

"Donna, you ever see *The Abyss?*"

Donna laughed as vast tentacles of water rose from the floor and took the fiery monster in their watery embrace. A cloud of steam arose again, Fiona pushed back, willing the water molecules to retain their liquid form rather than breaking out into unseemly vapour. The flame demon roared in its torment as the water clung to him like frosting to a cupcake.

The Voyagers, recovering, laid into the stricken creature with everything they had—but they needn't have bothered. The creature fell to its knees, slowly, then toppled forward onto its face. Fiona released the water, and its molecules dispersed into steam. There was nothing left of the thing but charred bones that fell into grey-black dust.

# 40 Belinda is Helpful

Christian had not been at work the day the meteor struck. He was glad of that. He worried every time the glass skull picked up a spot of dirt, and the thought of a scratch terrified him beyond belief. The whole Handy Pavilion shaking at the impact... that might have given him a heart attack, straight up.

Now he stood behind the Power Tools counter, polishing the skull with a soft cloth as Belinda told him about the incident. Buck Dusty had already told him, but since all the laconic cowboy had said was, "Reckon that was a bad'n," Christian was a little short on details.

"So was it an alien or something?" Christian said, once she got up to the part with the monster. He held the skull up to the light. Ostensibly this was to check his polishing, but even after all this time, he was hoping he could see his mistress, the Phantasm, in there. As usual, he could see nothing but his own reflection.

"Nah, it was a demon," Belinda said. "Like the one in Lord of the Rings, sort of. Only it didn't have horns or a whip."

"So it was a more generic sort of fiery demon?"

"Like a clone?"

"What?"

"Like it was cloned from another demon using generic science?"

Christian screwed up his eyes. When he opened them, she was still there. "No, like an average looking demon," he said, wondering what an average demon looked like.

"Yeah, I guess," Belinda said. "He was summoned by a sorcerer, I heard."

"'Scuse me, are you going to sell me a router, or do I have to try someplace else?" Christian looked up to see a red-faced old man glaring at him. He wondered how long the man had been there, unnoticed. He needn't have wondered.

"Ten bloody minutes I've been waiting here while you turkeys blab about some movie," he snapped. "Demons and Hobbits and stuff. I'm a paying customer! You don't have a lot of those at the moment, so if I were you I'd be tryin' to do me bloody job, right?"

Christian sold the man a router and, after a twenty-minute diatribe about poor standards, high prices, and some strange race of beings called 'm'lenyools', the old fellow stomped off with a new router and Christian retook his place at the counter. To his surprise, Belinda was still there, making faces into the reflective surface of the skull.

"Isn't your break over, yet?" he said.

"I'm not on a break," she said. "Meant to be working in Paints, but all the people from Bathrooms with nothing to do have taken over. It's bullshit."

Christian smiled half-heartedly. He honestly couldn't

give a damn. If what those plumbers had said was true, then the pocket dimension that had been underneath the Pavilion had collapsed into the skull that had once powered it, and the Phantasm was trapped inside. That was what mattered, the Phantasm. Yes, she had been a cruel and manipulative mistress to Christian but…

But…

Buck Dusty moseyed into the Power Tools section. He nodded at Christian and touched the brim of his hat to Belinda. "Ma'am," he said. Belinda gave an awkward smile. Christian was pretty sure she was keen on Buck. Better him than me, he thought.

"Back from your break, Dust?" Christian said.

"Reckon."

"Where are you from, Buck?" Belinda asked. "I always wondered. I mean I know you're from the States, but."

"I was born in Tombstone, Arizona, ma'am," Buck said. "My family lived there since after the war."

"World War II?" Belinda said.

"Other war."

"The Civil War?"

"No."

Belinda's knowledge of history seemed to come to an end here, so she didn't push matters. "So your family came from England?"

"Some," Buck said. "Some settled the West after they had to leave Roanoke Island. Others came a… a different way. My granpappy was from Baghdad."

Christian laughed. Buck turned on him wordlessly. Christian hated it when he did that. Buck was a quiet, gentle guy, but his stare was one of the most terrifying things Christian had seen.

"That funny?"

"Baghdad... To Tombstone," Christian said, swallowing hard to get that lump out of his throat.

"What of it?"

"Babylonia to Arizona," Christian said. "Like the song. Um. The Steve Martin song."

Without moving a muscle, Buck somehow made himself twice as intimidating. Involuntarily, Christian backed up a step. For a long time, nobody moved. A tumbleweed did not roll between the co-workers, but Christian wouldn't have been surprised if it had. With one last glare, Buck turned away.

"Got me some bench vices to unpack," he said, moseying off.

Christian breathed, realising that this was the first time he'd done so in nearly a minute. Unperturbed, Belinda was cleaning under her fingernails with a small chisel.

"So how do you know it was a demon?" Christian said. If Belinda wasn't going to go away, he felt he should at least make conversation.

"Pennington said."

"Who's Pennington?"

"He's an alchemist," Belinda said. "I didn't believe him when he told me he was an alchemist, but he's got it on his business card, so..."

An alchemist. Christian pursed his lips. The Phantasm of the Pavilion had warned him against alchemists. She despised them with a passion, but had never told him why. Still, someone who knew something about the occult arts might be just what he needed if he was to rescue the Phantasm from her transdimensional glass prison.

"Belinda," he said, "do you still have this guy's card?"

She rifled through her purse until she found it, then passed it to him. Christian realised that in all the time he'd known Belinda, this was the first time he'd ever felt grateful to her.

## 41 The Night Talker

Bruce was parked in his usual spot in the Handy Pavilion lot. He had a good position, not far from the main entrance. His existence had become more sociable since he'd merged with the killer robot, but that was a mixed blessing. Carol still came around to visit, trying to get him to tell her something mystical. Zorbar was still scared of him, but he came with his fiancé anyway, grateful to Bruce for saving both of their lives. On nights of the full moon, Seamus the gnome came by. And most evenings Marlon would discuss the ongoing struggle against the DIY Barn.

And then there was Karl Wintergreen. Bruce wasn't certain about Karl. There was something just… just not right about the guy. Karl was the only one outside of the Handy Pavilion staff who knew about Bruce, but Bruce hadn't yet told anyone about Karl. Maybe he should…

"As a ghost, you can walk around invisible and unseen, right?" Karl was saying. "You could go anywhere. You could walk into Cabinet meetings… Boardrooms of huge corporations… The Vigilancer's Justi-Building… Anywhere!"

"Yeah, nah, see…" Bruce began, but Karl Wintergreen was in no mood to be interrupted.

"And then you'd see everything!" he said. "The Masonic rituals, the alien conspiracies, UFOs, hymns to Yog-Sothoth…"

"Protocols of the Elders of Zion?" Bruce said, wishing that he could roll his eyes as he said it.

"Hey! No!" Karl said. "I'm not that sort of conspiracy nerd, alright?"

Bruce sighed, but relented. Karl adjusted his hat and stared at the parking lot ground, sulking.

"Some of my best friends…" he muttered.

"Bagels are delicious," he added.

"Not my thing," Bruce said. "Too chewy. Look, Karl, I'm not trying to give you shit about the conspiracy thing. Truth is, I just can't get very far. Never could, even when I was a straight-up ghost, yeah? There's only so far away from me bones I can get. That hasn't changed now that I'm possessing the body of a killer robot and making it transform into a concrete truck."

Hm. That sounded a little odd, when he said it out loud. Never mind, he thought. Just roll with it.

"I can just about get as far as the DIY Barn," he said. "Not that it does me much good. Security is good over there, and it's just gotten better since the times we *did* get through. For me to infiltrate the Trilobite Committee, they'd have to meet here, mate."

"It's 'Trilateral Commission,'" Karl muttered. "And I guess you're right. No secret society would meet in the Super Centre."

Bruce looked across the tarmac plain of the carpark to

the Square and Compass Kebab shop. The curtains were drawn. Chanting could be faintly heard on the breeze, though Bruce could not guess the language.

"Sure, whatever," Bruce said, not wanting to encourage Karl. "Look, mate. You've got a giant transforming robot that owes you a favour. That's pretty good on its own, isn't it?"

Carl looked up to the half-moon above as it passed from behind a cloud. "It's not enough. You can laugh if you like. Most people do. But... but the *secrets*. The secrets and lies! The world is made of truth, and all they ever let you see are the secrets and lies!"

Bruce's looked at the ground. He wondered how his gaze could shift since in his truck form he had no eyes. Again: just roll with it. There comes a point where existence is so absurd that there's no point sweating the details.

"What about that..." Bruce struggled for a name. He sometimes listened to news radio when he was bored, but more often he'd tune his internal radio to a classic hits station. "That embassy guy with the internet shit. Justin... Bieber? No, that's the kid that can't sing. Uh..."

"Julian Assange?" Karl scoffed. "I read through all his document drops. It's all just people being slightly dodgier and less competent behind closed doors than they try to seem in public. Nothing juicy. No reptilian conspiracies in the Pentagon or werewolf rituals at Buckingham Palace. Nothing *real*."

Karl spat into the gutter. "If the secrets of the New World Order were known then the established order would collapse. Since it hasn't collapsed, the secrets cannot have been revealed. Qued."

"I think you say that 'QED'," Bruce said. In high school, he'd been quite good at maths — though of course, he'd always been careful never to let this be known to the other members of his Rugby team.

"I'm pretty sure Assange is an MK-ULTRA plant."

"There are plant people?" Bruce said, genuinely confused. "As well as lizard men?"

Karl fell silent for a long time. When he spoke again, he said, "Ms Shan asked me to investigate the DIY Barn. I don't know if I should. Mr Smith seems like he's on the up-and-up, and yet you say those men in silver work for him..."

"Karl, they nearly killed me," Bruce said.

"But you're..."

"You know what I mean," Bruce said. "That meteor with the demon in it? The one that hit the Pavilion the other day? Everyone thinks it was an attack on the Pavilion in general, yeah? Well, it was aimed at me. My bones are buried in the concrete. It only just missed them. If they go, I go — and who'll be guarding the Pavilion then?"

"They summoned a demonic meteor?" Karl said. "They must be in league with..."

"I don't care, all right?" Bruce snapped. "I don't care which evil organisation you think they work with. All right? I don't care which pin they are on your bloody conspiracy corkboard. All I know is, they're trying to kill me. And mate? I've already been murdered one time, and I. Am. Fucking.

Over. It."

Karl stood back a step, looking hurt.

"You're a selfish man, Karl Wintergreen," Bruce said. "You talk about the truth setting everyone free? Well, I think all you want is to think you know more than everyone else. Well, you don't. There's plenty going on that you don't know, and don't even suspect. You're too busy telling everyone to 'open their eyes' to bother taking a look yourself."

The look of hurt on Karl's moonlit face deepened. Bruce felt awful — but he kept going.

"You know what? Don't worry. Don't worry about how the Barn got its unfair proposal through the local council. What does the Hertling Council matter, compared to the UN? What does half the people here losing their jobs matter against the Lizard Masons or whatever the fuck? Forget the people you actually *know*, you have shadowy figures to chase!"

Karl stood there for a long time, staring at the tarmac, his face shaded by his white hat. After perhaps five minutes, he reached into his pocket and took out a box, which he laid on Bruce's hood.

"Forgot to tell you, I got you this," he said. "You wire it to your horn. Plays the chorus of 'Underneath the Radar'. Know you like that song."

With that, Karl turned and walked away, a lonely white figure under the sodium lights of the carpark.

# 42 Time's Nature, Discussed by Gossiping Retail Employees

Nalda distrusted the thinking of the humans. It was erratic, contradictory, illogical. In her downtime, she'd seen many episodes of old television shows in which some character or other claimed that the erratic basis of human intelligence was a strength, not a weakness. But Nalda had seen the future Empire of the Machines crushing humanity beneath its chrome-plated jackboots, and she knew that those old shows had it oh-so-wrong.

Even so, she was dependent on Fanaka and his frail human brain. She was a war machine and her hardware was optimised for tactical reasoning, split-second decision making, and rapid calculations of vectors and trajectories. Worse, to keep her job at the Handy Pavilion, she'd had to reallocate much of her capacity for deep abstract thought into the arts and crafts. That didn't leave her with a lot of processing resources available. If she was to solve the conundrum of keeping her cold, robotic future intact, she needed Fanaka — even if he was something of a scatterbrain.

"Perhaps I should get a job here?" Fanaka asked. "At the

Pavilion. It would keep me close to the area I'm studying, and I wouldn't have to impose on you for food and lodgings."

Fanaka sat back in his garden chair. The two of them were sitting in Outdoor Furniture. Adam usually didn't like it when staff made use of the comfy benches. But he also didn't like speaking to Nalda if he could avoid it, so for the time being they were not bothered.

"I am a cyborg," Nalda said. "Even though I am on lousy wages, I am have few physical needs. I spend little, so I have a small fortune in the bank."

"Yes, but... But I have become distracted. I was talking about my graph of tachyon surges."

Deep inside Nalda, a processor performed an exasperation deletion subroutine. This had the same effect as an inefficient human sigh, but in a fraction of the time. Why was Fanaka like this? He was a tall, burly black man with that evenness and symmetry of facial characteristics that humans called 'handsomeness'. According to what Nalda had learned about humans from her television, he should be cool and confident—not an absent-minded nerd.

"Can we skip der graph, please?" Nalda said. The pair of them stood in a quiet corner of Outdoor Furniture, and at any moment a customer might ask Nalda a question. "And can we get on to your conclusions?"

Fanaka adjusted the circlet of brass gears that he wore around his shaven head. "Well, I have some good news for you. In a way. You see, time is a series of infinitely branching streams."

A fly buzzed between them, did a little circle around Nalda, and landed on a garden lamp. A moment later it flew away, seemingly disappointed by its new home.

"And?" Nalda said.

"What this means is that your plan to simply wait for your future probably won't succeed," Fanaka said. "But you make it happen. You can *cause* your future world to come to pass."

"But I did," Nalda said. "Dat is why I travelled back to this era. I was sent back by der world-spanning Computertron 2000 to bring about der end of…"

She stopped. Fanaka's eyes were wide open and his eyebrows were up as high as his circlet. Nalda knew that when he adopted this look, he was either listening intently or had zoned out completely but wanted to look like he was listening intently. Either way, she had to be careful what she said.

"To bring about der end of high bank fees and charges," she concluded. "Ja, that will do."

"How were you to accomplish that?"

"By killing der mother of der man responsible so he couldn't be born."

"Goodness me!"

Nalda grimaced. "Dat *was* der plan. But I couldn't find a big enough gun to do der job. Best I could get was a .22, and I could not kill someone with a little pea-shooter like dat. Most disrespectful! So instead I introduced der woman to dis charming guy who vas not der father of her future son. She marries der wrong man, and her son never got born anyway."

"That sounds needlessly confusing and complicated."

"Ja, well, dat's time travel for you," Nalda said. "So what should I be doing to get back to my future?"

Fanaka shook his head. "Now that I don't know. I need to do some more research. It shouldn't be difficult to get you where you're going, but I also need to get back to my timeline."

"Ja, dat's my priority, Poindexter," Nalda muttered. "What do we need to do to figure out how to get me into der right timestream?"

As she spoke, Axel Platzoff rounded the corner, whistling to himself as he constructed an origami slime mould. He stopped suddenly, his mouth dropping open.

"You're not messing with the timelines, are you, Nalda?" he said.

"So what if I am?" Nalda said. "You used to do that all the time."

Axel looked from Nalda to Fanaka and back again. "Yes, in my early days. But even *I* had to stop. You start messing with the timeline, all sorts of horrible things happen. Before I meddled with history, the only Spider-Man movie was that cool one with Dr Octopus. Clear cola was cheap and plentiful. Alvin and the Chipmunks were only mildly annoying. Hipsters were few, and the Janis Joplin/Jim Morrison All-Star Variety Hour ran from 1971 to 1999... You can't meddle with the past! You just can't!"

"Nein, I am meddling with the future."

"Oh. That's okay, then. How can I help?"

"I'd quite like to meddle in the past," Fanaka said.

"Yes, but you're from an alternate past, aren't you?" Axel said. "The dashiki printed with industrial designs is a hint, but that vivonium-powered time detector in the tamboti wood case is proof."

"Halt showing off, Axel," Nalda said. "Are you going to help us or not?"

Axel paused, his eyes wide open. He ran his tongue over his teeth and looked down at the origami eukaryote in his hands. "I…" he muttered. "I…"

A lumpy looking customer wandered over. "Hey, while you people are chatting, there are customers who need help, you know."

"I ought to go back in time to…" Nalda began.

"I don't work here," Fanaka said.

"How can I help you, sir?" Axel said glaring at the others.

The lumpy man turned to look at Axel. "I need a pulley. There are never any pulleys when I come here. Never! I just need a simple 100mm pulley, and it's driving me mad."

"Sorry to hear that," Axel said. "I think I saw a spare box out back. Hold on a tick, and I'll get you one."

Axel walked off with the man. "As for you two — don't do anything," he added over his shoulder.

"But you will be helping us?" Fanaka said.

Axel turned the corner. He might have shaken his head before he was gone, but even Nalda was not certain.

## 43 Never Pay Retail

It was almost a week before Christian saw Pennington again. This wasn't good news. Christian was holding onto his job by a thread, and he was terrified that he'd be fired before he could speak to the alchemist.

A whole dozen people had been fired. Low performers, chronic latecomers, suspected pilferers. To be fair to Ms Shan, she didn't play favourites—though to be fair, playing favourites would necessitate remembering everyone's names.

Only a couple of weeks before, Christian would have thought himself invulnerable to anything less than a complete shutdown of the Handy Pavilion, but his KPIs were all down since the Phantasm's disappearance. He might have escaped the last round of layoffs, but the next round would surely take him out.

He needed Pennington's help before that could happen.

It was a quiet Wednesday, although the word 'quiet' was both redundant and misleading. Every day was quiet in the Pavilion, and yet they were so understaffed that the workers were always busy.

The appearance of Pennington jolted Christian out of his idle thoughts. He hurriedly rang up change for a customer and told Ali that he was going for a break. Ali, who was in the middle of a conversation with a man buying a scroll-saw, was too preoccupied to tell him 'no'. With a final glance at the glass skull under his desk, Christian trotted off after the alchemist.

In a sudden burst of inspiration, Christian took a photo of Pennington's shopping trolley, then zig-zagged around a display of tomato frames to meet Pennington coming past hinges and fasteners.

"Excuse me, sir, can I have a word?" Christian said.

Pennington stopped and glared at Christian. He was a forty-ish gent with greying ginger hair. Christian didn't know much about fashion, but every stitch on the man read 'upper-middle-class.' The way he walked said 'cadets, but no actual military service', the smirk on his face proclaimed a man who'd spend more on a bottle of wine than Christian would spend on a meal for two. Without even asking, Christian could tell that Pennington could easily afford a Ferrari but had chosen to drive a Volvo—presumably to spite anyone who couldn't afford a Ferrari.

Was it too much to ask for an alchemist to be a hippie drop-out? Christian sucked down his contempt. This was good. This was usable. Know your customer—that's how you make a sale.

"Can I help you?"

"That's what I'm hoping," Christian said. "Word is, you're an alchemist?"

"That's right," Pennington said, handing Christian a card. "No offence intended, but I must warn you my fees are quite high…"

Christian suppressed a shudder of anger. "And well earned, I bet. But I was wondering if you could do me a little favour? Don't know if you can help, but if you're in the magic biz, maybe you can put me onto someone else who can…"

Pennington stiffened. Yes! Ego. That's the key to your Eastern Suburbs punter. Well, it's the key to everyone, sooner or later, but it works a lot quicker with your Scot's-old-boys types. "Perhaps if you tell me what the problem is, I can tell you if I can be of help."

"Well, it's to do with a glass Skull," Christian said. "It was powering this little pocket dimension, I reckon, but it's not powering it anymore. A friend of mine got trapped inside."

"Well, your dimension will be cactus," Pennington scoffed. "Hope you didn't leave anything valuable inside. But I miiiiight be able to get your friend back. He'll be in a sort of limbo, probably. I could make a dimensional bridge, as long as he hasn't wandered too far into the void."

"You have the power to do that?" Christian said, just the right note of awe in his voice.

"The power is in the Skull," Pennington said. "Just have to channel it correctly. It's tricky. As an alchemist, I usually deal more with matter than energy. But it's doable…"

Laura Cho came past, walking hard in pursuit of a fleeing Axel Platzoff, both screaming at each other in Cantonese. Christian's terrible mistress, the Phantasm, had a particular dislike for both Axel and Laura but, of course, had never explained why. The thought of the Phantasm made

Christian sigh. He missed her. He missed her.

Pennington cleared his throat, clearly not happy at having the wind taken out of his sails in mid smarm. "As I said, it's doable... but very expensive."

"Couldn't you do it *pro bono*?" Christian said. "I mean, if you can turn lead into gold..."

"That's more of a metaphor," Pennington said. "A metaphor for how expensive alchemical services are. Quite expensive. Yes. Very, very expensive."

Christian nodded. "I have a brother in the Federal Police."

"Are you trying to blackmail me?" Pennington shrugged. "I think you'll find that witchcraft is no longer a criminal offence."

Reaching into his pocket, Christian retrieved his phone. "That's a photo of your trolley. Looks kind of like the sort of supplies you'd be buying if you were running an ice lab. I bet the security footage shows a lot of your shopping trips look like that."

"Ice!" Pennington smiled. "I can make subtle and exotic potions that make ice look like weak tea."

"Sure you can, but my brother doesn't know that."

"If he investigates, he'll find nothing," Pennington sneered. "Is that all you have to work with? The threat of petty official inconvenience?"

"That's right," Christian said. "And me? That petty inconvenience wouldn't bother me. I'm used to inconvenience. But my guess is... yeah, my guess is you're *not*. My guess is, a bunch of AFP clodhoppers going to your house would find nothing—but try explaining them to your missus and your neighbours."

Pennington's face darkened.

"Look, like you said: making this bridge is not hard to do, and you're not using any of your own power," Christian said. "You won't be out of pocket, and you'll be helping someone who never did you any harm get out of limbo.

Pennington frowned at a pile of jerry-cans, as if they were the ones who'd bamboozled him. He breathed in deeply. Come on! All right, you're not happy—but it's costing you nothing but ego, and you have ego to spare.

"Ten dollars," Pennington said, at last.

"What?"

"I'll help you, but it won't be free, it will cost ten dollars. It's a nominal fee, but it's what's called a 'consideration', and it means we have a contract. Contracts are *very* important in my line of work."

Christian dug a five-dollar note and a handful of change out of his jeans. As they walked back to the Power Tools counter, Pennington counted every coin, before putting the silver in the charity box that was chained to the key cutting desk.

"You support 'UFO Abductees for 9/11 Truth?'" Christian said, squinting at the box's label.

Pennington reddened slightly. "I'll spend my money as I wish," he said. For emphasis, he dropped the gold coins in, too.

Back at Power Tools, Ali was ready to give Christian several pieces of his mind. Seeing Christian with a customer, he demurred. Christian went behind his desk and...

"Gone!" he wailed. "My skull... my skull!"

"Settle down!" Ali snapped. "Not in front of customers."

"Where's my skull?" Christian wailed, only quieter this time.

"Shit, mate, did some prick take your paperweight?" Ali said, actually sympathetic. "Too bad, that looked expensive."

"Did you see who took it?"

"If I saw, I wouldn't let 'em take it, would I?"

Christian dropped his head into his hands. He was roused from his despair by Pennington tapping on his shoulder. "Well, I did my best, not my problem now, 'kay, thanks, bye."

Christian arose from his despair, meeting the startled alchemist's eyes. "Oh, no! You're under contract. I find that skull and you're doing the deed. Consideration, remember?"

"Or," Pennington said, his voice dripping condescension, "I could just give you your money... Shit!"

There was nothing in his pocket but a crumpled fiver. He reached into his wallet, only to find it full of cards but completely bare of folding money.

"Shit!" he repeated.

## 44 The Party

Norman was late to arrive at the party in Outdoor Furniture. Adam had spread drop-sheets over all of his beloved display tables and chairs and though he seemed happy, there was a sub-strata of worry every time someone put a drink down.

Only a month earlier, Norman thought, Ms Shan would have balked at the idea of using the Handy Pavilion as the base for Zorbar's buck's night. Now, she not only gave her blessing, but invited herself as well. Wellsey — who, like many old rebels was a traditionalist at heart — objected to a woman attending a buck's night. But Fiona and Belinda also ended up on the invitation list, and then Zorbar's fiancee Carol announced she was coming. With that, any chance that the evening would involve strippers vanished in a puff of smoke, so Wellsey had to grin and bear it.

Norman surveyed the scene. Zorbar sat at the head of a huge long table. Perhaps in deference to the fact that he had to dress up nicely the following day, Carol had allowed him to come to his party dressed in nothing but a piece of zebra skin wrapped around his slender waist. Carol sat across from Zorbar, talking to Belinda and Marlon.

Axel—who had been looking more than usually haunted lately—had converted the café counter into a cocktail bar and was serving up drinks like there was no tomorrow.

"Have an Ouzotini, Norman?" Axel said.

"Why, because I'm Greek? That's kind of rac—hey! This is pretty good!"

Wellsey had brought a case of his famous home-brew for those that didn't care for cocktails, and Mrs Liselle from the Super Centre management had just 'happened' to turn up with some champagne from Emile's Vintage cellar. She sat at what she probably thought was a discrete distance from Ms Shan, which made Norman roll his eyes and feel jealous all at the same time.

And Buck was there, and the MacGregor sisters and Ali and Donna. People who worked in departments so obscure that barely rated a mention were all there. Former employees who'd been friends of Zorbar were chatting away, while some hipsters who sat in a corner playing with their phones were surely friends of Carol's. One table sat a couple of uncomfortable-looking rich boys, two chimpanzees and a lowlands gorilla—presumably Zorbar's family.

Drink in hand, Norman took a seat next to the groom. Zorbar was drinking something out of a coconut shell—something that turned out to be coconut milk.

"You not drinking, Zorbar?" Norman said.

"What happen last time Norman too drunk?" Zorbar said.

Norman gave an embarrassed little laugh. "Ended up

257

standing on a table with me shirt off, yelling at everyone, trying to start fights… Oh."

"Now Norman get understand," Zorbar smiled. "Zorbar stick non-alcoholic beverage."

"Fair enough mate," Norman said. "So… tying the knot, eh?"

"Carol not like other women Zorbar know," Zorbar said. "Not get captured by evil cult. Not need rescue from sacrifice altar. Ugh. Tiring on Zorbar day off! Carol not like that. Also Carol wear boot. Good ankle support. Not sprain during escape."

"Yeah, those are good points," Norman said, "but that's not all of it, is it?"

"Not all. All Zorbar will *say*. But not *all*."

Norman laughed. "Just looking out for you, mate."

Zorbar cut a piece of overcooked steak with his hunting knife. Norman could only imagine the number of compromises that the primal ape-man and his excessively woke hipster fiancée had needed to make to survive as a couple, but it looked like Zorbar had managed to avoid the perils of vegetarianism — although he did pick up the chunk of flesh with a paper napkin rather than his bare hands.

"How Pavilion going?" Zorbar said.

"It's stuffed, mate," Norman said. "Going down in flames. Ms Shan still thinks we can turn it around, but you know what those corporate types she works for are like. They probably won't even tell her they're closing this place until the last minute. Bastards."

"Where you go?"

"Well, not to the fucking DIY Barn, that's for sure," Norman said. "Other than that, I don't know. I'm a pretty good barista and technically I have café management experience but."

"But you want work Power Tools," Zorbar said. "Zorbar understand. Like working with Carol. Love Carol, but indoors all time. Zorbar think maybe he go TAFE, study landscaping…"

Zorbar's words were drowned by a huge echoing metallic clang coming from the great delivery bay doors. The partygoers looked around in confusion before the clang repeated itself. Norman looked to Ms Shan—for guidance, this time, not longing. The manager stood up from the table, wiped her fingers and walked towards the roller door. Norman followed, along with most of the rest of the staff.

"Who is it?" Ms Shan asked.

A"Open the fucking door!" came a voice from the other side. The voice seemed doubly distorted, first by some sort of megaphone and second by the door. But Ms Shan seemed to recognise the speaker anyway, visibly relaxing as she pressed the button. A terrible metallic clanking came from the door actuator mechanism, doubled by a terrible metallic clanking beyond. By the time the door was had risen high enough for Norman to see outside. There was nothing there but that old concrete truck that was always parked outside of the Pavilion.

Then Norman gasped. "Look!" he said. In the passenger seat lay the figure of a man. With his hat was missing and a huge red patch spreading over his trademark white suit, it took Norman a moment to identify Karl Wintergreen.

Zorbar sped forward and opened the door. Norman elbowed through the crowd to help the big man manoeuvre Karl's body from the cab.

"Don't move him!" someone yelled.

"No, that's back injuries. Looks like he's been shot."

"Could be stabbed."

"Granted, but…"

"Shut up!" Norman said. "Does anyone here know any first aid?"

A few people put their hands up, but Zorbar shook his head. "Better! There doctor in house."

Adam rushed forward to lay a cushioned sun-lounge cover on the ground just inside the loading bay. Zorbar and Norman lay Karl on the ground. Carol rushed over to stand closer to her fiancé. Norman glanced at Ms Shan and saw that she was holding hands with Mrs Liselle. He suddenly felt very lonely.

At Zorbar's gesture, the crowd parted, allowing a lowlands gorilla to knuckle his way through. Norman knew it was a 'he' because of the silver markings on the ape's back. What do you know? He'd learned something useful in high school geography.

The ape poked at the wound on Karl's chest. Zorbar grunted at the creature, which grunted back. "Someone get Dr Kagrat sharp knife and pliers," Zorbar said. "Also maybe call ambulance."

"I did that!" said one of Carol's hipster friends.

"Me too, except I used the ambulance service app," said another.

Axel appeared with a Stanley knife and a pair of needle-nose pliers, which he disinfected with OP rum. The gorilla took the tools and tore Karl's white jacket open with his bare hands. With a kiss, Zorbar released Carol and knelt on the floor, physically restraining the twitching Karl. Norman wondered why, until Dr Kagrat cut into Karl's flesh, and Karl began screaming and struggling in Zorbar's iron grip. Norman, feeling helpless, leapt in and grabbed onto Karl's legs. This had the unfortunate effect of leaving him facing directly towards the bloody operation.

"Come on! Come on! Give them some space!" Ms Shan said, shooing the partygoers away from the makeshift operating theatre. It took a while to get the gawpers moving, but Ms Shan was not to be ignored. She got them well back as a horrible metallic scrape told Norman that Kagrat had found the bullet with the point of his knife.

"It's the Barn," Ms Shan said. She said it low, relying on Karl's screams to make her words inaudible to anyone but Mrs Liselle, but Norman's superb hearing caught every word. Norman often resented his ancestry, but at least it gave him keen senses.

"I sent him there," Ms Shan said. "God help me. I sent him to find out what they were up to. It's a miracle he's alive. This is my fault!"

"Shush, love," Mrs Liselle said. "It's not your fault. It's

theirs. They shot him."

There was a long pause. The gorilla, a look of absolute concentration on his dignified face, reached into the hole in Karl's body with his pliers. There seemed to be a couple of false starts before the jaws bit, but then he had hold of something. With powerful, sensitive fingers, he started pulling it out.

"You're right," Ms Shan said. "You're right. They did it. Okay. No more bullshit. No more faffing about. No midnight pranks, no wait-and-see. They want a war? They've got one!"

Involuntarily, Norman's back straightened and his chin came up. Up until now it had all been killer robots and magic meteors and Phantasms and, for all Norman knew, witches' curses. Now it was *war* and, God help him, Norman would go anywhere, *anywhere* that Ms Shan ordered, follow any order that she gave him, even if it led to the grave.

"I *really* need a girlfriend," he said to himself.

But no one heard him over Dr Kagrat's grunt of satisfaction as, with a jerk, the bullet cleared Karl Wintergreen's body.

# 45 The Barn Door is Open

It was Buck Dusty who took the glass skull. Definitely. The security camera footage had been useless, so Christian wasn't sure how exactly he knew this. But he knew. There had always been something suss about Buck. Seriously, who wears cowboy hats to work?

Well, cowboys, obviously. Oh, and country singers. And truckers. And corrupt Texan mayors... but also honest Texas rangers. And that one guy in the commando unit who isn't the hero, but survives for a pretty long while before dying in a hail of bullets...

Okay, so lots of people wear cowboy hats. But even accepting that fact, Christian didn't trust Buck an inch. There was just something uncanny about the man. Something eerie had slowly overcome him. When Christian had first joined the Pavilion, Buck had seemed like a friendly, happy sort of cowboy, like in the old movies Christian's grandfather had loved. Someone like Audie Murphy or Hoot Gibson. Now, though... Now Buck didn't seem so much fun.

It was easy for Christian to sneak off to spy on Buck. His supervisor, Ali, was distracted. All the staff were distracted. Something had gone down at Zorbar and Carol's party the night before, and a fearful uncertain pall hung over the entire Handy Pavilion. Something about that idiot Karl Wintergreen getting hurt... Christian didn't care about the details, but he was happy to make use of the license the issue gave him.

He found Buck out the back, playing a mournful tune on a harmonica in a shady little cul-de-sac between a pile of discarded pallets and a broken-down forklift. Christian considered confronting him directly. After all, the cowboy was holding a bag that could have been big enough to contain the skull... But Christian found that he didn't trust his instinct as strongly as he might have. Instead of marching out to shirtfront Buck, Christian found a hollow in the unevenly stacked pallets and watched through a narrow slit.

What was Buck up to? What was he doing?

A newcomer joined Buck in his hidey-hole. It took all of Christian's strength not to cry out or move. It was Mr Smith! The manager of the DIY Barn. For all that he'd willingly participated in the Phantasm's schemes, Christian was at least enough of a Pavilionite to fear and suspect the Barnlings.

"Good morning, Mr Dusty," Smith said, extending a hand. "How are you this morning?"

Buck put away his harmonica, but did not take the offered hand. "Hot. Too many flies."

Smith looked annoyed, but he soldiered on. His presence of mind returning, Christian slowly, slowly began slipping his phone from his pocket.

"I hear Mr Wintergreen had an... unfortunate accident," Smith said.

"I hear tell one of your boys shot him," Buck drawled. "Did a bad job, too."

Smith reddened. Christian had his phone ready, but realised that he didn't dare take a photo. The angle of the sun meant they might see light reflecting off the lens. So what could... Voice recorder! Yes! That was even better. Christian turned it on, and stood still as a statue.

"You think you could have done better?" Smith said.

"I reckon there's some things a man can do by halves," Buck said. "Killin' ain't one of 'em."

"In a way, I'm glad to hear you say that. I hear Wintergreen has stabilised. I need him finished."

"I reckon even your boys can take care of a man lyin' in bed, and missin' half a yard of guts."

"I need *you* to do the job, Mr Dusty."

"Mr Dusty was my paw," Buck said.

"I don't have time for..."

"You can call me *Dr* Dusty," Buck continued. "I didn't spend all them years workin' on that thar dis-eert-ation to be *Mr* Dusty."

Smith blinked helplessly and brushed flies off his rapidly reddening face. "Damn it, you have to finish Wintergreen off. He knows too much. Your organisation..."

"COWBO has done plenty for you already," Buck said. "The Grey Barn may be aligned with the Barn of Shadows, but does not serve it."

Glad I got that recorded, Christian thought. Hate to have to figure out what this means as I go.

"You know I don't buy any of that mystical nonsense," Smith said. "I don't care why COWBO is supporting us, I need Wintergreen done away with. And yes, damn it, you're right. I can't trust my people. Subtlety isn't their strong suit. Can't have them creeping into a hospital."

It was hot in his alcove. Christian was sweating so badly, that he was barely able to keep hold of his phone. A fly landed on his upper lip. He snorted through his nose as hard as he dared, but the stubborn insect only took this as an invitation to wander about a little. Christian wished he hadn't shaved that morning. Some stubble would at least be some protection against the fly's tickling feet.

"That's too bad, hoss," Buck said. "Your boys are all you've got right now. I ain't never shot a man in the back. Ain't plannin' to start with a man in a hospital gown. They got enough reason to watch their backs already."

"Well, then what the hell am I going to do?" Smith wailed.

Christian tried to push the fly off his upper lip using his lower lip. It did not go well.

Buck sighed. "Find a killer that ain't too perticerlar about who he kills, is my advice. Or step up your plans so that you've won before Karl can talk. Or you could be a man and do the job yourself."

"Now look, you..." Smith began.

And then the fly went into Christian's nose.

He sneezed loudly, finally managing to dislodge the creature, and reflexively jerked a hand that was holding onto a badly stacked pallet. Decaying pine gave way, causing the pile to lean alarmingly. Buck and Smith spun around to look. Christian turned to run, but his feet got tangled up and he fell onto his face. Somehow holding onto a scrap of presence of mind, he slid his phone along the ground, watching as it came to rest under the forklift. Looking back, he expected to see the tower of pallets collapsing on top of him. Instead, it swayed back and forward, before coming to an anticlimactic stop.

Smith came bustling around to Christian, his face redder than ever, his shirt suddenly soaked with sweat. Buck followed behind at a mosey, rolling a cigarette as he walked. Smith tried to say something, but his words were swallowed by loud gasps for air. Buck put the cigarette in his mouth and drew a gun from his apron pocket.

"Reckon you're going to stay put and keep quiet?" Buck said.

Christian nodded before struggling to his feet. Help was only metres away, but he didn't like his odds if he cried out.

"What have you done with my Skull?" Christian said.

"Nothin'—yet," Buck said, whacking Christian's head with the gun. Christian's brain was full of angry digital fire for a second, then he crumpled to the ground again, dazed but not unconscious.

"Oh, good one," Smith said. "You know, we could have walked him out of here at gunpoint. Now we have to carry him."

"Was I supposed to leave a line like that hanging?" Buck said.

"Yeah… I guess that was pretty badass. What skull was he talking about?"

"Beats me. Come on, let's get him out of here."

# 46 Farewell

The skirmishing had ended and war had come at last to the Handy Pavilion. Employees that had once arrived by bus or on foot were now in mandatory car pools—safety in numbers. Every effort had been made to conceal from the public all the preparations for battle. Still, an observant customer might have noticed how the theft-prevention people on the door now focused their attention on the outside rather than inside; how the skylights all suddenly sported heavy iron grilles; how the woodwork demonstrations now seemed to produce nothing but baseball bats.

Axel Platzoff sat alone in the cramped little break room, building a matchstick model of the Reichstag and wondering about the role he would play in the coming conflict. Axel had been involved in wars before. He was a veteran of many conflicts—wars of secrets, wars of infinities, contested championships, invasions, onslaughts, civil wars and a seemingly endless series of crises. He wasn't even sure how many wars, but it was at least fifty-two. And they were always hard. Hard on survivors, harder on the dead.

A face floated up before his mind's eye. A kid of nineteen in a domino mask and a bad haircut. What had his name been? The Ghost something? Or the something Ghost? No one special. Just another cheap hoodlum with a weather controller and a limited understanding of bank security. Caught a piece of shrapnel when Baron Marianas' destructobot had detonated, back during the struggle over the Eclipse Glove in '94.

Sometimes, when he was sleeping badly, Axel could remember that look on the poor boy's face, the moment the penny dropped and he knew he wasn't going to make it. He could see the exact point where mocking, villainous sneer had vanished, and there was nothing left but a scared boy who knew he was going to die over a fucking *glove*.

Axel breathed deeply to calm himself. Ms Shan should call the head office and advise them just to close down the Pavilion. They'd do it. Do it in a second. They'd been looking for an opportunity. It would hurt the people who depended on the place for a job, but it wasn't like it *mattered*. The coming war was just the first catastrophe on the horizon. Even if the Pavilion got through that, there was a bigger disaster in the offing. Why not just let the poor, battered, bruised folk of the Pavilion go home? Enjoy their last months in peace.

Why did thinking that leave such a bitter taste in his mouth?

Never mind. Never mind the bitterness, never mind the worry. There was the craft. The craft would help. One matchstick after another. Simple. Occupying. It kept him on an even keel when the seas around were growing rougher. Forming shape of a building in his mind, and making it real with glue and pine. The faces of the past vanished, and for a while longer Axel was at peace.

Axel was somewhat aware of the door opening. It was Wellsey, but he didn't seem to be on his break. "Axel," he said. "There's someone here to see you."

Axel knew who would be there, so didn't bother looking up from his work. "Captain Stellar," he said.

"Hey Axel," Stellar said. His voice was quiet, awkward. "I, uh, I saw your Etsy store. A friend pointed it out to me. Don't think I ever saw a crocheted Henry Kissinger mask before."

The door closed, signalling the departure of Wellsey. Axel finally looked up. Stellar looked thinner than he had. His face was narrower and he sported a neat beard, the extra hair almost making up for the visible bald patch.

"What happened?" Axel said. "Cancer?"

Stellar laughed. "No. Just stopped working out. Stopped using that hair regrowth formula that Dr Wizardry made for me. I plan to act my age, and so I guess I should also look my age. I've quit, Axel. Quit for good. No more being a superhero. I meant... I meant to go back to it, you know? When I had my life sorted out... But people with sorted-out lives don't make great superheroes. Don't even *want* to be superheroes, not really."

Axel looked at Stellar as if seeing him for the first time. It struck him that of all the people in his life, he'd known Captain Stellar the longest. When had they first fought? Back in the late '80s, some time. An attempt to sell Lord Howe Island to North Korea… God, it seemed so silly now. The things you do when you're young.

"And please, call me Vincent," Stellar said. "Vincent Pizano. I'm a lawyer. I'm working for an LGBT community organisation now. It was a bit of a pay cut, but it's important work."

"Always the do-gooder," Axel smiled.

"Just can't help myself," Vincent said. "Anyway, your friend Wellsey… He figured out what was going on with you. And he figured out my secret identity. He's smarter than he looks, is what I'm saying. He told me that… Anyway, I came to say I'm sorry for messing with your head like that. It was… Look, you were being a dick, letting me take the blame for that explosion. You were being a dick, but my being passive-aggressive didn't help. It made things worse for you and for everyone, and I'm here to say I'm sorry."

Axel grimaced. Stellar was sincere. Of course he was. He was a hero, and sincerity was what he did. There was no doubt in Axel's mind that the apology was real and heartfelt. It still felt odd.

Stellar just seemed so… so ordinary, now. Standing there in his shirtsleeves in a white-walled break-room. When Axel had come to work at the Pavilion, that had been what he'd wanted. To walk away from the nonsense world of heroes and villains and just be a real person again. And here was Stellar… here was *Vincent*… who'd made it back to the real world before Axel had.

It looked like the Captain had beaten him. Again.

"You never did say why you did it," Vincent said.

"All those crimes?" Axel replied, absently. "The end goal was world domination, you see..."

"No, I mean why did you reform?"

Axel wrinkled his nose. "I'd just escaped from the Barrier Dimension. I was on the run, dodging Barriarite surveillance drones. Oh, it was bad, so bad. I was barely holding it together. And, just by accident, I ran into an old school friend. I thought he'd turn me in for the reward, but he had no idea I was a supervillain. Never was one for following current events. He saw I wasn't well. It was zelgonium poisoning, but he thought I was hungover. Bought me a coffee and a croissant, hah. He started telling me about his life... Not much of a life, honestly. Divorced, boring job, constantly passed over for promotion, behind on his rego... But nothing exploding. No friends trying to betray him, never getting mind-controlled or lost in a dimensional warp or thrown into his own death-trap. Vincent... Vincent, it sounded like heaven. I knew then I had to get out. To stop being evil."

"And become good?"

"Not at first, no," Axel said. "Not *good*. Just not evil. Maybe I should have been more ambitious, I don't know. But how do... How *do* you do *good*? How *do* you do the right thing?"

Vincent seemed to consider the question. "Are you asking me as a superhero or a lawyer?"

"Superhero. Definitely."

Vincent scratched his beard. "Hm. Well, even so, the

lawyer in me would like you to be more specific. But, ah, not so specific you incriminate yourself."

"There's a conflict coming," Axel said. "Who it's between doesn't matter. I've chosen my side, and I think it's the right one. But after that... Vincent, I was shown the future. Voyager showed me, the future Voyager. She showed me... Nalda... Fanaka. It's... I made a mistake, a huge mistake involving a pulley and Voyager showed me what happens next. The world is doomed. What does a little fight matter if there's something worse coming right behind it?"

"That's one way of looking at it," Vincent said. The door behind him opened, briefly. Someone looked in and quickly closed the door. A red-headed figure. Sadie MacGregor or Angela? Axel couldn't tell from the short glimpse.

"But look at it another way," Vincent continued. "If the world is doomed anyway, then there's nothing to be lost by fighting now."

Axel rubbed his head. "Sounds like a villain's way of looking at things."

"Yeah, I was pandering," Vincent said. "Look, you're not going to like this, but here's how it is: you already know what you're going to do. I can see that. You're worried about whether it's the right thing. Well, you should worry. Worrying about doing the right thing is the only way to make sure you *do* the right thing. But don't let that paralyse you. My advice: keep doing what you're doing, but just don't stop worrying."

"Isn't that a little pat?" Axel said.

"*Extremely* pat," Vincent laughed. For just a moment, he

looked like his old self—the laughing daredevil who had thwarted so many of Axel's plans. But then his smile faded, and there was no one there but a middle-aged lawyer. "Monumentally pat. Simplistic, bordering on the facile. But hey, you're new at this. Got to start you on the basics, you know?"

"I guess."

"So what are you going to do?"

"Do? I'm going to build some super-weapons," Axel said.

"Officially no longer my problem," Vincent said, quickly. "Take care. Be good."

"Take care," Axel said.

Vincent left, closing the door behind him. Axel pulled the plastic garbage bin over to the table and pushed his building in, then the matches, then the glue and his craft knife. He breathed in deeply, his skinny chest puffing up like an angry toad.

"All right," he said to himself. "Time for work."

## 47 Hearts and Skulls

Fanaka was beginning to feel an attraction to Nalda. This bothered him. He wasn't a stupid man, after all. He was a physicist with advanced training in transtemporal-dimensional topography, which is about as far from being stupid as you can get and, not being stupid, he knew perfectly well that Nalda was an emotionless, murderous cyborg. Even if he hadn't known that about her, sleeping on the sofa in her spare room had shown him quite a lot of warning signs. The impossibly neat piles of *Soldier of Fortune* magazine. The fact that no DVD in her collection didn't have a gun prominently displayed on the cover. The way her kitchen contained two dozen razor-sharp knives but no food. None of these suggested a person with a lovable nature.

Still, when the light struck her face in a certain way, it made her thin lips and square chin…

"Could you repeat that?" Marlon said.

Fanaka shook his head, bringing himself back to the present. He was seated in a small office on the other side of a beaten up looking MDF desk from Marlon. Damn it, he'd lost his train of thought. Nalda and Axel had given him so many tips to get through the barbarous ritual that the people of this weird future called a 'job interview', but he had forgotten them already.

Coughing, to imply that his vague answer had been caused by his throat, Fanaka said: "Well, sir, in that situation I would attempt to calm the customer, while walking her away from the affected area. I'd deploy one of those yellow 'wet floor' signs, and bring the matter to the attention of the Air Force."

"Air Force?"

"I mean Police! You do things so differently here."

"Where did you say you were from?"

"Nineteenth-century Nairobi, but in an alternate Afrocentric steampunk timeline."

"From… overseas," Marlon said, as he made a note. "And you're legally allowed to work in this country?"

"Oh... Uh... Let's go with 'yes, why not?'"

"Then we're good to go," Marlon said. "Congratulations, you start in Cleaning Products tomorrow. You're lucky; we're not really hiring at the moment. But we're kind of going onto a war footing and Nalda said you have some useful skills in that area. Welcome aboard!"

They shook hands and Fanaka left the office, which opened onto the Plumbing department. Wellsey shot him a disapproving look as he trotted over, past curtains, past carpets, to arts and crafts, to speak to Nalda.

Nalda was stacking plywood moneyboxes. She turned her head to look him in the eye, without ceasing her stacking. It should have been unsettling, but Fanaka found it endearing.

"They hired you?" she said.

"Yes, Nalda."

"Good. You will be able to spend more time here," she said. "If Laura was correct, then we have much to do, even if der Barn is defeated."

"I love your voice," Fanaka said.

"Vas?"

"We have a choice," Fanaka said, hurriedly. "The Laura who came from the future said a particular man buying a pulley would somehow set off a cascade of events leading to…"

He couldn't quite bring himself to finish the sentence. Neither could the stoic Nalda. "Ja, it leads to *dat*."

For a while, neither of them could speak.

"So we have to do whatever we can to prevent that timeline coming into being," Fanaka said. "But that means winning the war with the Barn first. My experiments… You see, this hardware shop is built on some sort of dimensional thingy."

"Thingy?"

"I'm not sure yet if it's a rift or a nexus. Precision is important. Could be a singularity? I just don't know. I think that's why I ended up here after my time travel accident, rather than in your world's Nairobi."

"That would have made a lot more sense if you think about it," Nalda said.

"A *lot* more sense."

Fanaka and Nalda both fell into silent contemplation for

a moment. Nalda cleared her throat. Fanaka looked at his shoes. Nalda cleared her throat again.

Somewhere in the distance, a cricket chirped.

"Anyhoo," Fanaka said, "like I said, this place is a dimensional deally, and it will be much easier to work if we can hold it."

"How do you know?" Nalda said. "About the dimensional vague noun?"

"Simplicity itself, my dear Nalda! My testing apparatus turned up some anomalous readings. I traced them to the glass skull which that oily young man in Power Tools uses as a paperweight. There's no way he could have known of its strange properties of course, so I borrowed it. Not only does it have some very strange dimension-distorting characteristics, but would you believe that it is impossible to remove from the Super Centre? It took all of my physical strength to get it out the door of the Handy Pavilion, and by no amount of effort could get it out of the Centre itself."

Nalda frowned behind her dark glasses. The creases in her skin... No! Concentrate, Fanaka, concentrate. "Christian is very possessive of that thing. You asked to borrow it?"

"No, but I left a note."

"Did you weigh the note down?"

Fanaka laughed. "How could I? I just took the paperweight... Oh. Hm. Well, I am done with my experiments. I shall return it with an apology, and I assume all will be well."

"Ja, that seems reasonable," Nalda said. She turned her head back to her stacking. "But look, this theoretical physics must not be our first priority. We must defeat the Barn. How are you in a fight?"

"I'm a lover, not a fighter," Fanaka said, his voice full of hope.

"Then you can help Axel with the weapons," Nalda said. "Perhaps some sort of phased plasma rifle in der 40w range."

"That would be vastly underpowered..." Fanaka said. "I mean seriously, 40w is barely..."

"Whatever, whatever. Just make something dat can kill people. Ach!"

Fanaka noticed that Nalda had put some acrylic paints back into their rack all out of order. Why would such a supremely efficient machine do such a thing? Unless... unless there was something on her mind. Something distracting...

"Nalda..." Fanaka said.

"Ja?"

"Would... when this is all over... would you... care..." Fanaka felt sweat on his brow. In his world, courtship wasn't a thing. Matches were arranged by parents, or at least they were among people of his class. And everything he'd learned about courtship on this world was weird and contradictory.

Still, Nalda probably knew as little about it as he did. How would she know if he got it wrong?

"Would you care to accompany me to some sort of social event?" he blurted.

Nalda stopped what she was doing. She didn't turn back to look at him as she said. "Ja. Maybe. Do you like monster truck rallies?"

"I don't know. I've never been to one," Fanaka said.

Nalda's head drooped a little.

"So you can tell me all about them," Fanaka said.

Nalda's head straightened. "Ja. Ja, maybe we do dat."

"Excellent. Well, we'll sort out the details later."

Fanaka marched off to Cleaning Products with a spring in his step and a song in his heart.

## 48 Timing

Sadie McGregor stood by a showerhead display and watched Fiona from a distance. The young woman was talking to a customer, an elegant woman in her middle thirties, who seemed confused about the differences between sink plungers. Sadie knew her assistant, Donna, had been talking to Fiona, talking to her about important things. Matters of guilt and honesty. Crime and punishment.

Light and dark.

"Timing, Sadie."

The voice belonged to her sister, the severely misnamed Angela.

"What about timing?"

"Timing is everything," Angela said. "Fiona is on the verge of confessing her role in the armoured car heist. This will inevitably implicate Axel. With him in prison, it will be very difficult for the Handy Pavilion to win this war with the DIY Barn. If only you'd pushed her harder, Axel would already be in prison, and Ms Shan could have planned for his absence. If you'd pushed more gently, she wouldn't be ready to go to the cops until after the dust had settled. You've lost the war for the Pavilion."

Sadie felt her lip curl into a sneer. She was good at sneering, and she knew it. And a sneer was the only appropriate response to her sister's goading.

"That is nothing to me," Sadie said. "It is not my concern who wins the hardware war. My interest is with how the conflict is conducted — not who emerges victorious."

"Hypocrite!" Angela snorted, stalking off. Sadie didn't watch her go. Why bother? It wasn't like she hadn't seen her twin leave in a huff before. Besides, Angela was wrong. It didn't matter to Sadie if the Pavilion lost to the Barn. Did it?

Sadie did not like doubt, and so she refused to feel it.

She took one final look at Fiona and her customer. The elegant plunger buyer would not have gotten her highly paid job if she hadn't lied on her resume. Sadie strode off, past a carpenter who habitually bullied his apprentice. She turned left at Garden Tools, where a welfare fraud and occasional car thief was looking at hedge trimmers. She passed thieves and liars, drunkards and addicts and who knew what else. For once she could not bear to look at their consciences.

She took a seat in the Pavilion café, hoping to see Norman. Of the three people involved in the armoured car heist, Norman was the most difficult to read. Fiona had never done anything criminal before, and predictably she felt the most troubled about her deed. Axel, the ringleader of the crime, had an enormously complex relationship with his conscience, but balanced against that was a lifelong commitment to never dobbing on his co-conspirators. Norman, though... Norman wasn't a bad person by any means. No one could say that about him. But he just seemed to have joined in a major crime as if it were nothing but a silly little joke, and what did that say about him?

Norman wasn't in the café. A greasy blue sign on the counter assured Sadie that he would be back at two forty-five. Since it was already five past three Sadie found it less than convincing.

"He's in the dunny," said the only other customer in the café, a burly old man with olive skin and a grey beard. "Probably trying to avoid me. That's why he's taking so long."

The old man smiled in what was probably intended to be a charming way. Sadie had a long-practised glare that could shut down any attempt at charm. It took a little longer than usual to make the old man drop his smile in favour of a neutral expression, but it worked in the end.

"I'm Norman's dad, by the way," the old man said.

Out of curiosity, Sadie tried to read the old man, to see what evil lurked in his heart. She saw nothing. Not 'saw nothing' in the sense of he'd done nothing wrong, so much as 'saw nothing' in the sense of invisibility. It was like he wasn't there.

"Oh, I get you," the old man said. He smiled—not a charming smile this time. More of a knowing smirk. "Yeah, that won't work on me, love. Things don't go like that where I come from." He hopped to his feet, spry for his age. "You want a coffee? Norman won't mind, and I'm sure someone like you won't skip out on paying."

Sadie watched with baffled interest as the old fellow

went behind the bar and started making cappuccinos. "My name's Zeus by the way, love. As in *the* Zeus. King of Olympus, and all that shit. Well, in title, anyway. The missus got the real estate in the divorce."

"I know of no God, but one," Sadie said.

"If you reckon," Zeus said, with a shrug. "Best things about being a deity? Theology is someone else's problem. You know, like how starfish don't bother to study marine biology. Now, what's your interest here?"

Sadie sighed deeply. She'd come here to take another look at Norman, to reconsider the question of whether his dark deeds ought yet to be brought to light. Because that was where Angela had it wrong. Even in the face of disaster, Sadie had a job to do, and that job would be done. But there was no reason that that job might not wait until things settled down.

"Your son was involved in a serious crime," Sadie said.

"Hercules had some problems when he was young," Zeus snapped. "But he's over that now. He's a pillar of the community. Besides, those records are supposed to be sealed... Hang on... Wait, a mo... You mean Norman? Serious crime? Huh. How about that? Didn't think he'd have it in him. Take a seat. How do you have your coffee?"

"I dislike caffeine," Sadie said. "And I believe I'll stand."

"Suit yourself," Zeus said. "And I'm not making some pissy herbal tea. You don't want coffee, you can go thirsty. So what did Normy do?"

"Armoured car heist."

The old man whistled. "What do you know? The boy

always tells me he doesn't like adventures. Good to see that he was lying."

"Are you trying to get a rise out of me?" Sadie said.

"I know better than that, love. Met your type before. None of you can handle a joke. Too black-and-white in your thinking. Now white-*is*-black... *that's* funny."

Sadie glared at him. "So, you'd laugh at a minstrel show?"

"Lady, you don't even want to *know* how lowbrow I can get," Zeus said.

"Your son's crimes must be brought to light," Sadie said. "They will be. Ideally, he will confess of his own accord, but if he is informed upon, that will suffice."

Zeus shook his shaggy white head. "You people! Minds of inquisitors behind faces like..."

"Faces like what?" Sadie said, feeling the muscles of her jaw tighten in spite of herself.

"I was going to say 'models,'" Zeus said, pursing his lips. "But what you *thought* I was going to say? That works too."

A man darted around the corner, a hat down over eyes that were already obscured with heavy dark glasses. Before either Sadie or Zeus could react, he ducked behind the counter and shed his obvious disguise, revealing himself to be Norman.

"No one looking?" he muttered, shrugging off the light jacket that covered his Handy Pavilion t-shirt. "Good to go! Oh, hey, Sadie."

"Hello, Norman," Sadie said, feeling the initiative

sliding ever further away from her.

"Okay, now, just so you know: I've been here for the last half-hour, okay?" Norman said to his father. Zeus nodded, an impressed-in-spite-of-himself look creeping up from under his beard.

Norman turned to Sadie and looked her square in the eye. "Okay?"

Later, Sadie would wonder again and again, just why she said what she said next: "Okay."

A second later she heard the explosion.

Norman grinned. "Now how's *that* for timing?" he said.

# 49 Another Newsletter

From the South Hertling Super Centre Newsletter November 27th, 2016:

## Explosion rocks Megacenter

by Harmony Sunshine, owner/manager EarthLife Health Store

Peaceful greetings! Unfortunately, Karl Wintergreen who usually makes the newsletter is still in hospital. I hope we are all sending our best thoughts and healing energy to him to help in his recovery. Hopefully, now that he is away from the hateful meat fumes from the kebab shop, he will be able to gather the necessary positivity he needs to actualise his own inner health, projecting it on his broken body. Until he gets back, I'm sharing newsletter duties with Barry from the other health supplement store, the one with all of the big jars of whey powder and what have you.

Anyway, there was a big explosion at the South Bannerman Megacentre across the street, you know, where that park used to be, back in the day. The DIY Barn over there was doing its best to deny rain to the soil by extending its carpark, when an asphalt spreader exploded, like the very planet itself was fighting back. The so-called 'incident' (if you can even *call* it that) happened when the workers were on one of the *few* work breaks that bloody Abbott von Turnbull hasn't abolished.

Work has been set back on the DIY Barn carpark by weeks at least, though in planetary terms that's just a blink of an eye. An eyewitness (ie, me!) was round between Carpets! Carpets! Carpets! and the Gulf of Carpet-eria when the explosion took place, smoking what, in a just world, would have been a perfectly legal substance, I saw a geyser of asphalt rise from over the roof of the Place O'Pets.

After crossing the road, I found a scene of confusion at the site of the alleged supposed explosion. When my attempt at restoring order through Tibetan chanting was rebuffed I said, "Okay, whatever," and stood back and watched them try to put out fires on the parking lot-making machines and shit.

Remembering that I was meant to do the newsletter this week, I decided to talk to the head of the DIY Barn, Mr Smith, who said "My car! My car! How did all this asphalt land only on my car?" The Earth Mother was targeting his karma, but he didn't get it. He was screaming something incomprehensible at the Handy Pavilion, and then he threw his hat at the ground and stamped on it like he was a sheriff in that movie with the truck. If he keeps getting that angry, it will seriously disturb his Chi.

~~Pigs~~ Police are treating the explosion as 'suss', but have ruled out terrorism. "We are looking into the matter," said Detective Sergeant ~~Badvibeson~~ Babbington. "We are particularly interested in how that guy's car got totalled. I mean, I think that stuff that gets tar off of tires only comes in small bottles right? And it costs a f-ing fortune anyway. By the time the owner of this car gets it tar free, he'll have bought so much of that shit he might as well buy a new car. Oh, and our investigations are proceeding, yadda yadda.

"As a personal aside," he added, "this is not what I expected when I joined the police. Could someone please just rob a bank, so I can chase them? Thank you."

I attempted to speak with DIY Barn's head of security, but he just pointed at me and screamed wordlessly. After five minutes of this, I left to calm my nerves with a bee pollen enema.

### Temporary Alterations to Traffic in Hurley Road

by Barry Wilberforce, owner/manager XtreemMaxPowerXtra Health Supplement Store

Oh yeah! South Hertling Council reports that it will be *blasting* the traffic lights on the corner of Hurley Rd and Crowe St! The current weak lights will be replaced by *three tonnes* of hard, solid *roundabout*.

"Traffic in the vicinity of the South Hertling Supercentre has been too puny!" is something similar to what that council said. "Seriously, it was time for that intersection to *step up* and *get real!"*

Since the *massive increase* of traffic to the **Supercenter** (and its wussbag neighbouring megacenter), the weary old traffic lights have become as useless as a ten-kilo dumbbell to a *real man*. The fact that they're as weak as some sunken-chested OH&S-lover has not gone unnoticed to Supercentre customers.

"Those lights suck, dude," said the first customer I spoke to with a respectable BMI. "A new roundabout will put hairs on that intersection's chest—and then *immediately* wax them off."

Disruption to Supercentre traffic is projected to be *minimal!* Way to go South Hertling Council! Keep *pushing that envelope!* I'm sure we'll all be *crying ourselves to sleep* in our *weird-smelling apartments* in the knowledge that you're on the job!

**Other Supercenter Newsletter News in this Newsletter:**

- Just Desks! Customer Already Dreading Assembling Purchase
- Gift Certificate Mislaid
- We Review the ~~Three~~ Four New Carpet Shops to Open in 2017
- Report: 90% of Storage Universe Purchases Used to Store Other Storage Universe Products
- Weird Looking Teenager Stands Outside Guitar Shop, Considering Options

# 50 Third Wheels and Fifth Columns

Claudia Liselle sat across the desk from Jasu Shan. Jasu sat behind the MDF desk in her little office, her fingers steepled in front of her. The office was small and while it had some very pleasant associations for Claudia, right then it seemed oppressive. It was airless and the only decoration was a small brass statute, a dying peace lily and one of those posters that are intended to inspire, but somehow only serve to bring the spirit a little closer to breaking.

"Officially, I can take no action," Claudia said.

"I understand," Jasu replied, and it was the worst thing she could have said.

If Jasu had argued, Claudia had arguments. If she'd shouted, Claudia could have stalked off in a huff. If she'd threatened, well, Claudia could have reminded her that she was in no position to make more enemies.

Instead, she'd simply agreed.

"If this... this war between the Handy Pavilion and the DIY Barn gets underway, that will be bad for the Super Centre. But if the Super Centre gets involved, that could bring the Mega Centre into the conflict, and who knows where that will lead?" Claudia said. She stood behind the rickety chair that faced Jasu's desk. There had been times when she'd been more comfortable in that room; much more comfortable. Now, the windowless, airless little space seemed like a prison cell. It took all she had not to fling open the door and run for safety.

"Of course," Jasu said. She did not meet Claudia's gaze. Her eyes were fastened to a little brass figure on her desk of a woman on horseback.

"I... I wish I could help."

"I know you do," Jasu said. "But let's be honest, an actual shooting war between hardware shops is a pretty unusual occurrence. And what do the other shops have to lose if the Handy Pavilion goes down? Nothing. But if they fight and lose, then they risk all. Karl from the stationary shop tried to help and he's struggling for his life. That's a warning to the others, as much as a call to action for us. Why are you standing? Take a seat."

Claudia sat, only part of her discomfort coming from the wobbly chair. "How is Karl, anyway?"

Jasu sat back and sipped at her tea. "His doctor tells me he was conscious for ten minutes yesterday," she said. "Apparently, that was enough time for him to explain the connection between the Knights Templar and the Banana Splits. The doctors think he'll recover—and I think they'd prefer that he does so as soon as possible."

"I'm glad he's out of the woods," Claudia said. "But Jasu... I... I don't want you to get..."

A knock on the door stopped her mid plea. It turned out to be big, bald Ali from Power Tools. His eyes flickered from

Jasu to Claudia and his cheeks darkened. Ali was usually polite enough to Claudia, but right then he was clearly making up his mind not to acknowledge her. Claudia sighed. That seemed to be a common reaction amongst Pavilion staff, to seeing their manager's lover. Frankly, Jasu didn't help, refusing to acknowledge the situation even though clearly everyone knew.

"Yes, William?" Jasu said.

"My name's Ali, miss. I found this," Ali said, holding out a scratched-looking mobile phone.

"Lost and found is behind the Key Cutting counter," Jasu said, without much emotion.

"Yeah, usually," Ali said. "I found it out back, in the loading dock. Figure it probably belongs to one of us or maybe a delivery guy. It's got a password, so I can't check who owns it."

"Maybe I can fix it?" Claudia said.

Jasu started slightly, looking up from her brass horsewoman. With no option to do otherwise, Ali looked at Claudia. She held out her hand and, after a moment's hesitation, he passed her the phone.

"Used to manage a phone repair place," she said. "Learnt a trick or two. Battery's low, but I think it will hold up long enough for me to get in."

Ali looked impressed in spite of himself. "Don't you need a computer? USB cable, that sorta shit?"

"No, I know a trick with this model. It's not that hard to bypass the password. That's why they took it off the market. Hang on, it'll just take a minute."

The room was barely spacious enough for two people, and Ali was a big guy. He stood awkwardly in the narrow gap between the door and the filing cabinet.

"How are your people?" Jasu said.

"Goin' good, Ms Shan," Ali said. With the change of subject, Claudia noted, he stood up straighter and spoke more certainly. "Been drilling the fu — the fellows in unarmed combat after hours. They're getting better, mostly. Keep trying to tell Belinda not to go below the belt. Save it for the Barnlings, yeah? But she won't listen, she's a vicious b— Uh... battler. Vicious battler."

Ordinarily, this would have annoyed Claudia, but honestly, she had too much on her plate to care, what with her love preparing herself for war and the fact that the reset button on the phone seemed to be damaged, requiring extreme finesse to engage it with a paperclip. But if she could make it happen... that was the weak point of that model of smartphone, the short-lived Yonggary 1000. Once you'd engaged the reset, you had a second in which to swipe the screen, bypassing the password. Once the phone turned on again, it would go straight to the main screen.

"Belinda?" Jasu said. "Ghanian woman with a wooden leg?"

"No, Ms Shan," Ali said. "That's... Uh... Actually, we don't have anyone here like that."

"And any sign of that missing guy?"

"Christian? No, Ms Shan," Ali said. "I thought maybe those Barn cu — cowards, those Barn cowards might of got him.

But Buck Dusty says he spoke to Chris just before he left and reckons he's a deserter."

"Well, technically, what happened is he quit without notice," Jasu said. "Which, as a casual employee, he's perfectly entitled to do."

"One way to look at it," Ali said.

"It is the legally correct way of looking at it."

"Legally, hardware shops don't go to war, Miss."

Perhaps that was why, Claudia thought, she was having such a hard time processing this. Because what was going on was not... a thing. Not a usual thing, anyhow.

"Got you, you fucker!" she shouted.

"Ay! Language!" Ali snapped.

The reset window popped up and she swiped frantically until the 'Yongarry' exit screen lit up.

"Let's see... Oh! It's Christian's phone!" Claudia said. "Selfie of him and that scull as a wallpaper. Yikes, I know he liked that thing, but... Phone's on very low power."

"Must of left it when he run away," Ali said.

"Maybe. But then why wouldn't he come back to get it?"

Jasu stood and walked around to Claudia's side, causing Ali to flatten himself against the door. "Are there any recent calls?"

"Isn't that an invasion of pr..." Ali began.

"Damn it, if Buck was wrong then Christian might be in trouble," Jasu said.

"Most recent call is a couple of days ago," Claudia said. "To a number labelled 'Mum'. Nothing recent in texts... Voice recorder app open? That's strange. Only one file... I don't think he used it much."

She looked up from the phone, to find both Jasu and Ali looking at her with deep concern. Which one was Christian again? It didn't matter. The Pavilion personnel shouldn't have been Mrs Liselle's concern at all. But somehow, they were.

Claudia hit play, and heard two voices talking. She recognised one of the voices as that of Mr Smith, the manager of the DIY Barn. "Who's the other guy?"

"Shh! It's Buck Dusty, ay?" Ali said. His face was frozen into a frown, and his hands shook like he was itching to punch someone. They all listened to the end in silence.

"They still want to kill Karl!" Claudia said.

"What happened to Christian?" Ali said.

"Buck is a traitor," Jasu said.

Yes, Claudia thought. That was probably the most significant takeaway from that.

"Well if Buck doesn't know we're onto him, we can use that to our advantage," Claudia said. "We can feed him false information. Follow him to see who he talks to."

"Or bash his fucking face in," Ali said, his face darkening, his hands trembling.

"Or that," Claudia conceded.

"Ali," Jasu said. "Where's Buck now?"

In a second, the blood drained from Ali's face. "He's on bodyguard duty, miss," he whispered. "He's looking after Axel!"

The room was small. The chaos caused by all three of its

occupants running out the door at the same time was considerable—but they got to Axel just in time to save him.

Or rather, *originally* that was how it worked.

Later, Mrs Liselle found it very difficult to reconcile her recollection of very definitely stopping Buck and saving Axel, with the certain fact that things had quite certainly gone very wrong indeed.

# 51 Betrayed

Axel didn't work much, in those days. Or, at least he didn't work much at his actual job. He arrived a little before the start of trading, took what materials he required from the shop floor, and retired to what used to be the staff lunchroom.

The staff ate outside and seldom complained. The lunchroom was for Axel's work now. On the Formica table in the middle of the room sat an extraordinary arrangement of timber and steel. It was designed to look like a found-material sculpture suitable for a large garden, but work like a military-grade automatic weapon.

Fanaka was already hard at work when Axel arrived. He was a brilliant engineer, and Axel appreciated the help. Unfortunately, Fanaka lacked something as a weapon designer. Killer instinct, perhaps?

(But then, how many people had *Axel* killed? *Really* killed? Not shrunken or frozen or propelled into another dimension or turned into bandicoots. How many people had he made run-down-the-curtain-and-joined-the-choir-invisible *dead*?)

"Hello, Axel," Fanaka said. "Been ironing out some of the kinks in this anti-aircraft gun. Turns out, we were nearly there. Just needed more tension on the occy straps that drive the secondary kerosene pump. But one question..."

"Ask away."

"Why do we need an AA gun?"

"There have been reports of gliders," Axel said. "The Barn has been sending them up for low-level night-time surveillance. Cunning. Nalda and I have been running an RF blocking system to prevent them from using drones. Gliders, though... silent and easy to miss if you aren't looking for them."

Axel couldn't help noticing the wistful look that crossed Fanaka's face when he mentioned the name 'Nalda'. This was not a time for love. The man was soft.

(As a villain, Axel had worked alone, so he'd definitely never done that thing where he murdered one of his own henchmen, just to show how evil he was. Oh, wait... he killed Captain Antarctica that one time, didn't he? But she'd been up and about again in under a month, so probably that didn't count.)

"You mean to shoot down surveillance gliders?" Fanaka frowned.

"No," Axel said. "Ms Shan has been organising some canvas decoys to feed false information to the glider spies. You know, like that fake army they made in World War II to confuse the Nazis... Oh, sorry. I keep forgetting you come from an alternate timeline."

"I think I know what you mean, though," Fanaka smiled. "We did something similar when we were retaking

Ghana during the Third Aztec War."

(Surely *someone* died during one of Axel's crimes. He'd attacked Brisbane with mutant starfish. Twice. That had to kill *somebody*.)

"Okay, well if we're happy with the AA gun, perhaps we should move on," Axel said, checking a clipboard. "Let's see... earthquake ray has been vetoed as 'likely to cause collateral damage.' I guess that means we're moving onto ramping up the power on those nailguns."

There was a knock on the door. Fanaka tossed a tarpaulin over the AA gun as Axel answered it.

"Yes?"

"Just me, sir. Buck Dusty."

Axel let Buck in. He carried two cups of coffee and wore a Stetson hat, faded jeans and leather chaps as well as his Handy Pavilion shirt.

"You're on guard duty for today?" Fanaka said.

"Yes, suh."

"Good man."

Axel looked from Fanaka to Buck and back again. Buck was not soft. Axel had never seen Buck commit even the smallest act of violence, but you only had to see the man's eyes to know. If Buck ever did come to kill a man, he'd never lose a second's sleep over it.

(The Human Sea Wasp! A fellow villain. Axel had shot him in the head, point-blank during the BloodSlaught, back in '99... No. Wait. That turned out to be a robot duplicate. Damn it!)

"I was about to say, Axel," Fanaka said. "I have this interdimensional energy source. It's Christian's I think, but since no one's seen him lately I don't think there's a problem in our using it."

"Interesting. Use it for what?"

Fanaka shrugged. "Make a teleporter device? Walk right past the Barn perimeter. Or gather power from outside our universe, bypassing the laws of conservation of energy. Or, if things get bad, we could just summon Cthulhu."

Axel lit a cigarette. "Last I checked, the Great Devourer was *not* taking my calls. Let's see this thing."

Fanaka reached his hand into a brightly-coloured woven bag. When it came out, it was holding a crystal skull. Axel sucked his breath in so hard, that it drew his cigarette into his mouth until it burned his lip. He coughed it out into the sink, aware that someone was pounding on his back. When he stopped choking, he looked around to see a very worried Fanaka, while Buck was trying to dislodge an ice-cube tray that was locked into the bar fridge by a crust of frost.

"Fanaka, that's... Holy crap! I haven't seen one of those since... I thought they were destroyed when... The power, Fanaka! The power! Even the power of Magalagenica, the Star Cluster that Walks Like a Woman couldn't... Shit."

"Axel, you're babbling."

"Fanaka, the power you hold in your hands could crush worlds and rewrite time," Axel said. He grabbed the ice-cube tray from Buck, shook out a cube and pressed it against his burnt tongue. "Improp'ly used, it could burn cont'nemts...

deftroy milliyes."

"And if *properly* used?"

"If properly used, it *wouldn't* do that," Axel said. "That's what 'properly' means."

The door opened wide. Axel, Buck and Fanaka looked up as one. It was only Sadie McGregor, her usually austere white face had flushed red, and her auburn hair had escaped its tight bun.

"Axel, the police are outside," she said. "It is about the armoured car heist."

The horror of seeing one of the skulls had taken all of Axel's attention and he hadn't been in the least self-conscious about forming the centre of a Stooge-like tableau. That changed rapidly, and he felt the blood rush to his face. He stood up straight, dusted himself down and placed the ice-cube tray on the table with an ostentatious flourish.

"Armoured car heist?" he said. "That was months ago! Are things... Don't tell me crimes are *still* illegal even when you committed them *in the past*? That hardly seems fair."

"'Fraid so, Prof," Buck drawled. He seemed oddly pleased, Axel thought. He filed that fact away for later consideration.

"And you on parole and everything," Buck continued. "Even if they can't convict, it ain't lookin' good."

"Oh, no," Sadie smiled. Axel realised he'd never seen her smile before. This was just as well because apparently, her smile was a horrible manic rictus. "No, no, no. No, you shall meet justice, Axel, yes, sweet justice. But not yet, no. No! Justice delayed is justice denied, no you shut up! You!"

"Uh…" Axel said.

"I confessed," Sadie said. "I confessed to the heist. No worries. The greater good. The greater justice. The Barn must not prevail, no, no. The weight is lifted from you and Fiona and Norman. I take that burden, and I shall carry it for you. No, a lie! A lie! Yet how can I not? Others carried greater burdens, greater sins for the good of all. Can I do any less?"

She stopped talking and stared twitchily at Axel. Even without seeing them, Axel could feel Buck and Fanaka staring at him too. For reasons that were not entirely clear, dealing with Sadie's meltdown seemed to be his responsibility. Still, he *was,* after all, one of the most intelligent human beings ever to be born. Shouldn't be too hard to think of something.

"Er…" he said.

Axel felt Fanaka's arms propelling him out the door. He didn't know why, until he saw the uniformed policemen, and heard the door close behind him. Yes! Hide the weapons. Good call.

"We're looking for a Sadie McGregor?" said one of the cops, a burly sergeant.

"Me!" Sadie said. "I am guilty. Take me away!"

"Caution this woman, constable," the sergeant said. "Who are you three?"

"Co-workers," Fanaka said. "Surprised, baffled co-workers."

The sergeant looked at Axel more closely. "Don't I know you?" he said. "Yeah, reckon I do. You're Professor Devistato, aren't you? See that?" The sergeant rolled up a blue sleeve. "I got that scar during your acid attack on Dapto."

"But you didn't die," Axel said. Damn it, had anyone died in one of his attacks?

"Guess I didn't," the sergeant said, unimpressed. "You on parole, Devistato? Well, I'm glad you're on parole in *my* neck of the woods. You set one foot out of line, and you'll be back at the Bay before you can count ten."

"Axel!" a frantic voice called. "Axel!"

Axel looked away from the sergeant, to see Ms Shan, Mrs Liselle from Centre management, and Ali from Power Tools, all jogging towards him. What was happening? Was the skull cursing him? He hadn't even touched it yet. Did that seem fair?

Buck grabbed Axel by the shoulder and leaned in, his mouth close to Axel's ear. The move suggested friendly advice, so Axel stayed still and listened:

"I work for the DIY Barn, Axel," Buck whispered. "Helped 'em capture Zorbar, and helped 'em capture Christian. Been reporting to 'em on your work, too. Told 'em *everything!*"

Buck let go of Axel and stepped back. Time seemed to stand still. Axel was aware of what was going on around him, but only in a distant way, as if what he was seeing was nothing but a vivid memory. Sadie was being cuffed. The sergeant was snarling. Ms Shan and the others were quickening their pace. Fanaka, opened mouthed, had one hand on Axel's chest, trying to hold him back. For a second, it could have gone either way.

Then Buck winked.

The next thing Axel was aware of was a pain in the knuckles of his right hand, and Buck Dusty sitting on the concrete floor, blood running from his smirking lip.

The sergeant's snarl turned into a warm smile. "And you, my friend, are under a-bloody-rest!"

"Good one, Axel," Sadie muttered.

# 52 Incoming!

Seamus the Gnome no longer made his life a secret. He couldn't really. There were just too many people in the Garden Centre when the full moon rose and brought him to life and he just couldn't be bothered to hide from them anymore. Besides, one of the late-night gardeners already knew him. Was that his name? Wellsey? Something like that

Whatever his name, the old feller wore a plastic safety hat that some keen artist had painted in camouflage colours. He stood in the gap between the impatiens and the camellias, right next to a huge thing of cast iron and bamboo that looked somewhere between an ugly garden ornament and a surprisingly attractive anti-aircraft gun.

Beside Wellsey was a young woman, also in a hard hat, scanning the skies with a pair of binoculars. A young man was also supposed to be watching the skies, but his work here was hindered by frequent breaks to look at the young woman.

"Saints preserve us, and what's going on here?" Seamus said.

"Oh, it's you, Seamus," Wellsey said. "Laura, Carlos, this is Seamus."

Laura grunted a hello, and Carlos stared, boggle-eyed at

the gnome.

"Whoi not take a picture? Sure and it'll last longer!"

"Stand down Carlos," Wellsey said. "He's one of ours. I should have warned you, I forgot he comes to life under the full moon. How have you been Seamus?"

"Inanimate, thank you very much. But yer ain't said what's going on?"

"Ack-Ack gun."

Seamus looked into the end of his pipe. He picked a twig from the ground and with it he cleaned out the bowl. "Go on," he said.

"We're worried about an aerial attack," Laura said. "And we think they'll use the full moon's light to their advantage."

"I see," Seamus said, raising his pipe to his eye to inspect his work. Finding it wanting, he went back to cleaning.

"So we're waiting here in case they attack," Carlos said.

"Sure, and that was implied," Seamus said, sticking the stem of the pipe back in his mouth. "Now d' thing is, y'see, the thing is... Why is a hardware centre about to bomb another hardware centre? Ain't dat... a little... you know... feckin' insane?"

The gunners looked at each other, then back to Seamus. "You kind of had to be there," Carlos said.

"Faith and bedad!" Seamus said. "Well, sure and if you're right, I'm in wit' ye. Won't have 'em causing no trouble with me plants, so I won't. I got good eyes and better ears and I stand ready to help."

Wellsey squatted down and laid a calloused hand on Seamus' little glazed shoulder. "Thanks, mate. I'm bustin' and I didn't think anyone would be relieving me for another hour."

As he marched off — double, or possibly triple time — Seamus climbed up the AA gun and sat behind the target finder, fighting the urge to make machinegun noises.

Carlos stared at him, his round face full of wonder. "So you're a living gnome?"

"If ye call dis livin'."

Confusion replaced wonder in Carlos' features. "I mean, you're like a garden gnome somehow animated? Are you, like, an actual gnome? A spirit being? Or..."

"No, no, I'm a very tiny golem, so I am," Seamus said. "One o' dem Jewish priests..."

"A rabbi?"

"No, one up from dat," Seamus said. "Like a Jewish monseigneur, or maybe a bishop. He put a spell on me, so's I can protect the Prague ghetto. Guess it ain't as big a job as it once was, so and it ain't."

Confusion fled Carlos' face, to be replaced with the look of a man who wants to call someone a liar, but is only ninety-five percent certain that he's right. It was a very specific look.

"I'm going to see what's keeping Wellsey," he said, walking off.

Seamus looked up at Laura, who looked down at him wryly.

"You know I was just pulling his leg?" Seamus said.

"Yeah," Laura said, going back to her binoculars.

"You're a Type III mineral animate, probably the result of excessive Class 2 mystical energies in or near the manufacturing facility you come from. Golems are Type I mineral animates."

Something about this response irritated Seamus intensely. "Sure, you're Voyager, the superhero."

"You do have good eyes," Laura said. "Most people can't spot that. No idea why that is, exactly. I only wear this tiny little mask. You'd think people could tell, but."

"Oh," Seamus said. "So why don't you just go smash up the DIY Barn with yer powers?"

"Rules. Being a superhero doesn't work like that. Besides, I need to save my strength for…"

"You know that Carlos is sweet on ye?" Seamus said.

Finally a reaction. Laura put her binoculars down, then quickly put them back to her face. "You think so?"

"I think so. What's more, I think you're sweet on him."

Laura twitched very slightly but said nothing.

"Ah, big people!" Seamus laughed. "You can't do nothin' without some sort of drama. Here's an ideal situation — all parties want the same thing. So what do yer do? Do yer say great, 'we all want some, so let's have sex with our weird meaty genitalia?' No. Yer gets feckin' paralysed."

Laura turned and glared at him, but whatever she was about to say was interrupted by the return of the boys, adjusting their belts as they passed the azaleas. Laura narrowed her eyes at Seamus, who beamed at her, his teeth pearl white against the brown enamel of his beard.

"Thanks, Seamus, I needed that," Wellsey said. "We're being relieved around midnight, but I needed some relief before then, if you know what I mean."

"Faith and... shhh!"

The big people fell silent as Seamus cocked his ear. "Incoming!" he said in an urgent whisper.

A black shape darted in front of the moon and was gone into the black.

"Glider," Wellsey said. "Too fast! Axel said if they were carrying explosives or something, it would slow them down."

"When did he say that?" Laura asked.

"When they were shovin' him in the back of the police van," Wellsey said. "I was taking notes. He was doing his villains voice. Never heard him do that before. It carries well."

"That's for sure," Laura sighed. "Uh... I've heard."

"That's impressive, hearing a glider," Carlos said. "Those are some good ears."

"Sure, and I heard no glider," Seamus said. "I heard *that*."

The others could hear it now, the low rumble of propellers over the rear wall of the Garden Centre, somewhere behind the cast iron wall-art and mounds of faux-Tuscan pots. It was over the wall in a moment—a silvery cigar-shape, perhaps the size of a large bus.

"Okay," Wellsey said. "Okay. Fucking seriously. I mean... Okay."

They all watched a little longer as the airship struggled forward.

"How strong d'ye reckon that headwind is?" Seamus asked. As he turned to ask the question, he noticed that Laura and Carlos were holding hands.

"Two knots, maybe," Wellsey said. "Barely a breeze. Well, no rush, but we should probably aim that AA gun."

Laura and Carlos began cranking handles on the gun furiously, while Wellsey stood behind and watched the airship through the viewfinder.

"Steady," he said. "Steady. All right, got it in sight. It's moving backwards a bit, reckon the wind is picking up. I think we can just about hit it. It'll land in the Place O'Pets loading bay, I reckon. Whoever's inside it won't fall far. Just need to pull the trigger. You want to do it, Mr Gnome?"

"Sure and why not?" Seamus said.

"Just press that," Wellsey said, gesturing to a doorbell button glued onto the back of the contraption."

"By all the Saints, today is a foin day to be alive!" Seamus said, pressing with his whole right hand.

The gun was surprisingly quiet as it spat a stream of glowing projectiles at the tiny airship. The blimp's envelope caught fire immediately, the bright flames spreading rapidly across its front section. A silver-clad man threw himself from the tiny one-man gondola but, as Wellsey had said, he didn't have far to fall.

"Shit," Wellsey said. "Just thought I'd puncture it. Let the helium…"

Wellsey never finished that sentence. With a damp, wet 'thump!' the burning blimp exploded.

"Don't reckon that was helium," Seamus said. Something burning caught his eye, and he looked upwards to see some piece of airship descending towards the gun. Instinctively, he leapt for safety in the sturdy branches of a nearby fiddle-leaf fig. Wellsey staggered backwards too, as the piece of burning metal came down like a falling star into the mechanism of the gun.

Seamus watched, horror in his ceramic eyes as Carlos leapt towards Laura. Probably he meant to push her to safety, but Seamus heard several of his bones break as he collided with her invulnerable body. She swung him away, shielding him from the gun. That was the last Seamus saw before the explosion threw his tiny body towards the Garden Centre wall.

The last thought that passed through his head before impact was: "Sure, and it'll be another four weeks before I even know if I feckin' died."

## 53 Inside Your Mind

"So," Fiona said.

"So," Norman said.

They sat at a wicker table, just by the plastic jerry cans in the Outdoor Furniture section. Not that long ago, Adam would have chased them away, but even he'd stopped caring. A grim, defensive mood had settled over the Handy Pavilion and customer numbers were at an all-time low.

"It's just *that* sort of a bloody morning, isn't it? Norman said.

"We have to give ourselves up," Fiona said. "We can't stay free while Sadie takes the blame for the armoured car heist. There's not even any reason for her to go to prison anymore. She was only confessing to save Axel."

"You got to remember," Norman said, "there's a bunch of shit to run through before Sadie is convicted. Yeah, we really should turn ourselves in, to free her. But right now, the Pavilion needs boots on the ground. We might not be as important as Axel in the grand scheme of things, but with Christian, Sadie, Axel and poor bloody Carlos out of the running..."

Fiona's head sunk into her hands. "So what are we

going to do?"

"Keep fighting until the fight is over. Then we can afford to think of ethics."

Fiona gestured around the empty store. "Why? What's the point? We've already lost everything worth fighting for. We've lost. Why does no one see that?"

Norman rubbed his eyes and swore. "What do you want me to say? 'You only lose when you give up' or something? I'm not a fucking motivational poster. All I know is a lot of people took a hit just so we'd still be here to take on those DIY Barn pricks. Are we going to win? Don't know. Probably not. But I'm not letting my friends down."

Fiona glared at him. "You know, Ms Shan will never want you. No matter how much you sacrifice for her."

Instantly, Norman's olive face went bright red. "Yeah. I know that. I'm not stupid. Of course, I know that. And you know what? It doesn't change anything. All right? It doesn't change anything at all."

"Excuse me," a well-dressed male customer said.

"Mate, you must be the only customer in the store," Norman said. "Can't you find another staff member?"

"Honestly? I'd love to. I'm looking for a guy named 'Christian' in particular. Been trying to find him for the last two days. Point me to him, and I'll be on my way."

"Christian is MIA," Fiona said.

"What does that mean? He on leave or something?"

"No, literally MIA. We think he's been captured by our enemies in the DIY Barn, but…"

315

"It's not *just* that I don't care," the customer interjected hurriedly. "Not caring implies a lack of interest. What I have is something like anti-interest. I actively don't want to know, you know? It's like I'd be offended if you told me. Look, forget Christian, he's not important. I just have to fix his crystal skull situation. Once I've taken care of my side of the contract I can move on. Christian can go to Hell."

Fiona and Norman looked at each other and shrugged.

"I have no idea what you're talking about," Norman said. "But last I saw that skull, Fanaka had it. I'll go see if it's still with him."

Fanaka was in the staff room/armoury. The customer, Mr Pennington, was left at the door as Norman and Fiona went in to see him. Fanaka was red-eyed and twitchy—both things probably related to the dozens of empty coffee cups that littered the room.

"Oh, hello, hello, Forman and Nioma, yes. Finished repairs on the AA gun, yes, all done."

"Are you okay, Mr Fanaka?" Fiona said.

Fanaka gave a broad smile and pulled back his hunched shoulders to show that he was fine. The effect was undercut when he replied in some unfamiliar language for several sentences before realising what he was doing.

"Fine..." he said, switching back to English. "Perfectly fine. Axel getting arrested was a setback, that's all. I can take care of his side of things, as well as my own."

Fiona glared at Norman, who ignored her. "Do you still have that glass skull that Christian used to have?"

"Oh, yes, yes," Fanaka said. "It's right here!"

He gestured at a bathroom cabinet, on top of which was part of an industrial workbench. Clamped into the jaws of the workbench was a thick length of copper pipe, in which was nested several narrower lengths of pipe. A flexible length of silvery shower hose ran from the cabinet to the end of the pipe. Fanaka opened the cabinet to reveal the glowing Skull.

"That some sort of death ray?" Norman asked.

"Probably," Fanaka said with a handwave. "No time to test it, no time, never time... Kuna tu si masaa ya kutosha katika siku..."

Again, Norman and Fiona exchanged glances. It was that sort of morning.

"It's a focused R-Beam emitter," Fanaks said. "Powered by a sort of pan-dimensional-artifact-crystal-skull-deally-o. Axel had some issues with using it, but he got arrested before he could say why."

"Well, can we borrow the skull?" Fiona said. "Seems like one of the last things Christian did before he vanished was ask this alchemist guy to use it to rescue his friend from some sort of dimensional prison."

"I didn't follow any of that after the word 'skull.'" Fanaka said. "But I can't let you borrow it, it's a thing of unimaginable—dare I say, unspeakable..."

"Oh, please?"

"Okay, fine. But don't scratch it."

Norman watched as Fiona carefully removed the skull from the nylon clamps that held it in place. "Are you sure this is a good idea?" he said. "We're sure this guy doesn't work for the Barn or nothing? I mean, maybe that's why they grabbed Christian in the first place? To get their paws on this?"

"I don't know," Fiona said. "It's not that I trust Pennington it's that... it's his story. *He* rings false, but *his story* rings true, somehow. Like it's the last thing you'd come up with if you were trying to lie to someone."

"Yeah, whatever," Fanaka said. "Just take it outside."

Pennington stood outside, impatiently tapping his foot. "Right. Let's do this. Open portal to skull's internal dimension, pull Christian's friend out, get the fuck out of here, and start shopping at that other Handy Pavilion in East Westville. Let's get started."

The alchemist placed the skull on the floor in the space between the concrete planters and self-watering pots, just opposite fertilizer. Taking a stick of chalk from his pocket, he drew a circle around the crystal and began silently dancing around it, his arms and legs describing strange angles in the air as he moved.

"My God, it's true," Norman whispered.

"What?"

"All those black people were right. We really *can't* dance," he said, grinning as Fiona smacked him in the arm.

Pennington finished dancing. "Right, that should do it. Dimensional bridge formed. Now it's just a case of Christian's friend finding the door."

"The door... to the bridge?" Norman said, raising an eyebrow.

"Mate, nobody likes a smartarse," Pennington said.

And then, with a pop, a large pile of black rags was sitting on the concrete.

"Done and dusted," Pennington said. "You see Christian, you tell him 'contract concluded'. And if you want to add something about him fucking himself, that would suit me fine. Goodbye!"

"What a wanker," Norman muttered as Pennington stalked away.

Fiona nudged the pile of rags with the toe of her boot, but jumped back when the pile moved. Groaning, it rose to its feet, a stocky figure in the filthy remains of a black velvet cape. As the rags resolved themselves into a human shape, Fiona gasped as she recognised the battered black hat that sat above the bone-white mask that covered the newcomer's face.

"The Phantasm!" she squeaked.

Norman swore. "This just gets weirder and weirder."

The Phantasm staggered groggily, leaning a hand against a shelving unit to stay upright.

Fiona looked at Norman. "You want to do it?"

Norman grinned. "Nah, you give it a go. You deserve some fun."

Fiona cleared her throat. "Let's see who you really are!" she beamed, snatching the mask from the Phantasm's face. "Gasp... It's... Gwen Harper? Wow. I should have gasped for real. That's genuinely surprising."

"Seriously?" Norman said. "Gwen?"

It was Gwen. She had a big scar that ran from above her

right eyebrow to her left cheek, and there were a number of smaller scars besides. But it was still recognisably her.

"And I would have got away with it too," she said, coughing something nasty onto the floor. "If it weren't for the sudden and unexpected collapse of my secret pocket dimensional headquarters."

Norman and Fiona exchanged disappointed glances. Gwen rolled her eyes. "Fine! *And* you meddling kids. Now, where's Pennington? Got to get that arsehole before he gets to his car."

The Phantasm turned, her ragged coat failing to twirl impressively as she did. She took off at a run, made it three steps, and slowed to a limping walk.

"It's just been one of those mornings," Fiona said, giving gentle chase.

"You said it."

# 54 A Very *Mysterious Aisles*

# Valentine's Day

It was Valentine's Day. This is probably a big day if you work in a florist's, a jewellery shop or a high-end restaurant, but for most sections of the Handy Pavilion, it was just another day, though there were exceptions to this general rule. The Garden Centre was busier than it had been in months, selling pots and pots of flowers. And Nalda in arts and crafts was struggling to keep paper-mâché hearts and red paint on the shelves.

"Excuse me, miss, where's the pink glitter?"

"Over dere. Next year, buy champagne."

Nalda muttered to herself. As a killer cyborg from the future, she'd long since decided that not understanding love was a cliché, and so had taken care to educate herself on the subject. Now, love did make sense to her. It just seemed stupid.

Sex — now *that* made sense. Biological imperatives were similar enough to programming to be comprehensible. It was the fact that sexual congress required high levels of personal approval that confused her, and the fact this approval could be won by displays of dying flowers or second-rate craftsmanship. Romance made no sense at all.

A lot of the organisms that worked and shopped in the DIY Barn were using the day as an excuse to pursue both their romantic and sexual agendas. Mrs Liselle had gone into Ms Shan's office on the pretence of a business meeting and was still there two hours later. Adam was trying to look like he was comforting Donna from Lighting over the arrest of Sadie, but his body language made it obvious that he had other things on his mind. Laura had taken the morning off to visit Carlos in the hospital...

"There's no price on this paint-by-numbers MDF tissue box."

"It costs 12.99."

"That much?"

"Der nearest jewellery shop is about three hundred metres..."

"Okay, okay. 12.99 it is. Geeze!"

A guy with the beard—a man who Nalda's internal biometric database clearly showed was Captain Stellar—was talking to another bearded, middle-aged guy. Stellar was laughing out loud at jokes that were barely scoring 23% on Nalda's humour recognition module. This was a sure sign of hoping to get some.

"Excuse me, is this suitable for a beginner's skill level?" said another customer.

"Ja. No need to improve yourself as a human being for love's sake."

"Damn right!"

Captain Stellar finished exchanging numbers with the other guy and came over. "Hi, uh, I'm looking for a guy named Fanaka?"

A weird, heavy, angry feeling flashed across Nalda's CPU. What did this man want with Fanaka?

"My name is Vincent Pizano, and I'm a friend of Axel's," Stellar said. "Or is friend the right word? I'm more of a 'no longer an enemy.' And I'm his solicitor, which is why I was visiting him in prison. I was given a message to take to Fanaka."

Nalda felt herself relax, but only up to a point. There was something suspicious about this man, but she couldn't tell which of her modules this assessment had arisen from.

"I will get him."

"Great. I'll just wait here, shall I?"

"Ja and I'll be here," Nalda said. What was this experience? Was this what being 'flustered' was like? "When I return. You see, I will go there, then I will come here."

"So... you'll be back?" Vincent asked.

"You could put it that way, yes."

Hesitantly, Nalda walked off towards the break room, where Fanaka was at work.

"Have you finished with the Skull...? Oh, it's you Nalda. Sorry, thought it was Fiona and Norman again." Fanaka wiped the sweat from his brow with a paper napkin. "They were just here a minute ago. I think. Maybe it was longer. I'm so tired..."

There was a brief spike in Nalda's CPU load as she

fought off an urge to tuck him into bed. Singularity alone knew where *that* came from. Perhaps the DIY Barn was using EM radiation to weaken Handy Pavilion electronics? It deserved further thought.

"Fanaka, dere is a man to see you. He brings a message from Axel."

Sighing deeply, Fanaka stood, swallowed a cup of cold coffee and adjusted his Pavilion polo shirt. "Okay, then." He staggered a little as he stood.

"Are you sure you are all right, Liebchen?"

"Fine, fine. Uh, what does Liebchen mean?"

Microprocessors worked hard to manage the blood flow to Nalda's face, preventing it from visibly reddening. "It is German for 'platonic work comrade.'"

"Oh."

The pair trotted out to the arts and craft section where Vincent/Stellar was examining a balsa truck kit. He put it down guiltily and shook Fanaka's hand.

A customer called Nalda over. Her hearing was exceptional and she could easily home in on a particular conversation through the surrounding din. She chose not to do so. Whatever the reason this man needed to see Fanaka, it was none of her business...

"My husband collects wooden models," the customer said, "but I'm not sure whether to buy him this jet fighter or this helicopter."

"Get him der chopper!" Nalda snapped.

Fanaka waved Nalda over, and she was surprised at

how relieved she was at this. The scientist rubbed his red-rimmed eyes. "Vincent says Axel has been suggesting I step up work on the Skull powered device. He's sent some ideas for improving it. They'll need work to implement but... Damn it, they're brilliant. Could you and Vincent go find the Skull? I need to... Need to sit down."

Why on Earth wasn't the Skull in its proper place? Nalda had no idea, but chose not to say so in front of the lawyer. She walked off with Vincent, searching. The Skull was vastly powerful. How could Fanaka have let it out of his sight? Was he not feeling well? Did he need some Panadol? A lie-down? Maybe he needed someone to get him some soup and plump his pillows, or go back in time and kill someone. What did Vincent/Stellar want with Fanaka anyway?

Through narrowed eyes, she looked at Vincent.

"So, you are homosexual, yes?"

"That's right," Vincent said, a defensive tone in his voice.

"You people have it easy."

"Do we?"

"It is we killer cyborgs dat are der real oppressed ones."

Vincent stopped dead by a pruning saw display. "I don't know what to say to that."

"Huh."

Vincent shook his head to clear it. "Are there many killer cyborgs?"

"I am der only one in dis time period."

"Must be lonely."

Nalda wanted to argue, but nothing came to mind. Perhaps her vocabulary database was glitching.

"Well, you're lucky in one way, at least," Vincent said.

"I do not believe in luck."

"Call it what you want. I just wish I had someone who looks at me the way Fanaka looks at you."

"Red-eyed and bleary?"

Vincent laughed. "No, I mean he loves you."

Nalda's CPU almost melted down. "No... Yes... You think?"

"Could it be any more obvious?"

"But... I..."

A worried look filled Vincent's face. He placed a gentle hand on her shoulder. "But you're a killer cyborg and he's a genius from an alternate Afro-steampunk Earth? Sweetheart, I've got to tell you: I've seen stranger relationships work. Much stranger."

Her processes were in such disarray that she barely noticed the Skull, sitting in the middle of a chalk circle, right next to the mushroom growing kits. Most customers were avoiding it, except for a handful of fourteen-year-old boys who were watching it in case it did something interesting. Nalda pulled herself together and damped down her reactor temperature and blood flow.

"Well, here it is. Are there any precautions we need to take?"

"Nein, it is powerful but inert. Let me just get it—"

Nalda reached into the circle. As she did, there was a

326

flash of green light. The mushroom kit boxes split open, scattering spores to the floor.

For a few seconds, nothing happened. Nalda's optimism module even dared to consider the possibility that this was all that was going to happen. But then the spores sprouted into mushrooms and in a few seconds, the mushrooms had grown to the size of human beings, long white arms by their sides and mouths full of jagged teeth in their caps.

The teenagers applauded politely.

"I don't *do* this anymore!" Vincent sighed, his hands beginning to glow yellow. Energy poured from his fingers, and a mushroom man exploded. Bits of the mushroom fell to the floor, where they started growing into additional mushroom men.

Vincent swore loudly. "Oh, uh... I didn't say that," he said to the teenagers. "Don't use bad language. Get out of here. And say no to drugs!"

Nalda's brain went into overdrive. Combat! This was easy. She'd been programmed for this. Concussive force was out, so there was no point getting her shotgun. Fire? Yes, fire would do it, but it would have to be extremely hot and fast, or else the sprinklers would kick in, and who knew where that would lead?

"Nalda?"

Nalda saw Fanaka standing at the entrance to the aisle, confused and exhausted. Her tactical programming crashed at the sight. Her desire to destroy the enemy faded to nothing. None of that was important. Fighting, killing, dying... What mattered was getting this brilliant, beautiful man to safety.

Though Fanaka was a foot taller than her, she grabbed him by the waist and with hydraulic arms, she swept him off his feet. He looked at her blankly at first, too addled by tiredness and cheap coffee to know what was happening. Then his weary eyes closed and he wrapped his arms tight around her neck.

"I must be asleep. Asleep and dreaming the most wonderful dream!"

"Nein, Leibchen, this is no dream." Nalda turned and jogged away from the conflict. "Oh, Fanaka, come with me... if you want to *love!*"

# 55 Deliver Us Not

Donna cast an eye over the morning deliveries of light bulbs and sighed. She had never realised just how much work Sadie had accomplished, until Sadie hadn't been there. Now, even though business was poor and customers were thin on the ground, Donna could barely keep up with doing the work of her supervisor as well as her own. Marlon had given her some extra hours to try to deal with the workload, and Donna's studies were suffering. Still, she endured.

She endured because that was what Sadie would have wanted. Sadie never quit or gave in. Sadie's job had been shedding light on her customers, and that is what she had done. She had never wavered, never faltered. Not until the end. Not until she had fallen into darkness.

A lump formed in Donna's throat. Sadie had been a strict boss, but a good boss. She had taken Donna under her wing and helped her protégé overcome her crippling addiction to *gesui*—a form of Japanese pornography so terrible that it cannot be found, even on the internet. Sadie had taken her, a lazy, deceptive young girl and helped her become an upstanding young woman.

As she carted the light bulbs from the loading dock to

the lighting section, she noticed Fiona and Norman chatting in Outdoor Furniture. She sighed. At Sadie's suggestion, Donna had befriended Fiona, hoping to be a good influence on her. Donna hadn't realised just how lost Fiona had been, until Fiona had confessed her involvement in an armoured car robbery.

And then, Sadie—Sadie of all people, moral, upright Sadie—had perjured herself and taken the blame for the heist. It made no sense.

Donna's new duties left her little time for her friend. She hoped that hanging around with Norman wasn't a sign that Fiona wasn't going back to her larcenous ways.

It was worrying, and she didn't need worries on top of stress. Maybe some *gesui*…

No! No, that was the old Donna.

"Excuse me?" said a customer.

Customers. Always customers, getting in the way of her work. It was this fancy looking guy, looking for Christian. Somehow, Donna misinterpreted this as 'looking for Norman', so she pointed him the wrong way and the man was halfway to Outdoor Furniture before she realised her mistake.

It didn't matter. Norman probably had a better idea than she did of what Christian was up to, anyway. Besides, she was beset with another customer, a lumpy looking guy.

"I need lights."

"What sort?"

"Don't care. I just need a lot. Cheap ones, I guess."

"What for?"

The lumpy looking customer looked sheepish. "Well, it

used to be that all my chores were done by a brownie."

"Not like the girl's service group Brownies," he added quickly. "I mean a literal brownie. A benevolent pixie."

Donna sighed. Asking more questions wasn't going to get this guy's house lit any better, but he looked like he wanted to tell his whole story. "Like a house-elf?"

"Right, yeah. You're meant to leave a saucer of milk out for 'em, but never give them any clothes, I think that's the deal. It always seemed a little hard, you know? Brownie working so hard, but always dressed in rags. So I think, what can I do for the poor guy that doesn't involve clothes. When I saw him struggling with my washing line…"

A chill ran down Donna's spine. She stood up straight, bracing herself for the coming blow.

"So I bought him a pulley," the lumpy customer said. "And the Brownie hasn't run away, but he's gone all… funny. Dressing in black. Growing a goatee. Running an email scam from my laptop. You know? And all that creepy running around at night-time. You know the deal, giggling, a pattering run, vague shadow. That sort of thing."

Donna shook her head slowly. She tried to breathe, but even as her lungs clawed for oxygen, she felt like she was suffocating.

"You know… You do know that you must never give a pulley to a brownie, right? You know that if one is 'feeding Gremlins after midnight' and a ten is 'invite a vampire into your home', what you did is about a fifteen, 'the only thing that can stop Godzilla is a robot Godzilla?'"

The customer pondered this. "Shit, ay?"

In the pause that followed, a man with a neat beard asked to see Fanaka. "Ask Nalda in crafts," Donna said.

Once the man had left, she addressed the lumpy customer. "Why am I everybody's social secretary today? Ad for you, you are going to need all the lights you can get. And probably an exorcism. My supervisor could have done that for you. She was good at exorcisms. But, for reasons that need not concern us now, she's in prison for a crime that she did not commit."

"Well, I'll be jiggered."

Donna looked down at her hands, then up at the huge range of lights that surrounded her. Did she have the strength to do this? Did she have the unflinching resolve, the deep personal holiness, the spiritual strength, the *light?* Well, there was only one way to find out.

"I will exorcise the corrupted spirit," she said. "Give me your address. I will drive out the unclean thing."

"We'll get a new Brownie, yeah?"

"My guess is no."

"The wife'll be spewin'."

"I can live with that. Now go! Leave me to prepare myself."

The lumpy customer walked away. Donna looked over her pallet of unsorted deliveries. Over by her counter was a stack of incomplete paperwork. Down the end of the aisle, Zorbar was screaming as he fought a band of humanoid mushrooms. It was one of those days—and yet this was the day where she had to reach inside herself and find the strength to do what needed to be done.

"Hey, Donna."

It was Angela, Sadie's twin. Donna knew Sadie didn't like Angela, but never quite understood why. But knowing Sadie's distrust for her sister made Donna a little distrustful in sympathy.

"Angela. I'm a little…"

"Won't take a minute. It's just that I know you're into that manga stuff, and someone delivered this to me accidentally. Do you know what it is?"

She handed a magazine to Donna. Tentatively, she opened the cover and… Oh! What were those space aliens doing with that goldfish? Why was that naked man dancing on stilts? *Gesui*! It had to be *gesui*.

"Is it like a Pokemon thing?" Angela asked.

"No," Donna said through clenched teeth. "It's… it's a little more specialist. Do you want this?"

"Don't know why I'd need it."

"Can I…"

"Be my guest."

A blood-curdling scream rang out, echoing from the tin roof. Sounded like Zorbar had got hold of one of his assailants. Donna barely took it in. She was busy, caressing the cover of the little pulp-paper comic. Angela smiled and walked away, leaving Donna to her thoughts.

# 56 The Principles of Retail Management

Wellsey leant against one of the pillars that held up the lofty roof of the Handy Pavilion and sighed deeply. It was just one of those days. Marlon, leaning on the other side of the pillar, sighed even more deeply. From his jeans pocket, he took a hip flask, took a swallow, and handed the bottle to Wellsey. Wellsey shook his head. Marlon shrugged and slipped the flask away.

"You and Joyce got Valentine's Day plans?" Marlon said.

Something came hurtling over the nearest shelving unit. Part of a toilet? Something porcelain anyway. Both men ducked as it hit a nearby shelf, smashing a pile of paint cans, sending blue acrylic dripping to the floor.

"Nothing fancy," Wellsey said. "There's a Valentine's special at our local restaurant. Free bottle of champagne. And we don't get out as much as we used to. How about you?"

"Off to dinner and the movies with Faisal from the Hoonworld Auto."

Zorbar Ofthechimps appeared on top of one of the great

shelves, seemingly the result of having sprung there, barefoot, wearing nothing but the remains of a pair of chinos. A terrifying scream pierced the air as he leapt onto one of the enormous ceiling fans, grasping a blade with one hand. He adjusted the shining knife in his grip, raised it to strike, and swung off the fan and into some melee below.

"Faisal?" Wellsey said. "Isn't that a bloke's name?"

"Yeah."

"I didn't know you were gay."

"Pretty sure I'm not. Still, I don't reckon it hurts to check, now and then."

Wellsey wasn't sure what to say to that, but there didn't seem to be any reply needed.

Ms Shan came out of her office, her blouse buttons done up all crooked. "Are we under attack?"

"Looks more like an own goal to me, somehow," Wellsey said.

"What's going on?"

"Well, near as I can tell, some sort of magical ritual went wrong. I think Fiona and Norman are tryin' to sort out the wizard behind it. And Zorbar was visiting; he and some weird guy with glowy hands are fighting these extra-dimensional mushroom people."

"So why is Donna banging on the door to the bathroom?"

"Probably in a rush to get in. Don't fancy her chances, but. Nalda and Fanaka went in just as everything started going to Hell—and I don't think they're coming out any time soon."

"So why are you two just standing here?"

Marlon fielded this one: "It's a hot day, and this spot's right under a fan."

Ms Shan looked up and blinked. "Isn't that the Phantasm trying to saw through the fan's shaft?"

"Yeah, ut I reckon we've got a few minutes before she makes it through. Good to keep cool, you know?"

Mrs Liselle snuck out of Ms Shan's office and crept away. Wellsey pretended not to notice. He was pretty sure that everyone knew about Ms Shan and Mrs Liselle. What's more, he was pretty sure that the management women knew that everyone knew. Still, they seemed to enjoy pretending it was all a big secret, and Wellsey saw no need to stand in the way of their fun.

"And the customers?" Ms Shan said.

"Mostly evacuated," Wellsey said. "I think Adam organised it."

"He's a good bloke, that Adam," Marlon added.

"Salt of the Earth."

In the distance, a ray of yellow force radiated upwards, knocking a small hole in the ceiling. "Sorry," called a voice.

Ms Shan took a very deep sigh indeed. Marlon handed her the hip flask, and she took a huge swallow. "Very well. I guess I knew a day like this was coming." She sighed again. "This is why I get paid the adequate bucks. YOU! Phantasm!"

The black-clad Phantasm started at the shout, and began sawing more rapidly.

"Stop that, right now! I have no time for your nonsense.

336

Whatever it is you want from the Handy Pavilion, we'll sort it out in my office, one hour."

"Fool! Dare you think that I..."

"Do you *like* being dressed head to toe in black velvet in the middle of summer? Because if you don't, hmm, maybe you *should* negotiate?"

The Phantasm paused. Wellsey saw the sinister figure tuck the hacksaw under one arm, freeing both hands to grab a hanky and wipe the face beneath the white mask.

"I guess," the Phantasm said. "No promises, but..."

"One down," Ms Shan said. "You two: with me."

Wellsey felt like a tinny being dragged behind a river ferry as he followed along.

"She should have been taking charge like this months ago," he whispered to Marlon.

"I can hear you!"

"Really?"

"No, but I'm good at guessing. Hm. Let's leave the violence boys to take care of the fungus men... You! What's your name? Donna? What's that magazine?"

Donna went white, then red. "It's... I... I was weak."

"Give it here."

Wesley watched Donna's hand tremble as she handed the magazine to Ms Shan. Without opening it, or even looking at the cover, Ms Shan tore the cheap paper into a thousand pieces. "Better now?"

"Yes, thanks." Donna breathed a huge sigh of relief— though Wellsey thought it might have been tinged with a little regret. Hey, he'd been there himself, once. Though not, of course, concerning anything quite so filthy. He'd been into drugs, which are comparatively wholesome.

Donna followed along as well, as the little group made its way to the door, dodging debris as they went. Up close, the damage wasn't as bad as Wellsey had imagined. Zorbar and the other guy were doing a pretty good job of keeping the fight contained to Aisle 5.

At the doorway, whatever dispute this 'wizard' had with Norman and Fiona seemed to have spiralled out of control. The usually good-natured kids had grabbed hold of him and they were pummelling him badly. Fortunately for all concerned, it was Norman who had grabbed the fellow and Fiona who was hitting him. It would have been much worse if it had been the other way around.

"Enough!" Ms Shan cried. "What's going on?"

"Your staff were punching me!" the man said.

"Give them back! Give them back!" Fiona yelled. She seemed ready to begin whaling on the fellow again, but Wellsey shook his head at her. Fortunately, that was enough.

"This prick stole Gwen's ears!" Norman said.

"Gwen... Seven-foot blonde man with severe emphysema? Works in Safety Equipment?"

"No, that's Egbert," Norman began. "Gwen used to work in timber until this asshole took her ears. She went crazy and turned into the Phantasm."

Ms Shan looked at the so-called 'wizard.' "Well, Mr..."

"Pennington," Pennington said.

"Pennington. I don't take kindly to customers abusing my staff. If you'd be so good as to return the ears, we'll say no more about the matter."

Wellsey pursed his lips. He'd been in confrontations with authority figures enough times that he could see that Pennington had two choices: he could defend himself on the appropriateness of his actions or with the *inappropriateness* of Norman and Fiona's actions. The latter would probably give him a stronger leg to stand on...

"I bought those ears, and fairly."

A smile came to Wellsey's lips. Wrong call! He could feel it.

Ms Shan raised an eyebrow. Pennington continued. "In exchange for those ears, I sold her a potion that was supposed to make this lunkhead fall in love with her."

He gestured at Norman. In fairness, Wellsey thought, Norman *was* a bit of a lunkhead.

"Hah! I'm immune to all potions!" Norman said.

Pennington stopped struggling. "Really?"

"Yeah. And minor wands, but that don't come up as much."

"Huh."

"Seems to me that wasn't much of a deal, then," Ms Shan said. "Working ears for a useless potion. So where are these ears?"

"At home."

Fiona slapped him. It didn't seem like a particularly ferocious slap to Wellsey, but it seemed to cow the already confused Pennington into submission. "Okay, okay. They're in my car. Part of my SUV's homemade sonar drive system. Built it myself. Won't work once I disconnect the ears, you bunch of arseholes."

"Norman, go with Mr Pennington, and make sure he hands over the ears. I'll give them back to the Phantasm, and that should be the end of that."

Across the wide front aisle of the Barn, Wellsey saw Zorbar — battered, bleeding, but grinning triumphantly from ear-to-ear. He was shaking hands with a bearded man wearing the ruins of an business suit. Ms Shan nodded at the sight, satisfied. She strode over to the Inquiries/Key Cutting desk and picked up the microphone used to make store announcements. She brought the mouthpiece up to her lips, and her amplified words echoed throughout the cavernous interior of the Pavilion:

"And *that* is how hardware shop management is fucking *done*."

She raised the microphone up over her head, holding it for a triumphant second, before letting it drop to the concrete floor.

# 57 Tall Tales Part 1

Darkness was falling as Laura Cho arrived for night watch duty at the Pavilion. A sad paper sign on the main door assured customers that the Pavilion was still open despite the damage. It almost brought a tear to Laura's eye thinking about the incident. Valentine's Day had been a disaster. The Pavilion had been dealt its greatest blow, and without the DIY Barn even making a move.

Laura had been away on the day that the mushroom men had gone wild. She'd been visiting Karl Wintergreen and poor dear Carlos in the hospital. She'd hoped that Carlos would have noticed her decision to visit on Valentine's Day, but he was still... not cold, perhaps, but distant. Very distant.

She'd had to come clean to Carlos about her secret identity as the superhero Voyager. What had happened to him made no sense otherwise, and it was not fair to leave him in ignorance. The simple fact was, he'd tried to save her by shoving her out of harm's way—and succeeded only in breaking a total of eight bones against her invulnerable body.

She'd had to explain this to him. Of course she had. And he'd been distant ever since. Perhaps he was still processing it. Then again, perhaps he felt threatened. Aquatic Woman had

341

warned her that this could happen in relationships between superheroines and non-super men. It was hard to say yet what the deal was.

Now she stood in front of this sign, this sad little sign… It made her want to fly right to the Barn, punch her way through the wall and destroy everything in sight. But that would be wrong. A misuse of power…

(But what was the point? What was the point of being a superhero if you couldn't defeat the genuinely evil? Was it all foiling alien gorillas and comical secret identity mix-ups? Was it never anything *real*?)

She shook her head. Bruce was parked nearby. He'd be waking up about now, what with the sun setting. Laura didn't know him well, but she needed someone to talk to so she wandered over and let herself in the cab. The door lock clicked open at her touch.

"Hi, Bruce."

"Laura." Bruce's voice sounded tinny coming through the car speakers. "To what do I owe the pleasure?"

Bruce was a ghost. Well, he had been a ghost. Now he was possessing the body of a killer robot which he'd somehow transformed into a truck… What the Hell was up with this place?

"Oh, it's young Laura," Bruce said. "I thought youse was that older version of you from the future."

Seriously, what *was* up with the place? Her older doppelgänger seemed to know, but that enigmatic pain in the arse never seemed to want to say.

"Does she talk to you a lot?"

"Yeah, fair bit. No offence, but she told me not to repeat anything to you that she said. She said 'time paradoxes' and I said 'what's time paradoxes' and she showed me that movie *Predestination* and it gave me a headache, and I can't take Panadol because I'm an undead robot, so I reckon I won't..."

"You're on night watch every night," Laura butted in. "You see everything that goes on here in the carpark?"

"That's right. Those DIY Barn arseholes run surveillance every night. They don't come too close these days, but. I think they want to see how near they can get before we react."

Laura shook her head. "This is so stupid. Ms Shan's finally accepted there's a war on, but she's waiting for them to attack first."

"Ms Shan's a hardware shop manager, love," Bruce said. "But she's also someone I wouldn't cross on a bet. When she's ready to move, I wouldn't want to be the Barn for love nor money."

"They still have Christian captive. She should organise a rescue."

"How do you know she hasn't?"

It must be so easy for Bruce to be optimistic. After all, for him, the worst had already happened. She checked her watch and saw it was time to get a move on. "Karl Wintergreen says hi. Oh, and he also said some shit about the Masons. But mostly, hi."

She left the cab. It had been an unsatisfying conversation and an unsatisfying shift was ahead of her. Perhaps it was the waiting that was getting to her. All this circling, looking for an opening. If only the battle would begin, then at least —

Laura felt a presence behind her. She spun on the spot ready to break the arm of whoever had been sneaking up on her. It was fortunate that the newcomer was not attacking, because for a second Laura was too shocked even to punch him.

"Buck!" she said.

"Ma'am," Buck Dusty said, touching the brim of his Stetson hat. He no longer wore the false colours of his Handy Pavilion shirt; instead, wearing an old-fashioned black suit under a long grey duster.

"You betrayed us! Sold us out to the Barn. What did you do with Christian?"

"Christian ain't happy, but he's perfectly safe," Buck said. "Pro'lly safer where he is then in there with the fungus monsters and air raids and whatnot. 'Sides, I don't work for the DIY Barn. Not directly."

A loud whirring noise told her Bruce was transforming into a robot. A robot that looked like it need a shave, but a robot nonetheless. His transformation complete, Bruce pointed an enormous ray gun at Buck. "I know killing people is against the rules for your sort, Laura," he said, his voice booming from massive speakers, "but I'm a robot. I can blow his head off before you can say 'crush-kill-destroy.'"

Buck hitched up his duster to reveal the six-shooter holstered at his hip. "Reckon you're fast?"

"Fast enough."

"All right, cut it out you two," Laura shouted. "I don't have time for idiot posturing. Dusty, say your piece and get lost."

"Very well, ma'am," Dusty said, unhitching his coat. "What you need to understand is that the DIY Barn ain't 'zackly what it seems."

"No, it's run by Nazis," Laura said. "I already figured that out."

"It is controlled by members of an ee-lete Nazi science institution who fled to South America after the war. But there's more to it than that. The Barn is in some ways a suburban big-box hardware store. On another level, it's an intrusion into our dimension of one of the Three Barns. As I say, I don't serve the DIY Barn. I serve the Grey Barn."

"That's the most I ever heard you say at one time," Bruce said.

"So you're the Grey Barn," Laura said, ignoring Bruce. "That makes the other two the White and Black Barns, right?"

"You ain't thinking multidimensionally. Your vision is too narrow. Predictable. The world's bigger'n you imagine. Your petty imaginin's can't barely comprehend the majesty of the eternal cosmos.

"Fine! What are they called?"

"The DIY Barn is an aspect of... the Barn of Shadows."

Laura looked at Bruce. Bruce looked at Laura.

"But not the Black Barn?" Bruce said. "Because that's pretty similar to the Barn of Shadows, if you ask me."

"What's the other Barn called? The Barn of Light?"

345

Laura said.

"Yeah, because if it was, you could just about call 'em the Black Barn and the White Barn, I reckon."

Buck Dusty took a deep breath. "Well, as it happens, the other Barn is called the Barn $18n = \cos \Phi /$rabbit. So why don't you both set quiet a spell and listen, and maybe you'll learn something?"

# 58 Gnome Time to Lose

Seamus the gnome awoke under the full moon to find himself alive and well. He felt himself up and down for cracks or chips. He soon noticed that the arm with which he was feeling was sore and stiff, and observed that it had been glued together in several places.

"Feckin' terrific," he said. "Sure and it's a hardware store here. Ye'd think there would be a better quality of glue."

"Oh, that's bloody gratitude."

Seamus looked up to see Wellsey lounging against a shelving unit full of trellises, munching on a sandwich.

"We had a man down and a destroyed AA gun that was looking like it might set fire to the Pavilion," Wellsey said. "I figured you wouldn't bleed out while I found some super glue and a clamp."

"Now, I ain't criticising ye for yer tardiness, I'm criticising ye for yer choice of materials," Seamus said. "Look at this arm! Sure and I'm a single man, I needs me right arm working!"

"The glue said 'suitable for ceramics," Wellsey said. "Besides, your pants are made of glazed porcelain, Seamus O'Consolodatedshanghaipotteryworks. You can't even open the fly."

"Tried, have ye?" Seamus said with a leer.

Wellsey just shook his head and went on eating his sandwich.

"So how come they have ye on alone, this time?"

"I'm not on alone. Laura is here. She's just outside with Bruce and that traitor, Buck. Looked like Buck was delivering exposition, so I didn't want to interrupt them."

"Exposition. Dat's important."

"Yeah. Not always interesting, but."

"True, 'tis often quite dull. But dat don't mean it ain't important."

Seamus looked around at his plants, and wished Wellsey hadn't been there. He wanted to check them; to ensure they were adequately cared for and watered. It was his chosen task in life. True, he hadn't had many options to pick from. It had been this or fishing, really, and he didn't have a fishing pole.

"So how's your war goin' then', big fella?"

"Awkward. Really awkward. How do yer expect a war between hardware centres to go? We're just not cut out for armed combat."

Seamus sneered. He often did. The curved lip his sculptor had given him to accommodate his pipe helped.

"Ye feckin' blatherskites," he said. "If you won't save me plants, who will?"

"We'll beat 'em," Wellsey said. "Somehow. We've beaten everything they've thrown at us so far. Ms Shan's planning a counterattack. She has big plans. She's a tough one, that one. Always thought of her as just another corporate type. Doesn't matter where you come from in the world, I guarantee that there's a private school there, turning out pricks like that with a cookie cutter. But no, I had her all wrong. She's one of us."

Seamus wanted to dismiss this speech with a joke, but a strange lump in his throat blocked his cutting remark before it could reach his lips. "You know who you need?" Seamus said. "That weird twitchy little fella who keeps hoidin' his cigarette butts under the bonsai section."

"Axel? He's in prison."

"So, he can bust out. Ain't he a supervillain?"

"Not anymore."

Seamus nodded knowingly

"But he used ter be?" he smiled.

"What's your point, mate?"

"Me point is, you people have big brains, but brains made of feckin' meat," Seamus snapped. "Are Nalda and Fanaka around?"

"Working in the arsenal," Wellsey said. "Or 'working' in the arsenal. I don't like to look."

"Well, have fun watching the skies. I've a plan, so and I do."

Seamus trotted off towards the Pavilion, leaving Wellsey scratching his head behind him. So Axel was in prison. That was too bad. Of all the Pavilion staff, Axel was the least likely to fold because of some moral qualm. The Pavilion needed Axel. The *plants* needed him. Ducking under the shelf that held the bonsais, Seamus salvaged a cigarette butt with Cyrillic characters around the filter. It was still a little damp. Sometimes having non-porous hands was a blessing.

Inside the Pavilion, Seamus considered walking right into the arsenal/break room, just to cause trouble. Unfortunately, the door was closed, so all he could do was knock on it with his foot. After a moment, the killer cyborg Nalda Teheinthausand opened the door. Seamus had been hoping to see her guiltily buttoning her shirt or something, but unfortunately, she didn't seem to have been doing anything untoward.

She looked left and right before looking down to see Seamus. "Ja?"

"'Ullo, love, may I come in?" Without waiting for an answer, he trotted past her. Inside the little break room, there was barely room to move for jerry-rigged infernal devices. Fanaka was up to his elbows inside one, and quietly singing a rhythmic African song. Seamus disliked the tune, just as he despised all songs that didn't contain reminders of Kilarney, or bid their listeners to go from glen to glen.

"Alright, you two," he said. "You're from der future, Nalda. And Fanaka, you're from some alternate past where der bastard English got what was coming to 'em, roight?"

"I think that's a little bit..." Fanaka began.

"Essentially correct," Nalda intoned.

"So we should see a build-up of potential temporal energy whenever you touch. Pure electricity when youse are skin to skin," Seamus leered.

Fanaka blushed and Nalda sneered.

"Right, so here's me plan. The Guarda have Axel, see? What we can do is bring a past version of him into the present. Pick him up from just before he got arrested, and put him back there as soon as the battle is over."

"Wait—what do you know about temporal physics?" Fanaka said.

"As much as any man with twenty-seven days a month in which to contemplate the mysteries of der cosmos," Seamus snapped. "I've done der maths, and I have here one of Axel's cigarette butts, with his DNA on 'em. Do one of youse yahoos have a transdimensional energy source?"

"Your accent is vildly inconsistent," Nalda said.

"Listen to who's talking, bedad. Do you have the source or not?"

Fanaka shrugged. "Yes, but attempts to use the Skull have been…"

"Aha! A Skull! Roight, I need you two to hold hands on top of the Skull."

Nalda looked at Fanaka. "I do not trust der liddle man."

"I thought it was humans you didn't trust," Fanaka said with a smile. "Look, I need to know more about the skull if we're going to be able to use it as more than just a battery. You know what I mean."

He placed his hand on top of the glass skull, which was sitting on top of a wooden chest, covered in dozens of lights.

"Very vell. If you try anything, little man, I vill destroy

351

you," she said, putting her hand on top of the skull, interlacing her fingers with those of her lover.

"Sure, and I wouldn't do nothing to endanger this place," Seamus said. "Trust me."

And with that, handed the cigarette butt to Fanaka, who placed it on top of the skull, in between fingers.

The lights in the room went out. A wave of force knocked Seamus back onto his ceramic rump. When the lights came back on, a little man stood next to Fanaka and Nalda. He sported a crewcut and a huge pair of goggles, and he wore a purple lab coat over an outfit that looked like pale blue surgical scrubs with knee-high boots. In a second, he had shaken a ray gun from his sleeve.

"All right! What's going on? Who are you? Who do you work for? The Society of Wickedness? N.E.S.T.? Les Frers Montgolfiers du Mal? *Who are you?*"

Winded, Seamus could only gawp. Fanaka's mouth opened and closed silently, his eyes focused on the ray gun aimed at his gut. Only Nalda seemed able to move. Ignoring the gun, she leaned in closer to the stranger.

"Axel?" she said.

"That's Professor Devistato to you, fraulein!" Axel snarled.

"Oh, moi word," Seamus moaned. "I think me calculations were a tad out."

He looked up at the ceiling, his fingers twitching slightly as he revised his equations. "Yep. My bad. Sure, and I forgot to carry der one."

# 59 Tall Tales Part 2

In the darkening car park in front of the Handy Pavilion, Laura listened patiently to Buck Dusty's rambling, seemingly endless tale of magic, conspiracy and the eternal peril approaching all dimensions. She nodded in silence as he explained the origins of the Grey Barn and how the fate of all dimensions is intertwined, all along the vast wheel of fate.

Once he had finished, she turned to Bruce. "You buying this?"

"Yeah, yeah, secret war, fate of civilisation," Bruce said. "Think I read this story I was a kid. Reckon it had the Silver Surfer in it. Hey — you're a superhero. Do you know the Silver Surfer? What's he like?"

Laura looked up at Bruce's immense robotic face. "Don't be silly. The Silver Surfer's not real."

Bruce looked so disappointed that Laura took pity. "Mind you, I met Aquaman once," she lied. "Total class act."

"I don't think y'all are taking my explanation serious, like," Buck said.

"Why should we?" Laura said. "It doesn't change anything. Before you explained all that crap, we were at war with the DIY Barn. Now we're at war with the Barn *and* we have to remember some stupid backstory that sounds like you were snorting peyote at a Twin Peaks marathon."

It was dark now, and the only illumination came from the massive overhead lights of the parking lot. Buck's face was invisible in the shadow of his hat, but he shifted uncomfortably from foot to foot.

"Do people snort peyote?" Bruce said.

"Yeah, I think so," Laura said, uncertainly. "Pretty sure."

"Enough!" Buck said. "This is important. The Pavilion's role in the cosmic..."

"Why are you telling us this anyway?" Bruce said.

"That should be clear," Buck said. "Remember what I said about the third epoch of the second conflict on the axis of..."

"Oh, so we have to win this fight because of the prophecy?"

"What prophecy? I didn't say nothing 'bout a prophecy."

"Yeah, you did. Didn't he Laura?"

"He might have. I was drifting in and out," Laura said.

"Look, this is simple, now," Buck said. "Since the days of Hammurabi, three Barns..."

"Hammurabi? I thought you said Nebuchadnezzar?"

"I mentioned Nebuchadnezzar. In passing. But it was Hammurabi that..."

"Hey, Laura! We have always been at war with Hammurabi! Get it?"

"Huh?"

"Oh, it's from this book I read in high school. Reckon the hero was a wuss, but. What's wrong with rats?"

Buck looked up at the sky and scratched his chin like he was trying to take the skin off it.

"Look," he said. "This ain't complicated. Let me tell it again, usin' small words. In the Time of Gardax, when the Sons of Horthan reigned supreme, King Zeblec was first of the Chosen Ones…"

"Choose this!" Bruce said, extending a mechanical middle finger the size of a bar fridge.

"You know what?" Buck said. "You can all go to heck, you consarned hoopleheads! I come over here to explain matters, let y'all know *why* it is you gotta die. Help you understand the cosmic purpose your annihilation will serve. But fine, you wanna die ignernt? Be my guest!"

Buck turned and stalked away. Bruce moved to follow him, but Laura checked him. "I put a tracer on him. With any luck, he'll lead us to where they're keeping Christian. In the meantime, we need you here."

"Why?"

"Because the final battle is coming in the morning."

"How do you know?"

"Because he wouldn't have told us any of that shit if he thought we'd have time to use it to our advantage."

Bruce stood to his full height and stared at the DIY Barn. A distant, determined look settled over his electronic eyes. "Seriously," he said, "what was with that bit about King

Arthur being a Sasquatch?"

"I know, right?" Laura said. "And the Great Wall of China is a spaceship? Puh-lease! I'd buy an Egyptian Pyramid spaceship, just about. But the Great Wall? That's just stupid."

"It was like a bad fantasy novel, written by an idiot."

For a second, both Laura and Bruce crumpled up their faces in deep thought. For a long moment, they were lost in deep consideration. They seemed to reach the same conclusion simultaneously and shook their heads.

Laura looked up at the full moon. Somewhere inside the Pavilion, she could hear noises. It sounded like a gunfight. Blaster pistol versus shotgun from the sound of it. She sighed, knowing that she would have to deal with it, soon.

Soon, but not now. Priorities, yeah?

"They'll attack at dawn," she said. "The Barn."

"You reckon?"

"They'll want light, but they also won't want to deal with the peak hour traffic on Wellington Road."

"Do you think... Do you think there'll be casualties?" Bruce said.

"Probably."

"Not worried for myself," Bruce said. "I'm dead, you know. But dyin' isn't fun. Wouldn't wish it on any of you. Not even Adam."

Laura was jolted out of her thoughts. "What's wrong with Adam?"

"Oh, *he* knows."

"I better call Ms Shan," Laura said. "Could you look

through one of the high windows and tell me what's going on? I don't want to know, honestly. But..."

Laura dialled Ms Shan's home number. Mrs Liselle answered, and turned it over to a barely awake Ms Shan. There was the slightest pause after Laura had said her piece. Just the slightest.

"Thank you, Laura," said Ms Shan. "I'll summon the troops. Stay where you are."

The phone slipped back into Laura's pocket. "So what's going on inside?"

"Looks like Axel is fighting Nalda," Bruce said. "Oh, now the Phantasm's gone and gotten involved. Looks like she doesn't like Axel. Oooh! That's gonna sting come morning."

Laura breathed deeply. A strange calm came over her. The alternate future version of herself had told her that she would not die battling the Barn, but she wasn't sure she trusted the older woman. No, tomorrow, she would live or she would die. If she lived, there was a greater threat to come, thanks to Axel's careless sale of a pulley. But, bottom line — if she lived, she lived; and if she died, she died.

There was something simple about that idea. Almost comforting.

# 60 The Call

Marlon was the first to be called. He was alone at home. He should have been in bed, he knew, but the empty bed was cold and uninviting. He sat on the couch watching old war movies. He'd bought a bottle of rum and another of Coke to drink while he watched, but he'd grown bored of drinking before finishing the first glass.

His heart leapt when he heard his phone ring, then fell when he saw the caller ID. Not a friend or a lover calling to chat. It was Ms Shan. He answered, knowing what the message would be.

"Marlon here."

"The battle's on," Ms Shan said. "Tomorrow. Dawn."

"I'll be there. Need me to help you call the others?"

"No. I have to do this."

"'K. Take care."

He hung up and looked at the flat, warm rum-and-coke on his coffee table. It looked even less appealing than it had before.

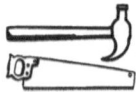

Fiona dreamed of Hell. She dreamed of fighting the

flames with her water powers and it not being enough to hold back inferno. Axel and Sadie were already trapped in the fire, which was rising to engulf her and Norman, and no matter how much water she raised —

But then the fires dissolved in the opening chords of *Royal*. Her phone. Blearily, she answered.

"Buuuuh?" she said.

"Fiona? It's Ms Shan."

"Guuuuh?"

"It's war. Dawn."

"Bluuuuuh. 'll be th're."

With the last of her consciousness, she set an alarm before drifting off to sleep. This time, she dreamed of redemption.

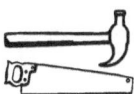

Zorbar woke and jabbed an angry finger ineffectively at the phone, until his wife sat up and swiped it for him.

"You speak, Zorbar listen."

Ms Shan invited him to the war. In deference to the neighbours who lived on the other side of the thin apartment wall, Zorbar did not respond with the terrible war cry of the chimps.

"Zorbar be there. Fight Barn."

"So you're going?" Carol asked once he'd hung up.

Zorbar looked down. "Zorbar know you want Zorbar keep safe," he said. "But Zorbar friends in danger..."

"Shhh, it's okay," she said. "Of course, I don't want you

to get hurt. On the other hand, those bastards captured and tortured you. You go fuck them up for me, okay?"

"Zorbar not think Carol believe revenge."

"Zorbar wrong."

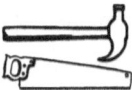

The phone woke Norman in his bedroom in his Mum's house where he'd slept since he was a child. It didn't wake the woman beside him, who was a sound sleeper.

He looked down at her hair, fanned over the pillow and smelling faintly of carob. He wondered if she'd stay with him. He didn't like one-night stands. They made him feel too much like his dad. He wondered if he'd still like this girl if he got to know her better. On the other hand, he wasn't sure if he could be in an ongoing relationship while he was still in love with Ms Shan…

The phone rang a second time. Ms Shan. A bolt of guilt pierced his heart for sleeping with someone who was not his love—followed by a jolt of regret for himself for loving a woman who could never possibly love him back. He answered the phone and heard the call to war.

It cheered him. All his confused emotions fell away, melting in the knowledge that he might be dead within twelve hours.

He was not the first young man to prefer the simplicity of a fight to the death, to the complexity of everyday life. Perhaps if young men did not feel this way there would be no wars—although of course there is no way to be sure of such a thing.

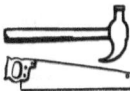

Karl got the call as a courtesy. Certainly, Ms Shan didn't expect him to rise from his hospital bed and fight.

But rise he did. He arose and retrieved his camera and tape recorder. He may only have run a shopping centre newsletter but that didn't mean that he wasn't a reporter... a journalist... a *newsman* damn it. If there was a war on, he planned to be a correspondent.

And so the call went out. Adam said little, then sat in the dark, silently sharpening a cleaver he'd borrowed from his cousin's butcher shop. Donna fretted and paced and wished that Sadie was there to tell her what to do. Ali took his children over to their mother's house. While he was there, he said all the things he wished he'd said; all the kind things he regretted not saying before the divorce. Jane Nguyen from the Key Cutting counter had dreaded this call for weeks, and now that she was hearing it, it came as such a relief that she just went back to sleep. There was no way to get a message to Axel or Sadie. They slept badly in their respective cells.

All the others were told. The cashiers and cleaners. The ones who knew where the washers were to be found and the ones who looked after the paint rollers. The people who knew a 6mm self-tapping wood screw from a 5mm plasterboard bolt. The ones who dusted the house numbers on display and the ones whose work lives smelled of mulch and manure. All of them got the call. Some wept, some bellowed in rage, others waited stoically for dawn. A handful gave Ms Shan their immediate resignations, which were accepted without question. But most of them—most of them readied themselves for the approaching battle.

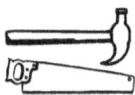

"I'm coming with you," Mrs Liselle said, somewhere in between calls.

"No. This isn't your fight," Ms Shan said.

"It affects you, it affects the Super Centre, it affects me."

"I know it affects you, my love," Ms Shan said. "That doesn't make it your fight."

"So you want me to just wait on the sidelines?"

"I don't want you standing anywhere near the sidelines."

"But—"

"No." Ms Shan laid down her phone and put a hand on her lover's shoulder. "You can't fight. Do you know why?"

Mrs Liselle nodded. "I know you're afraid of losing me. I know you don't think I can stomach conflict. Lord knows if I did, I would have been rid of my ex-husband long before I was. But...

"I don't want you to die," Ms Shan said. "But I know you're a fighter... when you have to be. And that's why I need you to stay out of the war: because we might lose. We might lose, and then it won't be Handy Pavilion vs DIY Barn anymore. The only thing standing in the Barnlings' way will be the rest of the Super Centre. You will have to take it from there."

"I... I don't know if I'm up to that."

Ms Shan lay a hand gently on her shoulder.

"Then I'll have to try not to die."

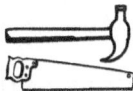

The last one to get the call was Angela McGregor. Her house was silent and dark, though she was not asleep. She never slept. But she also never turned on a light if she didn't have to. Lights cost money and accomplished nothing.

But a little square of light broke the darkness. Her phone. Ms Shan. War. The ground had been broken, the seeds planted. It was time to stand well back and watch the harvest.

The phone rang again.

Angela didn't need to be there at the end. It didn't matter now who won or lost. That was not her concern. As long as war was declared, her own victory was assured.

The phone rang a third time. Why did people make phones that shone so? Why did they need light to *see*?

She picked up the phone. "Hello?"

"Hello. It's Ms Shan. The fight's on. Dawn."

There was an unpleasant feeling at the back of Angela's throat.

"I'll be there," she said.

She hung up. For a long time, she just sat alone in the dark wondering 'why'.

# 61 Cat and Mouse (and Vole)

Professor Devistato hid behind some big bags of cement powder and pondered his next move in his running battle against the angry cyborg. She seemed to know him—she'd even called him Axel. That was worrying. Then that other woman had attacked, the one in the hat and cloak.

*Black* hat and cloak. That meant 'supervillain.' Old school supervillain. Retro.

No time for worrying about fashion. Focus! Where was he? Evidence suggested a hardware shop, but a far bigger hardware shop than he'd ever seen. Was he on some sort of giant planet? No, the hardware items were of ordinary size. He looked more closely at the label on a cement bag. English writing. Perfectly ordinary.

He looked at his blaster pistol. Running low on power, it was the only weapon he had. Damn the luck! They—whoever *they* were—had taken him while his Plasma Claw was in for repairs. He took a deep breath. He'd been in tighter situations than this. Usually, though, they'd come with a little warning...

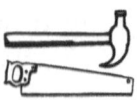

Gwen Harper already had her revenge on the Handy Pavilion as well as on Pennington. And revenge is great—but it doesn't pay the bills. It was past time to throw her white mask and broad-brimmed hat into the bin, say goodbye to the Phantasm and update her resume. Hell, the deal she'd cut with Ms Shan had even included the promise of a good reference. A new job wouldn't be too hard to find.

But there remained two reasons Gwen could not stop being the Phantasm. One was Christian. Her loyal servant was in the hands of the DIY Barn. If there was anything she could do to free him, she owed him that much.

The other reason was Axel. She may have cut a deal with the Pavilion. She may even have gotten her true ears back. But what she didn't have was revenge on Axel Platzoff.

If Fanaka was right, the Axel she and Nalda had been pursuing through the Pavilion was Axel's past self, propelled into the present by a misguided gnome. That meant she probably couldn't kill past-Axel without causing some sort of temporal paradox.

Couldn't kill him. But she could certainly kick his ass.

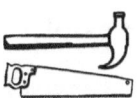

Nalda was detecting a class B temporal disturbance. This was probably caused by the arrival of past-Axel-Prof-Devistato, but more importantly, it was messing with her mind.

Her mind, after all, was nothing but a computer program. A hugely sophisticated program of massive complexity, but in the end, a program is just a program—a mass of nested strings of cause and effect. As a time-travelling cyborg from the future, she was designed with more than usual flexibility as to the *order* in which effect follows cause. Even so, there were limits to what she could handle.

Elements of her programs were fighting one another. Timeline protection subroutines demanded that past Axel must remain unharmed to prevent temporal paradox. Other, newer, self-derived programs said that since Axel had shot at her beloved Fanaka, he must die! Core programming told her that, Fanaka was mere flesh and must be destroyed for the Age of Machine to rise. And what about the Phantasm? She'd tried to harm Nalda's precious little students. But Ms Shan had ordered that the Phantasm not be hurt…

So many conflicting threads of thought fought each other in her electronic brain. Vital applications intended to harmonise internal conflict were down, and all their cycles diverted to keeping temporal paradox away from her core programming.

She looked down at the sawn-off shotgun in her leather-gloved hand, and her mind resolved into clarity.

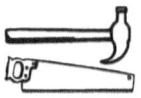

There was something colourful under the pallet opposite Devistato, just visible in the pale light of the full moon filtering through the greasy skylight. He looked around to check that he was unobserved before picking it up. It was part of a box whose label advertised a laser-level checker.

"*Laser*-level checker? The future?" Axel muttered. Yes. Yes, that made sense. He'd been working on a device for de-aging the hated Captain Stellar back to babyhood. Perhaps he'd weakened the time barrier while testing it? If so, had these people even brought him there deliberately? He reached for the most used pocket on his utility belt, and retrieved a hip flask from it. It reeked of aniseed. A large swallow made him shudder.

Whoever these people were, they were hostile. That was what mattered. Once they were dead, then he could figure out what was what. He climbed slowly to his feet, a plan already forming.

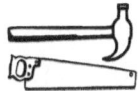

A black shape flitted through Nalda's field of vision. The Phantasm. A threat/not a threat/next to die. Axel, it was Axel that she had to kill, kill all humans, no not all…

"100001011!" she shouted, as some force struck her in the upper body. She looked down at her hands, to see that her left arm had been popped out of its socket and dangled uselessly in her leather sleeve. Where had the attack come from? She scanned the visible spectrum… nothing… wait! A tiny spark of coherent light. Someone using a laser-based invisibility system? She swung with her right hand, striking something fleshy. A neck. She had an enemy's neck in her hand.

You never forget that feeling, do you?

The air in front of her shimmered like a Christmas tree,

and then there was Axel, held off his feet by the throat, a crowbar slipping from his hand.

"I must break you," Nalda said. It was not the sort of thing she usually said, but somehow it felt right.

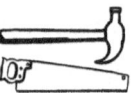

The Phantasm perched on top of an enormous shelving unit, looking down at what seemed like a fireworks display. Axel was showering sparks from his broken invisibility unit and Nalda was showering sparks from her dislocated shoulder. Gwen had never much cared for Nalda. She wished there was a chandelier to drop on the both of them, but no such luck.

She hopped lightly to the floor. Neither Nalda nor Axel moved. After a moment's thought, she picked up a broom handle from a display and prodded Nalda hard in the hand. Axel fell free, gasping, as Nalda staggered backward. What was up with the cyborg? Programming glitch?

Did it even matter?

Gwen gave the air a couple of experimental swipes with the broom handle, before stepping up to Axel's prone form.

"Should I hit a man while he's down?" she asked no one in particular.

"Dare I eat a peach?" she added, grinning under her mask. She aimed at Axel's head and the tip of the broom handle whistled as it swung through the air.

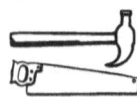

In his cell at Long Bay Jail's supervillain wing, Axel Platzoff awoke with a pain in his face. Must have been Autumn. The change in seasons always made the scar next to his eye throb. He sighed and breathed deeply. The prison was quiet that night. The only things he could hear were the faint crackle of walkie-talkies in the distance and Dr Crocodile in the bunk below, muttering sleeping threats to Aquaticwoman. He rolled over to go back to sleep.

He had nearly returned to his dreams when he suddenly sat bolt upright.

"Wait… What scar next to my eye?" he said. "And hold on, why am I in prison, anyway?"

"'F course I still hate you," Dr Crocodile muttered, "I j'st think I should battle other superheroines, too."

"Screw this noise," Axel said. "I'm breaking out."

# 62 On the Practical Applications of Cosplay

Belinda was kind of a pain in the arse. That was no great secret. If asked, she would have admitted without hesitation to being 'kind of a pain in the arse' and then she would have laughed annoyingly, just so that there was no mistaking she meant it.

She wasn't a terrible person, not by any means. Just one of those people who have no particular desire to be good, but who lack the ambition to be notably bad. She was a second-rate employee of the Handy Pavilion. She was an indifferent stock filler, with mediocre product knowledge and her tendency to see customers as unwitting spectators to her hackneyed impromptu comedy bits.

But no one is *completely* useless. There were two things that Belinda was very, very good at — and one of these things was cosplay.

Though she didn't know it, this skill was the only reason that she was still employed at the Pavilion. After her fifth poor staff evaluation in a row, Marlon had interceded with Ms Shan to let her keep her job, on the grounds that Belinda provide the

Santa costume that came out every Christmas. Not only that, she was the source of the Easter Bunny costume for Easter, a Leprechaun costume for St Patrick's Day, and of course not a single January 26th ever passed by without Australia Day Daveo making an appearance.

Thus, when inspiration had struck earlier that day, it had taken her a matter of hours to turn a thermal blanket into a close imitation of the silver uniform of the DIY Barn soldiers. When night fell, she simply marched up to the doors of the Barn, intent on rescuing Christian.

The guard on the door wore a costume similar to hers, though she had better goggles. He—or was it she? The uniforms revealed little—looked at her expectantly. Belinda had no idea what was expected of her, but this lead nicely to her second talent. She was a past master at never letting her own cluelessness get in her way. She guessed, and guessed hard.

"Hail Smith!" she said, thumping her chest with her right hand.

"We doing *that* again?" the guard said. Probably a guy? He had one of those voices that made it hard to tell. "I thought the 'hail Smith' thing died from lack of interest."

"Yeah, ha, I was being retro."

"Ugh," the guard said. "Whatevs. Just go on in."

Belinda walked in. The interior of the Barn looked… Well, honestly, it looked much like the interior of the Pavilion. Oh, the aisles were arranged a little differently. Paint directly faced the doorway, and lumber was on the left instead of the right. But basically, it was the same.

"Savages!" Belinda muttered. "*Blue* pricetags? What's up with that?"

"What's that?" the guard said.

"Uh…" Belinda needed to find Christian. But how? "Uh… Where's the prisoner?"

"Dungeon. Trapdoor's in aisle twelve, between rakes and shovels."

"Thanks."

"Wait a second."

Belinda stood stock still. The silver material made her sweat, but she'd had the foresight to stitch a terry towelling band into her headpiece.

"Look at that," the guard said. He pointed past the Place O' Pets to the small segment of the Pavilion that was visible from here. Bright lights flashed laser red in the windows. "Those idiots will destroy themselves before we even get to them."

Belinda had often thought the same thing, but didn't like to hear it from a Barnling. "Your fly's open," she said, as she marched off to aisle twelve.

No one gave her a second glance. There were dozens of silver-clad Barn Troopers around. They slouched against shelving units and stood in little circles chatting and scratching their backsides. An officious looking little fellow with a comb-over and a badge that read 'manager' came bustling by, and for a moment the Troopers stood rigidly to attention and moved with a stiff-legged march. Once he was gone, they went back to their lounging.

Belinda found the trapdoor in aisle twelve easily enough. It was painted black and yellow, and labelled 'WARNING: TRAP DOOR'. Even the forces of pure evil couldn't pull one over on OH&S, Belinda guessed. She lifted the door, and climbed down the ladder.

The dungeon was small, bland and surprisingly well lit. In it was a camp bed, a camping potty, a folding table and a director's chair. On the wall was a brightly coloured poster depicting a dead frog being eaten by ants, with the catchy slogan "YOU CAN'T SPELL 'CRUSHING DESPAIR' WITHOUT 'U' AND AN 'I'". Christian— unshaven, but seemingly unhurt—sat on the camp bed. A chain ran from his ankle to a ring in the floor. A silver clad guard stood at attention, revolver in hand, in a spot giving him a clear view of both prisoner and ladder.

"Hail," the guard said, with a halfhearted wave.

"Yeah, hail and shit. I'm here to move the prisoner."

"Oh, yeah? Who sent you?"

"Uh... You know, what's his name. That guy? With the glasses? The mirror shades, you know?"

The guard didn't move.

"With the wooden leg and the duelling scar down one cheek?" Belinda added. "What's his name?"

"Left cheek or right cheek?"

"Left?"

"Mr Hobson?"

"Yeah, him. I'm here to move the prisoner on orders of

Mr Hobson? Yeah?"

"Why was I not informed of this?"

"Because... Look, seriously, this is a small concrete room. You gonna fire a gun? You've got as much chance of killing yourself with a ricochet as hurting anyone else."

The guard looked at his gun. "You think?"

"Yes," Belinda said, bashing him over the head with the folding chair.

"Ow!" the guard said, dropping the gun and doubling over.

Belinda hit him again.

"Seriously!" the guard said.

And again.

"Ow! Stop it."

Belinda was seeing red now. She wasn't a fighter, and as such she had no idea when to *stop* fighting. It wasn't until the stricken guard literally yelled 'uncle!' that she put the chair down.

"Was that called for?" the guard said. His silver hood had been torn in half a dozen places, and thick brown hair was poking out the rips. "Was that *really* bloody called for?"

"Well Hobson said to do that, too," Belinda said. "Where's the key?"

The guard handed Belinda the key. She unlocked Christian's cuff.

"So what does Hobson want with me?" Christian said.

"It's me, you tosser," Belinda said, lifting her goggles. "Come on, I'm here to rescue you."

"Sweet," Christian said, standing.

Belinda clapped the cuff on the prostrate, sulking guard, and led Christian to the ladder. As he climbed, he turned to his former captor: "We're still on for karaoke, right Bazza?"

"Yeah, if I can find a sitter," the guard sighed.

"Oi! Stop stealing the drama from my rescue," Belinda said. "Remember, if anyone asks, I'm taking you to another location on Hobson's orders."

"What if we run into Hobson?"

"Knee him in the balls and run," Belinda said. "Do I have to think of everything?"

# 63 The Break Room of War

Christian sat in the staff room, a blanket around his shoulders and the nicest meal he'd eaten in days in front of him. The Phantasm was toasting him sandwich after sandwich and plying him with sugary tea. Most of his workmates were marshalling outside, but a few stood and listened as he spoke breathlessly of his ordeal:

"...And there was nothing to eat but Devon and cabbage, and we had to watch Barn employees confess to their crimes on black and white TVs, then we had to spend five minutes hating Emanuel Goldstein—I think he's Jeff Goldblum's brother or something—and there was nothing to read but *Jackboot Enthusiast Quarterly* and they tried to torture me with a slowly descending pendulum, but it squeaked and the torturer got annoyed and stopped it, but anyway, I know where the weak spot is on the Barn."

Marlon pursed his lips. "There's a weak spot?"

"Don't push him, he's been through a lot," the Phantasm said. "Scotch Finger or ginger nut?"

"Ew! Scotch finger please, my cruel mistress." Though she still wore her hat and cape, the Phantasm seemed to have given up her bone-white mask. It was an improvement.

Christian took his biscuit. While he was deeply flawed in many ways, on some level he was still basically a decent human being, with a decent human being's essential desire to do right. As such, he broke his Scotch Finger in half *before* dunking it in his tea.

"There's a weak spot. Round the back. Remember when they made that airship to attack us? Well, I heard one of the Barnlings say that the hangar roof had been damaged in a wind storm. He'd replaced it — but only with a bit of three mil MDF."

The Phantasm nearly dropped a plate. Marlon crossed himself. Even the usually impassive Nalda curled her lip into a sneer of disdain.

"Three mil? For a project like that?" Marlon spat. "They're disgraces to the hardware retail industry."

"And MDF when plywood would be optimal!" Nalda spat.

"Those are all good points," Christian said. "So I reckon, while we have them distracted with the big fight, we send some sort of elite task-force-thing round back to break into the hangar. We set charges on those hydrogen tanks and Emanuel Goldstein is a big jerk who looks dumb with his dumb hair."

"What?" Marlon said.

"Sorry, force of habit."

Nalda nodded. "This could be our chance. A small team could take advantage of this unexpected flaw in the defences. You know — like that movie... Um..."

"*The Guns of Navarrone?*" Marlon said.

"Nein, not that one."

*"You Only Live Twice? Independence Day?"*

"Nein. Come on, you know the one, were that one special person overcomes seemingly impenetrable defences using their power... Ach, vas ist es?"

*"The King and I?"*

"Ja, exactly. Dat woman uses the power of love to get through the emotional defences of the King of Siam. We will do something like that—only in more of a combat setting."

"Could work," came a voice. Christian looked around. He'd noticed the guy lying unconscious along a row of chairs but, in his capacity as the centre of attention, he hadn't bothered asking about him. Now he realised it was a guy that looked like he could be Axel's son, only dressed in a weird costume. The guy was sitting up now, rubbing his bruised face.

"Before you go rushing into things blindly, let's consider," the stranger said. "Christian here has clearly been brainwashed—pretty ineptly, but brainwashed nonetheless. He's leading you into a trap. What we need to do is out-trap them."

"Shut up, loser," the Phantasm said. "You're the reason I have these scars."

"They don't look too bad," Christian said. This was the first time he'd seen his mistress' face, and honestly, it was pretty okay.

"Yeah?" the Phantasm said, her voice laden with suspicion.

"Yeah. They add character."

A smile flickered across her lips. She bustled off to get

more tea.

"What was that about?" young Axel said. "Oh, wait. Just remembered: I don't care. Anyway, they're expecting the old 'small team bullseyes wamprats' plan. I say we run in with a *big* team, guns a-blazin' and hit 'em hard. Then we smash into the hangar, and blow up the hydrogen tanks."

"Why are you helping us?" Nalda asked.

"What part of 'blow up the hydrogen tanks' are you missing?" young Axel grinned. "I don't care who you idiots are, or what this fight is about, but... Kaboom!"

"I'll help you," Angela said. Christian had also forgotten she was there. She had been sitting quietly in the corner the whole time.

"That's great, but what we need is firepower," young Axel said. "Me, cyborg woman, hat lady, maybe some..."

Angela's pale face went jet black. The lights cut out and something darker than a mere absence of light filled the room with a blackness that hurt the eyes. Nothing was visible except for two glowing green eyes where Angela had been, and there was nothing to be heard except for a bowel-loosening wail of otherworldly horror.

The lights flickered and slowly the room returned to normal.

"All right, you're in," young Axel shrugged. "And if you have any more heavy -itters, we may need them too. All the rest of your force needs to do is hold the line until we reach the tanks."

"I should come too," Christian said, liking neither the

idea of his mistress going into battle without him, nor how quickly he was being sidelined. "I know where to go, after all."

Nalda shrugged. "That's probably a gut idea. I'll see if Fiona wants to come, too, or maybe Voyager from the future."

"We'll do it!" Christian said. "We'll make those Barnling bastards sorry they ever took on the Handy Pavilion!"

In the cheering that followed, no one heard him say, "Emmanuel Goldstein sucks balls" under his breath.

# 64 Twilight at Dawn

Sunrise found both sides of Wellington Road full of people in polo shirts and aprons. The occasional car drove by, and an observer in one might have noticed that the people on the northern side of the road wore their uniforms more neatly ironed than those on the south, that their work boots were more highly polished, that they stood in neat lines while those on the south side tended to favour rough circles.

This observer might have wondered what was going on. Probably some sort of charity event? Yes, that would be the most likely explanation. At first. Then this observer might have noticed just how many of the people on both sides carried crowbars, hammers, and Stanley knives. At this point, the observer's attention would have snapped back in the direction of the traffic lights as they frantically waited for them to change to green.

On the south side of the street, Ms Shan walked among the Pavilion troops. There were fewer of them than she needed. Her stomach twisted at the thought of every position she'd had to cut over the last year, each one a soldier lost before the battle had begun. The fear in the faces of those who remained was horrible to behold.

Her army was mostly normal people. The more powerful weirdos had been sent off on an important mission. There were still a few heavy hitters — Bruce, Zorbar, Fiona. That might have given the Pavilion the edge, had the Barn not possessed some powers of its own. Ms Shan didn't know which of the troops across from her had built a killer robot or summoned a demon, but some among them clearly had.

Most of her troops were just weary retailers, who'd come to the Pavilion for a job, not to fight against the forces of evil. Half of them wanted to run. She could feel it.

(Was it so long ago she'd wanted to run herself? Since she'd prayed daily that Central office would close down her branch and reassign her?)

Up the street, Marlon took charge of the left flank — Gardening, Cleaning Products, Paints. Wellsey had the right — Plumbing, Seasonal, Lumber. Ms Shan had the centre, while Ali stayed back with a reserve force from Power Tools and Safety Equipment.

The sun was nearly clear of the horizon. There was nothing in Ms Shan's gut but ice.

"I... I made this for you."

Ms Shan was roused from her reverie. It was Adam, and he was offering her what looked like a swagger stick made from pine dowel and electrician's tape. Ms Shan looked at it for a moment, then took it and stuck it under her arm.

"Thank you, Adam."

Adam saluted inexpertly, and Ms Shan nodded back. A glint of light caught her eye. Down the street was Karl

Wintergreen taking photos from the seat of his car. From conspiracy theorist to war correspondent. Karl was moving up in the world.

Parked cars. Hmm… There were a few small trees in the street, and a bus shelter, but other than that there was not much cover. This was not going to be a battle of manoeuvre and strategy, so much as an all-out brawl.

There was some consternation behind Ms Shan. She turned to see Axel Platzoff and Sadie McGregor moving through the ranks, Handy Pavilion shirts worn over their prison uniforms.

"Permission to join the battle?" Axel said.

"Granted. And you, Sadie?"

"I didn't want to break out," Sadie sulked. "He disintegrated my cell. I was lawfully incarcerated. This isn't right."

"But what *is* right, when you get right down to it?" Axel pondered.

Sadie glared at him, blue eyes between transparent eyelashes. "Don't get me started. You do *not* want to get me started, Axel Platzoff."

"Your time-displaced younger self is involved in a commando raid," Ms Shan said to Axel.

"Yes, I remember," Axel said, staring into the middle distance. "Something about hydrogen tanks? It was an episode of my life I never quite understood until now."

"Do you remember what happens next?"

"My memories are vague."

"A side-effect of time travel?"

"No. It's just that my younger self is drunk right now. I mean, *really* drunk."

"How drunk is really drunk?"

"A whole hip flask of pepper vodka and absinthe cocktail of his/my devising. I believe I used to call it a 'Montmarte Gulag.'"

Ms Shan nodded as she looked to the East. Not long now. A strange calm overtook her. It would all be over soon, one way or another. Perhaps she'd live and return to Claudia and live happily ever after. Perhaps she'd be dead. Either way, it would all soon be settled. It lent life a wonderful simplicity.

Across the road, Mr Smith seemed to be giving a speech. The wind was blowing the wrong way, so Ms Shan couldn't make it out, but she could see that the Barnlings closest to Smith seemed very bored.

A speech...

"Okay, folks, we all ready?" she said.

A ragged chorus of agreement broke out.

"Good. Because this is as ready as we're ever going to get."

And that was all she had. It seemed to be enough.

The sun cleared the horizon. On both sides of the street, weapons were raised threateningly as a fierce war cry sounded. The first ranks descended from the curb, ready to run across the street, when a huge semi drove right between them. It stopped at the light, even though they were only yellow and it probably could have made it. For three minutes, it sat there between the enemy camps, then with a growl of its engine and a sigh of airbrakes, it moved off.

Once again, two war cries sounded, and this time the armies flung themselves at each other, ferocious and unhindered by traffic.

## 65 Apotheosis Now

The battle was swift and the battle was merciless. Norman ran directly at a silver-clad Barnling, a length of two-by-four his only weapon. The Barnling raised his gun, but Norman's stout plank cracked his opponent square in the wrist, and the weapon went skittering over the bitumen of Wellington Road, landing under a car. The Barnling turned to face Norman, but too late. Another blow of the two-bee sent him sprawling to the ground with a shattered shoulder.

Norman almost laughed out loud. After the dread of the last few weeks, the actual battle seemed almost easy. Then something hit him in the head. Hard. He never saw it coming—never knew if it was an enemy strike or a misaimed blow from a friend. Either way, he fell to one knee, clutching his injury.

The sounds of screaming and shooting were gone. He could hear only the pulse of blood in his ears. He blinked hard. Was this what a concussion was like? If it was a concussion, he probably shouldn't go swimming for at least an hour... Or was that whooping cough?

To his right, Bernard from Storage Systems burst into flames. Norman blinked again. Through bleary eyes, he saw a man in a DIY Barn polo shirt waving his hands in an eldritch pattern. This was the Barn's fire sorcerer. The one who had summoned the flame demon. It had to be!

Norman forced himself up to his feet. Everything was moving slowly, like a week in Townsville. He realised that he wasn't the only one in the wild melee to see the sorcerer — Fiona had too. Fiona. The sister he never had. His partner in crime. How was it she'd never gotten over the guilt of robbing that armoured car? The Barn had it coming. Had *worse* than that coming.

As Norman staggered towards the fire-mage, Fiona clenched both of her hands into fists. The pavement in front of the mage exploded as the water mains burst, sending a geyser into the air. It looked for a moment as if Fiona had him, but the mage leapt back and sent a stream of flames from his hands into the geyser. The air filled with steam, scalding Norman and soaking him to the skin. He stumbled on towards his foe.

The throbbing in his head grew louder. He stumbled down to his knees. He hated himself for this weakness, but it turned out to be what saved him. From this position, he could see a pair of legs beneath a parked car — legs creeping ever closer to Fiona. Norman watched, gathering his strength.

The fire-mage was strong, but Fiona was stronger. The water from the mains began to take form, adopting the rough shape of a human, forming faster than the fire-mage could boil it away. As Norman watched, the mage's flames grew so fierce his plastic name tag melted down his shirt. Fiona sneered and turned up the water. She had this one — Norman could see that — but all her concentration was devoted to the battle. She had no way to defend herself against this new attack.

The Barnling behind the car leapt out at Fiona, a sharpened screwdriver in hand. Norman focused everything he had — what little he had left — into his legs. He hopped rather than leapt through the air, crashing headlong into his man, catching him in the midriff with his head.

The Barnling was surprised, but not slow to react. Norman felt the man's screwdriver enter his neck, the pain like a jolt of electricity. He wrestled the Barnling to the ground as he fell.

The mage-fire weakened before Fiona's onslaught... weakened... faltered... flickered... died. Then the wizard drowned, while standing on a suburban footpath on a clear day.

Norman wondered how it was that could see this, since he was lying face down on the stricken Barnling with the screwdriver, blood flowing from his wounds.

And then he was looking down at the battle from the sky. Men and women struggled in the street, their blood flowing through the gutters. A robot fought a demon. Two men duelled with deadly superweapons. A Pavilion footsoldier armed with a modified tile-cutter exploded into yellow gas. A sinkhole opened in the middle of Wellington road, swallowing a DIY Barn delivery truck. Police cars were converging from all directions. They could never arrive in time to stop the conflict. Never.

Suddenly Norman was whooshing through the air — across Australia, Indonesia, India, Arabia... Ahead lay Greece.

"No! No, no, no!"

Towering above Greece was Olympus. Not the mean little mountain that mortal eyes might behold, but the *true* Olympus that towered all the way up to the vault of the sky.

Norman's flight came to a halt outside the palatial home of the gods. The columned facade was carved of glowing marble, yet the front yard consisted of nothing but some green concrete. This, Norman's father was washing down with a hose.

"Normie," Zeus said. "Well done. Dead in an epic battle! Didn't think you had it in youse."

"Seriously?" Norman muttered. "This had better be one of them near death hallucination things. Fucked if I'm walking into the light."

"You think you've got problems, at least you're not still doing the yard work after getting kicked out of your own house. Seriously, you'd think this would be your new 'uncle's' job, but he's got a 'bad back,' so I..."

"You're using the wrong hose," Norman snapped. "You want less work? Get one of those high-pressure thingamos. Lauren in Gardening Tools can help you with that, if she survives the battle."

Zeus shrugged and turned off the tap. "Good enough, for now. If I volunteer to do the backyard as well, at least I can help myself to some zucchinis. Ah, look, Normie, I see where you're coming from. You've got friends down there, yeah? Well, you did your best for them. You saved that friend of yours, and that might be just enough to turn the tide of the battle. That's right, I was watching. Just because I'm an absent dad doesn't mean I'm completely disinterested."

"Uninterested," Norman said. "Look, spare me the bullshit and put me back. You need me to die for some fate thing? Okay, whatever. But my friends are dying down there. Just let me live until the end of the battle, okay?"

"Yeah, nah. Tell you what, though, I can make you into a constellation, yeah? I think that's a pretty good deal. All the best heroes get constellations. Who doesn't want that, eh?"

"No one wants to be a fucking constellation, you demented old pagan! Just put me back!"

Zeus took a deep breath. "I am way too old for this shit. Okay, screw fate, screw philosophy. Let's talk about respect. You've never shown me any."

"How much have you shown me? You think you can get respect without showing any?"

"I. AM. ZEUS!" A tremendous bolt of lightning came crashing down from the blue heavens above, engulfing the old man from his grey hair to his sandals. Electricity blazed from his eyes and ran up and sparked across his beard. The plastic of the hose nozzle instantly melted, turning into an orange lump in his hand.

"Zeus. *The* Zeus. Father of the Gods. Lord of Olympus. Respect flows *to* me, not *from* me. Do you get that? You're a barista at a hardware store cafe and I'm the ruler of the gods. What part of that do you not fuckin' understand, son?"

Norman stared sullenly at his father. "Fine. Okay, then. Put me back and I'll owe you a favour. That's how it works, isn't it? We mortals give sacrifices to the gods and in return we get favours."

"A sacrifice?"

"For a favour."

"Promise?"

"On me grandmother's grave."

The king of the gods stared at his son a while longer, his eyes alive with blue sparks.

"Kid," he said, "you just got interesting."

## 66 Scars

Old Axel was out the front of the Barn, fighting for his life. But that was something he'd done before. More significantly, he was fighting for the *Handy Pavilion*. He'd figured it out, in the end. Figured out about the shirts and what they meant and why it mattered if Pavilion staff lived or died.

He *cared*. It had taken him a while to figure this out because he'd never cared before. He cared about a weird, arbitrary workplace that stupid parole officer from The Hague had put him into, but that didn't matter. When your back is to the wall, what does it matter *which* wall?

Battle flowed on around him. The air was full of sounds of shouting, gunshots, and whirring engines. The scent of smoke filled Axel's nose. The tarmac beneath his feet was growing slick with blood.

The fighting *hurt*, now. That had always been his advantage back in the days when he'd been trying to conquer the world. He didn't care whether or not he won. World domination was just the challenge he'd set for himself. Axel was as apolitical as you could get. He had no idea what he'd do with the world if ever he had it. Fighting had never been about victory. Not really.

Not until now.

Axel had begun the fight armed with a propane flamethrower, but he'd had to abandon it when a valve had cracked. Now he had nothing but a shiv made out of a chisel, and a red mist in front of his eyes.

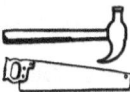

The rear entrance of the Barn was surely a trap, and the surest means Young Axel knew to disarm a trap was to spring it. Neither the Phantasm, Nalda nor Old Laura trusted him enough, so it was Christian and Fanaka that he sent right at the flimsy wooden shield that covered the back of the Barn.

Wait... Ha! Axel almost laughed out loud as he realised his mistake. The Barn was working a triple bluff! He could see it so clearly. There would be a token force behind the wooden cover, but when Axel's group moved in, a second force would engage. How did the Barn have so many troops to spare from the main fight? Were they so certain of victory on the main front?

It didn't matter. Young Axel didn't give a damn about this stupid little fight. He needed help to return to his own time, and for that, he needed to give a minimal amount of help to these jackasses. And the fact that he would get to make things go 'boom' was just a nice little bonus.

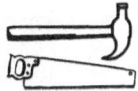

Most of the people getting stabbed would survive. Part of Old Axel's brain that he couldn't switch off told him that.

People are harder to kill than most people believe. Axel estimated that 80% of the people bleeding on the ground would survive if enough ambulances had been dispatched. If.

The stabbings and beatings were to be expected. It was the heavy hitters that changed the equation. The big guns on both sides were currently focused on each other. Axel ducked between the legs of the giant robot Bruce, as Bruce wrestled with a huge, bipedal lizard that had come from the Barnling side. If the giants on either failed, the opposing superweapons would be turned on the enemy infantry. It would be a massacre.

A Barnling charged, swinging a lawn aerator. Axel ducked the blow and slashed at his opponent's face. She recoiled—a young woman of perhaps eighteen. Axel grabbed her by the wrist, disarmed her and flipped her to the ground. If she were smart, she'd stay down.

He looked up, turning his attention to the huge lizard fighting Bruce. He wondered where the Barn had acquired it, and how they'd concealed it until the fighting had begun. Those were questions for another time. Right now, he needed to take it down.

And despite himself, Axel grinned.

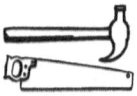

Young Axel slid forward, weaving between pallets, quickly catching up with Fanaka, the scientist from the alternate past. Fanaka seemed to like Axel. It seemed that Axel's future self was easy to get along with, which very much surprised the younger version.

"Change of plan," Axel said. "When we breach the wall, we don't wait for the others. We go in, hard and fast and hit these hydrogen tanks."

Fanaka nodded. The man was an engineer, not a fighter. He dealt with violent struggle in the way that many non-fighters do, through denial and blinking incomprehension, effectively standing in for courage. But the big man did seem very protective of Nalda, so Axel stopped short of explaining that the cyborg woman would be absorbing the force of the Barnling counterattack.

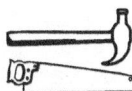

There was a bitter taste in Old Axel's mouth as he leapt onto the tail of the lizard. At first, he wondered whether the creature was secreting a defensive chemical. Then he realised that he was merely disgusted at the recollection of his own dishonestly.

It was an odd feeling.

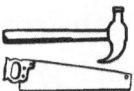

Christian swung the sledgehammer that he'd insisted on carrying. Axel hadn't thought much of it as a weapon, but he had to admit that watching the Barn's MDF defences crumple was kind of cool. Sure enough, there were a handful of silver-costumed Barnling guards waiting for them. Enough to make a creditable trap, but not too many to defeat.

Fanaka opened up with the gun he carried, which

seemed to be made of plywood and rechargeable motors. Behind him, Axel heard angry shouts and a shotgun blast. That would be the real trap, closing behind him.

A heavy dolly lay nearby—a battered square of wood on four castors. He dropped down, avoiding gunfire as he lay flat across it. His boot heels contained small rockets—useful for an emergency escape, but not much else. He activated them now, and thundered forward past Fanaka, past Christian, past the silver guards.

A moment before he hit the platform of the Barn's loading dock, he fired his wrist-mounted grapple gun at a beam in the Barn ceiling and winched himself to safety. He timed it wrong, unfortunately, and cracked his shin painfully against the platform's banister.

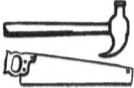

Old Axel held tight to the spines on the back of the giant reptile. He didn't have anything on him that might kill the beast, but his mere presence was distracting to the thing, giving Bruce the advantage. Perhaps that would be enough. The lizard had rough scales making it easy for Axel to keep his footing, despite the pain from the old wound in his left shin.

"There *is* no old wound in my shin," he muttered. "Please be careful, you young idiot."

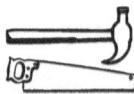

Young Axel limped desperately forward. The silver guards couldn't follow him, not without giving Christian and

Fanaka a free shot at their backs. Where were the hydrogen tanks? He could see an enormous promotional LPG container but... Oh, right. Hah.

Slipping a lighter from a belt pouch, Axel approached the tank. Timing was the issue. After touching off the explosion, he would have to be able to get back outside before...

"Axel Platzoff," came a familiar voice.

Around the side of the tank came Christian. The head had come off his sledgehammer, leaving him with a pointy handle.

"I knew you were brainwashed," Axel said. "But I never thought you were, you know... competently brainwashed."

"We meet again," Christian said. "Only this time, I am the master."

"Or you're incompetently brainwashed, but also an idiot. I have to admit, I didn't consider that... Ah!"

To Axel's shock, Christian had suddenly stopped posing and just swung at him with the handle. Axel stepped back, dropping his lighter. Even so, the end of the hammer's handle caught him in the hand, leaving a splinter deep in the flesh between his thumb and forefinger.

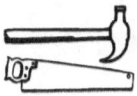

The lizard turned its massive face towards Old Axel. Immediately, Bruce whacked it in the side of the head, but the creature couldn't take its beady eyes off the irritation on its back. Axel smiled and held tighter. This time, he could see the old scar between his thumb and forefinger as it formed, fading into view like a Polaroid photo.

"Twice?" he muttered. "God, how much did I have to drink?"

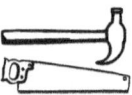

Young Axel reached into his utility belt with his injured hand, groping for a weapon. The first thing that he grabbed was an expanding fighting staff. He'd been hoping for a taser, but it would do. He shook the staff open and deflected Christian's next blow, but his hand screamed in pain as he did. Crap. And he'd cut off his own backup; that wasn't good. Through a haze of adrenaline and absinthe, his mighty brain searched for a plan.

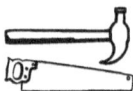

Bruce was whaling on the lizard like it was going out of style. "Stitch that, you prick!" he boomed through robotic synthesisers. Every blow was transferred through the monster into Axel's body as he clung on for dear life.

The lizard ought to turn to fight Bruce. The robot was the bigger threat, after all. Instead, it pulled back its head, flapped its crest and snapped at Axel with teeth like spearpoints.

Reflexively, Axel raised a hand to defend himself. As he did, he fell from the creature's back. He hit the ground and rolled until he came to rest against a parked van. There was blood all over him. Of course there was; blood was everywhere. Through dazed senses, he realised that his left hand was in agony. He lifted it, to see that the ferocious lizard had taken off the top of his index finger.

"Well, that was close," he said.

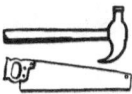

Young Axel held the expanding pole with both hands now, defending himself against Christian's inexpert but frenzied attack.

"Yo, Adrien!" Christian screamed. "I mean 'for the Barn!' No, wait... What? I thought... Aaaaagh!"

Slowed by his injuries, Axel put everything he had into defence. It wasn't enough. He was forced down onto his good knee, holding the staff above him, two-handed.

He watched, with mounting horror, as Christian's blows forced the staff downwards, towards him. Worse, the tip of his left index finger vanished. There were only two joints to the finger, which was capped with old scar tissue.

"Well," he said. "Strictly speaking, that shouldn't be happening.

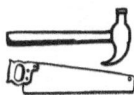

Old Axel sat on the ground, bandaging his hand, watching the lizard finally turn to face Bruce. "Takeaway points," Old Axel said to himself as he bandaged his hand. "Massive time distortion. Somehow connected to Buck and the Skull."

"And me!" said a voice. "Don't forget me!"

Axel turned his eyes sideways. Sitting slightly further along from him was a little man, about two feet tall. He had a little goatee and wore a black velvet waistcoat-and-knee-breeches combo that could be best described as 'Goth-Hobbit'.

"I'm not forgetting you," Axel said. "Because I have no idea who you are."

"Evil Brownie," said the evil Brownie. "Now that I think of it, you didn't know about me. Only Donna did, but Angela distracted her with freaky Japanese porn and she never got around to dealing with me. How do you do?"

# 67 Gaslight

Though the battle around her was bloody and cruel, Sadie MacGregor fought fair. That went without saying, perhaps, that even in the middle of a bloody battle she was Marquis of Queensbury rules, all the way. It didn't help her conscience. No matter what the terms of engagement, she wasn't supposed to be involved. Not this way.

A Barnling ran shrieking at her with a weapon made from a broom handle and two garden forks, and she simply felled him with a well-placed right cross to the chin. That was how you do it. The Barnling was unconscious, but would recover. Sadie checked the sleeping man's conscience and noted that he'd been padding his hours for weeks. That was morally wrong, and yet Sadie felt a brief flicker of sympathetic triumph on the man's behalf for ripping off the DIY Barn.

This mission. It had… It had weakened her. Watered down her resolve. Done *something* to her, anyway. The only consolation was that it had done the same thing to her sister.

Sadie's thoughts were cut short by the sight of poor Adam running from a silver-clad Barnling trooper, armed with a petrol-driven hedge trimmer. Sadie's doubts faded. She took chase, plotting how to tackle the trooper without anyone losing an arm.

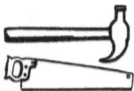

Angela MacGregor was pinned down by sniper fire from the roof of the Barn. She was in a little cul-de-sac of abandoned pallets next to Gwen Harper—who they were all now calling the Phantasm, apparently.

"Young Axel was an even bigger shitheel than our Axel," the Phantasm muttered.

"True. The amount of moral improvement Axel has undergone in the last few years of his life has been phenomenal," Angela said. "But he still hasn't quite reached the level of 'basically good'. I admire that."

The Phantasm wrenched a length of wood from a palette, balanced her hat on it and pushed it up over the top of their cover. The soft wood was instantly cracked in two by a bullet. The Phantasm swore loudly.

"Those bastards! Kill a defenceless plank."

"At least your hat's okay," Angela said.

"So what's your deal?" the Phantasm said. "You some sort of demon?"

"No. But that's the closest you'll get to understanding, so... I guess, yes."

"Don't give me that 'best you can understand' shit. I'm no human, I'm a bloody dryad."

A smile played across Sadie's thin lips.

"Well, there's nothing between us and the loading dock but wood."

Gwen grinned beneath her white mask. "Good point."

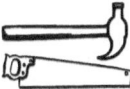

The hedge trimmer man was dispatched. Good. Sadie could see that the man was cruel to animals and... never phoned his mother? It was getting harder and harder to pick out little details like that in the roiling moral stew that surrounded her.

For a brief moment, no one was trying to kill her, so Sadie closed her eyes and concentrated, feeling rather than seeing the topography of sin and virtue. She opened her eyes again. Betrayal. Multiple layers of betrayal. Trickery, murder, revenge...

Where? Behind the dinosaur that Axel was falling off? Yes. Yes. On the other side of the Barn. It was...

It was Angela.

Angela was in trouble.

She hesitated, but only for a moment. Then fast as she could, she ran through the fight in the direction of the Barn. A Barnling tried to block her, but she kneed him right in the balls.

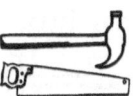

Gwen the Phantasm sang to the wood, and the wood listened and responded. Soon, there was a tunnel of pallets between Angela, Gwen and the rear entrance to the Barn. As they raced down the tunnel, the roof was struck again and again by sniper fire, sending up little eruptions of woodchips.

Angela stopped still for a moment. She saw splinters

cascade off the brim of the Phantasm's hat, but none of the bullets struck the dryad. Sadie took a deep breath, shook her head and hurried on.

They reached the loading dock in seconds. Angela climbed the stairs, while the Phantasm leapt nimbly up.

"Moves pretty well, for a big girl," Angela whispered to herself.

Inside the Barn, they ran into a silver guard. He looked more confused than anything and though he had a gun in his hand, Angela could see that more than anything he wanted to betray the Barn and run screaming from the battle.

Angela shrugged at him. "If not now… when?"

The guard turned on his heel and sprinted.

"Over here!" the Phantasm called. Angela looked and saw the younger Axel Platzoff fighting with Christian. Christian had taken a hit or two, but Axel was seriously on the back foot, barely able to defend himself from Christian's fearsome blows.

"Help me!" Axel shouted.

"Christian! What did he do to you?" the Phantasm bawled, reaching for a nearby broom handle.

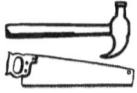

Sadie smashed through the enemy lines and ran for the Barn. The Barn carpark should have been full of the cars of the Barnlings, but it was empty save for a huge semi-trailer. Sadie ignored it.

There were no defenders between the battle and the

front of the Barn. Sadie wondered what the Barnlings expected to do if someone broke through their lines. Shout 'offside!' and wait for the referee's whistle? But a crunching sound and that odd sensation that mortals called 'pain' told her that there was some sort of defensive barrier.

Sadie looked down and saw that her leg was stuck in a bear trap. She frowned in annoyance. It was quite a powerful trap, and her shinbone was shorn nearly through. Sadie put a hand on either side of the jaws and pushed hard. The teeth met with a clank, sheering her leg through completely. The flesh fell to the ground, leaving nothing but a glowing white outline where it had been.

Sadie ran onwards to the Barn door. She kicked it off its runners with her glowing foot.

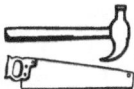

Angela watched the moral ebb and flow in confusion. Betrayal and loyalty. Freedom and oppression. Revenge and retribution. And an unfocused desire to just blow stuff up, which mainly seemed to be radiating from Axel.

"I didn't attack him!" Axel shouted, pointing at Christian. "He's a slave of the Barn!"

The Phantasm looked at Christian. "Is that true?"

"Call me, maybe," Christian said. "Don't have a cow, man. Incentivation!"

"Good enough for me!" the Phantasm said, launching herself at Axel.

Not to be outdone, Christian piled on as well. Axel

collapsed under the weight of his attackers, the three of them falling into an undignified scrimmage on the concrete floor. There was nothing and no one between Angela and the enormous hydrogen tank.

And it was down to her. Her alone. Set fire to the tank and destroy the Barn. Leave it be and risk the destruction of the Pavilion. What was to happen next was Angela MacGregor's moral choice.

She felt like vomiting.

A silver guard came flying out from an aisle of barbecue accessories. He hit the ground and slid across the floor, coming to a stop by the rear wall. The guard was followed by Sadie, still dressed in her ragged prison uniform.

"Sister," Angela said.

"Sister."

"I see you have injured your leg."

"Yes. My flesh-body will not last much longer. I see yours is well."

Angela laughed mirthlessly and opened her jacket. There was a hole just below her collar bone where the sniper's bullet had struck. Black smoke curled lazily from the wound.

"This body is as doomed as yours." Angela stared at the tank. "What should we do?"

"I… I don't… know…"

"Nor I," Angela said. "I've never made a moral choice before. I am the devil on the shoulder and you the angel. We say our lines, and others make the call. But you made a moral choice, once?"

"To take the fall for Axel," Sadie whispered. "It... did not go well. I finally see why mortals are loathe to make such choices. On the plus side, I think I helped some of my fellow prisoners to choose the path of reform."

Angela looked at the hopeless struggling mass of her allies. From the middle of the writhing pile, she heard the word "seriously?" but she didn't know who said it.

"Clearly we have to make a choice now," Sadie said. "For good or evil."

"Right or wrong. Which of us shall decide?"

"Both. On three: one... two... three!"

At the same instant, the twins spoke: "Blow it up."

The confused wrestling match had devolved into an exhausted tangle. Sadie took a fire extinguisher from the wall, and sprayed cold CO2 over the struggling Pavilionites. The fighters fell apart, whining bitterly.

"Get out, all of you," Sadie said. "Old Laura and Fanaka are still out back somewhere, keeping the Barnlings pinned down. Find her and she'll get you to safety."

"I'm seriously injured," Axel sulked.

"I'm physically okay, but I'm still pretty brainwashed, you know?" Christian added, nodding furiously. "Boiled beef and carrots."

"Two cases of man flu!" The Phantasm sneered. "I'll get them away. Good luck — you odd, odd ladies."

As the Phantasm helped the others out of the loading dock, the sisters approached the giant container. Sadie produced an old-fashioned cigarette lighter from the pocket of her apron. Angela took a small hatchet from a display.

"I did not think it would end like this," Sadie said.

"It never ends, sister."

"You know what I mean. How it ends for us."

"It's not the end for us, either."

"It's the end of us and the Handy Pavilion."

Angela breathed in deeply. "Perhaps… Perhaps we should not have interfered in the Pavilion. Perhaps we should have let events run their course."

To Angela's surprise, Sadie closed her eyes and nodded. "Perhaps. But it is done now, and there is no going back. Lesser beings may play with time travel. For us, there is no escape in that direction."

Sadie opened her eyes again. "Time to face the light," she said. With that, she swung her axe at the huge tank. It dented, but didn't break. She swung again and again, creating a small hole. Angela hesitated with the lighter. She didn't care for brightness as her sister did. But that was the wonderful thing about the darkness: it was always there. Always just hiding out of sight, waiting for the light to go away.

She smiled with false bravado as she flicked the wheel of the lighter.

# 68 War Correspondent

Karl Wintergreen used an old fashioned pre-digital camera and developed the negatives himself in a little darkroom he'd set up in the back of his stationery shop. This was partly because he preferred the warm tones that you only get with film photography but, yeah, mostly it was so that the Illuminati couldn't hack his pictures.

"The only way to keep your information safe is to keep it offline," he'd written in at least a dozen posts across five different social media networks.

To ensure the safety of his images, Karl's camera was a 1970s model, completely free of digital components. The use of a bulb flash could make nighttime photography problematic, but right at that moment, his subjects were beautifully illuminated by the rays of the rising sun, which suffused a golden glow over the field of carnage before him.

Frankly, Karl couldn't take it all in. The battle had quickly dissolved from a disciplined struggle between two organised groups, to a series of wild free-for-alls. He sat in his car, clicking his camera, winding on, clicking again. Once he'd developed the pictures he'd be able to make sense of it all. Maybe.

A large object flew out of the melee towards him. Reflexively, Karl covered his face, but the object missed his car and landed just next to it. It stood, resolving itself into a big, athletic-looking guy, naked except for a Handy Pavilion shirt wrapped around his waist as a loincloth. The figure dispassionately examined the road rash on his arm, sneered, wiped the blood from his lip and ran screaming back into the battle.

Karl thought he got a pretty good photo of the guy. His next photo was ruined, though, when Zorbar's loin-shirt fell off.

"Oh, I didn't need to see that," Karl muttered. "Why couldn't the Masons censor that shit, instead of covering up UFOs? That's... It's just unsavoury."

The passenger door of his car opened. Karl turned and found himself staring into the barrel of a revolver. But Karl hadn't gotten where he was today by looking just at what was in front of him. Behind the gun, he saw Buck Dusty.

"You! You're the arsehole who shot me."

"And that's why you're alive today," Buck said, climbing into the car. It was quite a small car, and his cowboy hat didn't fit through the door, so he backed away and took it off. He climbed back into the car, muttering. "Smith thinks it was his men who pulled the trigger, and you lived 'cause they can't shoot straight. Truth is, you're alive because I'm a *very* good shot."

"So *you* were the traitor in the Handy Pavilion the whole time!" Karl said.

"I don't recollect that being a question that anyone was trying to solve."

"I didn't say it was a big revelation," Karl said. "It's just a statement of fact."

"Uh-huh. I need you to drive."

"Where?"

"Away. This has all gone wrong. This was meant to fix the balance of the Barns, as created in time immemorial by the elders of…"

"Okay!" Carl sighed. "That's enough crazy conspiracy shit. I'll drive! I'll drive if you just *shut up*."

Buck glared at him over the top of the revolver. "Did saying that make you feel good?"

"Honestly? It was kind of cathartic, yeah."

Karl drove Buck away from the fight, into the car park of the South Hertling Super Centre. There was nobody there, although the Handy Pavilion car park was busier than usual at that time of the morning. Nothing moved in the centre but a whiff of sulphur-yellow smoke from the chimney of the kebab shop.

Soon the fight was behind them and there was nothing they could see on the road. Buck made Karl pull over. He parked in a little alcove in between Carpet Satrapy and whatever the music shop was called these days. It was as good a place as any to die.

"You going to kill me, Dusty?" Karl said.

Getting shot in a deserted carpark was sort of how Karl had expected to go. Now that this fate had moved from the potential to the actual, he felt strangely unhappy with the idea.

"One of us gonna die today. Ain't gonna be you."

"So you're going to die today?"

"That's what I said."

"Well, technically that's what you *implied*. But as a journalist…"

Buck rubbed his bushy eyebrows. "You ain't no journalist. You run a stationery store."

"And you sell power tools. But if you want to be a cowboy, I'm not going to burst your bubble."

The car rocked on its shock absorbers as a huge explosion shook the ground.

"What was that?"

"Explosion at the DIY Barn. Beginning of the end."

"Whose end? Yours or ours?"

"No, son," Buck shook his head. "It was never your'n or theirs. This fight is just a reflection of a greater battle, one in which I fight. Cosmic forces are…"

"Is that what I sound like when I'm talking?" Karl said. "God, no wonder I can't seem to hold onto a girlfriend."

"I will die in this battle," Buck said, in an I'm-still-talking-regardless sort of tone. "And then a greater battle will come. Win or lose, the balance between the Barns is lost, now."

"Greater… battle," Karl said, writing in his notebook. "Is that something to do with a pulley?"

"Yeah," Buck said. "How did you know that?"

"I keep my ear to the ground."

"The pulley ain't important. Not in itself. It's like the

first rock that starts the avalanche."

"Yeah, yeah, butterflies cause lung cancer, I get it," Karl muttered, writing furiously.

Buck let out a bellow of rage and fury as he fired five shots from his revolver through the windshield. The interior of Karl's Datsun filled with gunsmoke and righteous anger. This is it, Karl thought. Dead in a carpark.

"You. Don't. Get. Anything!" Buck thundered. "You're full of shit, Wintergreen! Your conspiracy theories are just crap you got off the Internet. You know nothing, see nothing. You reckon you're the one-eyed man in the kingdom of the blind. Well you ain't, you're the... the super blind man in the kingdom of the extra blind."

Karl watched, half terrified half annoyed as Buck gasped huge lungfuls of smokey air to calm himself.

"I'm gonna die, Wintergreen," Buck said. "I chose *you* to tell my secrets. I tried the others, but I don't think they even tried to remember... But you care! Somewhere in that addlepated noggin of yours, you care about the truth. And at least you write shit down."

Smoke plumed out of the bullet holes in the windscreen. "I believe," Karl said. "That the correct term is 'visually impaired.'"

"Shut up and listen. You have to know about the barns. Because the futures are coming. All of them. At once."

Karl looked at Buck. The cowboy's eyes were sincere, terrified. He genuinely believed that the end was coming. But genuine belief doesn't necessarily mean *accurate* belief.

"Tell me something," Karl said. "Tell me some vital truth that is hidden from the public. Prove to me you really know something worth knowing."

"Okay," Buck said. "You know God, right?"

"Know *of* him. Never met the guy."

"Well, I have. He told me this."

And Buck leaned forward to whisper in Karl's ear.

And Karl flinched back a little, mostly to get away from Buck's moustache.

And Buck sighed yet again, and just said what he had to say, quietly.

And Karl screamed at the top of his lungs, and drove his fist into the shattered remains of his windscreen, again and again. And he kept doing that until all the glass was gone, and his hand was just a bloody mess.

And Karl said: "You know what? I guess that does make sense."

# 69 Red Mist

Ms Shan turned and wiped blood from her eye just in time to see the DIY Barn explode into flames. Momentarily, the fighting slowed to a halt. The foot soldiers of both sides stopped in their tracks to watch the flames rise towards the heavens, taking chunks of roof with it. In the sudden stillness, Ms Shan could hear the approaching sound of sirens. Moments later, small pieces of burning debris began gently snowing down on South Hertling.

That should have been victory. That should have been the end of the fight. Barn gone. War over.

But it wasn't.

A Barnling—just a retail person, not a silver guard—threw a punch at a distracted Pavilionite. And Belinda—who had somehow gotten hold of one of Fanaka's superweapons—turned the Barnling into a pink mist with a push of a button. Then the giant lizard punched Bruce, and a silver guard struck Adam in the face and Fiona tried to drown what looked like some sort of war ogre, and before Ms Shan could demand the Barn's surrender the battle was on again.

On the Barn side of Wellington Road, she saw Mr Smith, partly hidden behind a bus shelter. He seemed... No, it wasn't how he seemed. It was how he *didn't* seem that caught her attention. He didn't look defeated. And he should have. He should have looked like his hardware store had been destroyed.

He should have looked god-damned heartbroken.

Ms Shan had thought that she had used up all her outrage by this point. Finding out that she still had a little left only served to anger and infuriate her further still.

She stuck her broken swagger stick in her belt. On the ground was a souped-up chainsaw, still clutched in the hand of Marlon's severed arm. She picked it up, restarted it and ran screaming towards Smith.

Through the red mist that seemed to be obscuring everything around her, she could dimly see that Ali and Wellsey were flanking her. There was some violence, and some blood—she was a little hazy on the details—and then she had fought her way to the curb. Smith saw her, finally. The look of abject terror on his face was a joy to behold as he turned tail and ran.

There was a flurry of movement to her left. A pale grey Barnling with huge black eyes made a lunge at her, but he was torn to pieces by something hairy in a Pavilion shirt and apron.

"Never knew Jane was a werewolf," she heard a voice say.

"Can't say I'm surprised, but."

But Ms Shan had no time to care. She was running after Smith as fast as she could. With unexpected agility, Smith leapt over a wooden barrier next to the DIY Barn carpark. Ms Shan cut the barrier in two without slowing down. Smith ran towards the door of the burning Barn, but secondary explosions rocked the ground. Probably the Barn's supplies of LPG and 2-stroke fuel finally going up.

Two silver guards came running from the burning building, protected from the fierce heat by their uniforms. Stricken as they were, they came running to their manager's aid. Ms Shan paused — just for a second, but it was long enough for Wellsey and Ali to surge forward, barrelling into the silver men. Ms Shan turned her attention back towards Smith.

Driven back by the flames, Smith looked around in desperation. The nearest cover was a huge semi-truck in the Barn parking lot. He raced towards it. Ms Shan ran faster yet, desperate to cut him off. Her breath was hot in her lungs, her blood was hot in her veins, and the chainsaw was hot in her hands. Smith would not escape.

She needn't have worried. Before Smith reached the truck, it sounded its airhorn and pulled away. Had Ms Shan been less furious, she might have wondered where it was going. As it was, all she knew was that it was no longer her problem.

Smith raced towards some construction vehicles. The ones that had been working on the Barn parking lot extensions, the *unfair extensions that Council never should have permitted!*

Ms Shan spoke four languages but she couldn't even tell which one she was screaming at Smith as she finally caught up with the horrible little man. The first slash of her chainsaw was shallow, cutting into his upper arm. Smith fell screaming to the ground from the pain. Ms Shan raised the chainsaw over her head and brought it down in a savage arc. Smith rolled out of the way, as the saw blade hit the ground. Luckily, the chain did not break, but the impact caused the motor to stall.

Alright, then. Barehanded.

But before she could strangle Smith, the red mist before her was dispersed by fireworks. She staggered and coughed up some bile. She struggled back to her feet and turned to see the *traitor*. Buck Dusty — the one and only person in the world she hated enough to distract her from Smith.

"You!" Ms Shan said.

"It's over, ma'am," Dusty said, holstering the six-shooter that he'd just used to pistol-whip her.

"The Barn is over."

"It'll be rebuilt. I'm afeared that the battle is over for your Pavilion."

As if in confirmation of this, a chorus of gunshots rang out in the direction of the road.

"You hit a woman. In the back. You call yourself a cowboy?"

"COWBO, technically. And yeah, I hit you. And I didn't. And I shot Karl and I didn't. And I'm talking to him now, and I'm here anyhow. It's all a mite confusing. But I'm going to die today. At least that much is for sure."

Ms Shan sneered. Behind Dusty, Ali and Wellsey were still wrestling the guards. She'd have to take care of Dusty *and* Smith.

"Want something done right," she grumbled.

The chainsaw was useless. The swagger stick tucked in her belt was sharp. As she reached for it, Dusty's hand covered his holster.

"Reckon you're fast enough?"

Ms Shan tensed her arm. "Reckon so."

Dusty shook his head. "No, ma'am. I'm gonna die, but I don't reckon it'll be *you* doin' the killin'."

Ms Shan locked eyes with Dusty. For a long moment, nobody moved. Dusty's hand was perfectly still over the butt of his revolver. She kept her hand, unmoving, above the handle of the stick.

A tumbleweed rolled between them

Dusty's eyes flickered between Ms Shan's face and her hand. Face. Hand. No movement was wasted. Everything he had seemed to be focused on those two things.

If only he'd also been watching her feet, he might have foreseen the boot to his groin before it was too late. As he doubled over in eye-watering pain, Ms Shan drew her stick. It made a cracking noise against his head.

The next moments were a blur—the red mist was returning. Then… then somehow, Buck had managed to draw his gun, and Ms Shan was trying to take it off him, and there was the sharp sound of a pistol shot. For a moment, Ms Shan thought that she'd killed him, but Buck cried out in pain and hopped backwards, clutching his wounded foot.

It was then that Ms Shan noticed that Smith had retrieved the chainsaw, and restarted it. Buck hopped backwards towards him. Smith really should have been holding the chainsaw more carefully. It was all very poor OH&S practice.

She shielded her face with her hand, and so the wet spray that had once been Buck Dusty didn't get into her eyes. Even over the roar of the chainsaw motor, she could hear Smith's horrified screaming.

When she opened her eyes, Smith was staring at something on the ground that Ms Shan took care not to look at. Smith was covered in blood, head to toe, and no longer seemed to be holding the chainsaw.

He saw Ms Shan coming for him, a moment too late. He tried to run, but she cornered him in between an asphalt spreader and a badly parked van.

In the end, he didn't put up much of a fight.

## 70 Bruce's Back

Bruce's back was starting to get to him. It didn't seem fair, somehow — dying, being reincarnated in a giant robot body and still having a bad back.

He hoped the huge lizard that he was fighting would go down soon, so he could have a sit-down. Technically, he shouldn't be up at all. The sun was rising above the horizon, and as a ghost, he shouldn't have been active during the daytime. Somehow though, he was still fighting on. He had no idea how.

He put the thought from his mind, just as he put from his mind the image of all the combatants dying in the street below. Concentrate. Concentrate on the lizard, the huge scaly lizard.

The thing was as big as him, and tough as well. Its bones seemed weirdly flexible, which was perhaps why the thing was able to absorb blows that should have crushed its skull. Bruce had been a big guy in life and he was a big guy in death, and like a lot of big guys, he'd never found it necessary to learn how to fight. All he knew how to do was trade punch for punch with the lizard and hope that the creature would go down before Bruce's back finally packed it in.

The creature hissed and snapped at Bruce's head. The fact that the thing hissed rather than roared disappointed Bruce. Sure, hissing was probably more realistic, just... disappointing.

And then, in a moment, everything changed. The lizard lost its footing. It was only for a second, but it was long enough. Before it could recover, Bruce had both massive steel hands around the creature's neck. The lizard was now held too close to use its claws, but it lashed Bruce with its tail. Bruce ignored it. If he held on, he'd win.

"Time to strangle the lizard," he said. This had sounded pretty badass in his head, but when spoken out loud it seemed more like a euphemism for something.

A sudden movement caught his eye. Without letting go, he turned his head and saw a semi driving out of the Barn carpark, bright red in front of the blackened building. It ploughed into the battle, running down and scattering Barnlings and Pavilionites alike.

There was a brief lull in the fighting as the bloodied combatants took in this new development. Then a door opened in the side of the trailer and out poured a half-dozen duster-clad cowboys mounted on horseback. They whooped and hollered as they fired into the crowd.

Perhaps because the truck had come from the Barn side of the road, the Pavilionites reacted first. But when the cowboys began gunning down Barnlings as well, both sides went into a panic. Some fought back against the newcomers but most combatants ran and hid.

One of the cowboys went down almost immediately. Zorbar—who had been halfway up a lamp-post for some reason—leapt down on one of them knocking him from his horse. Zorbar was covered in bruises and his long hair was matted with blood, but still he grinned wildly, as he slammed the fallen gunslinger's head against the ground.

The other cowboys met less resistance. Though the battle had been bloody, the actual death count had been low. Had been. Now, bodies tumbled in the street. Survivors fled in all directions. The air was filled with the sounds of gunshots and the screams of the dying.

Bruce watched helplessly; all of his servos dedicated to throttling the reptile, which still didn't sound right. A second cowboy was lost when he shot a Barnling at point-blank, setting off the super-weapon she had been holding. Half the cowboy and his horse evaporated in a puff of green fumes, the other half collapsed in the street.

At last, the lizard started to go limp in Bruce's hands (seriously!). Bruce squeezed harder and twisted until the creature stopped moving. He let it slide to the ground and turned to deal with the marauding cowboys. He aimed a kick at a horse. The horse was well trained and avoided the blow without throwing its rider. But the act did distract the cowboy long enough for Axel to smash him with a two-by-four. The rider dropped his gun, but didn't lose his saddle.

Bruce staggered. He looked down, saw that a cowboy had lassoed one of his legs, and was riding around him to wrap his legs together. He reached down a mighty hand to stop the rider.

Too fast! He bent down too fast. Pain—unimaginable pain—shot up from his lower back, filling his mind and crushing his will. It was so terrible that he didn't even feel himself fall, whimpering, to the ground.

When the spots of lights stopped flashing in his eyes, he saw that Axel had been surrounded by three of the cowboys. Reluctantly, the villain put his hands in the air. Laughing, one of the cowboys shot him in the head.

Bruce gasped—but Axel didn't fall. Tentatively, the little fellow reached up to his head, touching his skull gingerly as if afraid it would crumble under his fingertips. The cowboy shot him again. And again. Still, Axel stood, clearly just as baffled as the cowboys who were shooting him.

Concentrating all his willpower, Bruce reached out an arm. Though his back tried to murder him for this affront, his metal fist caught the cowboy who'd shot Axel. Bruce was a soft-hearted soul. He closed his eyes before squeezing.

When he looked again, he saw the other two cowboys galloping away. Axel was throwing something at their retreating backs. Bruce's hand was… still shut firm. He wanted to see what was in his palm, in the same way that a very sick man wants to know—yet dreads seeing—what he's just coughed into his tissue.

"I should be dead," Axel said. Bruce wasn't sure that Axel was addressing him, but he listened anyway as a distraction from the pain. "Those bullets… I felt them… I should be dead."

Two of the cowboys came thundering back, their hooves clattering across the bitumen. At first, Bruce thought that they were attacking again, but then he saw the last of the six horses behind them—no rider on its back, but with boots dangling from its stirrups. Someone had counterattacked, hard! The cowboys leapt their horses back into the semi. It was impressive to watch. The hatch on the semi slid closed, and with a belch of exhaust smoke and a grinding of gears, the truck started to pull away.

"Shit, I almost had the fuckers!"

Unwilling to risk moving his neck, Bruce swivelled his eyes to see Norman running after the cowboys. Except Normy seemed different. He carried a bronze-tipped spear and wore nothing but a sort of red toga arrangement that didn't leave much to the imagination.

"Don't even start, mate," Norman said. "Don't even start. Come on, you got to get me after those guys."

"No go, Normy, me back's buggered."

"Do trucks have backs, then?"

Oh, Bruce thought. Yeah. Fair enough. In a matter of moments, he had transformed his body into its concrete truck form. Norman hopped into the cab. "After 'em!"

"Okay, but there's only so far I can get from my mortal remains before—"

"Then you bloody better get going!"

Good point. So with that, Bruce put himself in first gear, sounded his horn that played 'Underneath the Radar," and drove off after the truck.

425

## 71 Laura's Future

Young Laura stood out back of the burning ruins of the DIY Barn, knocking the few remaining Barnling minions about. It was unrewarding work. She didn't quite understand the Vigilancers bylaws, but she was pretty sure she wasn't supposed to use her full superpowers on basic thugs. Her isotopic skin meant that none of the Barnlings could hurt her, but taking them down one by one with basic judo was time-consuming. She half hoped that the Barn would set a ninja or a war robot on her — but no such luck so far.

At least her future self seemed to have vanished. Honestly, this didn't bother her. The woman's deliberate mysteriousness had annoyed her from the start. Laura didn't even know why the woman was still hanging around in the present. She'd already given her warning of the future — for all the good it had done.

A black-gloved hand waved her over from near the burning Barn. Was it a ninja? No, it was just the Phantasm. Through the smoke, Laura saw that Nalda and Fanaka were supporting the injured Professor Devistato. Christian seemed to be leaning quite heavily on the Phantasm, even though he seemed fine.

"Angela?" Laura said. She'd already witnessed the deaths of Angela and Sadie with her electro-vision, but she understood the importance of setting up the emotional reveal.

The Phantasm shook her head. "She's gone. So's Sadie."

Laura considered crossing herself. As an agnostic, she decided that this might be a step too far, even in the service of drama.

"Well, that's the Barn blown up," Devistato said through gritted teeth. "One day you really must tell me *why* we destroyed it. Right now, though, you need to get me back to my own time."

Nalda sneered at him, and looked like she was about to drop him to the ground. She calmed down when Fanaka spoke up: "We'll need the glass skull for that."

"That wasn't your skull," Christian muttered.

"Yes, well," Fanaka muttered with a wave of his hand, "such is life. Anyway, the skull is currently wired into a super-weapon of my devising. I don't suppose we'll need the weapon now, so we'll just unclip the skull and... hm... speed of light... Earth's gravity... Moon in Capricorn... Carry the one... Yes, I think I can get our villainous friend here back to the past."

"Who has the weapon now, Fanaka?" Laura said, having been the only one present to catch the part about unattended superweapons.

"Oh, it was too dangerous for anyone to use if they didn't have an advanced understanding of hyperbolic topography," Fanaka said, adjusting the brass gears on his circlet.

"So you have left it with someone who understands science?" Laura said

"No, no," Fanaka said with a condescending look. "Someone with a scientific background might — wrongly — feel competent to use it. So I left the keys in the hand of the least scientifically qualified person in the Pavilion — Marlon."

There was a moment's uncomfortable silence.

"Who thought he was going to say Belinda?" Christian asked.

Four hands went up.

"Who almost shit themselves because they thought he was going to say Belinda?" Christian asked.

"So we can trust this Marlon?" Devistato said, rolling his eyes.

"He is reliable," Nalda said.

"Good," Devistato said. "Because —"

Devistato never finished his sentence. A bullet hole appeared in his forehead, smack between his eyes. Before anyone could react several more holes appeared in his face and neck. Fanaka and Nalda dropped him, his body suddenly a dead weight.

Devistato's corpse should have slid right to the ground, but instead his body fell slowly, so slowly, barely moving. Everything was barely moving. The people. The smoke from the Barn. Laura looked in horror as the whole world ground to a near-halt.

Her future self flashed into being, floating in the air above Devistato's body. "The futures! They're here! They're coming! You have to stop the Brownie!"

The sky above Laura distorted, writhed, split. To the east, the skies were black with smoke, as of a million factories running at once. To the west, the clouds were like blood and filled like men with the wings of bats. Through the middle ran a crack, and there was nothing on the other side but an endless void and an eye the size of a continent.

The skull. It had to be the skull. An artefact of vast, unimaginable power. What else could be causing this? Laura's superheroic reflexes leapt into action. The skull had to be shut down. Nothing else mattered.

She tried to fly, but there was something weird about the gravity, so she ran instead. Sprinting across the tarmac, she dodged burning pallets and unconscious Barnlings. The air was thick and warm as soup. Then somehow — somehow — she was in a shell crater, and it wasn't just the Barn that was burning but all of South Hertling. The sky was whole at least, though full of poison smoke. Everywhere were humanoid robots, like waking nightmares in chrome.

"Great. *Now* come the killer robots," she muttered.

What was happening? The futures, her future self had said. Was the timeline splitting? What was going on?

The robots were tough, but they were not expecting a superhuman. Laura knocked them about like tin soldiers with her isotopic ray hands. But there were so many of them. How long before they overwhelmed her?

It turned out to be a moot point. In a blink of an eye, the robots were gone. The sky above was no longer foul with smoke. It was blue—from what Laura could see of it between the skyscrapers. Cars, like wheelless 1950's Cadillacs, hovered up and down Wellington Road and people in one-piece jumpsuits strolled about in the morning sunshine. Laura barely had time to take this in before the skyscrapers changed shape and the road was filled with huge armoured vehicles, hammering each other with massive machine guns while pedestrians watched with polite interest.

"All the futures," Laura said. The monster cars were gone, and the buildings were small and grimy. A 1970s Datsun hatchback passed slowly down the street, drawn by a donkey. Future Laura had shown lies to her. The terrible fate that she'd demonstrated had only been one possible future. Why had she lied? To herself?

It didn't matter. What mattered was finding Fanaka's superweapon and shutting it down. It couldn't be far. She remembered Fanaka saying that the skull couldn't be taken from the Super Centre. That's where she had to go.

Block it all out. All the chaos around her. Block it out and run... No. That wouldn't work. What she needed to do was wait. Wait for a gap... she watched zombie apocalypses and reborn forests and alien invasions... *there!* The ultimate goal of Australian life—a future that wasn't all that different from the present.

Laura didn't know how long this reality would last, but she raced across Wellington Road, dodging traffic. It was an ordinary day in this future, with no huge hardware battle going on. As Laura smashed down the fence of the Super

Centre, she saw, there by the Centre water mains, was the superweapon, looking a lot like a bathroom sink and a bunch of PVC piping. It was being operated by a little man in a black waistcoat, knickerbockers and pointy shoes. Laura knocked him away from the contraption, and he fell beneath a planter full of agapanthus.

Deactivate the device… No time. Just smash the bloody thing! Laura summoned all her isotopic strength and drove her fist into the machine. Frankly, this was overkill. Any ordinary person could have made the flimsy contraption fold like a card house with a solid kick. As it crumbled, it spilled the skull onto the ground.

Panting, Laura looked up. The world was as it had been. Police sirens were approaching, the DIY Barn still burned and blood was running into the gutters of Wellington road. But at least the world was as it had been, and whatever future was coming was the one that people made. Unconsciously, Laura struck a heroic pose. The world was safe-ish again!

The ground began to rumble. The burning remains of the DIY Barn seemed to rise, distort, fall apart. Something was arising from the ground beneath it. Something white and smooth. It gleamed like polished marble. Laura watched in horror as it rose. The burning remains of the Barn spilled down its smooth sides, but left no trace behind of dust or ash. Other buildings within the Mega Centre tilted, wobbled, and collapsed as the thing rose.

The fighting in the street stopped. Every eye was turned towards the massive white pyramid that stood where the Barn had been. At its top was a vast golden capstone, decorated with the image of a closed eye. Laura's heart ran cold as the eye opened.

Laura felt a presence, of someone standing close to her. She looked, and there was Stavros from the kebab shop, munching on a falafel roll. He gestured at the pyramid with his free hand.

"Good, ay?" he said.

# 72 Pyramid Scheme

When the police arrived, Zorbar stopped stabbing a huge man in a gimp mask and a DIY Barn apron, and scrambled up a Moreton Bay fig tree that had somehow survived the battle. From there he escaped along the line of plane trees on Hurley Road.

Other than that, most of the survivors on both sides surrendered fairly easily. Old Axel seemed barely aware when the police strapped him into a Lechter gurney and affixed a hockey mask. Fiona was weeping in relief when she was bundled into the van, her guilt finally assuaged. Laura accepted the handcuffs with the bad grace of someone who knew she could tear the chains apart with barely a thought.

Jane and Donna were bundled into ambulances.

Marlon was zipped into a body bag.

Belinda was perfectly fine, of course. She even managed to talk her way out of being arrested.

Where the Barn—where the Megacentre—had once stood, a stark white limestone pyramid rose, looking down on the streets of South Hertling from a sapphire eye in its golden capstone. Its base reached almost to the pavement of Wellington Road, and it effectively screened off whoever had been behind it.

That included the Phantasm, Christian, Nalda and Fanaka. When the Pyramid had risen, they had been forced to flee across the shaking concrete apron of the Mega Centre, Nalda almost carrying Fanaka as the scientist explained how the specifics of wave motion effect showed that it was no natural earthquake. Now they stood in the little laneway between Hurley Road and Local High School.

"It was close," Nalda said. "I could *feel* it."

"Feel what, my love?" Fanaka said.

"Oh…" Nalda said remembering the cold robotic future that had been so close to condensing into reality, "nothing."

The little group started, almost panicking as something large dropped from a nearby tree. They relaxed when they saw it was Zorbar—battered and bruised, but alive. And naked.

"We didn't need to see that," Christian said.

"Speak for yourself," the Phantasm replied.

"Fight over," Zorbar said. "Cops come. They total buzzkill, man."

"Who won?" Fanaka asked.

"My people have saying," Zorbar said. "You alive? You won."

The ragged Pavilionites looked at each other and considered this. One after the other, they decided that it was probably the most positive thought on offer.

"Come on," Christian said. "My aunt and uncle are out of town and their place is just around the corner. We can lay low there for a while."

Then again, maybe *that* was the most positive thought.

"Hey, what happened to Axel... Young Axel... Devistato's body?" the Phantasm said.

Fanaka grinned. "It's vanished. All my theories about time have just gone out the window. It's quite exciting, really!"

Perhaps the others sighed when he said this. Or perhaps it was just the wind.

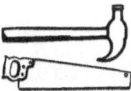

Bruce and Norman hooned after the truck full of cowboys.

"Who are those people?" Bruce said.

"Dad explained it, but it didn't make a lot of sense," Norman said. "They're like... Agents of some weird shit, but the balance of weird shit is all fucked up, so now we have to deal with their weird shit instead of the DIY Barn's weird shit."

"Oh, yeah, like with the Three Barns. Buck Dusty tried to explain it. It sounded pretty stupid."

"Yeah, well, stupid isn't the same as 'not dangerous'," Norman said, adjusting his bronze helmet. "We've got to stop them."

The truck ahead of them slammed on its brakes, and went squealing around a roundabout. Norman and Bruce could see why — a column of police vehicles approaching from the other side.

"Quick, Bruce! Handbrake turn!"

"That's not me bloody handbrake!"

Norman withdrew his hand quickly as Bruce spun

around to follow the cowboy truck. Before them was the Pyramid of Wellington Road.

Bruce sighed. "Sure. Why not? Hang on!"

Whoever was behind the wheel of the cowboys' truck was a very talented driver. He weaved the huge vehicle between the vehicles on Wellington Road almost perfectly. It only clipped a single police van, setting it wobbling worryingly.

"Now might be a good time to tell you, I'm not that great of a driver," Bruce said.

"Seriously? You're a bloody truck!"

"Yeah, well…"

Bruce turned off his optical sensors. In later days, he justified this by telling himself that he was using the Force—but actually it was the robotic equivalent of squeezing his eyes shut. He turned this way and that, his horn blaring "Underneath the Radar". There was no sensation of crunching into another vehicle or squishing a human, which was good.

Then there was a thump. Not a bad one, but palpable. He skidded to a halt and turned on his sensors. He'd knocked a police van over completely. But what were they going to do, give him a fine?

He was close to mounting the Wellington Road pavement. The Pyramid was directly ahead. A section of marble had cantilevered up, leaving a square entrance visible into the darkness of the interior. The cowboy truck was driving in. He paused.

"Hop out," he said.

"Nah, it's pronounced *hoplite*," Norman said, adjusting his helmet.

"I mean it. I'd follow them, but I'm dead. Don't risk your neck."

"I died too, mate. I'm in this, all the way."

Bruce had never felt close to Norman. Still, dead blokes have to stick together.

"Let's go get the bastards!"

Fiona started as the van rocked hard, then went tumbling as the van rocked again. Stumbling to her feet, she saw that the van was on its side and the rear door had popped open. She staggered out into the street, just in time to see Norman driving Bruce into the Pyramid. The entrance began to close.

To one side were the police—justice, final redemption for her crime. To the other, Norman—who she loved like a brother—was racing into peril.Her head jerked one way, then the other. One way, then the other as she tried to make up her mind about which way to go.

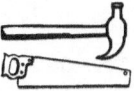

On the other side of the former Barn, the edge of the Pyramid had risen almost as far as a retaining wall, creating a little angled valley bounded on one side by marble and on the other three by cinderblock. From the ditch, Wellsey rose, groaning. Bracing himself against the wall, he reached a hand down and helped Ms Shan to her feet.

"You've got blood on your face," she groaned, handing him a handkerchief.

"There's a lot of blood on that hanky already, boss," he said.

A groan from further along the valley told them that Ali was alive, too. They helped him out from under a silver-clad corpse and to his feet.

"What happened?" he said.

Ms Shan looked up the side of the Pyramid and saw the great Eye looking down at her.

"I'm not one to admit when I don't know something," she said. Then she fell silent.

Ali took a tentative step up the side of the Pyramid, and had to be kept from falling as his feet slid from under him, sliding on the polished surface. Unperturbed, he tried to scale the retaining wall, but found it too sheer.

"Huh," he said. "Well. Looks kind of like we're fucked, eh? Ow!"

The 'ow' came when the end of a heavy rope smacked him in the face. As he rubbed his injury, he looked up and saw a familiar face.

"Hey, chief! It's your... associate."

"I think we can knock that off, Ali," Ms Shan said, a huge smile on her face as she looked up at Claudia Liselle. She tested the rope her lover had thrown and climbed up. As she crested the retaining wall, she saw that Claudia was not alone. Behind her was a whole crowd. Ms Shan was not the best with names, but she recognised a host of people from the South Hertling Super Centre—people who sold barbeques, health foods, sporting equipment, electronics, homewares, musical instruments, motor accessories and—above all—carpets.

As the others made the climb, Ms Shan looked in wonder, uncertain what to make of this.

"The war is lost," Ms Liselle said. "Yes, the Barn is destroyed, but still… the war is lost. It is down to us to be the partisans of the resistance. Ms Shan… Jasu… Will you be our leader?"

# About the Author

Australian SFF author BG Hilton spent most of his life doing jobs so tedious that his only escape was entertaining himself with crazy fantasy stories, and now he writes them down in the hope of entertaining others. He specialises in Speculative Fiction, Humour and Non-Fiction. His short fiction can be found in *Andromeda Spaceways*, *James Gunn's Ad Astra*, *Antipodian* SF and elsewhere. His debut novel, the Steampunk adventure *Champagne Charlie and the Amazing Gladys*, was published by Odyssey Books in early 2020. He lives with his family in Sydney, and consequently spends a lot of time in traffic.

You can find his blog at bghilton.com, where he writes about Frankenstein, the old TV series *In Search Of...* and pulp magazine covers. When he is online, many are his names on many websites. @bghilton among the Twitter, @bghilton.author to the Facebook. Ben_r0xX_111 he was in his youth, on the Geocities that is forgotten. To TikTok he goes not.